GREY
HORSES

GREY HORSES

HANNAH McNIVEN

POOLBEG

Published 2022
by Poolbeg Press Ltd.
123 Grange Hill, Baldoyle,
Dublin 13, Ireland
Email: poolbeg@poolbeg.com

A catalogue record for this book is available from the British Library.

ISBN 978178199-452-8

www.poolbeg.com

About the Author

Hannah McNiven is an Irish-born writer of Scottish and Irish descent. She has been longlisted (2017) and shortlisted (2018) for the Colm Tóibín International Short Story Award. This is her third novel.

Acknowledgements

Thanks to all the team at Poolbeg. Thanks also to Wexford Literary Festival for their continued support.

A massive thank-you to Dee, Barbara, Mam and Dad for their editing and notes.

Another huge thank-you that will never reach the often large and sensitive ears of the many animals who have inspired this book. Without them and the way of life they have introduced me to, there wouldn't be any characters or a book.

To everyone who has read my work, encouraged, inspired and helped me along the way – you know who you are – thank you.

Dedication

To women like Christine K. and Betty W. They may have passes to ride the bus, but don't need anyone's permission to continue riding their horses.

When I grow up, I want to be like you.

Chapter 1

1959

Estella's back ached. In fact, most of her body did. She could feel the collar of her shirt chafing the sunburnt flesh at the back of her neck, the stiffness in her shoulders, the strained ligaments and tendons of her forearms. Having spent the last four days sifting potatoes from dry soil, her fingers were constantly on the verge of cramping. Beneath the fabric of her trousers and the hessian sacks she had tied above and below her knees, she could feel the sting of raw, weeping flesh, rubbed by the continuous friction between skin and woven fabric. Even the arches of her feet twinged from the strain of kneeling with the toes of her boots pressing into the ground. She had tried a myriad of different positions over the last number of days but now, bone-weary, she did not try to alter her present one, despite the pain. It wasn't worth wasting her energy finding a better way to shuffle along on her knees as she removed soil-covered tubers of various sizes and shapes from the earth and placed them in a hessian sack. Besides – glancing up for the umpteenth time just to be sure – she was finally harvesting the final row of potatoes.

Half-filling the large, dust-stained sack, Estella laboriously

1

pushed herself up off the loose soil and stood with hunched back, afraid to straighten up completely for fear of a sharp spasm of pain. Stooping, she took hold of the two top corners of the sack, bent her knees slightly and with a practised jerk swung the potatoes onto her back. Dragging her feet across the dusty earth as if through mud, she walked up the hill to where Beryl, the donkey, munched contentedly on the grass by the ditch. Estella dumped her sack beside others collected by the wheel of the donkey cart which stood at the top of the row with its curved shafts pointing skywards like the legs of an upturned insect.

Estella tentatively stretched her shoulders, felt the strong but weary muscles catch, and stopped. Though no one would have thought it, there was real strength in her slim frame.

Beryl looked up momentarily, long stalks of grass with seeded heads protruding from the side of her mouth. There was such warmth and benign interest in her liquid umber gaze that Estella smiled. She sauntered over to the donkey and scratched the tufty grey-brown hair above her eyes. Beryl nodded her approval. Estella enjoyed the sensation too. There was something comforting about the soft warmth of an animal's coat running through her fingers. "Good girl," she murmured, giving the donkey a parting scratch on the rump before turning and grabbing an empty sack from the pile beside the cart.

She put no effort into walking down the field, instead allowing the gentle decline of the slope to carry her to the last few unemptied yards of the potato drill. However, before she knelt to her work, she glanced to the north and the mountains in the distance. It was said that if you wanted

2

the Irish weather to change, wait for five minutes. But this particular weather front was taking its time. Clouds billowed angrily above each curving summit, the inky-blue underside hovering with such menace that Estella shivered. She had been watching the clouds roil in the distance for the last hour, witnessing their transformation from innocent whiteness to corrupted black. Observing this change always made her think of her father. As the wind picked up, his voice seemed to be carried from the distant peaks all the way to where she stood. 'If you want to know what the weather's going to do,' he used to say, 'just look to the hills.' Breathing deeply, she tasted the metallic tang of electricity and the scent of water in her nostrils. There was a storm coming and, if she didn't finish up quickly, she would be caught out in it. And so would Beryl.

Finally dragging the last bag of potatoes up the hill, Estella harnessed Beryl to the cart, loaded the potatoes and led the donkey along the top of the field. The large evergreen trees along the top ditch, which had been susurrating gently in a light breeze all day, were beginning to creak. Their shaggy green branches whipped through the air as if, like errant children bent on rushing away from their mother, they were trying to break free from the main trunk. But they were always dragged back to heel by the vice-like grip she maintained, slumping back to their original position before making another attempt to dash away. Walking beneath their boughs, Estella felt the fine spray of pine needles pitter-patter on her bare skin. She brushed them from Beryl's back as the donkey twitched in irritation, her furry ears flicking

3

back and forth as she listened to the rush of air swirl around them.

"*Shhh,*" Estella intoned in a calm, even voice. "It's all right. *Shhh.*" She gave the donkey a reassuring pat on the neck. As she walked along, she could feel the ground shift as the tree-roots close to the surface strained to hold on to the trunk-mother and child-branches above – the anchoring fathers of the many-branched families who lived a life exposed to the elements. Estella thought of the strength it must take to cling on while the wind buffeted, doing its best to pull the roots from the depths. She considered how important it was for a family to have roots to bind them together. Without their mooring, they had nothing to hold them together, no nutrients to feed them and allow them to grow. Nothing to keep them from withering away, enduring a slow death until they were finally felled and cut into many disparate pieces. When a family lost its anchor, sometimes it was hard to keep the branches connected.

Passing through a gap in the evergreens, Estella led the donkey along a passage at the back of a single-storey dairy. The sound of the impending storm was muffled now that they were shrouded by the towering conifers. Beryl's unshod hooves echoed dully off the wall as they clip-clopped a neat little staccato rhythm on the packed earth and stone of the pathway. In response, there was a muffled lowing of cows from the far side of the dairy as they acknowledged the presence of a fellow creature. Estella could have wept with relief. The cows had made their own way up to the yard for milking which would save her getting them in the rain once she had unloaded the potatoes.

4

Just as the thought crossed her mind, she felt the first droplets hit the freckled skin of her face. Quickly opening the gate and traversing the cobblestones with Beryl, she led the donkey through the carriage doors of the large barn which ranged along the opposite side of the yard to the dairy. The cows' gazes followed their progress with only mild curiosity before returning to the loose hay dropped by the men unloading the hay bogies over the last few days. Estella hunched her shoulders as she thought of the hay harvest. There would be hell to pay if the neat rows of dried grass were still lying on the fields when the rain came. In her mind's eye, she could see the men glancing at the sky just as she did and redoubling their efforts to gather up and cover the hay before the storm arrived.

As she unloaded the sacks of potatoes from the cart, she listened to the sound of the rain on the shed's galvanised roof. The tinny pebble-rattle built to the roar of deep-bellied drums. Beryl's ears twitched but, otherwise, she didn't move. She stood stoically still as Estella heaved the bags to the ground, ready for carrying up the stairs to the loft. That was a job she would have to do after milking the cows. Unharnessing the donkey, she stood gazing out across the yard through the distorting grey-whiteness of the falling rain. She knew Beryl would likely refuse to cross the threshold of the barn into such a downpour. She did not resent the animal's obstinacy. In fact, she rather admired her stubbornness.

"All right, lovey," she sighed, fondling the thick tuft of hair again. "You stay here and I'll get you some hay."

Taking a deep breath, she plunged out into the now

5

torrential rain and immediately felt the fabric of her shirt stick to her back. The droplets landed with such force that they soaked straight through the material, chilling her skin. But she carried on regardless, collecting an armful of hay and a bucket of water for the donkey. Beryl watched proceedings from the barn door without even venturing her nose into the open. Estella then turned her attention to the cows who had very sensibly retreated into the shelter of the dairy. She longed to change her shirt and get a coat but decided to keep going as she was. She wanted to have milking over and done with so she could sort the potatoes into their crates before the light faded. Although, with the sun now obscured by steel-grey clouds, working by daylight looked more and more unlikely. And she doubted the rain would lift by the evening. There was nothing she could do about that. All she could do was keep going.

It was late and still raining steadily when Estella finally got into the house. The distance from the barn where she had been sorting the potatoes to the house was only a hundred or so feet but, as she crossed the yard, her body felt agonisingly heavy.

Entering the generously proportioned farmer's kitchen that was supposed to be the centre of her home, she saw that her brother, Graeme, had been in for his tea and already left. There was a loaf of bread, butter, jam, a knife and a plate still sitting on the table. He had, however, rinsed out his mug which was sitting on the draining board. Crossing the room, she picked up the mug and sniffed. All she smelt was the cold of the glazed interior. A furry tortoiseshell cat watched her from a chair by the fire.

6

"Thinks he's clever, Sophie," she told the cat. "Probably washed the mug to hide the smell of the whiskey. He thinks we don't know. But we've known for a while now, haven't we?"

Estella had heard him arrive back from the hayfield while she was just beginning to sort the potatoes from the sacks up in the loft. But Graeme hadn't looked for her. And it never even crossed her mind to call to him for help. There was something comfortable about working in solitude as the rain battered out its tattoo overhead.

It allowed her time to remember previous potato harvests when the strange train of travelling women would appear without fail every autumn. It was as if they were part of the earth that they worked with. The child-Estella had often wondered if they were like the nymphs in the stories her mother read to her and her sister Joy – living in the trees and hedges, their apparition precipitated by the need for labourers. They had always looked a ragged bunch, arriving with patched shawls draped around their massive shoulders. Some wore cloth bonnets, others battered straw hats with edges frayed and spiky – hats that couldn't cover the shock of wiry black hair that curled from their scalps.

Their hair fascinated Estella. All the women she remembered had black hair yet the children had assorted colours of bushy locks. The band of squabbling, scrape-kneed, foul-mouthed offspring that traipsed after their varying mothers, aunts and grandmothers, consisted of any number of tousled brunettes, rat-tailed redheads and lank, dirty blondes. She had vivid images of women with babies cocooned in shawls draped around their shoulders too. She

7

often wondered how these little bundles came into being as she had only ever known babies to be born when there was both a mother and a father. She wondered if they had fathers or if, perhaps, these women, mystical as they were, bore and raised children without men. A few young boys were always among the motley band but, once they were older, they disappeared, consigned to a lifetime in the recesses of memory. Besides, she only ever saw these children at a distance so she was never free to question them about their strange, fairylike existence. Her mother had warned her against conversing with them and, in truth, Estella had been relieved. Watching as boys resorted to fist-fights over scratched marbles and girls sang bawdy songs while skipping over plaited ropes made from scavenged bits of string, she knew she was not of their ilk. She had neither the pluck or the self-confidence to approach. She knew there was no way for her to insinuate herself into such a tight-knit group.

She had carried that same lack of self-confidence through to her adulthood and now, at twenty-five, still struggled to engage with people. If the itinerant potato-pickers had returned, she still doubted whether she would have the courage to talk to them. But there was no fear of them returning. Graeme had turned them away the year before last and they had not returned since. According to him, there was no need to employ a band of 'gypsies' to harvest the potatoes since there wasn't enough of a crop to warrant employing them. Besides, Estella had much less to do now so she would be free to do the bulk of the work. And if she couldn't manage it all, surely he could pick up the shortfall.

What Graeme had not factored in was that the last of the

hay crop would also be harvested at the same time as the potatoes. Or maybe that was exactly what he was hoping would happen since he really had no urge at all to partake in the laborious work of digging up and bagging potatoes. That, like many tasks now, fell to Estella. Just as clearing the table fell to her as well. Wearily, she removed the detritus before sitting down to her own simple meal. Her clothes were still damp from the rain but she was so ravenously hungry she forwent changing and just wrapped herself in a blanket.

It was in this state – hunched like a vagabond at the head of her own table – that a damp-but-glamorous Dolly Greer found Estella when she walked into the kitchen with a, "*Yoo-hoo*! Only me!"

Estella barely roused herself to manage a croaky, "Hello," in response to her best friend's cheery arrival.

"God Almighty, Stella! What's wrong?" Dolly strode around the table and caught her by the shoulder to better scrutinise her. This wasn't the first time she had walked into this house and found Estella sitting dull-eyed at the table.

"*Ow!*" Estella pulled her shoulder from Dolly's grasp. The persistently aching muscles from earlier had contracted into rigid lumps after her exposure to the cold rain. She knew she should have worn a coat, but something in her always made her feel that it was her lot in life to endure these small sufferings with silent stoicism.

"What have you done to yourself now?" Dolly asked in exasperation. She had known Estella since they were little girls in school together and, despite being the same age, often took on a maternal role in their friendship. "Estella

Frayne, you're soaked!" she admonished her, opening the blanket wrapped loosely around her friend's shoulders. She picked up the rat-tailed end of Estella's plait which was a wet, dark brown though her hair was actually a much lighter colour. 'You're a fine bay mare!' her father used to joke.

Estella batted Dolly's hand away. "Got wet."

"Well, I can see that!" Dolly said crossly. "What were you doing out in the rain without a coat and hat?"

Estella didn't answer.

"I was out in the rain too and you don't see me looking like I tried to drown myself in the village pond. *I – wore – a – coat – and – hat*." Her tone was that of a teacher explaining a lesson to a particularly obtuse pupil. She gestured to her own mostly dry immaculately dressed figure and bright blonde hair. "Look: dry as a bone. And I cycled over to see you and everything."

"Why *did* you cycle over to see me in the rain?"

Dolly's face lit up in the way Estella knew so well. She wondered for the umpteenth time in her life why someone as charismatic as Dolly was still living at home with her parents and siblings. She was a handsome girl with such cheery vitality that it was impossible not to feel better in her company. She would likely make some man very happy in the future but that day was yet to arrive. Indeed, one of her last men had left for England with four stitches above his eye from a well-aimed sugar basin hurled by his dearest. Dolly was inclined to read a lot of romantic fiction and had acquired a connoisseur's taste in men from her beloved books. She expected a lot from the opposite sex and they rarely lived up to her expectation of what a 'real man' should be. Though it never seemed to occur to her that the real, ideal

10

men she set her standards by were, in fact, fictitious.

"Do you remember the whole debacle at the start of the summer over at Leclercs'?" she asked, knowing already that Estella was perfectly familiar with what had happened on the estate next door.

"Yes," she muttered unenthusiastically.

The Leclercs were a wealthy middle-aged couple who lived in a grand house on the even grander estate of Ellendale that bordered Robin Hill – the land of Estella's family farm. At the start of the summer, it was discovered that Ellendale's manager, Tony Dillon, had been overcharging the owners of mares for the privilege of a foal by one of the Leclercs' stallions and pocketing the difference. Not only had he been fooling his employers but also almost every horseman and woman within a forty-mile radius. The betrayal meant Dillon had all but been run out of the county overnight – with all his cadged earnings still in his possession – and had not been seen or heard from since. The scandal had provided rich fodder for gossip. And, after her long day, Estella wasn't in the mood for outdated gossip.

"You'll never guess what's happened now," Dolly gushed, barely waiting for Estella to speak before she said impatiently, "Well, aren't you going to guess?"

"No." She almost laughed when her friend's face fell with comical rapidity. "No point guessing since you're just going to tell me anyway."

"You're no fun when you're in a grump," Dolly huffed. "In fact, what am I doing rabbiting on? You're wet through. Let's get you into a bath. Oh, what I would give to be able to say that at my house!"

"Well, you come over here so often to get a bath you hardly need one at your house," Estella pointed out as she allowed herself to be led to the bathroom.

Once or twice a month, Dolly arrived into the kitchen and announced she was there to use the bathroom. She had been doing it for years since the Frayne family were one of the few houses locally who had an actual cast-iron bathtub with almost constant running hot water thanks to the Aga.

"The water's hot, yes?"

Estella nodded. "I put some anthracite on at dinner and topped it up when I came in just now." She hobbled to the bathroom ahead of her friend, unable to straighten out any of her limbs.

Dolly studied her critically. "What have you done to yourself?" she repeated, exasperated, as she gently caught hold of Estella's elbow and helped her up the stairs.

"Digging potatoes then got caught by the rain."

She'd already scolded her for not wearing a coat so now Dolly tried a different tack. "And would you not get some help doing the potatoes? They will keep, you know."

Estella shrugged.

"You could have waited until the hay was done and got Graeme to help you."

Estella blinked owlishly at her.

Dolly grimaced. "All right. Fair point." She knew as well as anyone that Graeme was not the sort of person you willingly spent any time around. "Why don't you leave the awful bugger to shift for himself, Stella?"

"And go where?"

It was a familiar call and response between the two of

them. Dolly always with the same question, Estella with the same reply.

Dolly didn't answer. She knew there was no point. Estella wasn't going anywhere. She was a martyr for a cause and her cause was the farm she had grown up on. She wanted to save the place – to preserve it just as it had been during her childhood but, so far, her attempts had not been particularly successful.

Once they got into the bathroom, Dolly knelt on the linoleum floor and ran the bath while Estella laboriously stripped off her sodden clothing. It was something of a challenge, given that the material of her shirt and trousers seemed to adhere to her skin, turning every item inside out as she peeled it from her body. Though the air in the bathroom was beginning to fill with steam from the gloriously hot water, there was still a lingering chill which pimpled her exposed flesh. Bath filled, Dolly sat on the floor with her back to the wall so all she could see was the top of Estella's head once she got in. It was a position she had taken up many times over the years. They had shared hundreds of conversations and solved many problems with one of them in the bath and the other sitting on the floor. The familiarity between them was a bond deeper than that shared by sisters. Their love for one another was untainted by rivalry, arguments or the interference of others. What they found in their friendship was the pure affection of two people who needed each other. There was no one else in their lives who filled that void of a female confidante of a similar age.

"Right – what was it you came over to tell me?"

"*In the rain,*" Dolly added for emphasis. She primly

13

clasped her hands around her knees. "Well, you know the Leclercs've been looking for someone to manage the place since old Tony Dillon got the heave-ho? They've found someone! *And*," she paused for effect, "he's young!"

Estella listened to her friend's gurgling laugh and smiled. "Planning your winter wedding, are you?"

"Well, there may be a *wee* issue with that. I think he might already be married."

Peering over the edge of the bath, Estella was confronted by a doleful gaze. She ducked down again to hide her grin. "You *think*? So, you're saying you cycled all the way over here –"

"– in the rain –"

"– in the rain, to tell me that there's a new farm manager who is young and who might be married? Are you sure it was worth it?"

"Yes, but he only *might* be married which means he *might not* be married."

"And who told you about this new – possibly married – man in the neighbourhood?"

"No one *told* me," she answered in an affronted tone, as if she would not stoop so low as to listen to second-hand gossip. Yet, working in the telephone exchange, she often *did* listen in. "I *saw* him. On my way home from the shop. You know the old gardener's cottage? And how it's got a high hedge but you can see all the way into the house from the gateway? There was a removal van outside and I saw this fella who seemed to be organising those lads in the brown coats. Unloading furniture and the like. And there was an older woman – his mam because he called her 'Mam' –

wandering up the little driveway looking at all the plants. So I just stopped and said the hydrangeas were lovely and she agreed with me. I asked were they new to the area and she said her boy is the new farm manager at Ellendale and they'd been given the house as part of the arrangement. But I thought it might be rude to ask exactly who 'they' were. And anyway, he called her away to ask her something and she didn't come back so –"

"And what made you think he was married?"

"I don't know. The way she said 'they?' It sounded like more than just her and him. And they seemed to be bringing in an awful lot of stuff for just the two of them."

"Oh, so you had a really good look then?" Estella sniggered.

"Only so I could tell *you*. I thought you'd want to know."

"Give over! You were just having a good snoop for yourself." She leant forward and was pleased to find her muscles were much looser than they had been. Pulling out the plug, she waited a moment for some of the water to drain away before topping it up with more hot. "I assume you liked the look of this new fella, otherwise you wouldn't have come over to tell me about him."

Dolly's eyes and forehead appeared at the edge of the bath, her hands clasping the rolltop. "*I did!*" She vibrated with excitement. "He's *tall* and he's got lovely chocolatey brown hair. *Lovely* thick hair that swept in a wave like this." She wiggled her hand above her head from left to right. "And he just looked so *strong* and *capable*." She sat back against the wall, basking in her own remembrances. "I *really* liked the look of him."

"You'll have to keep looking if he is married."

15

"*Stella!* Don't ruin the moment!" she huffed.

"I don't know why you're so interested anyway. What happened to Jonathan Sanders? Or do you no longer think he's – what was it – the closest thing you'd seen to a real-life Gregory Peck?"

Dolly shouted out a derisive laugh and launched into a lengthy explanation of all Sanders' failings. How he was always late – 'Leaving me standing there like an eejit.' How his teeth weren't clean enough – 'I mean, it just looks unhealthy.' That he was forever talking about his livestock – 'How much time can you actually spend thinking about bloody cows?' And the way his mother told her how Jonathan's socks and underwear had to be ironed as he was quite particular about such things – 'You wouldn't think it to look at him.'

As she ranted, Dolly absentmindedly picked up Estella's wet clothes and folded them into a neat pile even though they were just going to be put in the wash. Though she wasn't prepared to iron a husband's undergarments, she would willingly have done anything for her best friend. For instance, had any another woman been wearing a man's trousers, Dolly might have teased or criticised her for her inappropriate attire. But she didn't comment. She simply pulled the thick leather belt through the loops, knowing her friend would need it again tomorrow. And she knew that Estella's weren't just any trousers. They were her father's.

Dolly never questioned it when Estella told her she was wearing the contents of her father's wardrobe so as not to waste good work clothes. If she wanted them used, her brothers could have taken them. Wearing them herself was

16

her way of keeping him close, keeping his spirit alive, even though he was now gone more than a year. The shirt was also his, only slightly too big for his daughter to wear given that he had been such a slight, wiry man himself. And Estella had such a boyish frame it was barely noticeable that she wore a man's shirt instead of a woman's.

Reaching the end of her tirade against the hapless Jonathan Sanders, Dolly concluded with, "*Anyway*, are you not shrivelled up like a prune yet?"

"Almost. Here, hand me a towel."

"I'll go and get you some dry clothes."

With both now dressed and warm, the two young women descended the stairs to the kitchen where Dolly made tea while Estella dried her hair, standing over the open top of the Aga.

Talk turned to general things. As Dolly's voice skipped and dipped over stories of farming, families and her new favourite bread-making recipe ("Buttermilk's the key, you know. I'm convinced of it."), Estella's mind wandered. She lost the train of Dolly's chatter and, eventually, the talking ceased. The two friends sat in companionable silence until the noise of the rain on the roof made them both look towards the ceiling.

"You'll stay here tonight."

It wasn't an offer. The comment precipitated both washing their mugs, saying goodnight to the cat and heading back upstairs to the bedroom they had so often shared over the years. The two single beds sat in opposite corners just as they had when Estella shared the room with her sister. But in the last fifteen years Dolly was the only

17

person who had ever slept in Estella's room. There was even an old nightdress folded in readiness in the bedside drawer.

Flagging once again, Estella struggled out of her clean clothes while Dolly used the bathroom. When Estella returned having also performing her ablutions, Dolly was sitting on the side of the bed but got up as soon as her friend closed the door.

"Night, night, lovie." She crossed to give Estella a hug.

It was a lovely feeling to be held. Estella hugged her back. "Night, night."

Chapter 2

By the time a week had passed, the surrounding area was abuzz with talk of the new manager at Ellendale. Dolly had been back for a second visit and took pains in relaying everything she had discovered about the new residents of the old gardener's cottage. However, details were thin on the ground.

"Keep to themselves mostly," Dolly informed Estella as they sat and ate supper. She seemed rather frustrated by the lack of concrete evidence she was able to pass on to her friend but ploughed on nonetheless. "Aylward's the name. She's Edna – the mother. Mai Craven cornered her in the shop. They were up the country before – don't know where – and her son was running a yard of cattle, horses, sheep – everything. Thing is, I still don't know *his* name." She scowled. "Apparently, she only said 'my son' when she was talking about him."

"And did Mai Craven not ask?"

"Mustn't have."

"Funny. She'd usually ask what colour underwear you have on."

"She did say *something* interesting." Dolly leaned in confidentially though there was no one else in the house, Graeme having gone to the pub. "*Apparently*, Dickie Jones had a good look over the hedge going by on his horse and cart and saw a woman in the garden playing with a little boy." She sat back, smiling triumphantly. "What do you think of that, then?"

"I think it sounds like he's married and you'd better stop poking around. I know you love a good story but it wouldn't really do to cast yourself as 'the other woman' now, would it?"

"A girl can dream," Dolly sighed.

"Anyway, I don't know why you're telling me anything that came from Dickie. This *is* the same Dickie who told anyone who would listen that he met some fairy folk down by the Rathole Bridge? Are you sure he didn't see a woman with glittery wings when he was spying? Maybe the little boy was green."

Dolly tittered. "Or maybe he ran up to Dickie and offered to grant him a wish. Ah no, I think he really did see it. It was Saturday afternoon."

"What's Saturday afternoon got to do with anything?"

"Well, when he saw the fairies, he was legless."

"And you think he can't be legless on a Saturday afternoon? We are talking about the same Dickie, yes? Dickie who has to rely on his horse to get him home because usually it's the only one of the pair of them sober enough to find it."

"I tell you something, when that horse dies, old Dickie'll be in real trouble."

"Maybe the fairies'll point him on his road home."

"He's more likely to go and live with them."

"Although, assuming Dickie doesn't snuff it before his horse is really a bit unfair on the horse," Estella pointed out.

Dolly nodded. "His liver must have spent the last thirty years pickling in whiskey."

Estella laughed but then found the sound caught in her throat. An image of her brother huddled in front of the Aga cradling a glass flashed before her field of vision. Would two different young women be sitting in a kitchen in thirty years' time saying the same thing about Graeme Frayne?

"Still bad?" Dolly had watched her friend's face change as the sound died in her throat.

Estella nodded but said nothing.

"Are you sure Austin can't do anything?"

A humourless laugh escaped Estella's lips. Austin, her other brother, hadn't spoken to Graeme since Christmas last year. "Still not speaking, remember? Or, neither of them have said anything to *me* if they've spoken."

"Do they not talk about the farm?"

"No." Austin still had his half of the land rented to Philip Scott. And he had told Philip to talk directly to Graeme if there are any problems with access or stray animals. It saved Austin having to talk to him.

Conversation flowed on various topics, including the Aylwards, for another while before Dolly stood and announced she was leaving before it got too dark. "And in case Dickie Jones mistakes me for a fairy and tries to kidnap me as proof."

Estella watched her cycle down the driveway and heard the cheery ring of her friend's bicycle bell as she turned onto the road out of sight. Even though there was nothing to see, Estella stood and watched the gravel track long after it had been vacated. She wondered guiltily why she hadn't told Dolly what she had seen earlier that day.

She had spent part of her afternoon on the farm picking blackberries for jam. Twenty years' experience taught her the best berries were found on the hedgerows between Robin Hill and Ellendale land and she had tramped to the bottom of the farm to find them.

It was while gathering a clump of particularly juicy fruit that she heard the familiar booming voice of Mr Henry Leclerc at the other side of the ditch.

"*No, no, you silly bugger*! Get out of it! *Percy!*"

Estella knew that Percy was one of the Leclercs' most errant canine companions. She looked up, expecting to see Percy burst through a thin patch in the hedge but, instead, she heard another voice.

"*Percy!*"

A man – powerful, commanding. There was a pause of a few moments and then, straining her ears, Estella heard Mr Leclerc again.

"Well, I'll be damned! How on *earth* did you do that, Aylward? I can never get the silly bugger to listen."

The other voice answered. "Beginner's luck, I suppose. Once he gets used to me, he likely won't listen at all."

As she listened carefully, Estella almost absentmindedly climbed up the ditch to see over it. Reaching the top, she gingerly peered through the twist of leaves, branches and briars. On the far side, two men were standing in a large, recently harvested field. A collection of dogs was gambolling to and fro. She spotted Percy a little distance away, sniffing

22

intently. No doubt he was trying to find something disgusting to roll in. However, her eyes quickly left the dog and focused on the men.

Henry Leclerc was easily recognisable. With his tweed suits and startling red or yellow waistcoats, he could be picked out at a distance of three-quarters of a mile. Though quite an active man, he still carried a distinct drinker's paunch. It preceded him everywhere, given that he walked with his shoulders thrust back and his head held high. Watching him stroll, anyone unfamiliar would have thought him supercilious – the long, commanding strides, the swing of his unnecessary walking stick. But that impression could not have been further from the truth. Mr Leclerc was a generous, hearty, avuncular man who had time for everyone no matter whether they were the village vagabond or a visiting duke. If someone was inherently decent, he treated them as they deserved to be treated.

Throughout her childhood, Estella had spent many hours and days on the Leclerc estate since her father was one of the family's closest friends. She fondly remembered being plied with cream cakes and milky tea by Henry's wife, Barbara. Riding around the yard on some of their largest hunting horses while Mr Leclerc judiciously held on to one of her short little legs, just in case. And she remembered being engulfed by the loving arms of both Leclercs at her father's funeral. She had taken such strength from their embrace and the way Barbara had squeezed her hand. All of this she knew and thought of when she glanced at Henry Leclerc. However, the majority of her focus was on the man who walked by his side.

This was obviously the man who had caught Dolly's eye.

Estella could see why. The new farm manager was half a head taller than his employer. He was lean and long-limbed with the easy movement of someone who had faith in their own abilities. Yet his head was bent as he listened attentively to what Mr Leclerc was explaining with free use of his walking stick to gesticulate. Their backs were to her but, in the weak autumn sun, she could make out rich brown hair peeking out from beneath his cloth cap. He was walking with such deliberate slowness that she suspected he was the sort of man inclined to walk much more quickly than the pace being set. And even though they were now at a distance from her, Estella could see his hands. He clasped his right wrist in his left hand behind his back and she could see the fingers beating out an almost constant rhythm against the pale skin on the underside of his arm.

Though the two men disappeared around a corner out of sight, she continued to look for a while longer until her foot slipped and she was forced to catch on to a tree branch. The sudden jolt shocked her out of her daze and she gave her head a little shake. Ogling over a ditch at a stranger! What on earth was she doing? She had enough jobs to fill her time without wasting it on such rubbish.

Redoubling her blackberrying efforts, she continued to search the briars for another half hour until her basin was overflowing with deep purple fruit. Yet the task was so mindless she did find her thoughts drifting back to the figure on the other side of the ditch.

Estella's mind continued to wander once she got home and began to weigh out equal amounts of sugar to fruit and pour both into the cavernous jam pan.

It was another mindless exercise which she had performed hundreds of times over the years with various fruits – gooseberries, blackcurrants, raspberries and strawberries – but blackberry was her favourite. It was, therefore, a little worrying when she almost let it boil over while drying her clean jam jars.

Testing its thickness, the jam was just beginning to rumple before her spoon when Dolly arrived. But Estella kept going, knowing that the jam couldn't be left to sit while she chatted to her friend. By the time she had it all potted and the lids securely fastened while the jam was still hot, to prevent mould, Dolly had prepared their supper and they were able to test out a little of the fresh jam.

As she had listened to Dolly gossip about the Aylwards, Estella's account of her own sighting of the elusive new farm manager grew heavy on the tip of her tongue. The more Dolly spoke, the more Estella felt her own information recede into the distance. It would be awkward to butt into the middle of Dolly's monologue with her own meagre knowledge of this Mr Aylward. The details of his person were as hazy as an unfocused photograph. And what could she tell Dolly that she did not already know from her own sighting of Aylward? And then there was the fact that Dolly would, no doubt, squawk indignantly and chastise Stella for withholding information. It was simpler to sit and listen while occasionally making appropriate exclamations in the right places.

When she went to bed that night, Estella's mind began to spool through all the evidence she had gathered about the Aylwards. Firstly, she surmised that they were not exceedingly sociable people. If there was information to be had, you were guaranteed one of the local snouts would turn up on your doorstep with an empty jug looking for cream or a week-old cake that needed eating. Yet these prospectors had remained unusually silent which meant they had obviously failed to gain viable nuggets to pass on.

Whoever these Aylwards were, they were good at keeping to themselves. And yet ... such reticence had given rise to plenty of speculation. Why had they come to Ellendale? Was there a local family connection? No one had ever heard of any other Aylwards in the area. But perhaps there were relatives on the mother's side. After all, they hadn't managed to winkle out her maiden name. *Was* her son married? If so, why had no one but Dickie Jones seen that woman who might be his wife? Dickie was hardly daft enough to invent an entire scene between a small boy and his mother – although Estella had her doubts about that assertion. And if they were real and not a figment of Dickie's imagination, why had both been hidden away? Were mother and son ashamed of them? Was there something wrong with one or both?

Tossing and turning in her bed, Estella couldn't find any answers. She was still awake when Graeme lumbered up the stairs, shoulders bumping dully on either side of the narrow ascent. She listened to his movements for a little while longer, heard him grumble when he dropped something on the floor of his room. Eventually, the noise subsided and the house was once more shrouded in heavy silence.

Estella turned over and slept.

Chapter 3

"Stella!"

Estella emerged from the cowshed, holding a yard scraper. She had finished milking the cows and was cleaning out the mess left behind so that everything was ready for use in the morning. She had heard the car arrive but assumed it was either Graeme or someone for him so hadn't bothered to investigate.

"Austin!" Her face split into a grin. Her other brother was there to collect her for their table tennis practice that evening. She always loved the few hours a week they shared with one another. It was the start of a new season and she was looking forward to the distraction over the winter months. "What are you doing here so early? Or am I late?" The smile slid off her face, concerned that she had let the evening slip away from her.

The younger of the two Frayne brothers stood in the yard beside his car, hands in his pockets. He was so like his father – short in stature, square-headed, yet had surprisingly delicate hands. These hands had served him well in a professional capacity. Like his father, Austin was a veterinarian. Those hands were perfect for the delivery of many species of animal. It was the part of the job which he loved most and he enjoyed telling his sister about the many successful births he attended. He loved to talk about his work. It made him immeasurably happy. And when he smiled, his eyes shone bright and the skin around them crinkled with contentment.

"No, I'm early. I saw Graeme's car outside Nelly Sweeney's when I was passing and thought I'd head straight here rather than going home first. Is there any food in the house? I'm famished."

"You go on in and get something," Estella told him as she turned back to the shed. "I'll just finish here and be in in a minute." However, as she ducked into the cool dimness of the building, Austin passed in beside her. "What are you ...?"

He shrugged. "Helping so you'll be done quicker."

"I thought you were hungry?"

"I'll live."

"You just want me to wait on you," she teased, giving him a shove.

"How do you know I'm not waiting around so I can wait on you?" he asked innocently.

For a moment, she was mollified but then she snorted. "Because I know you."

They worked together companionably, knowing the rhythm of things from their childhood. One scraped dung from the floor while the other filled the mangers with hay ready for the morning. The weather was good so the cows spent the night out at grass. On fresh pastures, they always produced more milk than when fed on dried fodder.

Job done, they both went into the kitchen where Estella forwent her usual bread and jam, instead frying some eggs and rashers of bacon in honour of Austin's presence. They were just mopping up egg yolks and bacon grease with brown bread when the phone rang, making both jump. It was attached to a bell just outside the back door so that it could be heard ringing out in the yard. But this also meant that it was deafeningly loud when you were sitting in the kitchen. Estella hurried out to the hall to answer it.

"Hello, Stella! How are you?"

The voice was comfortingly familiar. Marion Ward was the secretary at the veterinary practice her father had co-owned. Austin now worked there too.

"I'm fine, Marion. How're you?"

"Oh, you know, chipping away. Listen, I'm just about to go home but you wouldn't happen to be seeing Austin this evening for table tennis, would you?"

Estella glanced up to find Austin standing in the kitchen doorway. "He's here now. Do you want to talk to him?" She was just about to hand him the receiver when Marion spoke.

"No, no. Just if you let him know Henry Leclerc rang. Wants him to look at a lame horse. I said he'll be able to do it this evening."

"Yes, I'll get him to do that. No problem." She saw Austin mouth 'What?' but waved him away.

"Is that Marion?" he asked. "What does she want?"

Estella hung up the phone. "Henry Leclerc's got a lame horse. Wants you to take a look."

"Oh. Right." Austin nodded. "We could go on the way. Happy to tag along?"

29

"Course I am!" Her face lit up at the prospect. She had always loved attending calls with her father when she was little. Nowadays, it was rare she ever got to see anything as interesting as a bullock with a puss-filled cyst the size of a football or a ewe with a uterine prolapse. A lame horse was unlikely to be quite as gloriously disgusting but it was still fascinating watching her brother work. And then there was the added prospect of perhaps getting to see the illusive Aylward.

Estella quickly ran upstairs to wash her face and change into clean clothes. She could have worn a dress or skirt. She had many of them. But instead, she donned another of her father's pairs of trousers even if it did give rise to comments about her apparel. Others did not know the depth of longing which was associated with the wearing of her father's old clothes. How, for twenty-one long and painful months, she had cared for Reg before his death. She put everything into what remained of his health and happiness. She had shunned social occasions, devoting herself in a kind of pseudo-religious servitude to her earthly father.

When he died, he left her a tidy sum of money. Her brothers both received large tracts of land – tangible reminders of a paternal presence. Graeme had been gifted the house and yard. But Estella was left in a kind of limbo. It was as if the anchor which moored her to the solid ground of her home had been washed away. There was nothing tethering her to a place now that the connection to her father was severed. She was cast adrift, lonely and lost, not belonging to the place she had called home for more than twenty years. Yet, when it came to emptying out her father's wardrobe and drawers, she suddenly found something she could hold on to, hold close and once again feel like she belonged. Something still tenuously connected to Reg Frayne and the life he had inhabited. She had meant to divide the clothes between her brothers but, instead carried them down the hall to her own room where they had stayed ever since.

"Hurry up, Stella!"

Austin stood with mock impatience at the foot of the stairs, tapping his watch, when she appeared at the top. She clattered down past him and, grabbing her table tennis bat off the kitchen dresser, headed straight out into the yard and sat into his Morris Minor. It was a moment before he appeared. She rolled down the window.

"*Hurry up, Aussie!*" she jeered in a sing-song voice, leaning out the window. However, her smugness was ruined somewhat when the glass panel dropped suddenly, disappearing into the cavity in the door. "Oh, bugger," she muttered.

Austin shrugged. "Happens all the time lately. Here." He went rummaging in his equipment and produced pointy-nosed forceps. "See if you can grab it with that."

He drove off while Estella struggled with the glass. She was rather hampered by the bumpiness of the road which repeatedly jolted the glass out of her grasp. Eventually, she managed to catch it between her fingers and jerk it up. She smiled triumphantly at her brother.

"Don't be too pleased with yourself," he warned. "Given the state of Ellendale's back lane, it'll likely have fallen down again by the time we get to the yard."

As they turned into Leclercs' lane, Estella asked, "When did they take down the old oak tree?"

"Blew down in the spring. Have you not been up this way since then?"

"No, I haven't been to the yard in years. I just go up to the house."

"You get to use the posh entrance, eh? Not the tradesman's entrance like little old me."

Estella grinned. "Some of us just can't help being more refined than others."

On arrival into the stable yard, they were greeted by a cacophony of yapping and barking as dogs of various sizes issued from three different open doors. A stable lad was by the water trough and pump, washing off a sweaty bay stallion with a thick neck and proud carriage. Beside him stood Henry Leclerc resplendent in a bright-red waistcoat, plus fours and thick, knitted, khaki-green socks. He doffed his cap and waved it above his head in salutation. The horse's ears barely twitched at the sudden burst of enthusiasm beside him. Estella knew not all horses would have maintained such serene nonchalance.

"*Quiet!*" boomed Mr Leclerc as the dogs worked themselves into a frenzy.

The two Fraynes got out as the dogs subsided, contenting themselves to sniff around the wheels of the car and ankles of the visitors. Estella breathed in the scent of horses – the sweet hay, the sweat, the dung, the unique musk of the animals themselves. It was all so familiar to her and yet she had not smelt it in a long time. She looked around the yard with fresh eyes, marvelling at the whitewashed barn and stable block that ran along two sides of the paved square at its centre. The tiled roof overhung by several feet to protect the horses' heads on rainy days and outside each stable door was a hook welded onto a horseshoe with numerous bridles, rollers, headcollars and ropes on each. Yet, despite the multitude of objects filling the space, everything was immaculately tidy. The small square paving blocks were swept clean of hay, straw and other forms of equestrian waste. The usual pile of horse rugs and tack left outside the stables had miraculously disappeared. There had clearly been a regime change and Estella thought she might know who was responsible.

"*Two* Fraynes!" Mr Leclerc beamed. "We *are* honoured." He bowed and doffed his cap once again.

"How are you, sir?" Austin asked, shaking his hand.

"Well! I'm well." He turned to Estella and kissed her on the cheek then held her by the shoulders to better observe her. "And how's Little Iris Kellett?" It was the nickname he had given her after her many successful years in the competition ring. Back when she was still riding horses. "Gosh, I haven't seen you in far too long." His smile was warm.

"What's this about a lame horse?" Austin chipped in, beginning to head for the stables.

Glancing up, Estella caught sight of the clock tower and the wind vane that had always fascinated her as a child. It was in the shape of a large mare and foal perpetually frozen mid-gallop with their manes and tails streaming out behind them as if tossed by the wind they always ran into. And then there was the timepiece below it, its large face forever blank. Except it wasn't. Checking her watch, Estella realised that, for the first time in her life, the clock was actually telling the time. When she was a little girl visiting with her father, the hands had resolutely remained between quarter and ten to five and never moved an inch from the dozen or so minutes to home time for the stable boys. As she watched, she saw the minute hand jump to the next little black line and felt a little thrill of gladness that the workers might finally be able to go home and not be forever stuck with twelve minutes of work to do.

She gave her head a shake then realised she'd been left behind and hurried to catch up. Just as she reached her brother's shoulder, another figure emerged from a stable to their right, pushing a wheelbarrow of manure, and Estella stopped again.

It was Aylward. He wore braces and a shirt with the sleeves rolled up past his elbows. As he heaved the barrow with effortless ease, turned left and began pushing it away, she momentarily saw the fabric stretch across his shoulders. His dark hair was covered once again by a cap pulled low over his eyes.

"*Ivan!*" Mr Leclerc called.

Aylward looked up. So his name was Ivan. Estella peeked at him and wondered if he really looked like an Ivan. It was a good, strong name and he appeared to be a good, strong man. Ivan Aylward. Yes, it suited him very well.

"Ivan, this is the vet, Austin Frayne. A natural with horses, this one. Like his father." He clapped Austin on the back. "Austin, Ivan Aylward, my new farm manager. And one of the best horsemen I've come across in years."

Abandoning the loaded barrow to another stableboy,

Ivan ignored the compliment and wordlessly shook Austin's hand. However, he did glance at Estella.

"And this is Estella Frayne."

"Hello," Ivan said quietly.

"Another natural around horses. Although I haven't seen her on one in an awfully long time," Mr Leclerc admonished gently, with a stern glance in her direction.

Estella looked away.

"She gave up a while back," Austin answered quickly. "*Anyway*. What's the matter with this horse of yours?"

Ivan turned about and, grabbing a headcollar and lead rope, opened another stable.

Against the back wall of the square box, Estella could make out a dark, dappled grey horse. It was raw-boned and had a certain wild look in its eye. Immediately, she knew it was only a youngster.

"Three-year-old. Just in from the field," Mr Leclerc said. "We've brought in a few lately. Handling and breaking for the hunting season, you know. This one was fine for the first few days but now … well, he's lame and … who knows." He gestured vaguely at the animal and puffed out a noisy stream of air. The horse flinched. "Oh! Sorry," Leclerc muttered.

Ivan was softly approaching the animal, murmuring all the while. The horse viewed him suspiciously but didn't pull away when he slid on the headcollar.

"He doesn't lead that well," he muttered. "Best keep out of the way. Although he's a lot less flighty now he's hobbling."

They moved aside. Man and horse came marching purposefully out of the stable but, despite its best efforts to

35

make a bid for freedom, the animal was immediately struggling to bear weight on his front right hoof.

"I won't ask you to trot him up," Austin said blandly. "We can see he's got a real problem there with the off-fore. Any falls or strains or jarring when you were bringing him in and getting him going?"

"No," Ivan answered confidently.

"Heat, swelling, bumps, hardness in the muscle?"

"No."

Austin turned to his sister. "Well, Stella?" He winked.

"A gravel?" she suggested.

Mr Leclerc nodded approvingly but Aylward viewed her with mild surprise. Yet she held firm on her diagnosis. She had seen her father work many times over the years and, more often than not, sudden, unexplained lameness in a horse was due to an infection in the hoof. Gravel was always the first thing that was investigated in such cases. Both she and Austin knew that so she assumed he allowed her to guess because he thought the same thing.

"Run to the car, Stella, and get me out the testers and the hoof knife." He turned to Aylward. "Bring him back into the stable and we'll see what we have."

When Estella returned half a minute later, Austin was carefully rubbing his hand firmly down the horse's leg, talking to it all the while. Calmly entering the stable, she silently passed him the hoof knife. With neat movements, he scraped all the packed dirt out of the hoof and studied the golden-coloured surface. Wordlessly, he handed Estella the knife and she offered him the hoof tester in return. It was shaped a little like a salad-tongs and he caught the hoof between the two halves and closed the handles gently, testing to see if the horse reacted to the pressure exerted. When he got close to the front of the hoof, the horse jerked his foot away.

"There it is," he muttered. "Knife again, Stella."

With quick, deft movements, he cut away small chucks from the bottom of the hoof. The horse tried once again to wrench its foot from his grasp but he held firm until –

"Yes!"

The horse grunted. An unhealthy-looking stream of yellow pus oozed from the hole Austin had dug into the flat of the hoof and dripped onto the straw. Even standing a few feet away, Estella could smell the foul stench of infection. But she smiled nonetheless. They had found the problem and eased the animal's pain. That was worth a bad smell or two.

"He should feel a little bit better now." Austin stood and stretched his back. "But I'd get a bran poultice on that soon just to draw out the badness. He should be right as rain in a few days." He gave the horse a scratch on the shoulder. "You're a good lad, aren't you?"

They filed out of the stable with Mr Leclerc issuing an order to the lad leading the stallion to fetch the materials for the poultice. Bran poultices were one of Estella's favourite treatments as when you poured boiling water over the cereal in preparation, it gave off the most wonderful rich, malty smell. Every time she used one, she wondered who it was that first discovered a bran poultice was a universal treatment for lame cattle, sheep and horses that worked by drawing infection out of a hoof. Was there science behind it or had the discovery been a fluke? Whatever it was, it was a highly effective treatment and that was all that mattered.

"Where are you two youngsters off to on this lovely evening, then?" Mr Leclerc asked as Austin washed his hoof knife and hands in the trough.

"Table tennis is back for the autumn."

"Oh, yes! I'd forgotten about that! In fact ..." he turned back to the stables, "Ivan!" At his employer's behest, he appeared. "Ivan, I never thought to mention the table tennis club. You remember, when you asked was there much to do here in the evenings? Austin and Stella here are members so you know the two of them now."

Estella glanced at the farm manager, trying to gauge his reaction. There were many people who looked on table tennis as a foolish pursuit. It wasn't really a physical game, was it? Hitting a little ball back and forth over a six-inch net on what was essentially a kitchen table. Surely there was no skill in that? But there was and Estella knew it. On occasions, she had seen grown men drip sweat as they slogged over points, neither willing to give in.

Ivan Aylward gave little away. "Oh right – I'll keep it in mind," he said, before disappearing to find the stable lad in charge of the poultice.

"Right. We'd best be off." Carelessly wiping his fingers on his trousers to dry them, Austin shook hands with Mr Leclerc.

"Lovely to see you both again. Just like old times, eh? Well ... almost." For a moment, Mr Leclerc's jovial manner slipped and each stopped to watch Reg Frayne's shade walk across the paved yard with familiar, confident strides. "Oh, and Stella, you must head up to the orchard and get some apples soon. The trees are laden. And Barbara wants as many of them used as possible before the wasps get at them. So, tell everyone to come along with a basket or a bucket or, frankly, a *barrel*. I've never seen anything like it." He shook his head in wonder. "Anyway! I'd better let you get off." He guided Estella to her door. "Don't take so long coming to see us next time. Barb would *love* to see you." He laid a hand on her shoulder. "I mean it, Stella," he said quietly. "Don't be a stranger. We want to see you out in the world again. You shouldn't hide yourself away forever. You're too good for that."

Henry Leclerc's parting words shocked her. It was easy to forget there were people who remembered her when she never saw them. Yes, she went to table tennis practice, to church, to the shops and to town once a month. But, for years now, she spent the majority of her time at home. Firstly, it was caring for her father that tied her to the place. Now, it was trying to keep his memory alive.

Chapter 4

When Estella was growing up, Robin Hill had been filled with every domestic animal you could think of – cattle, sheep, goats, ducks, hens, donkeys and horses. There were never large amounts of stock, given that Reg had plenty of veterinary work to do. But one thing the family always had in abundance was horses. Mares and foals, yearlings up to the old pony the whole family had learnt to ride on.

Reg adored everything about horses. He waxed lyrical about the way they moved – the float of a trot, the confident marching walk. Their individual personalities and behaviours fascinated him. There was the mare that tried to stand on your toe when you were doing up the girth on the saddle. The little chestnut gelding who simply lay down whenever you asked it to do something it didn't want to. And then there was the pony who acted as a guide to every horse who passed through the yard and was never fazed or scared of anything ... except donkeys whom he was mortally afraid of.

The Frayne children had ridden from an early age. But Estella – the youngest of the family – had displayed an aptitude for equestrianism that easily outstripped her brothers'. One of her first memories was being held on the back of a fat little skewbald pony that belonged to Graeme, her hands entwined in its mane. As a little girl, she had been given her own pony called Poppet who was lovely until she saw grass. At that point, she would put her head down to gorge. And it didn't matter a whit if a tiny child ended up crying on the ground beside where Poppet ate having been pulled from the saddle. That pony taught her how to maintain a good seat (and not get dumped on the floor), the joy of cantering up a stubble field alongside her father and how to infuse the word '*Get!*' with just enough growl to make the pony do what you wanted it to. Over the years, her father had bought her numerous ponies of varying abilities and temperaments, each teaching her something new and making her a better rider. She competed in showing classes, show jumping and, in the winter months, she hunted alongside Reg, the Leclercs and hundreds of other like-minded equestrians.

Even as he aged and struggled with a bad hip, Reg could not be dissuaded from continuing his love affair with horses. With his sons, he had the common ground of a shared gender which made it easier to talk to his boys. With Estella, he had horses.

No matter what was going on in either of their lives, their shared love of the same animal brought them closer together.

It had happened in the spring of 1957, almost two and a half years before. Over the New Year, Estella had been breaking a young horse her father had bred out of his favourite mare

– a smoke-grey gelding called Burt. That January, his hip had been excruciatingly painful in the cold mornings and he was forced to come down the stairs on one leg with both hands on Estella's shoulders. The ache had been so bad he had forgone his beloved hunting for the season but was determined that he would be fit and well enough to compete when show jumping began later in the year. He watched impatiently as Estella trained his horse and was exceedingly jealous but also immensely proud that she was the first person to ever sit on Burt. It was a thrill he had experienced many times in his life so it was only right that his daughter was given the same opportunities.

Burt, however, was tricky. Some days he was a perfect gentleman and others he was inclined to be completely uncooperative. He especially did not like riding on the road and was inclined to nap as soon as he realised Estella was guiding him down the road. He would stop dead, plant his hooves and refuse to go forward. Sometimes he would begin to hop on the spot, back up or spin around. On two occasions, he reared straight up in the air and left Estella with no other option but to hold on around his neck and pray that he didn't lose his balance and fall over backwards on top of her. Eventually, however, Burt's fits of pique subsided and he became an animal Estella was proud to say she had trained. It was, therefore, with great confidence she handed over the horse's reins to her father.

From the off, Reg and Burt didn't get on. With his hip still giving trouble, Reg was in need of an animal that was completely docile and unlikely to challenge him as a rider. Having hobbled around for years, he no longer had the muscle tone in his right leg to grip the saddle properly or use his lower limbs to control the direction of the horse. A green youngster like Burt needed all the guidance he could get. Really, Estella should have told her father not to ride the horse – that she would show jump it for him. But how could you tell your father not to ride his own horse? She didn't want an argument. And she didn't want to upset him. In the months that followed, she often wished she had not tried to spare his feelings. It would have saved so much pain.

One evening, just as the weather was beginning to improve, Reg came home from work and wanted to ride Burt. He'd left the horse off for a week having hurt his bad hip lying on a cold stone floor to calve a cow. But on that particular day, his hip felt – if not good – better.

Estella was getting ready to feed the horses. She suggested that they wait until after tea when the animals had had a chance to digest their food and she could also get up on the horse first just to be on the safe side. But Reg was determined and set to tacking up Burt. He wasn't going to do much, just bring the horse for a quick hack down the road and come straight home. Hacking on the road was often seen as a good option for horses that were a little fresh since they usually weren't foolish enough to try anything silly on the hard surface for fear of hurting themselves. It was why, when breaking a horse, most people got up on them on a stone or paved yard.

Mounting up, Estella heard Reg grumble under his breath as he sat into the saddle. He rubbed his hip vigorously, then gathering his reins he clicked his tongue and nudged the horse out through the yard gate with his heels.

She never knew why but, for some reason, Estella found herself following her father through the gate so she could watch him trot off down the lane to the road. It was as if a thread had been tied to the horse's tail and she was being pulled along behind, compelled to trail in his wake. When Burt moved, she moved. When he stopped dead in the middle of the lane, she stopped. In slow motion, she watched the animal back up and felt her own feet retreat. She saw her father dig his heels into the horse's sides. And she watched in horror as the animal suddenly went up, up, up in the air and then down, down, down backwards. On top of her father.

Had Reg been a young man or even in the fullness of health, he would have easily managed the rear. He would have leaned forward, grabbing on to the horse's neck, just as he had shown Estella aged eleven when her pony took to dancing on his hind legs. But hampered by a bad hip and leg, Reg had lost his grip on the saddle's knee rolls and slid backwards, automatically pulling on the reins to try and regain his equilibrium. It was enough pressure to throw Burt off balance and, rather than come back down on his front feet, he had done the one thing Estella feared he would do and fallen on his back, sandwiching her father between three-quarters of a ton of horse and unyielding packed stones.

The air left Estella's lungs. She could not shout. She could not utter a single sound. She felt the earth beneath her feet shudder with the impact of man and beast. Then she was running. Running as she watched the horse flail its legs, searching for purchase, finding itself out of its element and scrabbling at air instead of solid ground. Finally, Burt

44

managed to roll himself over onto his belly, his head now facing Estella, his eyes white and shining with fear. But she wasn't looking at the horse who continued to lie on the laneway, completely winded and unable to get up. She was looking at her father who lay prone and diminutive beside the shivering bulk of his horse.

"*Daddy!*" she finally screamed. "*Daddy!*"

Graeme had been feeding sheep when he heard his sister calling. He knew by the pitch of her voice that it was bad. He abandoned the meal bucket and ran. When he saw man and beast lying on the lane, he could not bring himself to approach. He could not look into his father's blank face. Instead, he ran inside and phoned an ambulance.

They took him straight to a hospital in Dublin. Estella travelled all the way with him, still wearing her soiled yard clothes. Her teeth had chattered so badly she had clamped her hand over her mouth.

Once he was placed on a ward, Estella could not be parted from her father. She wanted to be there when he woke up. *If* he woke up. She wasn't even sure he would want to wake, given the doctors' prognosis. He had suffered significant damage to the lower thoracic and lumbar regions of his spine. They surmised – though were reluctant to say definitively – that should Reg Frayne regain consciousness, he would never walk again.

For three weeks Estella sat by his bedside, barely eating, drinking or sleeping herself. Eventually, a kindly nurse intervened and forced her with a mixture of coaxing and chastisement to take better care of herself for her father's sake. Another week passed with Reg neither improving nor deteriorating. Estella began to take regular meals and sleep when she felt tired. When her father finally did wake, she had gone to the shops to buy herself some fresh fruit since the supply in the hospital cafeteria was somewhat ... wrinkled. Walking through the door to his room, she had dropped her shopping bag, bruising the apples at the bottom.

"Hello, Stella," Reg croaked, just managing to lift his fingers off the blanket. "The doctor's jus' told me'll never ride ... horse 'gain 'r walk."

"Yes." The tears silently streamed down Estella's face as she grasped her father's hand and kissed it.

"Good thing 'bout par'lysis." His tongue stumbled over the final word, unused to its formation and also thick with lack of use. "Can't feel sore hip ... can't feel 'nything."

And with that, Reg Frayne began to sob like a child.

Reg was in hospital for months. The damage was severe and permanent. His spinal cord had been crushed and nothing could be done to bring back the feeling in his legs. The gnawing pain in his hip was replaced by an excruciating pain in his lower back. He could not move without gasping or even crying out, despite high doses of painkillers. There were also crush injuries to his organs which were difficult to treat, given the fact that Reg could not feel discomfort when something was wrong. He was constantly monitored for signs of infection or blood loss. There was the risk of urinary tract infections from the catheter, blood clots in his legs and bed sores which could become infected if they were not immediately spotted and treated. He required so much care in those first weeks that it would have been impossible for anyone but experts to treat him. Eventually, however, he was deemed well enough to be moved to a hospital closer to home.

Austin, who had completed his sixth – and final – year of exams had returned home shortly before his father. It had been the plan for years that Austin would work in the veterinary practice alongside Reg. But now, barely a month out of college, he was stepping into his father's shoes. It was an impossible task for anyone, never mind a twenty-four-year-old who was yet to officially graduate from university. However, the goodwill which Reg always courted and the Frayne name were enough to give Austin an advantage over anyone else who might have filled in. Austin also had a calm head and, aside from six years of education, he had spent almost all of his life following his father around the county's farms learning what they didn't teach in textbooks.

Having been away at university so long, Austin hardly recognised the sister that watched at their father's bedside. Once, Estella had been bubbly and quick to smile like her friend Dolly Greer. Now, she was quiet, introspective and inclined to shy away from conversation with others, leaving Austin to talk to the nurses and doctors even though she was in the hospital more often. He thought that once their father began to improve, the old Stella would return, unaffected by the experience that was Reg's alone. After all, Reg was the one who had suffered the pain and trauma of paralysis. All she had done was watch.

Estella travelled in the ambulance with her father to the local hospital where he was to be cared for and begin his physical rehabilitation. Once Reg was settled in for the night, Austin picked Estella up and drove her home. If she had not been with Austin, she would not have been able to face the drive up the laneway where her father had fallen. She held her breath as they trundled over the spot where it happened. The car hit a bump and, for one horrifying moment, Estella had the terrifying thought that they had somehow driven over their father or the spectre of what had once been the whole man. Shakily, she released a long, slow exhalation as the tears streamed down her face. The thought was absurd, she knew that, but she could not help it. She might as well have driven over Reg. It was, after all, her fault that the horse had reared and fallen on him. She had failed to train the animal well enough. She had allowed her father to ride an unsafe horse. It was her fault he was condemned to live the rest of his life in a wheelchair. Her fault. Entirely her fault.

Getting out of the car, Estella looked towards the stables, expecting to see Burt's speckled white muzzle gleam like a beacon above the half door at the end of the row. He was always curious about the goings-on in the yard. But he was not there. Two other horses nickered in recognition but otherwise there was an empty stable where there should have been a horse.

"Did you …?"

She couldn't bring herself to say it. The temptation was there, even for her. Part of her – even if it was a small, cruel, remorseless part – wanted Austin to get his gun and shoot the horse for what it had done to their father. It had destroyed Reg's life and it, therefore, deserved destruction as well. But Estella knew in her heart that the horse was not to blame. It was simply an animal being an *animal*. Yet she did wonder if either of her brothers would have been tempted to put the horse down anyway rather than have it serve as a constant reminder of what happened. In an irrational moment, it was possible that their anger would boil over and they would take it out on the animal. Suddenly, she had a horrible fear that the horse was dead and that that too would be her fault for having failed both man and beast.

"Henry Leclerc took him," Austin answered her unfinished question. "Said he'd keep him or buy him or sell him or … whatever you want done with him. Up to you."

Estella simply nodded. She did not have the strength of mind to make such decisions. All she wanted to do was go up to her own bed and sleep.

When she eventually lay her head on the pillow, her brain began to whir incessantly. The bed felt unfamiliar, the covers damp, icy-cold. She turned onto her side, cocooning herself in the eiderdown, and switched on the bedside lamp, bathing the room in warm light rather than the chilly blackness of night. Her eyes fell on the empty bed pushed up against the opposite wall. Lying there, just looking, she tried to work out how long it had been since her sister had slept in the other bed.

Chapter 5

Estella had turned nine at the beginning of summer, 1943. Though the memories of the day were almost completely erased by what happened two weeks later, she remembered having a small party with her friends and how everyone had been sunburnt by the unusually hot weather. The tops of her arms and the backs of her legs had been particularly bad. Her mother had diligently rubbed calamine lotion over the inflamed skin while Estella lay face down on her bed. Her elder sister, Joy, had watched wordlessly from the other bed, compulsively rubbing the felt waistcoat of a stuffed bear. The waistcoat was a new addition that Prudie Frayne had sewn with motherly affection to save the already threadbare belly of her daughter's teddy.

The bear's waistcoat was already shiny with wear and Estella's skin was still peeling when Prudie Frayne died.

Graeme, aged fifteen and home from school for the weekend, had been drawn by a clatter and thump out in the yard. He emerged from the barn to find his mother face down, one arm caught beneath her body, surrounded by a flock of busy hens. She was crossing to the hen's feed trough

50

with a pan of chicken feed when, mid-step, she lost her balance, staggered and fell – dead before she even hit the cobblestones. She had suffered a sudden and massive intracranial bleed which could not be explained by anyone. She was a fit, healthy mother of four children. There was no family history of sudden haemorrhages or stroke. She was simply alive one moment and dead the next, scattering chicken feed everywhere and sending the hens into a wild fit of ecstasy as they gathered around her to pick at the spilt grain.

In the chaos that followed over the next number of days Estella's sunburn was forgotten and Joy, for the most part, sat mute as ever stroking her teddy's waistcoat. On the occasions when she found her voice, she screamed and struck out at anyone who tried to touch her or calm her down. No one in the family knew what to do with her since it was always Prudie who dealt with her eldest daughter's uncontrolled fits of temper. For fourteen years, Joy had been anchored by the presence of her mother. She had needed Prudie more than any of the other children in the family. Her mother was her voice, helped her understand the strange, terrifying world she had been born into. Prudie kept her calm and knew exactly how to head her off when the world became too much for her roiling mind.

Now that her mother was gone, Joy was completely alone in the small, frightening world that no one could reach her in. She was grieving yet had no concept of how to express her sadness. It built up inside her, slowly and inevitably until it came gushing out. She would throw herself onto the floor, against doors and walls, slap and scream and gouge with fingernails her mother was not there to clip.

None of the remaining members of family had the wherewithal to help Joy. Prudie had years of hands-on experience while the others had watched from the side-lines. She guarded her eldest daughter with the fierceness of a wild animal hovering over its offspring. By insisting on sole care of such a dependent child, Prudie never considered what would happen if she was not there to tend to her. And her self-sufficiency had condemned her eldest girl to live out the rest of her days in an institution for the feeble-minded.

That was the last time Estella had shared a room with her sister. The grief of losing a mother and sister, wife and daughter weighed heavily on the entire Frayne family. Estella and Austin did what was natural for them and clung to one another and their remaining parent. Reg, equally, focused on the two children who needed him most. At fifteen, Graeme was left stranded between the sorrow of his father and that of his younger siblings. He had always been a level-headed, determined, no-nonsense kind of chap. He was almost a man so he could bear the loss better than the two youngest members of the family. No one seemed to notice as Graeme's boldness melted away. No one noticed as his silences stretched for hours – sometimes days – just as his now-absent sister's once had. With every passing day, the distance between the four members of the family grew, splitting them into a group of three and a solitary figure. Still a brother and a son but not one of *them*. No one noticed but Graeme.

The family rift was most evident after Reg's accident. While Austin and Estella developed a rota for visiting their father, Graeme remained at home. There was work to do. He couldn't leave the farm. There were cows to milk, crops to plant, sheds to clean out, lambs to sell, ditches to be trimmed. Yet, Graeme still managed to go to the pub every night. He still managed to sit and drink and play cards.

Eventually, when Austin lost his temper with him, Graeme visited his father.

He brought Estella to the hospital one evening and sat with ill-grace at the foot of the bed. Reg had experienced a painful day and had no desire to see anyone. In such a mood, he was inclined to think more of the weeks during which his eldest child had not deigned to visit rather than his immediate presence. Estella hung back, chewing on her thumbnail until it bled as the antagonism between the two men swelled into a noxious bubble that poisoned the air around both. Graeme's reticence and apparent lack of concern rankled their father in a way it would never have irritated him had it come from someone else. In fact, Reg hated it when people showed sympathy or pity. Yet it seemed to be all he wanted from his eldest boy. And it was the one thing Graeme, who barely answered the questions his father put to him, would not show. Reg had no pity for *him* when he was grieving the loss of his mother. Reg never thought of how traumatic it was to find your mother dead but still warm on the cobblestones of the yard she crossed every day. It was a cruel oversight Graeme could never forgive his father for. Though it may have been petty to hold on to such resentment, Graeme was incapable of letting it go – not even when his father lay propped in a hospital bed without the use of his lower limbs.

The resentment only blossomed further when Reg was finally moved home.

Though not yet fully capable of caring for himself, it was agreed by everyone that keeping him in hospital would not aid his recovery. Reg was restless and unhappy – longing to go home so that he could begin to feel less like an invalid and regain some small amount of privacy. Austin and Estella spent an entire day preparing the house for him. While he measured all the doorways to make sure Reg wouldn't catch his knuckles on the wooden frames while wheeling himself through, Estella removed boots and shoes from inside the back door and found a narrower table for the telephone in the hall. They dismantled his bed and brought it down to the dining room which was being repurposed as a bedroom. All the dining furniture was borne upstairs where their father could not see it and to make his new room look as though it was meant to be a bedroom and not a slapdash substitute.

Graeme's sole contribution was to remove his boots and leave them directly in the path of their father's wheelchair as soon as he crossed the threshold.

The bulk of their father's care fell to Estella. She was, after all, a woman and therefore the family member the others deemed best suited to the role. Though she adored Reg, it was not a natural role for either of them. Before, the understanding between them had always come back to animals – to Reg's occupation and Estella's work on the farm. Now, with nothing but each other, each suddenly felt exposed. It didn't help that Estella had to change her father's position every two hours to prevent pressure sores and check the skin of his lifeless limbs for redness, moisture, heat or swelling. She was in charge of daily physical therapy sessions to help with circulation, helping him to wash, monitoring his catheter, making sure he maintained regular bowel movements. There was a nurse who came for a few hours every second day as well but, for the most part, Estella managed on her own.

The arrangement upset Reg more than it upset Estella. She cultivated the pragmatic efficiency of a true medical professional and treated all her tasks with a business-like air. There was no point in being squeamish or embarrassed. She just had to get on with it. And it wasn't as if she lacked medical experience. Every opportunity she got, she stood at her father's elbow and watched him repair prolapses on cattle or sheep, perform surgeries, set broken bones and stitch gaping wounds. She had developed a keen eye for details and a strong stomach – both of which were invaluable when it came to treating a human patient. However, she did sometimes struggle not to constantly treat Reg as her patient. Sometimes, she had to remember that he was still her father.

Reg hated the whole situation. Always an active man, dependence on others was something he could never abide. It had always been he who had helped people, not the other way around. Before the injury, he was a man who had lived his life out of doors. Confined to a bed or a wheelchair, he could never go far on his own. The constant backpain made it difficult for him to push his own wheelchair. If he did go outside, the uneven surface of the yard and pathways shook and ground the bones he could still feel. His whole world had shrunk to the few square yards of the ground floor of his house that he could navigate. He became irritable and was inclined to brood. Though Estella did her best to entertain him, often all he wanted to do was wallow in his own sadness.

One thing that truly upset him was the absence of all the horses. Neither of his sons had any inclination to share his interest in the animals and Estella maintained that she had enough to do with housework, yard work and caring for him. This excuse wounded him deeply. He felt his daughter was blaming him for the removal of her beloved animals even though she did no such thing. Truthfully, she wanted rid of them herself. All they did was serve as a reminder of the time before – when her father was strong, capable, mobile. Every time she approached them, smelled their distinctive scent, the image of Reg going up, up, up and coming down, down, down flashed across her vision and left her blinking away hot, angry tears. It was her interest in horses that paralysed her father. If she had not shared Reg's love of everything equine, perhaps he would still be walking around, complaining of nothing other than his aching hip.

Gradually, everyone settled into a routine. Austin's reputation as a vet grew, Graeme worked on the farm and Estella cared for their father. The brothers still struggled to see eye to eye and, after twenty years of arguing, Austin reached the end of his tether and moved out to live closer to the veterinary practice. They had been snappish with one another for months and Estella usually got caught between them as she tried to keep the peace. Their father didn't help as, no matter the disagreement, Reg always took Austin's side. Sometimes Estella struggled to see why Graeme even stayed on the farm with the rest of the family. Later, she realised it was because

Graeme feared their father would give the farm to Austin who had neither the time nor the inclination to work it himself.

Winter was especially difficult. With the colder, wet weather, the dull pain that was Reg's constant companion increased. He struggled to stay warm. His bouts of depression lasted longer as he sat in his wheelchair staring out while rain and wind made the windows rattle. Estella began to notice unexplained bruises on his useless limbs. It was not until she snuck into the room without her father noticing and saw him viciously pinch his own legs that she realised he was bruising his own skin. It was the only time she lost her temper with him. She was furious that he would willingly cause himself harm. It hurt to think she was putting so much effort into keeping him healthy and his unfeeling limbs undamaged while he deliberately did the opposite. They both cried as each fought to have their feelings heard. She was worn out with the responsibility of caring for him and he was miserable living what he saw as a half-life, confined and incapable of doing the things he loved.

One morning, almost a year after his accident, Reg announced he wanted to go through all the veterinary equipment that had been left scattered around the house and sheds. It was a task Austin perpetually meant to do but never got around to. Reg therefore suggested that he would do it himself. Estella did worry that going through everything would upset her father, but Reg was in a particularly good mood that morning so she was inclined to let him do as he pleased.

Relishing the opportunity to do something that wasn't chopping vegetables to help his daughter make food or read another damned book, Reg sat in his wheelchair surrounded by boxes of medication and equipment. The faint chemical smells were so familiar to him that he began to hum contentedly as he sorted through the out-of-date and dried-up bottles. Then there was the paraphernalia for surgery – scalpels, saws, catgut, needles. There were syringes, hoof knives, a set of rasps for horses' teeth and some pairs of scissors that had seized up.

Estella left him to separate all of it into two piles – one for rubbish and one for things Austin or another vet might have a use for.

When she came back in from the yard, she could hear him in the kitchen. He was singing.

"Is it a sin? Is it a crime? Loving you, dear, like I dooo! If it's a crime then I'm guilty, Guilty of loving yooou!"

His rich baritone filled the space and made Estella's heart feel lighter. He was happy! Reg was finally happy! She began to dream up plans of how she could give him more opportunities to sort things out and be useful, since it seemed to bring him so much joy. She wondered if there might be a way he could work in the dispensary of the veterinary practice. He had nearly forty years' worth of experience treating animals and knew everything there was to know about chemicals and medicines and treatments. Perhaps he could return to working on small animals if they could manage to adapt a table that was low enough for him to sit at. She knew that helping owners and animals would give him a sense of purpose but, before that day, Reg had shown little inclination to return to work. Though he wished he was a whole man, the knowledge that he was not meant he was not prepared to think of the things he *could* do. He was too busy thinking of all the things he couldn't.

That night when Estella tucked him into bed, he gripped her hand in his own. She had noticed of late that they were no longer work-roughened. The calloused hands she had gripped in her childhood were now soft with lack of use. They were almost unfamiliar to her but she squeezed back when she felt the pressure of his strong fingers on hers.

"You know I appreciate everything you do for me, don't you, Stell?" he asked, studying her face intently. "I know I'm a cantankerous old bugger but … I do still love you."

"Still?" She laughed lightly. "You make it sound like one day you won't." She saw hurt flash though his eyes. "But I know you love me. *Still*." She winked.

"Doesn't an old man deserve a kiss then?" he asked, proffering his cheek.

"Just the one," she answered, giving him a peck.

Still holding her hand, Reg kissed her knuckles. "Night then."

"Goodnight."

At the time, she thought Reg's sudden need to show his love was down to his experiencing a rare good day. His cheerfulness spilled over and she was lucky enough to be touched by it. But, looking back, Estella knew what her father had been trying to say.

Around five o'clock in the morning she got up to help him change position to prevent bed sores, as she always did.

Before his injury, he always had the uncanny ability to wake exactly when he needed to. It was a handy skill for a vet to have – being able to sleep and wake whenever he wanted. But, for some reason, his body no longer wanted to wake close to dawn. Even with an alarm clock by his bedside, he still could not rise. It was, therefore, up to Estella to move him. Sometimes, he didn't even wake when she man-handled his limbs into their new position at the side of the bed closest to his wheelchair, ready for getting up in the morning. But this time he had already manoeuvred himself to the edge of his mattress ready for the morning. So she let him sleep.

When she went to wake him at eight o'clock, she did not immediately realise her father had not moved a single inch since five. He lay perfectly still, his legs and torso under the eiderdown, his hands and arms exposed to the morning's chilly air. She did note that the position was odd. Reg always slept with his hands under the covers. She always did too. It was a small similarity which she felt brought them closer together. But now, the flannel stripes of his pyjamas interrupted the fussy blue-and-white pattern of flowers on his bed cover.

Estella barely glanced at him as she crossed to the window to open the curtains. "Morning, Daddy! Did you sleep well?"

She turned and, for the first time, really looked at him in the watery light of the early morning sun. His skin was pale. He wasn't usually that pale. Immediately, all the things that could have gone wrong in the night, all the signs of illness or infection that she could have missed began to swirl through her brain. Taking a step towards the bed, she noticed how cold the room was. It was the sort of cold that existed when a room was empty. When there was no warm body to heat the air. She wanted to reach out a hand and feel his forehead but she couldn't seem to persuade her hand to touch the waxen expanse of her father's brow. Feeling suddenly lightheaded, she took a breath, not realising she had been holding it, waiting for Reg to exhale. She gulped in the air, watching the motionless body in front of her.

"Daddy?"

Her eyes raked over him. She searched every inch for some small sign of life but knew instinctively that he was dead. Despite all the care she had taken, all the hard work and long hours she had devoted to doing everything that was possible to keep his body healthy, she had failed. She had missed something and it had killed him, just like her failure to properly train a horse had paralysed his legs. It was always her fault.

"Daddy?"

Then she saw it. She had taken a step and the sunlight streaming through the window fell on something that glittered on the bedside table opposite. There were two identical medicine bottles with corks in the top, just like the ones he had spent the previous day sorting through. But they were completely empty. They should have been thrown out, not left by his bedside. And then there was what lay in front of them. A medium-sized glass syringe was resting at an angle across the corner of the small tabletop. The metal plunger looked tarnished but the fine needle attached to it was shiny with newness.

Estella did not need to read the stained labels on the bottles.

She knew what it would say. Sometimes it was called Veronal or Barbital. Seeing the bottle in the light of the sun, she remembered sitting with Austin in the veterinary practice's dispensary when they were children, pointing to bottles and testing each other on what each was called and what it was used for. For Reg, it was an easy way to keep them entertained. It was also useful since, if he was busy, he could ask them to fetch things needed either by him or by farmers. The children, therefore, had to know exactly what each drug did. But they were never allowed to touch the Veronal. Barbiturates were always kept on a high shelf. They were sometimes used in lesser doses instead of chloroform to anesthetise small animals. Or in bigger doses to euthanise them.

Slowly, she walked around the foot of the bed and sat by her father's body. She still couldn't touch him. She couldn't even look at his cold, dead face. Instead, she reached for the bottles. The contents of both would likely have been enough to kill a man much bigger than Reg. But then she doubted whether either were full. He had a habit of picking up whatever bottle was closest to hand and taking a little bit out without finishing anything. With that in mind, she managed to reach out a hand to her father's neck, searching for a pulse. But his flesh was cold. Nothing moved. She already knew this. But she had to check.

Reg wouldn't have done it if he hadn't had enough. He knew exactly what he was doing and, no doubt, gave himself a little extra just to be sure. It was the sort of mercy he showed animals. Always give them more than they need, he said. He could work out the correct cubic centimetres of an injection to the weight of an animal in the drop of a hat.

He would not have calculated it incorrectly – not when it was the last, most important calculation of his life. He would have shown himself mercy.

But he had not shown Estella mercy – or so she thought. The tears began to stream down her face as she returned her gaze to the empty bottles. She had worked so hard to keep him healthy. She had tried so hard to smile, to be positive, to make him happy. And for what? So that he would kill himself. She gasped, struggling to breathe against the bands that were tightening around her chest. Her father was dead. He was lying on the bed behind her. She shot to her feet. It was because of her that he was dead. Through her thoughtlessness, her lack of care, she had allowed him to take the needle, the syringe, the bottles. She should have watched him. She should have known he might try something. She had failed him again, just as she always did. Every day, it was an awareness that dogged her like the ticking of a clock.

Perhaps, then, he *was* showing her mercy. Perhaps by ending his own life, he was ending her responsibility for his care. On more than one occasion, he spoke of how unfair it was that she was tied to him. She was a young woman, he said. She should be out living her life, not cleaning up after him. He felt guilty for claiming so much of her time. Yet Estella was so hell-bent on giving it to him, he could not convince her to do otherwise. He did not want to be the object of her pity or something she was obliged to care for. Hard as he had tried to push her away, she would not leave him alone to wallow.

Reg tried to explain all of this in the letter he left for Estella.

He'd been planning it for months – how to go about it so she would not try to stop him. He thought about doing it when he first came home from the hospital. However, back then, he didn't have the courage to go through with it. Yet, that didn't stop him from thinking about it a lot. A barbiturate would be the best, he surmised. He knew his weight from reading his own medical charts. Working out the amount he would need was simple. But he needed time. He couldn't do it, not yet. He needed to put his affairs in order. He had to make provisions for all of his children. He had to make sure Austin settled in to his new occupation – offer him what help he could before leaving his favourite son to fend for himself. And then there was the small hope that he would get better – that some miracle would occur and give him back the use of his legs. But it didn't so, one year after the accident, Reg knew the time had come.

Graeme found Estella staring at the wall in their father's bedroom. He stood looking at the scene for some time, processing all the disparate parts – the body, the syringe, the bottles, his sister. Eventually, he crossed to her, gently took her elbow and led her from the room. He knew what it was like to discover a parent lying dead. Guiding her into a chair in the kitchen, he poured her some tea which had been keeping warm on top of the Aga. The liquid was so dark, it looked like he was pouring melted treacle into the mug.

Once he had seen Estella drink, he spoke.

"I've got to make some telephone calls." Then, without any further comment, Graeme walked out of the room.

Chapter 6

Estella decided to take up Henry Leclerc's offer to make a visit to their orchard to collect some apples. The large apple tree at Robin Hill had blown down years ago so almost all the apples they ate came from next door. In fact, half the local area made use of the two-acre patch of trees that always produced a bumper crop. Branches sagged under the weight of the fruit and the gnarled trunks seemed to bulge and fold under the pressure of bearing up such hefty loads. Every year the trees decorated themselves with the brightly coloured baubles, determined to outdo the Christmas trees later in the season – glorious bows bedecked with their luscious red, green and golden orbs.

Yet, for all the fruit that clung to the trees, there was an equal amount scattered in the long grass beneath them. On still days, flies and wasps sailed through the air, drunk on the fruit sugars which made them hum with pleasure. In other places, the hum turned to an angry buzz as insects gorged themselves on the bruised flesh of windfalls. Sometimes, the wasps became greedy and bored holes in the living fruit still clinging to the trees. They could strip the insides from an outer husk within a day, turning juicy plumpness into crispy, dry, wrinkled flesh. And there was hell to pay if you were unfortunate enough to be the person who touched these partially hollowed balls of crawling, stinging possessiveness.

Yet, despite the wasps, Estella enjoyed picking apples in the orchard. Like blackberry jam, apple jelly was a welcome taste of autumn preserved in a jar which could be enjoyed all the year round. By evening, she would have her fruit boiled and tied in muslin bags hung from the dresser to drain into a variety of receptacles. With two pannier bags attached to the bike as well as a large basket hanging from the handlebars, she set off for Ellendale.

Collecting up the choicest windfalls for chutney and apple jelly, eaters straight from the tree for storing and small or bruised fruit for animals off the ground, her only company was usually insects and the odd rabbit brave enough to nibble the grass nearest the ditches.

Halfway through picking eaters off her favourite tree Estella was, therefore, surprised and slightly excited by the appearance of strangers at the orchard gate. It was a group of three – two women and a boy of four or five. Immediately, she wondered if this was the rest of the Aylward family that Dolly had spoken of. The older woman was of a height with Estella but carried more weight than the younger who was short and elfin. The young woman's skin glowed and her chestnut-brown hair shone in the light of the sun. On their arms they carried baskets and without pausing made a beeline for the clump of trees Estella was combing.

"Hello!" she said as cheerfully as she could under their

blank gazes. "If you want to pick here, I can move on."

The older of the two women blinked then smiled a smile that didn't touch her eyes. "No, you're fine. There's plenty for everyone." She addressed the younger woman without looking at her. "Come on, Rebecca. We'd best get on."

Rebecca glanced at Estella. There was curiosity and light in her eyes. She had a much less serious expression than her companion. Bending down, she whispered something to the little boy, gave him a pat on the back and sent him scampering off to gleefully scatter the grazing rabbits. With stoic silence, the two women set to work picking windfalls into one of the baskets while keeping a respectable distance from Estella.

It felt somewhat uncomfortable being so close to two people who were so quiet. By the covert glances Rebecca was throwing Estella, she looked as if she wanted to say something. Yet she remained silent as Estella cudgelled her brain to come up with something innocuous but not completely trite to talk about. However, by the time she did think of something to say, it felt like she had waited too long and that speaking now would be even more forced than if she had said something earlier.

However, just as the tension became too much for Estella and she was about to move off, Rebecca spoke.

"We'll have to bring Ivan next time we come," she said, resting her hands on her hips and throwing her head back to look up at the apples beyond their reach.

"You're Ivan's family?" Estella blurted out.

Now that she really looked, she saw Ivan had inherited the shape and colour of his mother's brown eyes. Her hair, however, was a motheaten russet colour rather than his rich brown.

Still standing with her hands on her hips, accentuating the subtle curves of her body, Rebecca was simply beautiful. When she glanced up at the tree again, Estella noted the girl's long, smooth neck and her delicate hands with pianist's fingers. In her mind's eye, Estella could see Ivan and Rebecca standing together, gazing lovingly into one another's eyes. They made a fine couple.

"Mummy, look!" The little boy came dashing up with a long spike of willow herb covered in deep-pink flowers. He was a slightly pudgy, miniature version of Ivan but with golden hair rather than brown.

"Thank you, lovie!" Rebecca crouched and gave her son a hug.

Ivan's mother answered Estella's question. "Yes," she said crisply. "I'm Edna and this is Rebecca."

"And this is Harry," Rebecca offered, picking up the little boy, all the better to show him off. She radiated motherly pride as she smiled at her little boy, catching his fat little fist as it rested against her chest.

He, meanwhile, ignored his mother, instead viewing Estella suspiciously. She smiled warmly at him.

"Hello, Harry." She proffered her hand. It was something her father had always done with children on the farms and she knew how important it made them feel.

Harry slowly extracted his hand from his mother's grasp and shook it.

"My name's Stella. I live just down the road. So I think we must be neighbours, don't you?" She said the last part more for the benefit of the others than for the boy. But it felt easier to address him than Edna and Rebecca.

"Stella? Estella Frayne?" Rebecca's attention was suddenly focused. "Are you connected to the vet?"

She nodded. "Yes, I'm Austin's sister. I met Ivan when he brought me along to look at a lame horse at Ellendale."

"And you play table tennis locally. My brother said there was a group –"

"Your brother?"

"Yes. Ivan's my brother."

Estella felt herself blink stupidly as this news filtered into her brain. "*Oh!* I thought ... Sorry!"

"You thought he was my husband?" Rebecca screwed up her face but laughed.

"Uncle Ivan's my uncle," Harry added helpfully as his grandmother turned and walked away.

Rebecca threw a glance after her but quickly came back to Estella. "Ivan and I used to play table tennis when we were in primary school but there were never any older players. I'd love to play again!"

"Well, we're always happy to welcome new members to the club," Estella said enthusiastically. "The more the merrier. Membership for the year is a pound but that's just to cover the hire of the parish hall. But, of course, you can come along and see if you'd be interested in joining the group first. We meet at eight every Monday evening. And I'm sure we've a few spare bats in the club."

A grin spread across Rebecca's face. "If everyone's as encouraging as you, I don't see how we could resist. I'll have to see if Ivan's still interested though." Harry, meanwhile, began to squirm to get down. She plonked him on the ground and he hared off after his granny.

The two women watched him go. When he reached Edna, she looked back, a grim expression on her face. She stared at them for a few moments then pointedly turned away. It was clear from the set of her shoulders that she was cross about something. Estella immediately began to trawl through their meeting, wondering what she said that could have offended the woman.

"Have I …" Estella began hesitantly. "Have I done something to upset your mother?"

Rebecca's gaze continued to rest on her son and mother. "No," she answered eventually. "Mammy is just … distrustful of people. She always worries about … everything." The corners of her eyes tightened as she said it. It looked as if she were in pain. "It's the way she is."

Nodding, Estella didn't comment. "You know where we are now anyway," she said quietly. "If you feel like coming to table tennis some evening. There's a lovely group of people. We'd be delighted to have you."

A warm smile flushed Rebecca's face. "Thank you," then, decisively, "I look forward to it."

Luckily, the road from the orchard was relatively flat which meant cycling home didn't take too much physical effort. However, Estella did have to concentrate very hard so as not to crash her bike into the ditch. It was quite tricky since she had quite a weight of apples strapped to the front and back which seemed determined to overbalance her. However, it wasn't just that. She was used to carrying goods on her bike.

But now her head was addled with thoughts of the Aylwards.

Even though Rebecca told her that she was Ivan's sister rather than his wife, Estella could not help but think that the other woman was playing some sort of cruel prank on her. She had been sure Rebecca was his wife – had resigned herself to the fact that Ivan Aylward was a married man. There was no family resemblance between the siblings that Estella could see. Rebecca didn't even look like her mother. Her son was the child-version of her brother. And then there was the fact that Ivan was a handsome man with a good job who, at this stage in his life, should have a wife and children. Of course he would marry someone beautiful – beautiful like Dolly, like Rebecca.

Rebecca was his *sister*. It was only Estella's own foolish doubt that contradicted that fact. Why would Rebecca lie? Estella had looked into her eyes and knew there was no guile there. There was only warmth and potential friendship. She wanted Rebecca to be her friend. Yet, had she been Ivan's wife, Estella would have wanted nothing to do with her. Estella's bike wobbled precariously. *Stop it*, she told herself firmly. You don't want to waste all these apples by scattering them all over the road. And you definitely don't want to be picked out of the ditch by a passer-by – unless that passer-by was one of the Aylwards, some part of her mind thought slyly.

Unbidden, Edna Aylward's disapproving face floated before her. Obviously not *that* Aylward. Estella wondered what made her view the world so severely. But then, all the Aylwards seemed a little off at first. Looking back, she remembered how quiet Ivan had been. He had barely looked at either her or Austin. All his focus had been on the horse – though she could hardly criticise him for that. It was his job. Edna radiated dissatisfaction on finding her in the orchard. Initially, even Rebecca seemed deliberately distant. It was as if the whole family were trying to remain apart from the rest of the world.

She wondered why Rebecca and Harry weren't living in their own home with her husband. Obviously, something had happened to the man. Estella assumed he was dead. Rather than care for the child on her own, Rebecca had presumably gone back to her family who were helping her to raise Harry. It was an arrangement that was not uncommon, with several generations all living under the same roof and sharing the workload. But Estella was sure there was something else lurking beneath the surface. There was something aside from grieving the loss of a loved one that coloured the behaviour of the family. Estella knew grief. And it was not what the Aylwards were suffering from.

Chapter 7

Graeme was in the kitchen when she arrived back with jelly arms and heavy legs from pushing the bike up the lane. The small kick up to Robin Hill was a challenge – especially with all the apples. He viewed her critically as she waded into the house under the weight of the handlebar basket and heaved it onto the counter. She waited for a moment, gathering herself to go back out and get the rest but, when she turned to fetch the pannier bags, she met Graeme carrying them in.

"Thank you."

Graeme shrugged and sat down again. "Where'd you put the blackberry jam?"

"Cupboard." She pointed.

He huffed, got laboriously to his feet and opened the cupboard door. "Where?" he asked, staring at the rows of jars.

"Left. It's always on the left." Estella got herself a drink of water and sipped it. The water from the tap was always ice-cold and, if she drank it too fast, made her back teeth ache.

Leaning against the sink, she watched her brother shuffle back to the table where he already had bread, butter and a

73

mug of tea. He looked tired. His back was hunched and the dark shadow of stubble made his face look grey. He opened the jar of jam and cautiously sniffed the contents. His head jerked back and, putting the jar down on the table, he pushed it away.

"Is there something wrong with it?" Estella asked. Sometimes, if the seal wasn't up to scratch, the surface of the jam would go mouldy or ferment.

"It's fine," he muttered. "Just don't fancy it." Instead, he pulled the butter towards himself and carefully began to scrape thin curls from its surface. Slowly, he smeared the butter onto his bread, put the knife down and sat staring at his meal. With what seemed to be a concerted effort, he picked up the buttered slice and brought it to his mouth. He took a small bite from the soft, crustless edge and chewed morosely.

Lately, Estella had noticed her brother's appetite had waned significantly. There was a time when the siblings sharing a hearty dinner at twelve o'clock each day, without fail. Now, Estella often ate alone or endured the discomfort of watching Graeme push food around his plate before he made his excuses and left. Instead, he seemed to be eating copious amounts of bread at odd times of the day and night. She wouldn't have noticed this so much if it wasn't for the fact that he almost always left the loaf of bread, a plate and a knife on the table for her to clear up.

Fighting the urge to ask him if he was feeling all right, Estella turned her back on her brother. She knew such a question would at best receive one of Graeme's practised withering glances. At worst – well, Estella didn't like to think of her brother at his worst. Mostly, Graeme was the quiet, monosyllabic type. But when he lost his temper, he was frightening. Despite living together, the siblings had never been close and it was therefore easier not to engage with each other. Neither asked the other about their day. Neither asked the other where they were going later on. They simply got on with their own separate lives.

Theirs was quite a lonely existence. To share a home with someone and yet have no communication with them made Estella feel she had somehow failed in life. Homes were supposed to be places of laughter, conversation and love. That was what it was like in Dolly's house. For Estella, Dolly's family was a shining example of all that should suffuse the multi-layered fabric of a family home. Everything in their house centred around the kitchen. There was always the smell of food and a smile waiting for her when she visited. Jokes, arguments, discussions and advice abounded. When in the Greer kitchen, she could not help but sit and let the family's voices wash over her. Every time she cycled away from their house, the hollow feeling in her chest seemed to expand. Over the years, it seemed her grief and longing for a more wholesome family increased rather than eased, due to the slow fragmentation of her own. First her mother, then her sister, Austin and her father had vacated the Frayne home. And Graeme might as well not be there for all she saw of him.

Leaving her brother to his food, she slipped out to the yard. Despite the many things that had happened there over the years, it was still the place where she felt safe. There was something comforting in the familiar roughly plastered walls, the peeling red paint of the windows and doors, the play of the light through the trees and the shadows they cast on the cobblestones. And then there were the animals. The cows with their warm bodies, coarse hair and placid eyes. Floppy-eared pigs. The chickens who bobbed about with so little concern that they were, on occasions, found pecking beneath the legs of other animals. And then there was Beryl who held a special place in Estella's heart. She was the closest thing to a horse that still lived on the farm and, no matter how much it hurt to think about all the shared time with her father and horses, she still missed the heads sticking out of the stable doors every time she crossed the yard.

The cows had already shuffled up the laneway, ready for milking. Some white heads turned to watch her approach, their bottom jaws wagging slightly as they continued to nonchalantly chew their cud. Surveying the mottled brown and white coats of some and the brindled coats of others as they caught the light of the evening sun, Estella could not help but view the animals critically. There was no elegance in their solid, heavy bone structure. Their straight backs and jutting hipbones had nothing of the beautifully curvaceous silhouette belonging to a well-muscled horse.

In the dying light of the autumn, the thought hit her in the chest like a hammer-blow: she wanted to see a horse's long nose above the stable door at Robin Hill. No matter the painful memories, she wanted to feel a soft, curious muzzle in her palm once again. She wanted to hear the rasping sound of a brush through a tail and smell the nutty warmth that was a horse's unique fragrance. And while a horse would never solve all her problems, she knew that having one would bring her comfort and once again bring her closer to her father.

Chapter 8

As September turned to October and the leaves on the trees turned from green to orange, gold and burnt sienna, Estella donned her woolly hat in the mornings and began to wear heavier jumpers. Apart from her brief forays to table tennis, the local shop and church on Sundays, Estella saw no one at home other than her brothers and Dolly. Her best friend continued to bring brightness, laughter and gossip to a house that had grown increasingly dull from the protracted stretches of silence and depression it witnessed. Working as she did at the local telephone exchange, Dolly could gabble happily about who owed money to the local grocer and what neighbour was currently accusing the other of stealing their wether lambs. And then there was, of course, the obligatory discussion about the Aylwards whom Dolly was finding increasingly frustrating.

On multiple occasions, Estella found herself on the verge of telling her friend about meeting the Aylward women in the orchard but just couldn't. There was such dignity and severity in Mrs Aylward that Estella could not bring herself to break the family's confidence. Every time the words formed on her tongue, the woman's disapproving face flashed before her eyes and the sounds died before they could escape her lips.

Though Dolly noticed these moments where her friend almost spoke, she never knew their substance and, therefore, never forced Estella to speak. Years of experience told her that she could never compel her friend to say something she didn't want to. Their relationship had been defined by Estella's long periods of silence into which Dolly poured her pointless prattle. But it worked for both parties. Dolly loved to talk and Estella relaxed without the pressure of having to make conversation.

Unfortunately for her, Estella was always obliged to make polite conversation every Monday night at table tennis. There was always a part of her that panicked when someone asked her a question that required more than a monosyllabic answer. She felt her smile stiffen and her face grow cold as the blood drained. It was getting easier and Austin helped a lot but she was getting to the point where she thought she would never feel comfortable in company again. However, in late October she began to wonder if she herself wasn't necessarily the problem. Perhaps it was just that she was talking to the wrong people.

Hurrying into the parish hall one evening, Estella stopped short when she found two Aylwards chatting to the table-tennis club chairman, Edgar Chapman. Austin grumbled audibly as he bumped into her from behind but she paid him no mind since all her attention was focused on the small group at the other end of the hall.

Edgar was a balding man in his early sixties who, many

years before, had taught both Austin and Estella the rudiments of table tennis. In fact, there was barely a player in the parish who had not experienced the joyful enthusiasm and patience of Edgar's tuition when they first arrived with a new-smelling bat and a haphazard serve. For more than forty years, he had spent his Monday nights coaching the children then playing against the adult members of the club, regularly trouncing two players at once. Estella smiled to herself as she noted the broad grin and sparkling eyes of her old coach. He was, of course, delighted to have new members in the club but she guessed he was already planning to thrash the Aylwards later on in the evening. Though everyone loved Edgar dearly, they could not deny he was something of a show-off.

"Stella! Austin! You're late!" Edgar admonished in lieu of a greeting.

"Cow with a beet stuck in her gullet," Austin shrugged as they removed their coats.

Edgar tutted. "I do wish these animals were considerate enough to fall ill on a day when there *isn't* a training session."

"And I wish they wouldn't calve in the middle of the night. But what can you do, eh?" Austin directed this remark to the Aylwards who chuckled.

Estella noted that her brother's eyes lingered a little on the perfect form of Rebecca. She supposed her own eyes might have lingered on Ivan too.

"How did the youngster with the gravelled foot do after?" Austin asked him.

"No problems. Sat up on him myself for the first time last week, in fact. Although, there's another mare we'd like you

79

to come and look at. Just off-colour, you know. Not eating that well …"

Rebecca glanced at Estella and rolled her eyes. "This is all I ever hear at home," she said under her breath but grinned nonetheless. "Thought I'd get away from it a bit coming here. No such luck, eh?"

Estella only smiled in reply. She longed for a return of such talk to her life. She loved listening to her father and brother speak about the people, the places and – most importantly – the animals so vividly it was almost as if she was there with them.

"It's taken me a month to convince him to come with me," Rebecca grumbled as she linked Estella's arm and led her away as if it was the most natural thing in the world to do. "He said he wouldn't come until the clocks changed and the evenings were shorter."

"Working every hour God sends, eh?"

"You've no idea. You'd hardly ever see him in the summer."

"My father was like that."

The words were out of her mouth before she even knew she was saying them. She never talked about Reg. It hurt too much. But there was such openness and warmth in Rebecca Aylward's face that Estella wanted her to know about the person who was still the most important figure in her life. "He … my father … died. A year and a half ago."

"Oh, I'm so sorry!" Rebecca put a hand on her shoulder and rubbed gently. It was such an unconscious, affectionate, motherly thing to do. "Our father died quite a number of years ago now. He was away a lot and I was quite young at the time so it didn't really affect me that much. Ivan was only ten but he felt he had to become the man of the house once Daddy died. He was always such a serious little boy."

The two women glanced at their brothers who were now standing a distance away, deep in discussion. Austin was drawing a line down the front of his hip bone and Estella knew he was telling the story of a horse with a foot-long laceration he had sewn up. In response, Ivan was tracing a corresponding line down his forearm while screwing his nose up with a mixture of wide-eyed disgust and glee.

"They're in their element, aren't they?" Rebecca smiled. "And I hear you know what you're doing with horses too." Seeing Estella's questioning look, she clarified, "Mr Leclerc's been singing your praises to Ivan."

Estella shrugged uncomfortably. "Did you make anything nice with the apples you collected that day?"

"Oh yes! Me and Mammy and Harry picked blackberries the day before so we made blackberry and apple jelly. And a whole vat of apple jelly too. Mammy has problems with her teeth so she doesn't like the little seeds. They get stuck in between and drive her mad."

"My other brother is like that. He's had terrible teeth for years but he won't go to the dentist."

"Oh, I didn't know you had another brother!"

"Yes, another older brother. Graeme. We live on the farm together."

"So it's just the three of you then?"

Estella was about to say yes. It wasn't that she was ashamed of Joy. In fact, she was the only one who wasn't. Neither Austin nor Graeme ever spoke of their other sister.

It was easier to pretend she didn't exist and saved a lot of explanation. Generally, Estella followed suit so as not to contradict them but always felt guilty denying Joy's existence – even if Joy would never know. However, as the word formed, Estella looked at the woman beside her. There was such kind-heartedness in Rebecca's expression, such trust, that Estella couldn't lie.

"I have an older sister. Joy. She lives in a … in a home on the far side of town."

"What a lovely name! I had a great aunt called Joy and we all adored her! Do you get to see her often?"

"Now and again. Not as much as I'd like. Claybourne's is a bit of a distance to cycle."

"And would your brothers not give you a lift?"

"No, they don't visit her," Estella answered shortly.

Rebecca frowned but was saved having to reply when Edgar came bustling over.

"Now, now, girls! We're not here to chitter-chatter! We're here to practise. And I'm sure *you*, Mrs Bruce, need all the practice you can get! And your brother too." He turned on Ivan and Austin. "Mr Aylward! Mr Frayne! Chop-chop! Let's begin!"

Estella offered her bat to Rebecca who took to the floor with a cheerful, "Wish me luck!" and stood at the opposite end of the table to her brother. The siblings began making gallant attempts to serve accurately and string a few shots together under the watchful eye of Edgar who grimaced at their imperfect game. But Estella, who gave every appearance of watching too, was meditating on what she had just heard.

Mrs Bruce. At one point in the not-so-distance past,

Rebecca must have been married to a *Mr* Bruce. She watched the vivacious, pretty woman before her, laughing as she jogged down the length of the hall to fetch a misfired ping-pong ball. What sorrow must this young woman have known? She could hardly be much older than Estella herself and yet she was already a widow. How could someone who had known that much pain carry on? Thinking about it, the answer presented itself in the memory of a handsome little boy running through the Leclercs' orchard. Rebecca was a mother. She had to carry on for the sake of her child. But it wasn't just maternal duty that bore her onwards. She appeared to have such a thirst for happiness, such a sunny disposition, that grief could not maintain its hold on her. For her, life was for living, for enjoying. There was always a future, no matter what pain existed in the past.

"*Aaaand match*! Well done, Mr Aylward!" Edgar's voice cut through Estella's reverie. "Although I *must* say I see lots of potential with both of you. A little rusty, no doubt, no doubt! But with practice, why you might rival the *other* siblings we have here!" He winked at Estella.

"No chance," Austin scoffed. "Come on, Stell, let's show them how it's done."

The group stayed much later than usual that evening. The session ended with eleven adults hurtling around the table, laughing and shouting like children as they ran a circuit from one end of the hall to the table to the other end of the hall and back to the table, trying to knock one another out. It ended as such games often did with a long rally between Edgar and Austin which the former eventually won. Unusually, however, Estella had been knocked out early on, fumbling an easy shot when she was distracted by a whooping Ivan Aylward. But she didn't mind. It gave her the opportunity to observe the glee with which the two siblings dashed around the table with blazing grins stretched across their faces.

Rebecca's face was made for smiling. Her lips were a blushed pink that brought out a similar rosy shade in her cheeks. She had beautifully straight teeth. Her brown eyes sparkled brightly under dark, expressive eyebrows. But no matter how happy Rebecca looked, it was her brother that drew Estella's gaze.

Ivan had looked so serious whenever she had seen him previously. But watching him galumph up the room, the floor vibrating with the weight of his charge, Estella found herself laughing at his expression. It was that of an exuberant puppy who had suddenly been given the freedom to gambol about. Yet, every time he dodged around a strategically placed chair and up to the end of the table, the grin slid momentarily from his face as he concentrated on his shot. However, as soon as bat connected with ball, the smile reappeared and off he hurtled again.

When he finally fluffed a return, the fleeting disappointment left his face as he jogged across to Rebecca who was sitting to Estella's left. As he threw himself down on the chair beside his sister, he winked at Estella.

"Do you think Mammy would mind if we practised on the kitchen table?" he asked Rebecca.

"Well, we'll have to do something if we're to compete against the likes of Stella and Austin!" Rebecca smiled and gave Estella nudge.

"And Mammy mightn't be so inclined to shout at us for playing table tennis in the kitchen now that we're grown up."

She stared incredulously at her brother. "You have *met* our mother, haven't you?"

"No, I've never met my mother in my life. What's she like?"

Rebecca slapped him on the arm but all he did was laugh. She turned away from him in mock irritation. "You see what I have to put up with?"

Estella tittered but she was also trying very hard not to show the siblings how much she envied their easy friendship. "Oh, I don't know." She looked past Rebecca and caught Ivan's eye. "I'd say he's not the worst of them."

He smiled back at her and then – when his sister wasn't looking – winked at Estella once more.

Chapter 9

Since her father's death, it fell to Estella to handle Joy's care. For the most part, this involved making sure the home where she resided was paid monthly from the allowance Reg had put by for his eldest daughter's care. Prior to his death, he also made sure to visit her every now and again, just to be certain she was being cared for appropriately. Really, that was all he felt he could do since he had no way of communicating with her. Austin and Graeme were of the same opinion. Neither could claim to have ever had a relationship with Joy even when they had shared a home. But Estella was different. She still remembered the times when they had shared a bedroom – when they played with dollies on the carpet and lay cuddled together in Joy's bed, enjoying the feeling of being cocooned and safe together.

Every month, Estella cycled beyond the town of Mountlennon to visit her elder sister. The nurses said Joy wouldn't notice if she didn't come, but Estella could see the happiness her visits brought. But that could have been because the person who came to see her sometimes brought her little presents.

Each Christmas, there was a new teddy. She now had a collection of sixteen which she kept in a large basket by her bed and tucked in with a little crocheted blanket every night. Each tiny bear also had its own individual items of clothing. There were coats, jumpers and wool trousers, skirts and dresses. However, none of these bears were afforded the same privileges as a small, worn bear with a felt waistcoat who was the only one that slept in Joy's bed.

In truth, it would not have mattered who gifted these miniature items of clothing. But Joy now recognised that the blue-eyed, freckled young woman with light-brown hair who always arrived with a smile on her face occasionally carried gifts in her work-roughened hands. It did not matter that these items followed the same sewing and knitting patterns used by their mother all those years ago. It did not matter that Estella made a point of picking out the brightest colours and the softest material. When she trawled the shops looking for just the right shade of pink felt to complement the fur of a particular teddy, Joy never noticed. But it mattered to Estella.

She could have given her sister clothing made of any old off-cuts from the fabric shop. She could have used up the collection of half-finished balls of wool stuffed in their mother's old sewing cupboard. In fact, she had knitted two tiny jumpers out of the same wool Prudie Frayne used for her own favourite jumper more than twenty years before. But the significance was lost on Joy.

The trips Estella made to see Joy were always slightly more challenging when the weather turned. Yet, Estella was stoic. On the second Wednesday of every month, she visited Joy.

Though it wouldn't have made any difference to the eldest Frayne sister what day a visitor came, giving herself a strict routine to follow meant that Estella could not make excuses. It didn't matter if she had other jobs to do, wasn't feeling well or if it was blowing a hoolie outside – she sat on her bike and cycled the hour-and-a-half-long journey to the Ethel Claybourne Home for the Mentally Disabled.

Though the sign on the entrance pillar was of discreet brass, Estella always felt herself hunch involuntarily as she passed through the gateway. The home was viewed with such pity, such distaste among locals that it was hard for her not to feel as if the eyes of Mountlennon watched as she cycled up the beautiful sweeping driveway to the front entrance. The setting was so picturesque with its rolling lawns, tall deciduous trees and towering conifers. The old stately home had once sat in the centre of several hundred acres of farmland, much like the Leclercs' estate. Now the grand but dilapidated house boasted only a few acres of garden to which the residents were confined. As part of their routine, many worked in the garden growing flowers and even some fruit – especially alpine strawberries which were dotted throughout the flowerbeds.

The November weather for Estella's cycle into town was what could only be described as dull. Even the pretty gardens around Claybourne's looked distinctly lacklustre in the flat light of the winter sun. Propping her bike up against the low wall surrounding the house, she jogged up the steps and rang the bell. A harried-looking nurse bustled up to the door and smiled when she saw the pink-cheeked face glowing on the other side of the glass panelling.

"Hello, Estella! She's in the library today."

Without further ado, the nurse turned and led her off into the labyrinthine house, leaving Estella to firmly close the door and hurry after. Not many of the residents received regular visitors so Estella was noted by the staff. The two women chatted about nothing as they walked the corridors. Estella knew there was no point in asking about her sister's condition since the answer was always the same – no change. Joy floated through life in a bubble of contented general ignorance, confined as she was to her own internal world. The only thing that mattered was that she was happy and, from what Estella saw, that seemed to be the case.

When they entered the library, the sweet smell of mouldering paper filled Estella's nostrils. Casting about, she saw the browns, reds, greens and blues of dyed leather spines stamped with black and gold script. The walls were lined with books that likely hadn't been touched for half a century. Estella sometimes wondered why they never sold the books or the richly upholstered, deftly carved furniture that was scattered about the house. But now the whole place and the items in it were too worn. Much like the human inhabitants, the inanimate objects were unwanted by outsiders.

Despite the ever-present chill of the house – which meant everyone in it wore either a coat or thick jumper all year round – one of the large bay windows was open. Sitting in the alcove by it was Joy and another woman in her late fifties called Susan. Though you couldn't really say the two were friends, the pair were often seen drifting around together, one stopping occasionally to watch the antics of the other. At that particular moment, both women were intent on something just outside the window and, as Estella approached, a small brown blob came into view just beyond the peeling white edge of the window frame. She knew instinctively from the carriage of Joy and Susan that she should move with caution rather than suddenly looming over proceedings. Carefully placing one foot before the other until she was only a few feet away, she was able to observe her sister unnoticed.

Joy had her hand out the window and the brown blob – which turned out to be a plain-looking little sparrow – was pecking at a sprinkling of white dots on the window ledge. As she watched, Estella saw the sparrow hop back and forth on the cold grey stone then, with a tiny flutter of its wings, hop onto Joy's outstretched fingers where it began to peck at a small pile of breadcrumbs sitting in the depression of her palm. Beside her, Susan gave a tiny squeak of excitement and her hands flailed as she bounced in her seat. Joy turned to give her companion a dirty look but, out of the corner of her eye caught sight of Estella instead – or, more importantly, Estella's hands.

Immediately, bird and companion were forgotten about. Joy stood and came towards her sister with cupped palms, the residual crumbs still clinging to the skin where Estella wordlessly placed a miniature cardigan.

It was worth the effort of following the frustratingly fiddly patterns and cycling twelve miles just to see the light in Joy's eyes.

She carefully pinched the garment between her thumbs and forefingers, holding it at eye-level to scrutinise it properly. Estella saw her fingers move in a gentle, circular motion as she rubbed the wool between her fingertips. Ignoring her sister completely, she turned away and brought the cardigan to a table where she laid it out, making sure the ribbed knitting at the bottom was absolutely parallel with the edge. She stroked the dusty blue front panels then turned it over, lining it up with the edge again and exclaiming in delight when she saw the fuchsia-pink embroidered flower with a glowing golden-yellow centre. Kneeling on the floor by the table, she began to caress the silky surface of the threads, cooing softly.

It was why all the handmade items of clothing had little quirks and were made from such a variety of materials. Estella had become quite proficient at ribbed and plaited knitting patterns. She used angora wool, felt, velvet, satin and tiny bits of silk. Buttons were also important. There were tiny seed pearls, plastic discs – and once cold, shiny metal ones but Joy didn't like them so Estella never used them again. Though it had never really registered when they lived together, over the many years of visiting, Estella began to notice the way her sister's hands were constantly searching for something to brush, tap or hold on to. Joy was a connoisseur of touch. She seemed to experience so much of the world through her fingertips. It was unusual to see her sitting as motionless as she had been with her hand on the windowsill a few minutes before. She ordinarily found such stillness deeply frustrating. But then, aside from her bears, Joy had a deep-seated fascination with birds.

One of the few intelligible sounds she made was a murmured, "Chook-chook-*chook*!" Over the years at the institution, she had befriended many small birds whom she persuaded to fly to her window and feed from her hand. Often, when these creatures became regular visitors, she would sit for hours waiting for them to appear, muttering, "Chook-chook-*chook*!" under her breath.

After the initial inspection of the cardigan, Joy led Estella – or rather Estella silently followed – down a corridor and upstairs to the basket beside her bed. There, she selected a teddy, divested it of its bottle-green corduroy jacket and changed it into the new garment. The jacket was then neatly folded and placed in the top drawer of her bedside locker along with tens of other tiny items of clothing. Susan wandered in shortly after and sat on the bed where Joy was arranging her bears. Estella watched the older woman's hands creep tentatively towards the teddies but then stop short. Susan gazed covetously at the collection but knew they were not to be touched. No one but Joy was permitted to handle them.

Viewing the two women side by side on the bed, it would have been impossible to guess their ages had Estella not known already. Earlier that year, Joy had turned thirty while the staff had celebrated Susan's half-century a few years before. While everyone in the home was always neat, everything they wore was shapeless and gave no hint of the wearer's age or build. Though they were encouraged to spend time outside, their skin was universally pale and doughy. However, they always smelt fresh, looked clean and their hair was never greasy. Susan's hair was pure white, wispy like fog and so fine Estella could see the vague pink tinge of her scalp. Joy's was a darker shade than her sister's, beginning to turn prematurely grey at the roots. But it was the ends of her hair that drew the eye.

Joy always wore her hair loose as, no matter who tried to persuade her, she could not abide having it tied back. This, however, meant she was free to indulge the only true vice Prudie Frayne had never managed to dissuade her of. Hundreds of times every day and even at night when she slept, Joy chewed her hair. Close to her face, the strands were short and shaggy – just long enough to graze the edge of her mouth. Further back, the ends were equally uneven but they became slightly longer the further each lock was from her mouth, finishing in a point at the base of her neck just inside the collar of her shirt. It always gave her the look of someone who had fled the hairdresser's midway through their haircut.

Estella watched her sister fuss over her teddies for another twenty minutes until another nurse came in to collect the women and take them down to eat with a cheery, "Right girls! Din-dins! Come on now, dearies! Chop-chop!"

The nurse could not have been much older than Estella. In fact, recently there had been an influx of younger staff all of whom, like the older nurses, referred to the residents as 'boys' and 'girls'. Yet many of the inhabitants were likely more than double their age. However, given the developmental problems so many had, most were quite child-like and spoken to as such. It just seemed so natural for them to use childish designations even if, to an outsider like Estella, it seemed slightly derogatory. She had never seen patients treated with unkindness – quite the opposite. But they were all treated like overgrown children which Estella believed – though she admitted her own ignorance – left no opportunity for these people to mature or improve in any way. They were perpetually toddlers and children though their bodies marched on apace, decaying and degrading without their notice.

As her sister walked out past her, Estella put a hand to her shoulder. Joy shuffled on without acknowledging her sibling's touch. Instead, she reached for Susan's hand and gave it a little squeeze as their fingers interlocked. Estella watched as they followed the nurse. Standing alone in the room, she cast a final look over the neatly arranged teddies and left.

Chapter 10

The wind whipped at the edges of Estella's coat as she descended the steps of Claybourne's. She had not taken it off while she was inside since the temperature indoors was quite similar to the chill out in the open air. She looked back at the windows which stared vacantly at her, reflecting the steel-grey, ominous-looking sky that hung over her road home. She shivered, suddenly cold despite the warmth of her coat. She could see the tendrils of water coiling from the clouds and knew it would be a miracle if she managed to get home without being soaked. She cursed quietly to herself before mounting her bike and pushing off down the hill.

Only a few miles into her journey, cold droplets blowing on the wind began to spatter her exposed skin. As she rode on, the rainfall became more consistent. Muttering under her breath, she continued, squinting at the road ahead as she tried to keep the wet from her eyes. The surface was becoming slick and she could feel the water whizzing around her tyres before hitting her in the chest and back. And still it became heavier – a deluge the like of which she had not seen since the day she finished picking the potatoes.

Why was it she was always getting caught out in the rain, looking like she'd fallen in a local marl hole?

Her exposed hands were cramping on the handlebars as she freewheeled down a dip and shivered violently at the onrushing wet air. When she reached the bottom, she stamped on the pedals to begin the ascent and felt the water in her shoes ooze out between her toes.

Toot! To-toot! To-tooooot!

Estella swerved closer to the ditch. The road was narrow but it wasn't as if she hadn't left enough room. Yet there were always drivers who thought themselves more worthy of the road just because they had an engine. She heard the vehicle rumble closer and thought about giving the side of it a good wallop as it went by just to make her feelings known. But she was afraid of who might be in it and what they might do if she did lash out. Huddled by the ditch and still doggedly peddling on, she did not initially realise that the vehicle had slowed down beside her. It tooted again and she almost screamed something rude at it.

"Stella!"

The bike wobbled precariously as she jerked her head up to find the driver leaning towards the passenger window. Wretched from her fight with the elements, she stared dumbly at the shadowed figure sitting in a Morris Commercial van that was keeping pace with her.

"It's me, Estella! Ivan!"

Ivan. *Ivan Aylward!*

The front wheel of the bike twisted viciously and she came off the seat, only just getting her feet on the ground in time. Ivan Aylward was staring back at her, mouth agape.

"Get in, would you! You'll catch your death or get run over out in this."

She stood and stared stupidly into the cab. It seemed the rain had washed away her faculties and the cold had frozen her tongue into an uncooperative lump. She watched as if standing outside of herself and saw Ivan open his door, get out and run around to her.

"Stella, come on! You'll drown!" he shouted over the torrential thunder of the rain.

He placed his hand on her shoulder and it was only at that point that Estella realised she was shivering violently. Rather than try to reason with her, Ivan prized the bike from her stiff fingers, ran to the rear of the van and threw it in with little ceremony but a great deal of protest from whatever was already in the back. He then returned to bundle her – with a little more ceremony – into the cab of the van.

By the time he was sitting back in the driver's seat, the rain was dripping off the peak of his cloth cap. Wordlessly, he removed his jacket and stuffed it around Estella's shoulders as she sat hunched on the passenger side beyond the bulky metal lump of engine between them. She could feel the heat radiating from it on her cold hands, making her skin itch. But the warmth didn't touch the rest of her body. Now she was off the bike and immobile, the cold sank its claws into her, piercing her chest and stomach. She hunched forward, hugging herself, and saw a pool of water forming in the footwell beneath her feet. She threw a look of horror at Ivan.

"I'm s-s-s-sorry."

He dismissed the apology with a wave of his hand.

"Don't be silly. Mr Leclerc won't mind. And it'll dry. Given the state you're in though, I'm not sure you will. Are you all right?" He was speaking a little louder than usual, pitching his voice above the sound of the engine.

"'M fine."

"Are you sure?"

She nodded jerkily. With a sigh, Ivan grabbed a grubby-looking towel and wiped his windscreen which had completely steamed up. He reached across and wiped Estella's side too. Then, stuffing the towel down beside his seat, he put the van into gear and moved off. There was a slight kerfuffle and a squeal or two from behind their seats that Estella was only vaguely aware of. She was trying, with little success, to control her shaking body and hoped he couldn't hear her teeth chattering above the tinny clanging of the engine. Keeping her eyes fixed firmly forward and her head slightly bowed, she didn't even want to look at him for fear of seeing disapproval in his eyes.

"You all right?" he asked again after a while.

"*Mmph*." She managed a small glance in his direction and rather than seeing pity or disapproval, saw a quick closed-lipped smile before he returned his gaze to the road.

Becoming curious as to the origin of the snuffling, squeaking noise behind her, Estella turned and peered through the gap to the back. Though the light was dull, she could make out her bike sitting in the middle of a thick layer of straw. However, her eyes were drawn to a bumpy white-pink mass huddled against the side of the van. As she watched, a tiny snout appeared, caressed by two comically floppy ears. Sitting up, it swayed unsteadily with the movement of the vehicle then dived back into the pile of warm bodies, rootling itself into a better position. She knew there was a pig sale in the market every Wednesday. When she was younger each of the Frayne children were given a pig once a year which was their responsibility. It became a competition between the siblings as to whose pig would be the heaviest by the end of the season and would, therefore, gain them the most profit at auction. Estella had fond memories of the rivalries and schemes each of them entered into to try and find their pig the most fattening feed.

"They're for the Leclercs' orchard," Ivan told her.

"Good idea."

"Mammy was saying there were so many windfalls that'd never be picked up and it was all untidy and long grass and everything. So I thought it might be an idea to clear the place up and fatten some pigs in the process. Mr Leclerc said if I bought the pigs to clear it myself, I could sell them when they're fattened and keep the profit."

Estella nodded. "They're like that, the Leclercs."

"He's a good man," Ivan agreed. "And Mrs Leclerc's been good to all of us as well. Making sure we settled in all right. Inviting Mammy and Rebecca up to the house."

"And Harry."

"You've seen Harry, have you?"

"Met him when I saw your mother and Rebecca in the orchard. Lovely little fella." She saw a smile quirk the corner of his lips.

Every now and again, a convulsion ran through her body when she became aware of how cold the underside of her upper arms or the front of her thighs were. She noticed how much the small of her back ached too. However, the heat from the engine and the numerous bodies in the van were taking effect as was evident from the constantly fogging windscreen. Ivan gave up putting the towel away and simply held it constantly in his hand.

"Warming up any?"

"A bit," she shrugged.

"What were you doing out in that weather in the first place?"

"I was …" She stopped. She could say she had been to town because it was technically true. She had cycled through the outskirts on her way to Claybourne's but the empty basket on the front of her bike made it seem unlikely she had been shopping in town.

"Were you visiting?"

"Yes."

It was a good minute before he asked, "Were you visiting your sister?"

"How do you know about my sister?" she asked rather sharply.

Ivan didn't seem to notice. "Rebecca mentioned it on the drive back from table tennis. Joy's her name, isn't it? Said she was in a home outside of town."

"Yes." Usually, Estella would have changed the subject. She always thought the people in the village who knew the most about her sister seemed to treat Estella herself differently. As if they thought she was also touched by Joy's affliction – talked down to her and always gave the impression that they were studying her for any signs that she too lacked the wherewithal to function independently.

But for some reason, she wanted to tell Ivan. However, she couldn't quite manage to keep the challenge out of her voice when she said, "Joy lives at the Ethel Claybourne Home for the Mentally Disabled."

Ivan simply nodded. "Has she been there for a long time?"

"Fifteen years. My mother cared for her before that."

He nodded again but said no more. They lapsed into silence, and Estella felt her head droop slightly. The rattle of the engine began to grow faint and her eyes wouldn't focus on the road in front of her.

Suddenly, she wrenched herself upright, unaware of how long she had been drifting in and out of wakefulness. She gazed out the rain-slicked passenger window and saw the trees and hedgerows of her own neighbourhood. "I'm just along –" She cleared her throat and started again with more volume. "I'm just along here. You can drop me at the end of the lane."

"I will not! I'm taking you back to Mammy and Rebecca first – let them see to you."

"*No!*" she shouted at him in a panicked voice.

"I'm not letting you home in that state! You'll end up with pneumonia or something."

"I'll be fine."

"You won't – you'll –"

"*I'll be fine.* I'll change once I get in."

"It'll take more than that to warm you up. You'll need a hot meal and a good warm drink besides. Have you eaten your dinner?"

Estella remained resolutely silent.

101

"You haven't, have you!"

"I was going to get something when I got home! It's there all ready to go. And I had a big breakfast," she added defensively.

"I'm bringing you home with me."

"No, you're not!"

"I am!"

"*You're not!* Look," she took a deep breath to calm herself and stop her voice sounding quite so screechy, "just bring me home – to *my* home –" she cut in before he spoke. "Please, Ivan."

"Fine," he capitulated with ill grace. "But promise me you'll get something warm into you as soon as you get home."

"I promise," she answered, not wanting to argue just as they approached the laneway to the house. "You can just drop me off –"

"*No.* I'm going to watch you go in the front door," he said as he swung up the stone track.

With an exasperated grumble, Estella crossed her arms and threw herself back into the seat with the petulance of a disappointed child. Staring straight ahead, she saw fresh rain stipple the windscreen while water ran down either side of the track in mud-coloured rivulets. Her spine quivered at the thought of going back out to milk the cows once she had eaten and changed. Though she wanted to say something to him, stubborn silence seemed to be the best way to make sure Ivan knew she was cross with him for not doing exactly as she had asked. She didn't know why his consideration irritated her so much. Maybe it was because it didn't read like care. He just seemed overbearing. But there was something more to her annoyance.

She had *decided* to set off into the onrushing storm. She told herself she was confronting whatever difficulties were placed in her path. Like the characters she remembered from her Sunday school Bible studies, it was up to her to welcome these struggles. She had to bear them with stoicism and without complaint. But then Ivan had ridden up and ruined her martyrdom.

Pulling into the yard behind the house, they were greeted by a particularly vocal Beryl who was standing in the arch of the carriage doors, sheltering from the rain.

"Yes, yes, I'll feed you in a minute," Estella answered her testily as she eased her stiff form from the passenger seat.

"No, you won't," Ivan replied shortly as he hopped out of the van. "You're going in to eat and change. Where will I put the bike?"

"First stable on the left." Her reply was equally abrupt and, ignoring him, she walked across the cobbles to another stable to fetch some loose hay for Beryl. Turning back, she nearly walked into a grim-faced Ivan who was standing with his hands on his hips, the rain leaving dark spots on his pale shirt.

"*I'm* feeding the donkey," he told her, snatching the hay from her and taking it to Beryl.

"Are you always this bossy?" she asked.

He turned back. "Are you always this pig-headed?"

They stared at each other for a moment, eyes locked as they dared each other to say more. Estella looked away.

"Thanks for the lift."

He watched her in silence then replied, "Any time."

"I'd best go in."

"Yes." He walked over to Beryl and gave her the hay and a quick pat.

Awkwardly, they both crossed the yard, heading in the same direction. Ivan stopped at the van and stood making sure Estella went inside. She turned at the door.

"Bye then."

"Yeah, bye. You take care of yourself, Stella."

Hearing the words, she bristled. But then noticed the softness with which he had said them. It wasn't an order. He really meant it. The fight went out of her. "Will do. You too, Ivan." And with that, she went inside and closed the door between them.

Chapter 11

Once she was alone, Estella gave in to her misery. As she put her dinner on the stove to heat, the tears flowed down her cheeks and sizzled as they hit the open hotplate. Leaving her food to warm, she tramped upstairs to change out of her sodden clothing, peeling it off just as she had only a few weeks before. Except now there was no Dolly there to comfort and distract her with gossip. She stood in the cold bathroom, damp skin stippled with goose pimples, completely on her own. Catching sight of herself in the mirror, she saw the off-white and glowing-red blotchiness of her skin. She looked away. She didn't want to see herself – didn't want to know how pitiful she had become. Once, she had been a strong, bright, capable young woman. Now she was just weak and pale – a shadow of the person she had been. Cold, unhappy and lonely, she sobbed freely as she dried herself and changed into her father's old clothes. Automatically, she sniffed the collar of the shirt, expecting to smell the familiar chemical and animal smell that suffused his clothing. But now, after almost two years, there was nothing.

* * *

The rest of Estella's day was little better. When she got down to the kitchen after changing, the stew she was heating had welded itself to the saucepan. What remained tasted good but afterwards she had to spend a good deal of time scrubbing the charred black gravy from the bottom of the pan.

Radiating foul humour, Graeme arrived in his car while she was in the middle of scouring the blackened metal.

"Jesus Christ, what'd you bloody do now?" he fumed as he stormed across the kitchen to the bread bin and wrenched it open.

Estella said nothing but felt the tears begin to leak down her cheeks once again. She kept her back to her brother as he stalked back and forth, slamming cutlery and crockery on the table. When he subsided and sat chewing mutinously on buttered bread, it took him only moments to turn on her again.

"Would you ever stop with that bloody *sniffling*! God Almighty, can't a man have peace in his own home?"

Estella cringed at his harsh voice. Fighting for control, she choked and a strangled sob escaped her lips.

Graeme turned. "Are you *crying*?"

She didn't look at him.

"Stella! Are you *crying*?"

She couldn't tell if there was anger, concern or simply disbelief in his voice. Whatever her brother might be feeling towards her, she didn't want to know. Abandoning the pan, she left the kitchen, donned her hat and yard coat, then hurried out into the rain again. Despite the cold and the wet, it seemed like the safest place to be – the place she always retreated to when things became too much. Even before her father's accident, living with three men was not always simple. Sometimes it was easier to walk away than get into an argument. And there was always something to do outside which gave her the opportunity to mull over her grievances or just forget about them altogether. Back then, the one thing she always found solace in was brushing horses. In the stables, it was cool in summer and warm in winter. The smell of horses, of hay and straw and the comforting warmth of their bodies always calmed her. Then there was the way they felt under her fingers. The relaxed yet still firm muscles, the bones covered by taut skin and all hidden under a fine-haired, soft, smooth coat. And while it soothed her to run her brush over their bodies, it was never a pointless exercise. Brushing the horses helped to clear dust from their coat, increased blood-flow to their muscles and allowed Estella to examine their bodies for small cuts or uneven patches of skin. Plus, it was a chance for younger horses especially to get used to human contact, helping to forge a bond that often lasted a lifetime.

But now there were no horses. Yet Estella still craved animal contact. Fetching the brushes from the old tack room, she ran across the yard to Beryl who was still hiding in the barn. The donkey's coat was long and coarse compared with that of the horses. Having been out in the rain but dried slightly, the hair had clumped into thousands of little Vs along her sides. She had the jutting bones of an underfed yearling despite eating more than any other animal on the farm. But she was soft and warm and glad of the attention so Estella did her best to make the animal feel loved. It was also a good way for Estella to warm up her own still chilled body. There was no point in lightly brushing an animal. The best thing to do was put some muscle and weight behind each stroke. That way, the bristles of the brush went deeper into the coat and did a better job of cleaning and stimulating the skin. Within minutes, Estella was breathing hard and considering taking her coat off. But she kept it on and simply enjoyed the cosiness and started to feel that things were perhaps not so bad after all.

By the time she had finished ministering to Beryl, Graeme was long gone, storming out to his car and disappearing down the lane. Since the evening was getting on, Estella thought the cows should have made an appearance but when she peered out into the failing evening the yard was resolutely empty.

"Of all the days," she muttered angrily then set off in the now-misty rain to fetch the herd. When she arrived at the field, she saw the cows had quite sensibly decided to huddle up by the ditch for shelter. But that meant Estella had to walk all the way to the back of the paddock to round them up.

Darkness had settled on the yard when she returned. The cows dripped water from their coats as they stood munching their hay while Estella sat on her stool and milked. All was going as it usually did until she got to the second last cow. Just as she was in the process of sitting down to milk the particularly large Ayrshire, the cow lashed with her back leg and caught Estella square on the side of the knee with her horny hoof. It was years since she had been kicked and, caught completely off-guard, she fell hard on her backside.

But it wasn't her backside she was worried about. White hot pain exploded from her knee, radiating up and down her leg. Immediately, she burst into tears. They were tears of shock, pain, anger, frustration and exhaustion.

The cow continued to eat, completely unconcerned by the prone figure beside her. It was as if her kick had been totally casual rather than carrying a great deal of weight and force. There was no reason behind it at all that Estella could see. In fact, part of her really wanted to get up and give the cow a wallop for hurting her unnecessarily. But a greater part of her just want to lie on the stone floor of the cowshed and forget everything.

For a time, Estella did just that. She lay on the floor, allowing the chill of the concrete to seep through her clothing, her skin, muscle and bone. It was easier to give up than contemplate carrying on. She simply stayed in the moment, watching clumps of hay and cow fluff eddy in the draughts that wafted across the floor. She saw the many cloven hooves of the cows shift as they rested weight on one foot, then another. She heard the grinding of the cows' back teeth as they chewed their food and the soft hiss of the rain still falling on the tin roof of the shed. And then she heard the sound of an engine.

At first it was distant. On the road, she thought. But it grew steadily louder and she knew that it was coming up the lane. Perhaps Graeme was back. Maybe he could finish milking the last two cows for her. Maybe she could call out to him. But then she remembered the mood he had been in earlier. Even if he offered to finish the milking, she would say no just to get rid of him. And it wasn't Austin. For one thing, his Morris Minor had a distinctive rattle. For another, he wouldn't come this early on a Wednesday evening for fear of coming face to face with Graeme.

The roar of the engine ricocheted off the stone walls of the courtyard as it finally arrived and then abruptly cut out. The silence was eerie for a moment then she heard two doors open, two sets of footsteps on the cobblestones and two voices – one male, one female.

"– no light on."

"Maybe they're away."

"Maybe."

Estella laboriously dragged herself up into a sitting position and felt her knee smart in protest. She hissed through her teeth in an effort to ignore the pain and stayed as quiet as possible, straining her ears, hoping against hope that the pair outside would simply get in their car and leave.

"There's a light on over there. Look."

"No, I'll go."

The footsteps drew closer and Estella clumsily tried to arrange herself in a more dignified position. She was cold, stiff and disorientated from lying on the floor too long. All the blood rushed to her head and she now felt as if it was twice the size it should have been – much like her knee.

"*Hello?*"

Estella thought about staying silent. Because she knew who the voices belonged to. But then a long shadow began to creep down the passage behind the cattle and she knew he was going to see her.

"*Hello,*" she croaked back.

The shadow loomed suddenly and then a head peered

110

around the rump of the cow that had kicked her. He stood for a moment then leaned an elbow on the jutting hipbone of the cow opposite.

"You know, that's probably not the best place for a sit-down."

"I'm aware of that," she muttered, not looking at him. It was too embarrassing to try and stare up at him from such a compromising position.

"Ivan?"

He glanced towards the doorway then at Estella again. "Come on." He proffered a hand. "Up you get."

Estella reluctantly stretched out and felt his firm grasp enclose her fingers. Putting all her weight on her left leg, she allowed him to haul her upright but, given the slope of the ground and her still fuzzy head, she overbalanced and fell straight forward, colliding with Ivan's chest.

"*Oof!*" He stepped back, trying to maintain his own balance while Estella hopped on one foot, afraid to put pressure on her right knee. Steadying them both, Ivan caught her by the waist and held tight.

"What's happened?" Rebecca Aylward stood a few feet away, viewing her brother and Estella with wide-eyed surprise.

Estella hastily pushed herself away from Ivan and stood on one leg. Yet, despite the distance she put between them, he still held on, giving her something to brace against so that she didn't topple over. She couldn't look at either of them as she mumbled, "Cow kicked me."

Rebecca had a hand on her shoulder immediately. "Oh God, are you all right? Where?"

"Knee."

Both Aylwards dropped their gaze to her knees.

"You're all damp, Stella," Rebecca said, patting her coat and then brushing her hand across Estella's cheek. "And you're freezing too! We'll have to get you inside. Come on."

"Can't. Haven't finished milking."

Ivan rolled his eyes. "I can do that. Who needs done?"

"I can do it –"

"Get in, would you!"

He sounded deeply irritated and though Estella was inclined to argue since they were her cows and it was her job to milk them, her reply died on her lips when she saw the tautness of his jaw. She could even see the strain in the tendons of his neck. "Just these two." She pointed to them. Then, with a small, bitter quirk of the lips and a nod towards the culprit, "Watch her. She kicks."

Without further ado, Ivan righted her low stool and plopped himself down to milk. He looked ridiculous. Being so much taller than Estella, his knees were almost at his shoulders when he bent forward to reach the cow's udder. But he seemed confident in what he was doing and as Rebecca gently yet firmly supported her down the passage, Estella heard the familiar hiss as the milk hit the bottom of the bucket.

Once they were inside, Rebecca deposited her in front of the cooker and warned her to stay put. As she was unfamiliar with the kitchen, it took a few moments before she located an old tea towel and soaked it in cold water. She found an egg crate in the porch which she used to prop up Estella's foot before rolling up her trouser leg to expose the injured knee.

"Oh my goodness!" Rebecca bent her head to better examine the large bruise spreading across the knee. "Look at that! It's purple!" She tutted as she tenderly wrapped the cold, wet tea towel around the limb. "Is it sore?" She laughed. "Sorry. Silly question."

Despite Estella's embarrassed protests and assertion that she would be fine on her own, Rebecca continued to bustle about. She boiled water, scalded the teapot, made the tea, added milk and sugar then handed it to Estella before beginning to clear away the mess Graeme had left on the table.

"*Leave that!*" Estella almost shouted at her, feeling her cheeks redden at the state of the room. "It's – I can clear it away later. I should have done it earlier but I left before Graeme was finished. And I had to leave early this morning too. That's why the counter's in a mess. And I didn't know you were coming over either. If I had, I would have tidied up a bit. The kitchen wouldn't usually be in such a state, you know."

"Stella," Rebecca turned, her hands on her hips, "would you ever just calm down. You don't have to do everything yourself. Sometimes, it's nice to just sit down and let someone else do something for you."

"But you shouldn't have to –"

"But I want to," she answered firmly. "Look, I'm going to be very blunt and very honest with you, Stella. Things haven't been easy for us over the past while. And I'll admit that we were scared – or, at least, Mammy and I were – coming to a completely new part of the country. It's been a challenge and … and given what happened before we came here, we were cautious about meeting new people and

113

having them know our business. Because people love to know each other's business. It's human nature, I suppose – to ask questions. But you haven't really asked questions at all. You've just been kind to me when we've spoken. And we all need kindness now and again. You haven't tried to force your company on me, you haven't pried or tried to corner me outside church. And, most important of all, you haven't made any comments about my son." Her voice hitched a little on the last word.

Estella didn't know how to answer so she said nothing. She wondered silently what people might be saying about the little boy. What was there *to* say? He was a handsome, affectionate, bright boy who had all his limbs and a perfectly polite way of speaking. What would prompt anyone to say anything negative about him? Because clearly someone had. And what *had* happened before they arrived? She watched as this pretty young woman pottered aimlessly, her buoyancy suddenly absent. Coming over, Rebecca wordlessly changed the old tea towel for another cold compress. Though she was gentle, there was now a weariness to her movements – as if she were abruptly aware of the cares and worries of her life and they weighed heavy on her delicate limbs. Unconsciously, Estella reached for her hand and held it in her own, squeezing gently. With a little encouragement, Rebecca sat down opposite.

"I've been judged too," Estella said quietly. "By people who I thought were friends. When my father –" She looked away, clearing her throat and felt a small increase in pressure on her clasped hand. She continued on a different tack. "I've been stared at, whispered about behind hands. People love

114

a tragedy, a scandal and … and my family have had a few. If things are getting a bit slow on the gossip front, the Fraynes are always fair game to talk about."

"You're probably not getting much of an airing at the moment." Rebecca watched her own foot scuff the floor, head bowed. "Within the first week of moving, Mammy was all for going back. We moved to get away from talk. I suppose we should have known better … She's so protective of us. Always has been. Even more so now."

Rebecca gazed off into the middle distance, pulling unconsciously at her bottom lip. She looked older, worn. The light in her eyes that gave her such a youthful appearance dimmed. She had the expression of someone racked by constant stress and worry – the expression of a wife, a mother. Estella was neither and yet she had seen the same look on her own face staring from the mirror in the bathroom upstairs. But, unlike Rebecca, she had not yet mastered the art of either burying or overcoming the pain and worry that beset her life. The young mother sitting in front of her was clearly resilient.

But then, Rebecca had a mother to guide and care for her. For the first time in a long time Estella felt acutely aware of Prudie's absence. Her grief at the loss of her father had eclipsed the previous undertow of her mother's death since it was Reg who had always been there when no one else was. It was Reg who had guided her through her teenage years as best he could, Reg who had given her confidence, pride and the knowledge to live a life in which she barely felt her mother's absence. But he never thought to teach her how to live without him. Perhaps if her mother was still alive, she wouldn't feel alone, so sad. She would have an ally, a confidante – someone who would give her the strength and the courage to continue. Someone like Edna Aylward who was there to hold her family – her children – together when their lives fell apart. Because, by the look of pain that grew on Rebecca's face with each tick of the clock in the hall, what happened before was not something she could have dealt with on her own.

A knock at the door shook both women from their reverie.

"Only me!"

Ivan appeared in the doorway and leaned against frame. "You all right?" he asked. His eyes lingered on the exposed white skin of her calf and the cold compress swaddling her knee.

"I'm fine," she murmured and made to push up out of her seat.

"Don't you dare get up!" Rebecca warned.

As if to second the order, Sophie appeared and hopped onto Estella's lap.

"She'll have to get out of it at some point in the future, Bec." A slow smile warmed his face and he winked at Estella.

Estella became suddenly engrossed in the cat. She was unused to seeing someone so tall in her home. Yet he looked so comfortable standing in the kitchen door with his sleeves rolled up and his arms crossed. Once, their kitchen had been a thoroughfare with farmers collecting medicines or bringing ailing small animals to her father. In all that had happened since, she had forgotten what it was like to have strangers in her house – to be relaxed and happy in the presence of other people. There was a time when she could have talked to anyone, discussed their farm, their animals, their family just as easily as Reg could. Now she sat mute between the siblings and could only think about the flowing lines and contours of Ivan Aylward's exposed forearms, the strong weathered hands. And the way his eyes danced when he smiled at her.

Lifting the cat from her lap, Estella subtly tested the pain in her knee. There was a dull ache and it felt about twice the size it really was but otherwise it was just cold from the wet cloth. She thought it might not be too bad but still wasn't brave enough to defy Rebecca while her brother was watching. Abruptly, she realised how rude it was to have visitors in her house without offering them something to drink. But then they were catching her at a distinct disadvantage.

"Do you want some tea or supper or …" She glanced between the two Aylwards, feeling foolish for not offering them something immediately. "You should at least sit, Ivan. And … and not be standing there looking so out of place."

He didn't look out of place at all but it was a line she had heard her father use on countless occasions. It always elicited the same grunt of humour and resulted in the removal of a farmer's cap and boots before he padded across the kitchen floor in his socks and took a seat at the table.

The siblings glanced at one another and Ivan shrugged.

"We'll have a cup of tea," Rebecca agreed, "but I'm making it and you're staying put," she said firmly.

"Doesn't that defeat the purpose of me being the host?" Estella grumbled.

Ivan chuckled as he undid the laces on his boots then stood on the heels to pull them off. Head still bent, he slid his cap forward, pulling it from his head. Estella watched as wavy strands of brown hair fell across his forehead. Absentmindedly, he pushed them back, the palm of his hand almost seeming to drag his head up by his hair … to look directly into Estella's eyes. She looked away and felt her cheeks warm, having been caught staring. It was something of a shock when her mind presented her with the thought that she would quite like to run her hands through his hair, pushing it back out of his eyes. What a stupid thing to think! She could now feel her skin burning with embarrassment, hoping she hadn't betrayed her wayward thoughts with a look or movement. A distinctly male grunt emanated from the space close by and her head snapped up to find Ivan settling himself in a chair at her end of the table just past her right shoulder. Often when farmers came in, they would sit at the far end of the kitchen just inside the door rather than come all the way in to be close to the Aga. Perhaps it was so they didn't get too comfortable basking in the warmth the cooker threw only halfway across the room. Or maybe it was something to do with being closer to the outdoors rather than the kitchen.

"Here we are now." During Estella's musings, Rebecca had arranged bread, butter, jam, milk and sugar on the end of the table along with mugs and plates. Using the old, stained pan holder, she lifted the pot of tea off the hob and carried it over as if she had done it a thousand times before in Robin Hill's kitchen. Her confidence and brightness from earlier returned as she doled out tea then helped Estella from

118

her low armchair to the table. Ivan made to get up and help but his sister brushed him off. Despite her small stature, she was well capable of ministering to the patient alone.

Estella couldn't help but feel a twinge of disappointment that he wasn't the one helping, despite Rebecca's kindness. Rebecca even draped a blanket around her shoulders, noting the cool dampness of her clothing.

Ivan suddenly focused on Estella. "You did change your clothes when I brought you home earlier, didn't you?" he asked sharply.

Estella scowled. She didn't like his tone at all. "Of course I did. I just got wet again is all."

His left eyebrow rose in a smooth dark curve – like a question mark on its side. Shaking his head but saying nothing, he went about adding milk and sugar to his tea.

Each took care of buttering and jamming their own bread in silence before Ivan cleared his throat and stated, "I cleared the cow-house passage and poured the milk into the churn at the end. The donkey looked happy enough where she was. And I closed the hens in. You'd already fed the pigs, yes?"

Estella nodded. She was touched that he had taken it upon himself to finish the little jobs she would otherwise have had to do once they left. But his next words dampened her rush of gratitude.

"There's nothing in any of the stables though."

He phrased it as if it was a question but she knew by his tone that it wasn't. She gave a curt shake of her head.

"Pity," he added conversationally as he examined the slice of bread and jam in his hand. He took a large bite, chewed deliberately then swallowed without looking at her.

"They're fine stables."

She didn't know how to reply.

"You used to ride, didn't you?" Rebecca piped up. "I think I said before that Mr Leclerc mentioned it. Or was it Mrs Leclerc?"

"Both," Ivan said directly to his sister. "Hardly a week goes by without someone regaling us with a story about Stella Frayne and horses. Little Iris Kellett, they call you."

Estella stared unseeing at her plate of food as her jaw worked on a mouthful of crust that seemed to have turned back to flour on her tongue. She didn't want to think of those days, didn't want to remember, didn't want to be Noted Horsewoman Stella Frayne anymore. She didn't deserve their remembrances because she had failed when her skill mattered most. This was why she didn't talk to people. She didn't want to be reminded of the time before. She didn't want to join their conversations – to force words out around the hard lump in her throat. Suddenly, she wanted to be alone again.

"Mr Leclerc still keeps some of your horses, you know."

Estella's heard her stiff neck crunch as she turned swiftly to gape at Ivan. He was looking directly at her, a neutral expression on his face. She hadn't known that. She assumed Mr Leclerc would have sold them over the last three years. Or that Tony Dillon would have at least lined his pockets with the proceeds of her horses – no, they weren't her horses. She didn't have horses anymore. And they weren't her father's either. Because Reg was dead. Burt had killed him.

"Does he still have a horse called Burt?" she blurted out.

Ivan frowned. "I don't know. Mr Leclerc just said 'some

of these are the Fraynes' horses' when he was giving me the grand tour."

"You didn't know," Rebecca said softly.

Estella shook her head. "He never said. I never asked. I wonder …" She wasn't sure what she wondered. Did Austin know? Had he asked the Leclercs to keep the animals? Had her father? Did they think she would want them back some day? *Did* she want them back? All of them? How many had there been? Four mares and their foals, three yearlings, two two-year-olds, and then all the horses that were broken and riding, ready for selling on or competing. But then two of the mares were old and could have died in the interim. About twenty? "How many are there?"

"Dunno. Fifteen or sixteen maybe."

Which animals had been kept? As if she was flicking through Reg's old album of pictures, she saw each of the family's horses in her mind's eye – the chestnut coat of one, the bay with four white socks and a flash down its nose, the dark-grey Burt who would now be well on the way to white. Was Burt still there? She wondered if she would recognise each one when she saw them. When? If. She didn't even know if she wanted to see them. If she saw them then she would remember … No – she thought too much about her father as it was. Sadness heaved through her body. Why was it the person she had loved most in the world was so inextricably linked to the animals and the thing she loved to do most in the world? Why couldn't she separate them and move on? Why did her father's death have to colour almost every good thing she had?

Your fault …

121

The voice was always there, ready to explain, ready to make sure she never forgot.

Wordlessly, Rebecca began clearing up the remains of their supper. Ivan absentmindedly scratched at a narrow scab that curved across the back of his hand. As she brushed by, Estella caught a glance that passed between the siblings, then slid to her. They both looked away, noticing they were being watched. Rebecca seemed to want to say something but Ivan gave an infinitesimal shake of his head. Estella was glad their silence persisted. One wrong word from either of them and she would disintegrate at the end of her own kitchen table.

"I think we should be heading home," Rebecca eventually said quietly.

"Sorry," Estella muttered, waking from her reverie. "I've been a terrible host."

Rebecca placed a gentle hand on her shoulder. "We didn't come here to be hosted. We came here to make sure you were all right. We came here to help."

"You did." Estella nodded. "Thank you. For the help." She glanced at Ivan but looked away quickly when she found him observing her.

"Now don't you get up!" Rebecca chided as Estella tensed to push herself from the chair. "We can see ourselves out, can't we, Ivan?"

"Do you want me to come over in the morning and do the milking?" he asked, ignoring his sister.

"*No!*" Estella almost shouted at him then, more quietly, "No. I'll manage some road. You've done enough already. Thank you. Again."

She watched the two Aylwards saunter from the kitchen,

waving their goodbyes. Ivan bent to put on his boots and lace them. She noticed the back of his hand shine as the light caught it and saw a glow of red. The scab was bleeding. Immediately, the urge to go to him and wash the blood from his skin overtook all her other thoughts. She could imagine holding his solid hand in hers as she sponged it clean. The strong bones, sinews and tiny muscles flexing beneath her ministrations. The soft swell at the base of his thumb under her fingertips ... But then perhaps he was the sort of man who wouldn't let her tend to his wounds. She blinked. *Stop it*, she thought. He glanced at her before nodding and disappearing from view.

She heard the door close behind him, heard the engine start up and move off, the lights sweeping through the kitchen window.

She continued to sit long after they were gone, allowing the eerie peace to invade her body, cooling the flush of human contact. She had felt the warm of these two people, their humanity, their liveliness, touched them as they touched her, no matter how briefly. It was not until she became aware of its absence that she realised how much she craved physical contact. The only person who ever touched her now was Dolly and she hadn't made an appearance in more than a fortnight. She was like that sometimes, especially if there was a new man on the scene as there was now. Roy... something was his name.

Two weeks, Estella guessed. Two weeks and no one had touched her. Not even a hand on her arm, a hand on her shoulder, until today. Until Ivan had helped into the van earlier today. Until she collided with his chest in the barn this evening and he held her upright while she clung on to him. Rebecca had supported her across the yard, tended to her swollen knee with gentle touches. She was clearly a tactile person. The small brushes of her fingers were so unconscious for her but so noticeable to Estella. Little Harry was lucky to have such a naturally affectionate mother.

Musing on her loneliness, Estella wondered if her new friend had inherited such warmth from her mother. The brief encounter with Edna suggested she was not one to show affection. But then some people were much colder, more formal in public. Also, she was from a different generation and there was no telling what challenges life had thrown at her to make her so distant. Prudie Frayne had been a woman of that same generation and while she had been quite reserved with her sons and youngest daughter, it seemed the love she denied them supplemented the affection – physical affection – she offered Joy. Estella didn't resent this memory exactly. In a way, she understood her mother's need to express her love for her eldest daughter in a way that Joy might comprehend. Words didn't seem to reach the depths of the girl's mind but the small touches – when wanted – seemed to give her real pleasure.

Perhaps it was this early lack of physical contact that made Estella crave and set so much store by the touch of another human being. They had never been a touchy-feely family. And now her brothers considered themselves too manly to show they cared with something as intrusive as a hug. Her father rarely cuddled her but when he did it was a moment to be treasured. Even when he was paralysed and could barely look at her, never mind touch her, she relished the moments when he was forced to wrap his arms around her so that she could help him move. When she sat by his body, there was a fraction of a moment when she had considered lifting his lifeless arms around her shoulders just so she might experience one last embrace with him. But deep down she knew that cold, empty embrace would become the only one she remembered. She had to make do with the few they shared when he was a living, breathing man with warm flesh.

Slowly, she came to the realisation that Ivan Aylward was one of the only men to have held her close in years. Since her father's accident, she hadn't really gone anywhere except to table tennis. The men there shook her hand after a game but nothing more. Such touches didn't really count since it was nothing more than a formal gesture. No doubt she had also shaken the hands of many men at Reg's funeral but she couldn't remember the feel of their touch. Henry Leclerc had hugged her that day. When he and Barbara had engulfed her, they were sharing their grief, uniting it with fellow feeling. It had meant a lot. But it had also hurt.

In the last three years, the only man to hold her for any amount of time had been her father. And he had been dead for more than nineteen months now. If she closed her eyes and thought about it – *really* thought about it – she could remember the weight of her father's arms around her, usually a little stiff and unsure but caring nonetheless. Dolly's were different again – her arms were lighter but she held on tightly, squeezing Estella close. Dolly's embrace was the closest thing she had known to true affection in … well, she couldn't remember anyone being so openly and unaffectedly affectionate with her.

But Dolly, much like Henry Leclerc, was the sort of person who could not help reaching out to someone's shoulder in greeting, guide them through a crowd with a hand on their back, grasp their arm as they laughed at the same joke. Age and gender made no difference – they took care to make everyone the centre of their attention. Though she knew both cared for her, the attention they offered was not unique to her. There was no effort involved. They were just affectionate by nature. As she gingerly got to her feet to make her way – hop her way – upstairs to bed, Estella surmised Rebecca Aylward possessed a similar nature.

And absentmindedly, she also wondered if Ivan Aylward did too.

Chapter 12

Estella slept badly that night. She was prone to restlessness as it was. On occasions, wild-eyed grey horses careened through her dreams making her flail both arms and legs. Now, the constant ache in her knee burned viciously with every toss and turn, jerking her awake. The two soakings she had suffered also made her muscles stiff and sore. When her alarm rattled its angry little bell, she was quick to shut it off before its insistent metallic buzzing entered her head. She lay in the darkness of the early morning, wishing she didn't have to get up and haul herself through the soggy ground left in the wake of the previous day's weather. Yet she still dragged herself out of bed. However, it did take her somewhat longer to dress as she awkwardly hobbled about the room, fearing the twinges of knotted muscles in her back and shoulders. She *must* start taking better care of herself, she thought.

As she crossed the hall to the bathroom, an unhealthy hacking cough escaped from her brother's room. It was now a familiar sound throughout the house and yard. When it started in the summer, Graeme had brushed off her concern by telling her that it was nothing more than an unseasonable sore throat. She had silently left honey and lemons on the counter in the kitchen but the lemons had done nothing other than wizen into putrid green-brown lumps. He preferred adding whiskey to his hot water to soothe his raw gullet. Sometimes, she heard him coughing during the small hours of the morning too and wondered if he was so used to his body reacting to the irritation that he slept straight through it. No doubt she would have heard him swearing after each fit if he was conscious of them.

By the time she had eaten her breakfast, the blue light of dawn was filtering through the grey clouds above the yard. Since the farm buildings and tall evergreens surrounding them overshadowed the back of the house, the kitchen was quite a gloomy room. It was always difficult to tell the time of day since the natural light was so poor. Estella found the dimness oppressive and was strongly of the opinion that spending too much time in the kitchen had furthered her father's descent into inescapable depression. She often tried to gently persuade Reg to sit in the bay window of the sitting room which had a beautiful view out across the fields and woodland beyond. The sun also shone directly into it for most of the day, making it a brighter, happier place. But the more she encouraged him to occupy the other room, the more he pushed against the suggestion until she stopped altogether, thinking he was simply refusing to go because she wanted him to.

The cold air nipped at her exposed flesh as she left the house and limped across the yard to the cowshed. It was always a good place to be on such occasions thanks to the numerous large warm bodies that radiated a welcoming heat on chilly mornings. Estella didn't mind milking the cows in the winter. The jobs she hated were the ones where her hands or gloves got wet. And mangling frozen turnips for the pigs was one of the worst. It was a task she had loathed since childhood and yet here she still was at the age of twenty-five, cursing the fact that she would soon be mangling turnips in the freezing cold –

"*Aaaahhhhh!*"

Grumbling audibly with head down as she thought of all the things she needed to do during the day, Estella was not prepared to find herself colliding with a man's chest for the second time in as many days. It was hard to be sure which of them got more of a fright. Estella, who thought herself completely alone, or Ivan Aylward whose friendly, "Hello!" just before she walked straight into him was drowned out by her scream. He grabbed her by the arms to steady her as she smacked into him, momentarily knocking the air out of his lungs. She reacted instinctively, flailing her arms in panic, not knowing what she was aiming for or connecting with.

"*Wha – No, no, no! It's all right! It's all right. Ow! Stella!*"

Her elbow connected with his jaw just as she realised who stood in front of her.

Giving up on reason and with a smarting chin, Ivan grabbed her by the wrists before she did any more damage to him. "Stella! *It's me!* Christ!"

She froze. The whooshing sound in her ears wasn't enough to drown out the hammering of her heart as it fought to burst from her chest and flee to a safe distance. Though somewhere deep in her tired and shocked brain, she recognised the man standing in front of her – no, holding on to her – she still stared up into his face, uncomprehending. Ivan – somewhat ruffled by her sudden assault – was equally concerned by the abrupt stillness of her body and the glassy stare she gave him. Struggling to see her clearly in the poor light of the barn, he bent down and looked directly into her eyes, hoping she had not lapsed into some sort of catatonic state. If you gave someone enough of a fright, was it possible?

"Stella?"

His voice was soft but deep. She felt his breath on her skin when he spoke her name. Yet she still could not speak. As his eyes searched hers for any sign of recognition, she saw in the light streaming in behind her that his were the same dark brown as the lock of hair that brushed his forehead. Despite the early morning, he was clean-shaven and smelled of carbolic soap.

"Estella?"

He took his hand from her wrist and touched her cheek. She jerked back, suddenly aware of what he was doing. His fingers closed when she pulled away – as if he were trying to hold on to something that slipped through them.

"Wh – *What are you doing here*?"

The question came out much harsher than she intended. Though she would never admit it to anyone – not even Dolly – Ivan had drifted in and out of her restless dreams the previous night. However, he was never within her grasp, always standing tantalisingly out of reach by the doorway of the kitchen. She felt her cheeks flame, thinking that he might somehow know that his shade had kept her company while she slept. It was part of the reason she got such a fright when she ran into him. The man in front of her was altogether real. The liveliness of his face, the scent of his clothing and the immoveable solidity of his body were enough to make her sure of that. But she reached out and touched the front of his jumper just to be sure.

He stepped away. "I came to do the milking." Turning, he walked down the row to a shorthorn three from the end. "I haven't finished but I thought I'd do what I could before I left for work. Just to make things a bit easier for you. I saw your knee last night when Rebecca was … Anyway, it looked a bit nasty so …"

"But I could have asked Graeme to do it!"

"And did you?"

"No."

"Why not?"

The answer was on the tip of her tongue but she halted, unsure whether she should say it. "Because he was … I didn't … see him this morning."

"He's gone already?"

"No, he's … still in bed. I think."

Ivan gave a small bark of laughter. "Well, he's not much use to you there. Why didn't you just get him up?"

"No." Estella shook her head emphatically.

Ivan was about to reply but something in the way she said that one word made him bite his tongue.

"I said I could manage," she grumbled indignantly. "Don't you think I'm able?"

"Of course you're able! But that doesn't always mean you have to, Stella. I knew I could make things a little easier for you … so I did," he shrugged. "Take the help when it's offered."

His gaze was direct, kind.

She looked away and sighed. "Don't think I'm not grateful – I am. Of course I am! But you didn't have to. Thank you."

He smiled then. It was the same boyish grin that crinkled the skin around his eyes when he played table tennis. "See! That wasn't so hard, was it?"

Estella fought the urge to swat him the way she might have swatted Austin when he teased her. Instead she huffed, making Ivan laugh.

"I can come this evening too, if you want –" he began, but she cut him off.

"*No!*" Her voice rang loudly within the confines of the barn. "No," she said more quietly. "I'll manage. I'm sure you've enough to do without me bothering you."

He nodded and reached past her to collect his coat from the hook on the wall. Estella footed about awkwardly as he pulled out the folded collar, fixed his cuffs and did up the buttons. Turning to leave, he stopped as he reached the door and focused on some loose hay blowing up the passage. "You're not bothering me, Stella. You're my friend – our friend – and I want to help." He offered her another small smile. "Look after yourself."

With that, he was gone and Estella was left to stare at the empty space where he had been. If it had not been for the pail of fresh milk on the floor further up the passage, she might have thought she had invented the whole encounter. But he had been there with her and they had spoken and he had shown her real kindness. Again. She wondered what she had done to deserve it. And he had said she was their friend, *his* friend.

Finishing milking the cows, she allowed herself to indulge in his final few words, replaying them over and over again in her mind.

You're my friend, you're my friend ...

Chapter 13

Ivan did not return over the following days but Rebecca came often.

It seemed the primary goal of these visits was to chastise Estella for always being on her feet rather than resting her injury. Despite her protestations that it was healing nicely, her knee was still stiff and sore, the bruises having changed from purple to a kind of black tinged with sickly green.

This being the case, on the second day Rebecca arrived with a pot containing some funny-looking cream and a promise that it would soothe her aches. She assured Estella that it was her mother's own secret recipe and could attest to its effectiveness, having used it many times herself. "And, of course, Ivan uses it all the time too. You know the way men like him are always coming home with bumps and bruises."

Rubbing the lavender-scented salve into her bruised flesh did indeed offer some relief but she wasn't sure if it was the smell, the cooling sensation or the knowledge that Ivan used it that made Estella feel better.

However, it also seemed that Rebecca got some relief

from her daily visits. Although her relief was from simple irritation rather than any physical pain.

"You know, I do love my mother dearly. And I'm so grateful for all her help with Harry and taking me back after … But good Lord! When you've run your own house for more than three years and then you're suddenly back in the middle of someone else's …" She shook her head trying to convey her frustration. "I love my mother," she repeated. "But she's got her own way of doing things and her own ideas about how I should be raising Harry. And sometimes I just want things done *my* way …"

"I suppose that's one advantage of managing things yourself," Estella replied as she sat in front of the Aga with her foot on the egg crate and watched Rebecca make tea. It was a routine they had easily fallen into and, though it was her kitchen, Estella had given up protesting. "But sometimes I do wish I had someone to just ask simple questions of. Ask their opinion, you know?"

"Oh, I know!" Rebecca nodded enthusiastically. "I could never leave Mammy alone after … after I was married. I was forever in and out asking her how to do this and that." It was the first time she had ever mentioned anything to do with her married life. Estella noticed the small hesitation but said nothing. Rebecca barrelled on. "But now we're back in the same house again … Different kettle of fish altogether. And you know, I *am* here because I want to visit and make sure you're looking after yourself – which you're *not* – but sometimes I just need to get away from Mammy. Before I – I don't know – strangle her with her apron strings!"

Rebecca seemed happy to rattle on and though Estella

never said very much – just as she didn't with Dolly – she enjoyed listening. She thought that Rebecca had perhaps been starved of company before and, now she had a ready companion, was enjoying the advantages.

Ivan's sister probably said more than she ever would have if she had been asked to explain her history directly. Given that both women had lost fathers, it was a topic of conversation they came to early in their daily meetings. John Aylward was a second son and had crossed the water to join the British Army fighting in the war against Germany. For him it was a way to earn enough money to buy a farm of his own and give his children a better future rather than work for his brother earning a pittance. However, his grand plan for improvement ended abruptly when he was killed during the North Africa campaign. Rebecca was ten and Ivan eleven.

It was the first and only time Rebecca had ever seen her mother cry. She had wept inconsolably for three days but on the fourth had emerged from her room dry-eyed and never let anyone see her tear-streaked face again. As they spoke about Edna, the two women could not decide if her husband's death had made her or broken her.

"She always loved us. And let us know it," Rebecca explained. "But it was so hard for her without Daddy there. I can't imagine what it was like – well, actually, I can a bit. I suppose." She left her obligatory pause when touching on the subject of marriage and husbands. "And she did get the widow's pension but she always scrimped and saved trying to put a bit by for our future. Ivan, of course, didn't need it much since he started working when he was fourteen. But I went on in school. And what Mammy saved helped get me through college too."

"What did you do in college?" Estella asked when her companion lapsed into silence.

"What? Oh! I was a school teacher. Primary. Before I was married. But then I was a kept woman – that is –" her eyes suddenly widened and some of the soft, warm colour left her cheeks. "What I mean is I kept house for ... for my husband. He worked and ... and then I had Harry. I was supposed to go back to teaching when he went to school. I was going to teach his class and I was so worried he'd call me Mummy in front of all the other children." She forced a laugh then sobered abruptly. "But, well, that didn't happen, obviously."

It was moments like this that made Estella's heart beat a little faster. She was worried Rebecca would say something she regretted but also longed to know what on earth lay behind her new friend's unhappy moments. The oft-dormant gossip in her raised its sleepy head and sniffed the air hoping for a titbit to be thrown its way.

Yet, as they entered the last month of the year, Estella's curiosity remained hungry.

Chapter 14

With the arrival of December came the end-of-season table-tennis matches. Having missed several practices due to her injured knee, Estella felt distinctly rusty. However, she did find herself truly looking forward to going back after her absence and not just because she missed playing. Rebecca's detailed accounts of each practise session and the mischief everyone got up to made Estella pine for the company of all the other players in a way she had not before. It was perhaps because of the way Rebecca spoke about each individual, infusing them with a kindness Estella could not always see. She was so used to viewing people more pessimistically. Rebecca's positivity was infectious, so it was with high hopes that she bounced out to Austin's car on the last Monday evening training session before their competition the week before Christmas.

"Knee's better, I see," he muttered before heading off down the lane.

Estella deflated a little at the sour expression on her brother's face. Usually, Austin was happy to see her. She wondered what she might have done wrong to receive such a lukewarm welcome. Was he angry with her for missing training? Or was it something else? However, rather than sit in silence worrying, Estella took a more direct approach.

"What's wrong?" she asked bluntly.

"Nothing," Austin snapped.

She snorted. "You're a terrible liar, Aussie."

Her brother's eyes widened in surprise. When he didn't want to tell her something, she usually left him alone. He wasn't used to her calling him out.

Huffing, he eventually said, "Graeme."

Estella rolled her eyes. She considered leaving it at that since she didn't want to end up in the middle of another of her brothers' disagreements. Graeme always accused her of siding with Austin and, since she lived with him, she preferred not to antagonise her eldest sibling. But, yet again, the creeping influence of Rebecca's forthrightness compelled her to ask, "What is it this time?"

"*Nothing.*"

"Austin –"

"I was in Kennedy's getting some bits and, I don't know, he must have seen the car outside." He hunched his shoulders at the memory. Then he sneered. "On his way to the pub for the evening, no doubt."

"Just now?"

"Yes."

"What did he say?"

"He – I was there in front of everyone!" Austin ran his hand through his hair, making it stand up on end. "He … he was angry with me over a bill."

"A veterinary bill? Why?"

"He said I was overcharging him. Which I'm not! And

139

that he's my brother and he of all people shouldn't be overcharged. In front of *everyone*."

"You didn't overcharge him, did you?"

"*No, I bloody didn't!*" he shouted, making Estella cringe. "All I charged him for was the medicine. I didn't even charge him for the call-out."

"And did you explain that to him?"

"Of course I did. But it's not that, Stella. It's the fact that he said it in front of everyone. The shop was packed and there were about six people there who I've done work for. Now everyone's going to start questioning their bills and Marion's maths. *My* maths." His fingers dragged through his hair again. "It was just a really bloody dirty thing to do."

"Yeah," Estella answered quietly. The irony was she handled most of the farm's paperwork and had seen the bill Austin was talking about. She thought the invoice was very reasonable, considering the amount of work he did for his brother. Most people were reluctant to have the vet out to an animal unless it was absolutely necessary but, since Graeme had a brother in the profession, he was more inclined to call. The strange thing was, Estella had opened the bill and filed it away once she had written the cheque, signing Graeme's name herself as she usually did when paying things off. She wasn't sure her eldest brother had even seen the invoice. She had never seen him looking at them before. He probably didn't even know where they were kept. It seemed to her that Graeme was attacking their brother for the sake of it.

However, one benefit of discovering what had angered her brother was that he was not so sullen by the time they arrived at the hall. Nevertheless, the moment she entered,

140

she made a beeline for Rebecca.

"Good to have you back!" She smiled, taking Estella's hands. Rebecca had visited Robin Hill earlier but seemed just as glad to see her now. "You're going to stop the boys from teasing me every time I lose a match."

"And what makes you think Stella here will stop us teasing you?" Ivan plopped down in the seat beside his sister. "Hello, Stella, how's your knee?"

"Good, thank you –"

"She'll stop your teasing by beating you," Rebecca cut in. "Won't you, Stella?"

She laughed. "I'll do my best. But you've had a lot more practice recently than I have."

"Rebecca's been practising on the kitchen table with Mammy when I'm not there," Ivan informed her. "She thinks I don't know, but Harry let it slip."

"The little scallywag! Still doesn't mean I can beat you though, does it," she grumbled, making her brother chuckle.

Just then, Ivan was called away to play against Austin, leaving the two women to watch.

"I used to practise on the kitchen table with Austin too when we were little," Estella murmured. "We'd put mugs along the centre as a net."

"Yes, we do that too!" Rebecca nodded. "But our kitchen's a bit piddly to get a full run at a game. Your kitchen's much better suited to play in than ours. You've all that room and that lovely big oak table."

"It feels like wasted space now though, when it's just me and Graeme." The house had never really felt full, but now it was distinctly empty.

141

"Maybe Graeme will get married. Or you? You wouldn't be long filling the place then."

Estella's shocked laughter drew several gazes. She covered her mouth, reddening with embarrassment. "No," was all she managed to get out.

"No? No, you mean he won't marry or you won't?"

"No," she said again, shaking her head.

Rebecca frowned. "Come on! Surely you've thought about it. You can't expect to spend the rest of your life alone. And I know I've never met Graeme but don't most men want to marry eventually? It's what you do."

"Graeme's more interested in going to the pub than finding a wife," Estella muttered. This wasn't a subject she felt comfortable with at all. Though Dolly often wittered happily about her own marriage prospects, Estella didn't join in. Dolly was so used to her oldest friend's silences on certain subjects that she never tried to cajole a response. But since Rebecca didn't know her so well, she was more inclined to press.

"Well, it's not *completely* impossible to find a wife in a pub," Rebecca reasoned. "Although whether you'd want a woman who frequents the pub as a sister-in-law is another matter."

"And what about Ivan?" Estella blurted out, trying to deflect the discussion away from herself. "If all men want a wife, why doesn't he have one?"

A quizzical look creased Rebecca's features. "Oh, Ivan's had the interest of a few girls over the years but nothing's stuck. Apart from one but that ended when, when –" she stuttered, then caught herself. "Why? Are you interested?"

"*No!*" Estella's answer was a high-pitched, mortified hiss. "No, I'm not – I wouldn't – it's not what I …"

"What, you don't like Ivan?"

"*No*! It's not that."

"Don't you think he's nice?"

"Yes!"

"And kind?"

"*Yes!*"

"So is he not handsome enough, is that it?"

"No – I mean yes, he's handsome but I didn't – I never –"

Rebecca threw her head back and laughed. "There's no need to get so flustered. I was only joking – actually I wasn't joking. The two of you would make a *lovely* couple," she mused. "But I suppose if neither of you are interested …"

They lapsed into silence and watched the game. Estella paid particular attention to Ivan. She *did* like him. And of course he was nice *and* kind. There were people she had known her entire life who would not have treated her with the care and kindness he did. During their short acquaintance, he had shown her he was a good man. *And* he was handsome. His height, his broad work-strengthened shoulders, the large angular face and the rich brown hair that had ripples like disturbed water running through it. But all of that didn't matter. 'Neither of you are interested' was what Rebecca had said. No matter how decent or good-looking he was, he would never be hers. He thought nothing of her just as everyone else did. She came to this conclusion just as Rebecca spoke again.

"Not saying Ivan's not interested, by the way. But you're not so –"

"Rebecca! Stop gabbing and get up here!" Edgar Chapman called bossily, his voice cutting through the noise of the room.

As Estella mouthed like a landed fish, Rebecca jumped up, winked at her and giggled as she trotted off to begin her game.

"What's up?" Austin asked as he took a seat beside her.

She tore her eyes away from Rebecca to look at her brother but found her gaze wandering straight past him. Ivan sat to the left of her brother, an enquiring look on his face. It was as if the contents of her brain had suddenly been removed. In the presence of Ivan Aylward, she couldn't seem to find a single word to say. He held her gaze for a moment – perhaps a moment too long then turned away to watch his sister. Estella blinked as the confused jumble of thoughts resurfaced just as abruptly as they had been removed. Out of everything that sloshed around her brain, she managed to find one thing to say to Austin.

"Nothing."

Her brother viewed her suspiciously. "Fair enough." He shrugged, turned his attention to Ivan and launched into a conversation about how many mares would be foaling at Ellendale next year.

An hour later, Edgar began pairing everyone off for doubles after everyone had played at least one singles game.

Austin rapped his knuckles on the side of Estella's leg before standing expectantly. "We're up."

"No, no, no!" Edgar wagged an admonitory finger. "I'm splitting up the dream team. Just for now. Austin, I want you with Rebecca. And Miss Frayne with Mr Aylward. Give our two green recruits the chance to play with a real player, hey?" He chortled.

"Don't be an ass, Edgar," Austin said cheerfully. "They're bloody good players for beginners. They'll be giving all of us a run for our money soon."

"Yes, yes, of course. The teams should be quite evenly matched. What with Stella missing so much practice."

"Maybe we should stick together then," Austin offered, misinterpreting the look of trepidation on Estella's face. He assumed she was afraid of losing, of letting the side down. But, in fact, her unease was down to the things Rebecca had said to her earlier. It had flooded her mind with so many thoughts she wasn't sure she could stand beside the man who was at the centre of them.

"It's like being picked for teams back in school," Rebecca whispered loudly, linking Estella's arm and dragging her from her reverie. "I think Austin doesn't want me on his team."

Austin spun to face her, looking aghast. "No! That's not it at all!"

"I mean, you're talking about Edgar being an ass ..." Estella tutted at her brother, patting Rebecca's hand.

"*No*! You *know* that's not what I meant." He looked ten years younger and distinctly lost.

The two women cracked at the same time and guffawed at the pained look on his face.

"Oh very *funny*," he muttered.

"Well, Austin, you're welcome to her because I'm *delighted* with who I have on my team."

Estella experienced a little thrill of shock when two large hands came to rest on her shoulders.

145

"Do you hear that? Even my own brother doesn't want me." Rebecca mock-sobbed.

Looking up, Estella found Ivan smiling down at her. Fighting the urge to tense at the contact, she felt his fingers squeeze gently. He bent down to her ear and his breath tickled her cheek as he whispered, "Let's give the cocky bugger hell."

She turned to him and smiled a genuine, bright smile. "Let's."

Despite having never played together, the siblings all worked well in their new pairings. What really stood to them was the fact that they were all competitive. Ivan, despite his size, could move almost as quickly as Austin but had the advantage of a greater reach. Rebecca, however, had better technique. And then there was the fact that each was as determined as the other not to be beaten by their sibling. By the final game of the match, everyone else in the hall had forgotten about talking and were watching the two pairs battle it out. Both of the men were sweating and Estella knew that by now her hair was a fuzzy mess since Rebecca's was the same. The scoreboard continued to seesaw in increments of one, passing the usual endpoint of twenty-one. None of them were willing to surrender as, with each shot, the cheers from the gathered players increased in volume, egging them on.

Estella was in her element. For once, she did not feel like the weaker member of the team and that knowledge bolstered her confidence. When she played with Austin, she rarely got effusive praise. He would encourage her with comments like, 'Good shot!' but he was reserved with her in a way he didn't seem to be with Rebecca. He showered Rebecca with praise, making her glow with happiness and strive to do better. Equally, Ivan hailed Estella's abilities and made her determined to keep them in the game. But it was more than just the words Ivan spoke. It was the way he smiled at her when she cheered his winning shots. And it was the small touches he offered in between each rally – a hand on her shoulder, a touch on her back. Each made her skin burn with more than mere exertion.

The final passage of play was a long rally. Estella didn't even try to count the shots since she was too busy concentrating on not being the one who ruined it. Luckily for her, it was Austin's cockiness that got the better of him. Ivan hit an acute cross which had Rebecca reaching to make the shot. Her ball was slow and allowed Estella to put some topspin on it. Seeing the ball slow down, Austin wound up to smash just as the little white sphere jinked on landing. He fumbled, smashed and missed the end of the table by half an inch.

The hall erupted.

Between the cheers and shouts of the other players, Edgar Chapman's squeals of glee could be heard above all else as well as his pronouncement that he now had two more of the best players in the county. Austin swore horribly, drawing looks of deep consternation from several others and a shocked giggle from Rebecca who smiled brightly despite their defeat.

But it was Ivan's reaction that Estella enjoyed most.

"*Yes!*" he roared then launched himself at Estella.

Caught by surprise, she screamed as he grabbed her around the waist, lifted her off the floor and swung her in a circle. Shock made her cling to him even though he held her tightly, burying her head in his neck. It didn't matter that he was hot and sweaty. His was the scent of masculinity and exertion and she enjoyed it for a brief moment, breathing it in as he held her. Gently, he returned her to the floor and disentangled his arms from her. Although she was sure his hands lingered on her waist for a fraction longer than was entirely necessary.

"Well, I defy anyone to follow that performance!" Edgar cried as he named the next two teams to step up.

"Yes," Rebecca said as they all shook hands, then quietly so only Estella could hear, "I defy anyone to follow that celebration at the end."

She cackled gleefully at the scowl Estella threw her.

"What?" Ivan asked.

"Nothing," Rebecca replied sweetly before catching Estella's eye and they dissolved into a fit of giggles together.

"You're coming for Christmas, aren't you?"

Austin was driving at snail's pace. The road home was blanketed in a thick white fog which hid the ditches along the sides. Edgar had kept them late making sure who would be available for a little tournament he was organising the weekend before Christmas. When his plans were finalised, he had sent them out into thick white clouds and eerie quiet. Estella had heard several people cursing his name as they fumbled for bikes and car keys to head home.

Squinting through the windscreen and leaning over the steering wheel as if it might improve the view, it took Austin a moment to answer.

"Well, I don't know, do I!"

Hearing the snappishness in his voice, Estella considered whether she should have let him win that evening just to improve his mood. However, she concluded that a more cheerful Austin was not worth forfeiting her celebration with Ivan. She sighed. "I just said I'd ask so I have an idea of how much food I need to buy when I'm in town."

It took Austin a while to reply again. "I don't know if I want to be in the same house as him."

"Ah." Estella stared out the windscreen – as if a solution to her problems might present itself to her. But all she saw was white.

"I want to come for you. You make the best Christmas dinners, but Graeme – it got to me this evening."

She ignored the last part. "How would you know whether or not I make the best Christmas dinners? You've never had anyone else's."

"Because no one cooks the way you do, Stell." They were almost home when he gave a long, controlled exhale as if he was letting go of something. "I'll come. For you. I'm probably going to be on call, though. So even if you do cook for me, there's no guarantee I'll be there to eat it."

"You'll get to eat it eventually. I can keep it warm for you. Don't forget, I had years of practice doing that for Daddy."

Estella blinked, taken aback by her own words. It had been so easy. She hadn't been building towards talking about it. She was relaxed and happy and it had just happened. She had spoken about her father and it hadn't hurt. It had been a good memory, untinged by guilt or regret. Thinking about Reg, talking about him was becoming almost … easy.

149

As he turned into their laneway, Austin glanced at her, aware that there was a strange quality to her silence. But he didn't think much of it so turned his attention back to the track – and slammed on the brakes.

A figure was tottering up the lane a few feet in front of them. Graeme Frayne moved as if he was traversing the deck of a sailboat. His feet rose only to descend and hit the ground with a jolt that tipped him in the opposite direction. Sometimes, it was as if he missed the ground altogether and stumbled forward looking for a steady foothold. And while he used his right hand in vain attempts to balance himself, his left hand swiped repeatedly down the side of his jacket. It was a gesture Estella was familiar with. No matter how drunk or sober her eldest brother was, he always sought to put his hand in his left pocket.

"Should've just run him over," Austin sneered quietly as Graeme staggered to the verge.

Estella didn't reply as she stared at the formless black shape of her brother stumbling on the uneven grassy edge. It was a while since she had seen him so drunk. But that didn't mean it wasn't a regular occurrence. Usually, she didn't see him at all because she was tucked up in bed. She did, however, hear him quite regularly as he lurched about the house, sometimes making himself a plate of bread and butter, other times simply careening into walls as he attempted to navigate the stairs and passage to his room. She didn't ever want to see him like that. And she also didn't want to be seen *by* him. She knew how that would end. He would reject her help then say something cruel before disappearing into another room to get away from her. Deep down, she thought his dismissal of her was perhaps rooted in shame. He did not want her to see him like that so he said something hurtful just to make her go away.

Parking in the yard, Austin kept the engine running as he asked, "Do you want me to stay just, you know, to deal with him?"

She shook her head. "No, I'll just go to bed. He'll manage." That seemed the most peaceful solution for everyone.

"Right. I'll see you next week."

Estella climbed out. But before she closed the door, he leaned across. "Well done tonight, by the way. You and Ivan make a good pairing. I hope he doesn't steal you away from me."

Estella smiled. "Give over! You and Rebecca made a fine partnership too."

"Not as good as you and me, though. But who knows, maybe playing with someone else would be good for you. We'll see."

With that, he sat square in his seat and Estella closed the car door. Watching his taillights disappear, she hoped he wouldn't be tempted to really run over their brother when presented with a second opportunity to do so. Shivering in the oppressive fog, she headed inside and straight up the stairs, listening all the while for Graeme to crash into something and announce his arrival. Minutes ticked by and still the house remained silent until she eventually heard a thump and foul swearing. No doubt he had stumbled over the pile of boots and shoes inside the back door. She kept all of hers neat but his were often left exactly where he had taken them off. If he fell over them, it was entirely his own fault.

Breathing evenly, she heard every bang, every curse. She allowed the sound to float in the air around her without it ever touching her. She was warm and safe in her cocoon of blankets, free to dwell on the better things in her life. Lately, it was her conversations with Rebecca that often came to the forefront. Dolly now had Roy and hadn't been visiting much, so it was no wonder Estella's new friend took precedence in her thoughts. However, it was their earlier conversation which prevented her finding sleep tonight.

Seeing her brother stagger up the laneway, she couldn't imagine any woman wilfully entangling herself in such a mess of a human being. Because her brother was a mess. And it hadn't started recently. She remembered the smell of alcohol on his clothing when she began to take over the household chores – including laundry – from her father around the time she finished primary school. In her mind's eye, she remembered coming home from boarding school for summer holidays to see Graeme sitting hunched at the end of the kitchen table – pale, red-eyed and liable to flinch at loud noises. How their father sneered and criticised him.

No woman in her right mind would shackle herself to Graeme Frayne. So then perhaps it was up to Estella to fill the house with life once again. She snorted into her bedcovers. The idea alone was ridiculous. Other people got married and had children. It was what they dreamed about from childhood, through their adolescence until the opportunity to realise their fantasies presented itself – usually falling well below their still-childish expectations.

Estella's only plan for the future had been to work with horses and her father. The outer edges of this narrow dream were completely blank. There had been no back-up plan. Maybe that was why her life ground to a standstill when her father had his fall. She never factored his absence into her prospects. And now she had neither father nor horses to work with and shape a life for herself.

Perhaps, then, it was time for a new plan. As she heard her eldest brother fall up the stairs, curse then continue, she began to speculate. What could her future hold if she was willing to work towards something? Something new, different, exciting, rewarding. Would she pursue a career? Could she do it alone or would she need help? If so, whose help would she ask for? And might there be a man in her future too? A husband, perhaps. Marriage and children? Would this husband be tall, athletic and have dark, wavy, brown hair?

She stifled a giggle in her pillow, covering her face with her hands. "Go to sleep, Estella!" she admonished herself aloud then closed her eyes, rolled over and slowly fell asleep.

Chapter 15

After finding her half drowned the previous month, Ivan – via Rebecca – had offered or, rather, insisted that Estella catch a lift with him into town the next time she was visiting Joy.

"He says I'm not to take 'no' for an answer. And that he knows you're very stubborn and independent but he's *still* not going to take 'no' for an answer."

Estella had stewed for a moment as Rebecca's gales of laughter subsided and accepted the offer with comic ill-grace. However, as the day drew closer, she felt nervous about once again sharing the confined space of a vehicle with him. What would she say to him and he to her?

As it was, she needn't have worried. Graeme had decided to sell some empty ewes at the market. Unlike the others in the flock, they did not sport the gawdy red mark of the raddle on their behinds that showed which females had been impregnated by the ram. Rather than overwinter them any further, he was cutting his losses and making a few bob before Christmas. So, having helped him to separate out the sheep earlier in the morning and loaded them into another farmer's trailer, they set off for Mountlennon.

Driving along, however, Estella silently thought a journey with Ivan would have been considerably better. At the very least, it would have been safer. Graeme was still pie-eyed from a drinking session the night before and his driving was erratic at best but downright terrifying at worst. They weaved across the road from ditch to ditch with Graeme apparently making no attempts to avoid potholes or even other vehicles. He was also snappish and irritable which made conversation – no matter how polite – impossible. In fact, Estella's very presence in the car seemed to irritate him since he kept throwing her disgusted looks as if she had just loudly broken wind.

These venomous looks probably had something to do with a brief exchange they had shared the previous morning concerning Austin.

"So. Was Austin saying aught to you at table tennis on Monday?" Graeme had asked with forced nonchalance.

Even if she hadn't known what he was alluding to, the fact that her eldest brother was saying anything about his younger sibling would have set off alarm bells. He never asked her anything about Austin, never even acknowledged his existence, unless there was something amiss.

"No," she answered. "Spoke about work mostly. He's on-call over Christmas. And then he was saying that the Leclercs have a lot of mares to foal this year and it's a good thing they've got that Aylward fella working for them when they have so many and that he seems to know what he's doing –" She had to force herself to stop talking. She tended to ramble when she was lying but hoped Graeme had never realised this. He hadn't. He simply stared at her until she said innocently, "Why? Was there something he was supposed to tell me for you?"

Her brother had huffed. "No. Is he coming for Christmas then?"

"As far as I know."

"When did you ask him?"

"Monday night."

Another huff and a long silence ensued. "Right," he finally sneered.

Estella supposed that was not the answer Graeme had wanted to hear. He had wanted to hear that he had riled his brother. That Austin was so angry he wasn't coming for Christmas. Graeme wanted to know that his words had affected him. He did *not* want to hear inanities about Ellendale's foaling schedule. If Austin had said nothing to Estella, that meant she didn't know she was supposed to have taken a side. And if she hadn't taken a side, then there was nothing to argue with her about.

When he dropped her off at the gate of Claybourne's, Estella asked, "Do you want to come in for a minute?" though she already knew the answer.

"No," he said vaguely. "I've got to meet Pat Kavanagh to unload the sheep."

She knew he didn't have to be there for an hour since she had heard Pat say what time he would arrive. Plus, there were always ample numbers of men and boys at the market to unload animals. Nevertheless, she said nothing and walked away up the curving path to the grand old house alone. She had a new bear in a purple waistcoat wrapped in shiny silver paper held firmly in her hands as per her

Christmas tradition with Joy. She had bought the gift months ago when she saw it in the toyshop window in Mountlennon and had fashioned the bear's attire herself. She had no idea what her sister's favourite colour was but she herself liked deep, darker colours so made the waistcoat to her own tastes hoping they would chime with Joy's.

When she entered the main doors, the nurse she met was grim-faced. "Not a good day, I'm afraid. We're under the weather and feeling very sorry for ourself."

Despite being inside, Estella shivered in her coat as the nurse led her up the stairs and down the hall. With each breath, she saw the mist of her exhalation hang in the air before she walked through it.

When she got to the dormitory, she found Joy facing away from the door curled up on her bed snuffling into a sodden handkerchief while Susan sat in a chair beside her stroking the bedcovers, concern evident in her eyes. Grouped around her on the bed were all of her teddies, ranged at the foot and head, glassy eyes all focused on her as they kept their silent vigil.

Estella didn't dare break the cloister-like hush of the room as she tiptoed in. Wordlessly, she passed Susan and gently placed the shiny package on the cover beside Joy's hands. For a moment, the childlike woman lay motionless, a tiny bead of clear moisture clinging to the end of her luminous red nose. It looked raw and painful, but Estella knew better that to try and get her to use the Vaseline that was sitting on her bedside table. Joy's gaze drifted down to the gift. Though her hands moved slowly to retrieve it, her eyes shone avariciously, knowing there was doubtless a true treasure wrapped in the gleaming paper. Momentarily, her sickness was forgotten as she removed the string and paper, pushing both off the edge of the bed. As Estella bent to retrieve the wrapping, her sister gave a small crow of appreciation before lying the bear down on her pillow so that they might stare into each other's eyes and bask in the glow of unwavering attention.

Estella absentmindedly folded the shiny paper in a neat square. Susan stood and began rocking on the soles of her feet. When she was closest to Estella, her hand jerked forward, extending almost involuntarily then withdrew. Throughout this little performance, her eye darted from Estella's chin to the folded paper in her hand. No matter how many times Susan had met her over the years, she could never manage to make eye contact. But her meaning was plain.

"Would you like to look after my bit of paper for me?" Estella asked quietly, still unwilling to disturb the quiet room.

The other woman positively vibrated but said nothing. Taking that as an affirmative, Estella offered it to Susan. With delicate, hesitant fingers she reached out and slid the paper from between Estella's fingers, glancing repeatedly at Estella's chest as if she expected her to snatch it back. However, once she had it in her possession, she had eyes only for her gleaming new prize, turning it over and over between her hands. Once her inspection concluded, she moved away to the next bed. She knelt in front of the locker on the far side and Estella heard her knees crack loudly. Joy whimpered but the sound didn't seem to affect Susan at all.

Curious, Estella stood on her tiptoes to see what else her sister's friend might have deemed worthy of safe-keeping. The space surrounding Joy's bed had been plastered with pictures of birds and flowers and, of course, there was the basket for all her teddies plus some of the keepsakes she had brought with her from home all those years ago. Susan's space, however, was completely blank. Estella knew no one ever visited her. There was no one to bring her trinkets or even meaningful possessions. Instead, she scavenged things. Silently stepping a little closer, Estella saw a plethora of tat. There was a folded square of cellophane, a line of six odd buttons that had possibly come off other people's clothes, a tiny clear glass bottle with a chipped mouth that had obviously been dug up since it was still a little dirty and filled with dried soil. Then there was a ball of baby-pink wool that Estella sometimes saw her carrying or fondling as she sat in the dayroom. The pale-rose colour had a grey tinge now from being handled so much. In the top righthand corner was a selection of short pieces of string, wool and thread taken from clothing and one piece of blue silk ribbon with a frayed end that had pride of place in the centre of everything. Considering carefully, Susan placed the shiny paper behind the row of buttons, patting it down in place as if to make it comfortable.

Glancing at the floor, Estella spotted the piece of string she had used to tie up the parcel under Joy's bed and bent down to get it. From there, she could see the edges of Susan's skirt at the far side of her bed as she continued to kneel, examining her treasures. Not wishing to disturb or cause Susan to withdraw, she rolled up the string and carefully aimed it under her bed. Bending further in order to see if it had reached its target, Estella saw the red-and-white twisted ball had come to rest by Susan's leg. She watched as pallid fingers crept down the brown fabric of the skirt and plucked the end of the string from the ball, unwinding it as she lifted it from the ground.

"Miss Frayne?"

Estella popped up to find one of the nurses standing in the doorway.

"Will you be needing anything?" the nurse asked kindly.

"No, no. I'm done, I think. Let Joy rest. Hopefully she'll feel better tomorrow." She looked across at her sister who was still in thrall to her new bear. "Thank you."

The nurse nodded and left her to it. Getting to her feet, she brushed off the knees of her trousers which had a fine dusting of grey-white where they had touched the floor. She glanced across at Susan who was still sitting on the floor, running the string through her fingers, a look of pure wonder on her face. Estella smiled. Though it was a pitiful gift, she hoped it might give her sister's friend some happiness, however small. With that thought, she left – the clack-clacking of her hard-soled shoes incongruously loud in the large rooms and cold empty corridors.

Estella made her own way back to town on foot. The day was bracing but thankfully dry so the walk wasn't much of an exertion.

After visiting the large grocer's shop to purchase supplies for Christmas she hadn't previously collected, she browsed the chemist for pretty soaps for Dolly and Rebecca.

She had already made jumpers for her two brothers during the summer evenings when the natural light in the house was better. She found if she knitted using electric light, she couldn't make out the patterns as clearly and was more inclined to make mistakes.

Her purchases securely wrapped and stowed in a sturdy canvas bag she had brought for the purpose, Estella made her way to the market square. She found she was joining a general flow of people all heading in the same direction. Boys and men in flat caps and heavy tweed jackets hurried along to make the start of the sale, smoke issuing from many of their mouths and nostrils as they chugged along with pipes or cigarettes clamped between their lips. She smiled to herself as she thought how they all looked like absurd little engines spewing steam and smoke as they hurried onwards. Scanning the crowd, she saw other women bent on the same direction, carrying bags of provisions similar to her own. They must be the wives of other buyers and sellers on their way to find husbands and deposit shopping in cars. She wondered if any of them were looking at her with similar thoughts. Did she look like a wife? What did a wife actually look like? Maybe some of these women were sisters too and didn't have husbands either. But then she found herself automatically assuming all women over a certain age were wives because that was what you did as a woman: you grew up and you got married.

Drawn onwards by the stench and sounds of animals, each became more overpowering as she approached. The further into the melee she walked, the more she risked being trodden on by the gathered men and beasts. Some were in pens but others were driven or corralled by the crowd. She was surprised it was so busy, considering it was the depths of winter. Usually, it was the spring sales that commanded the biggest crowds. Snorting and squealing pigs in pens against the back wall of a house nearby where Estella walked could not override the bleat of sheep and the smell of lanolin. She assumed that many farmers, like her brother, were getting rid of empty ewes.

A commotion a dozen yards away attracted her attention as a particularly large haltered cow towed the boy leading it through a gathering of burly men. Catching some of the language and posturing of the group, she changed tack and headed in a different direction, unwilling to witness their displeasure. She wondered if some of the women she had seen were their wives. Once again, she began to consider why she never thought of herself marrying when she expected it of everyone else around her. Absentmindedly, she began searching the faces of the men rather than just looking for her brother. Could that man over there with the badly shaven jaw be her husband? He hawked and spat. She thought not. Another man bumped into her and walked on without apologising. Well, he wouldn't do either. Studying face after face, figure after figure, she discarded each man. A group of sheep trotted by and someone stepped back, standing on her foot. She clasped her bags close. It was beginning to get uncomfortable, hemmed in on all sides by strangers. She could feel her face growing hot. Don't panic, she told herself.

"*Stella!*"

She swung around and bumped against the elbow of a man carrying a sack of meal through the crowd. "Watch it!"

he admonished before adding, "Bloody women." Her gaze followed him until she heard her name again.

"*Estella!*"

She scanned the crowd again. Ivan Aylward was coming towards her, using his height to his advantage as he surveyed the market. Estella waved to him as another group of sheep cut a swathe through the crowd, blocking his path to her. His smiling, clean-shaven face was a bright beacon amongst the tan-stained browns and pasty greys of the gathering. He was laughing and shaking his head as he stood out of the way of an exceedingly portly man whose protruding belly cleared the mass before him like the prow of a fat little trawler. A gap opened just as the boat chuffed by and Ivan slithered through, exhibiting a litheness that was incongruous with his size. Suddenly, they were chest to chest and he was using her shoulder to steady himself and not topple over her after rushing forward to meet her. She caught his elbow and they both laughed.

"What are you doing in the middle of this mess?" he asked. His arm slid easily around her shoulders as he bent his mouth to her ear. But when he stood to his full height again and looked expectantly at her for an answer, his arm stayed where it was.

"Have you seen Graeme?" She pitched her voice slightly above the hubbub around them.

He stretched up on his toes, gaining another six inches, still clasping her shoulder protectively, his elbow sticking out to protect her back. The movement dragged her closer so that she was pressing against his ribs. She put her arm around his back as she regained her footing.

163

"Oh! Sorry!" he apologised, looking down as she used his solid form to right herself. "You're never going to find him in all this. Did you not have a place to meet up?"

"No."

He glanced at her. "Want to hop up on my shoulders and see if you can see better than I can?" His eyes sparkled with humour.

"No, you're fine!" She stepped away slightly in case he decided to try and pick her up. "I didn't realise it was going to be this busy," she added as two young men pushed past, forcing her to cling to Ivan once again.

"*Oi!*" Ivan shouted at their retreating backs.

Estella heard them cackle rudely in reply.

"Some bloke out past the Dell isn't well so his brother's selling off a whole load of the stock to cut down on work," Ivan said. "The son's in America or something and can't get home. And his wife's getting on so she's not able. Mr Leclerc's asked me to take a look. It's manic! Come on, let's get out of here."

Rather than take her by the hand, he pulled her in front of him and kept at least one hand on her at all times so as not to lose her.

Soon they had found their way to the fringes of the crowd and could stand apart yet Ivan still held her shoulder. "I've only just found you. I don't want to lose you again now, do I!"

"I haven't seen crowds like this since the last time I was at the Spring Show in Dublin." She brushed some loose hair out of face and blew out. "How am I meant to find Graeme in all that?"

164

Ivan slid his cap off his head and rearranged his own hair before replacing it. "Well, was he buying or selling?"

"Selling sheep."

"Maybe he's over at the sheep pens then."

Estella thought for a moment then tittered angrily at herself, hitching her shopping bags higher on her shoulder. "Not likely. He's probably in the pub. I don't know why I didn't think of that straight off."

"The pub's over the far side though, isn't it?"

"Over where that big carriage arch is. I'll head over there now. Sorry about that. Thanks for your help." She made to move off but hadn't gone two paces when she found herself held in a firm grasp.

"Oh no, no, no! I'm not letting you off into the middle of that on your own."

She rolled her eyes at him. "I'll be fine. I'm a big girl, I can look after myself." Mostly, however, she was worried what sort of state she would find Graeme in. And she really didn't want Ivan to see that.

But Ivan didn't let go. "I know you can look after yourself but how do you think I'd feel if I heard you'd been crushed in a stampede on market-day? Also, you're not *that* big a girl. I reckon I could pick you up and throw you over my shoulder without much effort." He stepped towards her, his other hand extended at waist height.

"Don't you dare!" she squealed, drawing the eyes of several passers-by.

His chest rumbled with laughter. "Come on."

With a hand still on her shoulder, they cut through the massing men and beasts. Though she wasn't going to admit

165

it, she was glad he was helping her. She felt safe with Ivan. He was not like the other men around her. Though she could not look into his face, she knew she would not discard him with one glance. But then, did she really know? If he had been a face in the crowd like the others, would she have brushed over him in the same way? The comparison wasn't really fair since she had no knowledge of these strangers. Over the last few months, she had come to know him a little. But on their first encounter at Ellendale, he had seemed distant. Maybe he was just a little shy. Meeting new people was difficult. Now that he was getting to know her, he appeared to be quite comfortable in her company. And she in his. It was possible that if she got to know some of the men around her, she would trust them too. Yet as her gaze moved from grim mouth to hooded eyes, she thought not.

By the time they were on the other side of the marketplace, Estella's eyes were watering from having walked through so many clouds of cigarette smoke. As she approached the pub, she surmised that the interior of the establishment would be no better – that was, if she could get in. They were only a few yards from the entrance when a voice boomed through a megaphone somewhere behind them.

"*Ah-lovie-day-fur-it-gelmen-lovie-day …*"

"Do you ever wonder whether auctioneers even know what they're saying themselves sometimes?" Ivan asked conversationally as he pulled her against the wall of the pub to protect her from the stampede of punters exiting the building.

Estella snorted in reply, carefully watching the stream of

men – just as she might count animals through a gateway – hoping that her brother might be one of them. "You should go," she said to Ivan. "I don't want you missing your lots because of me."

He shook his head. "Sheep are first. I'm here for the cattle. They're not on till two. Come on, we'll go in."

The smell of tobacco filled her nostrils and the bitterness of alcohol fumes coated her tongue as Ivan pushed the door open for her. Despite it being less than an hour since opening time and the mass exodus they had just witnessed, every seat, bench and stool in the place was occupied. Glancing around, Estella immediately noted that she was the only woman in the entire establishment apart from a middle-aged barmaid. Her entry drew the eyes of many and she was suddenly very thankful that Ivan had insisted on coming with her. Scanning the customers, she spotted Graeme sitting at a table with three other men. Each had a half-drunk pint of amber liquid and an empty glass in front of them – except for her brother who had two empties. She cringed internally but approached him nonetheless.

"Graeme?"

He slowly dragged his eyes away from one of the other men who was in the middle of a story, the smile on his face morphing into a frown as soon as he focused on her. "What're you doing here?" he asked, the irritation in his voice barely disguised.

She ignored his question. "Aren't you going out? The sheep sale's started."

"Why would I need to go out?" In the space of a few words, his exasperation had increased.

167

Estella did something she hadn't done in a long time. She reacted to her brother's sharpness. "I don't know, Graeme. Maybe you might be wanting to get a fair price for your empties?" She didn't care that the other men at the table had stopped talking and were now openly staring at her. Having Ivan behind her made her feel brave facing her brother.

Graeme's gaze darkened then darted over her shoulder. A slow leer expanded across his face. "I'm not finished my drink," he answered innocently, lifting the pint to his lips with deliberate slowness and taking the barest sip before replacing it on the table. "Why don't *you* make sure I get a fair price. Since you're such an expert." He chuckled then looked to his companions for their approval. They smiled half-heartedly.

"All right then, I will." Her voice was calm but she burned with fury. How could her own brother willingly make a fool of her in front of a group of strangers in a pub? She turned to leave.

"Who's your shadow?"

She looked back to see Graeme hugging his pint to his chest, a placid smile on his face, not even deigning to look at her.

"I'm the one who'll be taking her home this evening since you'll be too plowtered drunk to find your own backside, let alone drive."

There was no need to look at Ivan, she could feel the anger and tension radiating off of him. Graeme's companions tittered as she watched the grin slither off her brother's face, replaced by a twisted mien of rage. However, before Graeme could dredge up a decent reply, she felt a grip on her elbow guiding her towards the door. Once they were out in the open, she filled her lungs with the early afternoon air. Yet she gained no relief from it. She felt as if there was a crushing weight on her chest that was nothing to do with the shopping bags she was still carrying. Now she could feel the long handles digging into her flesh in a way she had not noticed when walking through the marketplace with Ivan.

"We'll have to go and see what lot your sheep are," Ivan said, all business as he marched towards the pens. "They'll be on soon. There wasn't that many of them."

She trailed after him half-running to keep up. It was abundantly clear that he was still angry – his back rigid, nose in the air. He was leaving her completely behind and Estella wasn't sure she would be able to find him again if they were separated. And there was no chance she was going back to Graeme. She'd rather walk home than share another journey with him.

Glancing back, Ivan seemed to remember her. "Oh! Sorry! Are you all right?" He began making his way back to her but she passed him, following the unintelligible drone of the auctioneer and ignoring the biting pain in her shoulder.

"Estella, wait!" He grabbed for her and instead caught the strap of one of the shopping bags, spinning her around by it. "Christ, that's heavy," he said, lifting it from her shoulder.

She snatched it back and pulled away from him. "It's fine," she answered shortly. She could feel the scalding heat on her skin where the strap had rubbed it.

"Why didn't you say something? You could have put it in the car rather than carrying it around."

"It's *fine*. Come on or we'll miss the sale."

He didn't argue but, as she forged onwards, she felt the light touch of a hand on the small of her back.

169

"Don't know why we're even bothering," he muttered. "Ignorant cretin deserves nothing for his sheep."

"But the sheep deserve to be looked after," Estella answered as she approached the pens. "There they are, third from the end."

"Chop, chop then. He's nearly at them."

Reaching her brother's animals, she immediately felt uncomfortable. There were too many people and they were all too close. And they were all men. Her arrival drew curious looks and she fought the urge to hide behind Ivan's large form. Several of the sheep in the pen were panting, their bulging eyes unsure which of the many two-legged creatures surrounding them posed the most threat. Estella sympathised. She wasn't sure either.

"Here he comes," Ivan said into her ear as the auctioneer approached. "How much are you hoping to get for them?"

Estella shook her head. Panic was beginning to overtake her once again. It flooded her brain until she couldn't think straight. She couldn't even speak. This was why she never went anywhere anymore. She couldn't deal with people. No wonder her brother had grinned so sceptically at her back in the pub. He knew she wouldn't be able to stand beside the auctioneer and talk to him in front of everyone.

"*Stella!*" Ivan hissed with a little more urgency. He turned her and bent down so that he could look her in the eye. She saw him frown momentarily before he said, "Do you want me to do it?"

All she could do was nod or shake her head to the hurried questions Ivan asked her about the sheep – their age, breeding and whether they were all definitely empty. As she stood silent and watched him step out in front of everyone, all she could do was be thankful for his bravery. But then what he was doing wasn't brave. It was perfectly normal behaviour. *She* was abnormal. She was the one who couldn't stand to have the eyes of the gathered punters on her. Allowing her glance to dart once again from face to face, she gave each *man* a reason not to choose *her*. She was weak, shy, unhappy, ugly, incapable, lost. She had nothing of value to offer anyone. Never mind *her* not wanting any of *them*.

"*Sold!*" the auctioneer roared, making her jump.

A moment later Ivan was beside her, guiding her back through the crowd. "Well, that wasn't too bad, was it? A grand price, I thought, eh?"

Estella blinked. She had absolutely no idea how the sale went. "Oh … yes … very good. Thanks. Thanks very much."

They pushed on until they were walking down a virtually empty side street. "Stella?"

"*Hmm?*"

"How much did I get for the ewes?"

Her head snapped up to find him grinning down at her. She huffed and walked on, a deep chuckle rumbling beside her. Wordlessly, he reached over and slid one of the bags from her shoulder then wrapped the strap around his fist and swung it playfully.

"If there's anything broken in that when I get home, you're paying for it," she warned. But she smiled nonetheless, feeling the ache in her shoulder subside.

"Nope. You can write off any damages against my commission for selling the ewes."

"Oh? How much commission do I owe you?" she asked warily.

"Let's say twenty per cent."

"Of what?"

"One hundred pounds," he answered without missing a beat.

"*What?*" she squawked. "Get on outta that!"

"Well, you don't know how much I got, do you? So I can say whatever I want."

"Tony Dillon thought that too," she said darkly. "And now you've got his job."

"Ah, but Tony got greedy and diddled everyone. If you're cute about it, you'd only do it when you know the other person hasn't a notion about how much something sells for."

"And are you inclined to swindle folk?"

"Me? Of course not! I'm as pure and honest as the driven snow," he replied with a beatific smile. "Here we are." He stopped beside an old grey VW Beetle and opened the door for her with a small bow. Snorting, she deposited her bags in the footwell and stepped back for him to close the door. "Well, in you get."

"What?" Then she thought she understood his meaning. "Oh, right! You're going back to the sale." She got in. It was probably better that she didn't go back to the market square.

Yet Ivan looked confused. "No, I'm not." He shut the door, walked around to the driver's side and got in.

"You're not taking me home, are you? You've got to go back to the sale!"

"Would you stop telling me where I'm going, woman!" He slammed the door in exasperation. "I'm getting something to eat." He extracted a nine-inch-square metal box from behind the driver's seat. "Is that allowed?"

"Yes," Estella answered in a quiet voice.

"Good. Now Mammy always makes too much for me so there's plenty here for you too –"

"Oh no! I'll be fine –"

He grabbed her hand and slapped a doorstopper of a sandwich onto her palm. "If I'm eating, you're eating," he said stubbornly. "If you don't, I won't."

She narrowed her eyes. "Have I ever told you you're fierce bossy?"

"Yes. You have. Now say thank you and eat your sandwich." He took a huge bite from his own and winked, his cheeks bulging.

With ill-grace, she nibbled at the edge of the brown bread. It was light, slightly malty and delicious. She took a bigger bite and found a filling of thinly sliced cheddar and, "Gooseberry chutney?"

He nodded and swallowed hard. "Mammy's favourite. We had loads of bushes back home or" – he frowned – "at our *old* house."

"Do you miss it?"

"A bit," he shrugged. "It's been harder for Mammy and Becca. Mammy's never lived anywhere else so it was a big upheaval for her. But the Leclercs ... I don't think you could work anywhere better. The best land, the best horses and the best people. I mean, people say Mr Leclerc is a bit ... full of himself. But he knows good horses and he trusts me. And I can't ask for more than that. *I like it here*," he said with real conviction. "Much more than home – I keep calling it that even though it'll never be again."

"You'll really never go back?"

His face darkened. "No. Never."

"So you're here for good, then?"

"Why?" he asked as he picked up another sandwich and grinned over it at her. "Would you miss me if I was gone?"

Estella looked away. She could feel the heat in her skin travel up her neck. "No, no! Just wondering."

"So you're saying you *wouldn't* miss me?"

"What? No, not – you're, I didn't mean – *ugh*! Leave me alone!"

"You're blushing!" he teased.

"And you're a – a – pain!"

He gaped at her then gave a shout of laughter. Reluctantly, she joined in. "Well, that's quite the comeback. I don't know how to respond to that at all."

"Good!"

The warmth in her face subsided and they continued to eat quietly until Ivan said, "I've seen Graeme before, you know."

"Oh?" She was suddenly wary.

"*Mm*. At Nelly Sweeney's. I went in for some Stockholm Tar."

"And what did you come out with?"

He grinned. "A wind-up radio, clothes pegs, a pound of bacon and some rat poison."

"Sounds about right."

"Your brother was there."

"Was he?"

"At the bar down the end."

"Yes."

"Regular occurrence, is it?" he asked carefully.

"Yes," she answered, then added, "Very." There was no point trying to deny it. If he asked anyone locally, they would tell him Graeme Frayne spent every evening of his life sitting on the last stool at the end of the bar in Nelly's.

"Ah." Ivan slowly chewed the last bite of his second sandwich. "And is he ... difficult at home?"

Estella didn't answer immediately. Instead, she focused on the tiny speckles of rain beginning to fall on the windscreen. "We see very little of one another, really. Ships passing in the night."

"Do you get on?"

"Not really, no. It's why we avoid each other. But then no one gets on with Graeme."

"Austin doesn't, no?"

She snorted. "No. They can't stand one another. Not since they were young."

"And you're caught in the middle," he said quietly.

She was surprised by the comment but nodded. Clearly, Ivan had been paying attention to what he'd seen over the last few months. She wasn't sure if that worried or pleased her.

"Right. Ready to go back to the madness? Or – you don't want to stay here, do you? You'll come back with me?"

"If you want," she shrugged.

"No, Stella. What do *you* want?"

She havered for a moment, uncomfortable with the idea of re-entering the hullabaloo. But then it wasn't so bad when Ivan was with her. In fact, it was rather enjoyable.

She opened the car door. "Let's go."

Chapter 16

The stress of preparing for Christmas quickly overtook Estella's reminiscences about her day at Mountlennon market with Ivan.

Exactly a week before the day itself, she cycled over to Oliver Pratt's to collect a small freshly killed turkey. Once she got it home, she plucked and hung it in the back kitchen. Of course, she already had the pudding in muslin cloth hanging from the dresser and the cake maturing in a tin. But the Christmas cake needed covering with apple jelly, marzipan and royal icing. She had never been particularly good at piping writing with coloured icing so her decoration mostly consisted of wobbly sprigs of holly. She had almost fallen in the river that ran along the side of the farm fetching real holly sprigs to hang over the picture frames all around the house. Although she forwent decorating the newel post of the stairs. Graeme had come home late the previous Christmas and had filled the house with voluminous swearing when he grabbed a handful of prickly green leaves to steady himself on his ascent rather than the familiar smooth wood.

She also purchased quite a small Christmas tree since, really, there was no need for a big one and it was also a lesser obstacle for her brother to complain about.

In the run-up to the twenty-fifth there were also the visits from the locals who still called. Mostly, it seemed these women came to scrutinise her preparations, comment on the quality of her pudding and criticise the neatness of her cake decorations. Dolly also finally reappeared to explain to her best friend that she really was absolutely, madly, totally and utterly in love … again. She had formed an attachment to Roy Oaks – the new huntsman who had come from England to manage the Ellendale pack. And he was the handsomest, funniest, most strapping man she had ever met.

"Honestly, Stell, you'll love Roy as much as I do!" she gushed. "Actually, you'd better not because I'd hate us to fall out over him!"

Falling for the new huntsman was the least of Estella's worries. Mostly, she worried about how Austin and Graeme would behave at Christmas lunch given that they hadn't – as far as she was aware – met since their set-to at Kennedy's. She worried her carefully prepared meal would end up scattered across the floor of the kitchen (they didn't use the dining room even though it had been refitted after their father died) and her brothers would be rolling around on the tiles with it. However, she didn't share her concerns with anyone else. They would have thought she was being overly dramatic. Austin's public face was always benign and relaxed. She doubted whether anyone else had ever had the misfortune to see him at his worst. She had because it was always Graeme who brought out the nastier side of their brother's character. And while most people locally knew how difficult the eldest Frayne could be, they assumed Austin had the composure to deal with him. Granted, neither had physically hurt the other since they were teenagers. But there also hadn't been so much tension between them since then either. And back then her father had been there to referee their skirmishes. If they did kick off, there was nothing she could do to stop them.

The day dawned dull but thankfully dry. Estella fed the animals before she came back in to prepare all the food for their dinner. There was no need to start cooking before breakfast since the turkey wasn't particularly large and she didn't want it overcooked. Dry stringy turkey was sure to ruin the day even if her brothers didn't. Graeme surfaced just before they went to church and declined breakfast. Though he was wearing his good jacket and a tie, Estella thought his shirt looked distinctly rumpled. It looked as though he had slept in it from the day before and there was a lingering smell of hops and cigarette smoke in the car and when she stood close to him in the pew.

Austin had rung her just before they left to tell her he would have to miss the service to attend a horse with severe colic. He still hadn't arrived when they got back to the house and were met by the mouth-watering smell of herb and onion stuffing mixed with cooked turkey. The smell always reminded Estella of waking up on Christmas morning and running downstairs to be enveloped by the smell of cooking meat. Her mother would be at the kitchen table halving Brussels sprouts she had picked fresh from the garden that morning. Tendrils of Prudie's hair would already have escaped from her neat bun and begun to curl around her face. Estella always thought these stray locks made her mother look pretty and much younger than she was – although Prudie had never reached any great age before she died. When her hair was scraped back from her face, it made her look irritable, severe. In Estella's memory, she was a kinder woman when her hair was loose. Or maybe she was the same woman no matter what and her youngest daughter just misremembered.

It was at Christmas that Estella missed her mother most. Never again would she come down to a meal that was already prepared. Never again would she and Joy sit side by side at the table and eat scrambled eggs with crispy bacon as a special treat for the holiday. That tradition had died with Prudie. Now, they had the same breakfast they always did. The main meal in the middle of the day bore the weight of all the festive expectations and was, therefore, something Estella took great care and pride in. Also, she didn't want to give Graeme anything to complain about or criticise. Because if he did then Austin would defend her, get angry about something entirely unrelated, attack his brother verbally and maybe even come to blows if the mood suited one or both. Really, there was a lot riding on the perfection of the dinner. And Estella felt the pressure.

While she checked and rechecked all her timings and put the pudding on to steam, Graeme poured himself a 'festive' whiskey and sat in the sitting room reading the paper. He didn't even appear when Austin's car rattled into the yard.

Austin knocked before coming in – something he never

did when he knew his brother wasn't there. Once he was in, he stood awkwardly in the middle of the kitchen, holding a small bag that smelled strongly of lavender.

"Happy Christmas," he muttered before thrusting the bag at his sister.

"Same to you," she answered, accepting his gift. "There's a present under the tree for you. Same as usual but I know you wear them." He leaned up against the counter as she opened up a small box filled with several lavender soaps and a hand cream. "Oh they're lovely! Thank you!" She reached out and touched his folded forearm in acknowledgement. It was the closest they would get to physical contact that day. "How's the horse?"

"Bad." He shook his head. "I'd say the stable lad was a bit too keen to get home and didn't close the door properly. Horse got out and gorged itself on oats. All sweated up when I got there. Kicking at its belly –"

"Wanting to roll." She'd seen it before. If it was gassy colic, sometimes horses could pass the trapped air themselves with very little help. But if there was a blockage or torsion of the gut then they were in real trouble.

"Curling its lip. All the usual symptoms. I'm hoping that it'll be all right though. I gave him some painkillers and they called the stable lad over and I left them walking it around a paddock."

Estella nodded. Forcing the horse to move might have sounded cruel but it was the best way to encourage movement in the gut and, if you were determined enough, it was the best way to stop them rolling and twisting their intestines into an unsalvageable knot. "Hopefully it'll be all right."

"I'll probably go back after dinner," Austin added. "To check."

There was little a vet could do so soon after treating a colicky horse but she pretended not to know that. Of course a vet might go back to such a patient – to give it more pain relief or perhaps fluids. But really it was just an excuse to make a quick getaway. If it kept things civilised then she was just going to have to accept it – even if she was disappointed he wouldn't stay for her.

Graeme shuffled in from the sitting room with an empty whiskey glass. "Well," he said without intonation.

"Well," Austin replied, equally bland.

"There's a present in under the tree there. From Stella."

Wordlessly, Austin pushed off the counter and went to fetch his present while Graeme refilled his glass. They almost met at the doorway as one left and the other came back.

Austin's narrow-eyed gaze followed his brother into the other room but, thankfully, he didn't pass comment. "Thanks very much for this," he said to Estella, holding up his new jumper. "They're great for late-night calvings and the cold days when I'm doing TB testing."

She glanced at the clock and put a little dish of cranberry sauce in the warming oven before starting her gravy. While she stirred, she considered whether to speak of what she was thinking. "Daddy used to say the longest days he ever did were when he was doing the tuberculosis testing in a parish. Because no matter how clear the priest or the vicar was about what day the vet was coming, there'd always be a few lads that'd have cattle out and they were always bound to be the wildest animals in the entire county."

181

"Do you remember how everyone used to look at him when the vicar announced testing during the parish notes at Sunday service?"

"Like it was all his fault," she smiled. "Do you remember how his shoulders used to shake?"

"Because he was trying so hard not to laugh."

Austin grinned in return, picking Sophie up off the floor where she was mooning about spilt titbits of turkey. "It really used to tickle him, didn't it?"

They stood reminiscing quietly to themselves until dinner was ready to be served. Austin offered to carve the turkey while she doled out the boiled vegetables, stuffing and roast potatoes.

Much like the cat, Graeme appeared once serving was imminent and mutely sat at the table, surprisingly leaving the seat at the head empty.

"You should sit there," he said to Estella. "After all, you're the one who cooked it all."

She looked at Austin who waved her to her seat. "Thanks," she said, pleased by this small show of respect and – more importantly – agreement between her brothers.

Dinner was eaten and roundly praised. The pudding had especially turned out well and Graeme didn't even pass comment when she served it with cream instead of brandy sauce. Estella had always hated the smell and taste of it so had decided not to use it, hoping it wouldn't cause problems. She was relieved, however, to find her brothers behaved perfectly reasonably. Only halfway through the meal did she realise neither of them had spoken directly to the other. All they said was directed at her and most of what Graeme said involved complimenting the food – though he didn't finish his plate. Austin prattled easily about work and people they all knew but hadn't seen for a while. It was only when she got up to clear the table that things took a turn.

With her back to the kitchen and the clink of plates and cutlery in the sink, she was at first unaware of what was happening behind.

"Couldn't you leave it alone for just *one* day?"

Austin's voice was harsh, deep.

The dinner plate in Estella's hand slipped but she held on to it … just. Her elder brother had spoken in her father's voice. Usually, Austin's speech was tempered by his genial character. Yet this time, the tone, the volume, the emphasis all belonged to Reg. And this was a version of her father that she had only seen when he was furious. It chilled her to hear him again in anger. Reg was dead and his rumbling bass would never again fill their home. She didn't want to turn and see what was going on. She wanted to simply take a step forward and be subsumed into the sink and wall behind it – to disappear completely. However, if there was anything she could do to head either of them off, she had to intervene and save what little there was of the day.

She took a breath, held it and turned to see Graeme with his whiskey tumbler in one hand and the other proprietarily clasping the neck of the bottle. He held his brother's gaze as he took an insolent swig from glass.

"Leave what alone for one day?" he asked calmly.

Austin turned white with fury, his fists balling on the tabletop. "You're a piece of work, you know that?"

Estella took a step forward. "Austin –"

"*Shut up, Stella!*" he snapped, turning his fury on her. "You don't defend him, you hear?"

"I wasn't *going* to defend him!" she replied, fighting the lump in her throat.

She and Austin had argued many times before. Of course they had – they were siblings with only a year of an age gap between them. But he had never unleashed such sudden, concise vitriol on her. Usually, their disputes built slowly yet when Graeme was the subject it seemed nothing could control her elder brother's rage.

"Well, what were you going to say then? If you weren't trying to defend him." Austin stabbed a finger across the table at his brother without looking at him.

"I was going to tell you to leave it. Just for *one day*. Please, Aussie."

"Don't *'Please, Aussie'* me. You always take *his* side and I'm fed up with it." He was on his feet and for one horrifying moment she thought he was going to lunge at her.

She stood tall – taller than she ever thought she would be able to. She was fed up with it. Just totally and utterly weary with their inability to act like adults for even a few hours.

"Grow up, Austin," she said coldly. "There are no sides. There's family and you're both part of mine, however much you might not want to be. And I thought for one day, just *one day*, we could get along."

"Well, we can't," he replied petulantly.

"So I see."

"Because *he* can't go a single day of *his* life without being pie-eyed."

Graeme, who had been following the back and forth between his siblings with the attention of a tennis connoisseur, took this opportunity to butt in. "Sure, all I'm doing is wetting the baby Jesus's head," he said pleasantly.

"You'd drown the poor little cretin with all you drink!" Austin slammed his fist on the table, making everything on it – as well as Estella – jump.

"At least he'd've died happy," Graeme murmured as he drained his tumbler once again. He poured himself another one. "Well, if no one else wants me … Thank you for dinner, Estella, it was lovely." He made to leave with the glass in one hand and the bottle in the other.

"*Oi!* I wasn't finished!" Austin shouted across the table.

Graeme spun very slowly and leered at his brother. "Yes, you are. Now get out of my house."

Graeme walked out, leaving Estella alone in the kitchen with the one person she had always thought was her ally.

"Austin," she began, but he held up a hand to stop her.

"Don't, Stella. Just don't."

"I don't take sides," she affirmed once again but he was already shaking his head.

"Why do you let him get away with it?"

"I don't *let him* get away with anything," she hissed. "*He* couldn't stop even if he wanted to. And he doesn't. What makes you think *I* could do anything?"

Austin shook his head doggedly. "You could do something." He picked up his new jumper and pushed his chair in. "You're his sister."

"And you're his brother. But I don't see you helping anything much, do I?"

Austin glared at her for several beats then, without another word, walked out.

When she heard the backdoor slam, she slumped against the sink. Her throat constricted as if someone had closed their hands around her neck – a pain almost as bad as the day she buried her father. What would he have said if he had witnessed such a scene? Would he have intervened? Most definitely. He would have placed the considerable heft of his opinion squarely behind Austin and the two of them would have ganged up on Graeme. No wonder her eldest brother found solace in a glass or a bottle.

Being on the receiving end of their anger hurt. She felt like she was to blame for something she had no hand in, like she had let them down, like she had disappointed them. Because Austin spoke with her father's voice and he disapproved.

But he didn't. Austin was not his father and she needed to stop seeing Reg in everything. He had not seen their argument because he was not there. If he had been, Graeme would not have drunk at the table. Austin would have been jovial, silly. And no one would have dared to say anything vaguely negative to Estella because their father would have walloped them so hard they would have finished up past New Year. She thought Austin offered her similar protection now Reg was gone. But she had been wrong. Her father was dead and she was on her own. She just wished it hadn't taken the ruining of Christmas Day to realise it.

Chapter 17

With heavy steps, Estella dragged herself upstairs to her room. She wanted to get out of her good clothes. They no longer felt appropriate since she wasn't celebrating anything. She could not celebrate the birth of her Saviour when he had not saved her the heartache that was ever-present throughout her life. She had felt unloved as a child since all of her mother's affection seemed to be reserved for Joy. When Prudie died, any chance to forge a connection was lost completely. She had to learn to be a woman in a household of men. And just when she thought her life was settling into some kind of enjoyable rhythm, Reg had his accident.

Automatically, she pulled on her father's clothes. She touched the cloth of his trousers. No – they were her trousers now. She had worn them so often they would no longer have recognised the shape of her father. But she could no longer claim that she wore them just to be close to *him*. Now they stood to remind her of the time when she rode horses.

She could still remember the first pair of corduroy jodhpurs Reg had given her as a little girl. He had sent to Dublin especially for them. In her mind's eye she could still bring to mind the feel of them under her fingers as she sat rubbing the plush this way and that, watching the colours of the kaki fabric change. She would wear them all day despite Prudie's irritation when she realised her youngest was *still* in her 'boy trousers'. At her father's insistence, she had learnt to ride astride from an early age. He had seen too many horses over his years as a vet with problems on the near side because they had been ridden side-saddle. If a rider didn't position their weight properly it put undue strain on a horse's left side. Reg didn't care how elegant or lady-like it looked – if he could do anything to improve the welfare of a horse, he did, and expected his daughter to follow suit.

Once her father had become an invalid and they got rid of all the horses, Estella wore only skirts and dresses. She didn't want to remember the feel of her adult-size corduroy jodhpurs grating on her bare forearms as she rested them on her knees to hold Reg's hand in the ambulance. She did not want him to see her in clothes that would remind him about what happened. He thought about it enough already even when there was nothing close at hand to prompt such memories. Thinking about it with the benefit of nearly two years' worth of distance, she had spent so much of her time caring for him walking a tightrope – trying to guess what would please or upset him before he even realised it himself. All of it – *all of it* – because of her *bloody* guilt.

She descended the stairs much more quickly than she climbed them. Storming across the kitchen, she had her boots on and was out the door, still donning her coat and hat as she traversed the yard, scattering chickens in her wake.

She needed to get out of that bloody house. She needed to *move*. All this guilt, all her pent-up frustration seemed to swell inside her like the bulbous throat of a frog. It pressed against her heart, her lungs, her throat. She'd had enough. She was fed up being the last person on everyone's mind – including her own. So much of the responsibility for the house and the yard fell to her. They were a woman's domain and if it hadn't been for her interest in horses and Reg's encouragement, she likely never would have gone anywhere.

What none of them appeared to grasp was that without her considerable input, nothing in their lives would have run as smoothly as it did. Where they fell short, she picked up the slack. Yet when she fell short, her brothers especially made sure she knew they noticed her failings. Why was it one rule for her and another for them? Was it because she was the youngest? Or because she was a girl? Because she was the reason their father was dead? Even Austin – Austin who stood by her for years – had become nasty and judgemental today. Striding across a field, she growled aloud. *How dare he!* When she did her best to make the day run smoothly and had made such an effort to have good food on the table for what remained of her family. And Graeme had even behaved. *Graeme!* But *why*, after all these years, had Austin turned on her today rather than continuing to direct his fury at his older brother?

It all made her so angry – and sad. They were the only close family she had left and they couldn't be alone together. Dolly argued with her siblings and gave out about them but they all managed to get on and clearly loved each other. The Greer brothers even worked together on the farm without

189

falling out. Yet each Frayne was an island. Graeme, Joy, Austin and Estella. She hadn't realised it until now. She always believed that she and Austin inhabited the same country, shared the same views, cheered one another on when they succeeded, commiserated when they failed. Now it seemed she had no one to cheer her on. She was truly alone.

"You stupid bastard. Austin! You stupid – ugh!"

Her voice was loud and carried across the empty space. She felt better for getting it out in the open. She shouted again without words and let her frustration be swallowed by the ether. She began to walk faster, striding along with her arms swinging. She kicked out at a clod of earth resting on the surface of the stubble field and it burst into tiny particles of stones and wet, clagged earth. It felt good and destructive. She found another lump and swung her foot into it, exploding the ball into a hundred little pieces. Striding around like a child looking for iced puddles to smash, her entire focus became finding something to obliterate.

By the time she had worked out all her anger, she had reached the bottom of the farm. To her left was a wood of mature conifers that had been planted decades before her father bought the place. To her right was the outer-reaches of Ellendale estate and straight ahead the countryside opened out before her, stretching for miles in varying shades of green and brown. There was a back lane to the farm buried somewhere in the woodland but she had no idea where. Graeme had hoped to get that woodland himself since he could sell the wood from it and make some easy money. Instead, Reg's favourite son now owned it.

As she cast her gaze over the gently swaying trees, she suddenly noticed the open spaces between the trunks and the pale discs of tree stumps flashing like beacons amongst dull browns and greens. Someone had been in to clear out some of the wood. Clearly, Austin was of a similar opinion to Graeme when it came to selling the wood to make a quick buck. It surprised her that Austin hadn't mentioned it. But then it turned out Austin wasn't perhaps the man she thought he was. Why would he tell her anything?

She turned away from the woods to stare out across the acres of grassland. Breathing deeply, a calm descended over her. She found comfort in the sights and smells of nature. Her brothers could sling their mud but she would not let them break her. She would not become bitter and vindictive. She would not let their cruel words touch her. Or, at least, she could try to do all those things. It was all very well to form such resolves when she stood alone in a field where she felt happy and safe. Once she was under the wrathful gaze of her brothers, her determination to stand firm would likely crumble. But the fact she was trying to make such a resolution in the first place was a step in the right direction.

Inhaling the scents of the countryside, she caught movement out of the corner of her right eye. Focusing, she saw two horses over the ditch less than a hundred yards away – one being ridden by a tall man who was leading the other alongside him.

Ivan Aylward sat astride a large bay and led a draught-type grey. He seemed to be away in his own little world, his posture completely without tension as he observed the ditch beside him. He had a light hold of the reins and, despite being relaxed, his back was straight and not at all huntsman-like. Reg Frayne would have liked that. He always said a hunch-backed rider was waiting to get dumped 'out the front door' if a horse unexpectedly decided to stop or turn around. Ironically, he also maintained that such riders would never have longevity as they would be crippled by rheumatism later in life. Reg never got the chance to experience a rheumatic spine. But Ivan rode like he walked – proud and upright.

Abruptly, the silence of the afternoon was shattered by a great commotion in the hedgerow between two starlings just ahead of where Ivan and his horses were walking. While the grey simply stopped dead, his bay suddenly realised it was mortally afraid of all noise, hedges, birds – possibly even the colour green – and took off sideways.

Sensibly, Ivan let go of the grey's rope rather than be dragged from his mount. Calmly and quickly, he took the reins of his horse in both hands. His voice did not betray even the slightest bit of panic as he said, *"Woah ... woah ... woah ..."*

The bay slowed but its blood was up and it skittered left and right rather than standing still. *"Woah ... woah.* Calm now, calm, Bella. You're all right, nothing's going to eat you,"* he promised, patting it on the neck.

Only when she realised she could hear every word he said to the horse did Estella notice that her feet had carried her towards the border between the two fields. She therefore heard Ivan's next sentence with perfect clarity.

The grey – gradually becoming aware of its sudden freedom – was coming to the conclusion that it quite liked being able to go exactly where it wanted and began to trot away.

"*Aw, bugger it!*" Ivan cursed as he nudged his bay forward to head off the other horse.

Sensing imminent capture, the grey slid to a halt, about-turned and began trotting in the opposite direction – directly towards where Estella stood on the other side of the ditch.

"*Woah!*" she called, climbing the bank and praying she didn't frighten the horse even more. She tried to cross through the ditch with fluid movements so as not to suddenly burst forth from the already-suspect hedgerow. It didn't quite work, however, as the loose horse took one look at her and backtracked, its tail up in the air, as it snorted its displeasure. However, she knew from years of experience at gymkhanas and on hunting fields that trying to catch one horse while either holding or sitting on another was decidedly tricky. Such tasks were always easier with help – even if that help initially made the situation worse.

Ivan didn't even bother with a greeting. "*I'll head her off and try and get her back towards you!*" he called.

Walking smartly after the grey, Estella waved a hand, acknowledging his plan. Though apparently highly agitated, the horse was heavy and quite slow. So despite its sudden fear of people emerging from ditches, it wasn't going very far at any great speed. However, as soon as Ivan tried to approach her on his own mount, she shied away again, ears pricked as if the whole affair was quite a jolly game. With the mare now heading back towards her, Estella carefully raised her hands in front of her as if she was about to push something. She didn't want to threaten the grey by sticking her arms out but she *did* want to command the animal's attention and respect. It was a fine balance to strike and she hadn't done it in a long time. But the movements came to her unbidden.

She heard herself speak without even thinking. "*Woah, girlie. Woah now.*" The horse's trot slowed to a walk and it stopped several yards ahead of her. She could see a ripple of indecision running through the mare's body. It was trying to decide if this person was to be trusted or if it would be safer to high-tail it once again. "No, you don't. Don't be silly," she said firmly. The words didn't matter. What mattered was the calm, even tone of her voice. It worked. The glassiness in the mare's eyes dulled and her head dropped slightly. Taking steady steps, Estella walked up, caught the trailing rope then proffered her hand for the horse to sniff. "There we go now. That wasn't so difficult, was it?" She gave the animal's long nose a rub and it nodded as if to agree with her.

Estella's heavy stomach dropped to the floor. As the mare encouraged her stiff, scratching fingers, suddenly she realised something. It was the first time she had touched a horse since the day of her father's accident. Her whole body fizzed with electricity. She felt hot and lightheaded all at the same time. Staring into the benign liquid eye of the mare, she could see the flecks of rust, gold and dark brown. There was no fear now, no judgement, just calm.

"Thank God for that!" Ivan rode up beside her, the look of relief plain on his face. "Good thing you happened to be here. I have the gate onto the road open and there's no telling how far she could have gone. Miles, probably. Did I say thanks?"

Estella shrugged without looking at him, running her free hand down the mare's neck. She could feel the firm ridge of muscles along the crest just below the mane. Smiling slightly, she weaved her fingers through the six-inch-long strands of hair.

"What is it?"

Ivan's question startled her. "W-What?"

"You're smiling. What is it? *Tell me*," he coaxed as she began shaking her head.

"Her mane's long."

"Yes?"

"Not hogged."

"No. Do you disapprove?"

"What? No! I think shaved manes look terrible! I hate it. And it must be awful for them in the summer when they've got nothing to shake at the flies." Still holding the rope, she brought both hands to the mane and began plaiting the strands between her fingers.

"Careful," Ivan warned, "or I'll be kidnapping you to come and help me plait manes for hunts and shows now that I know you can."

She grinned. "You've got plenty help in the yard already with all the stable lads. How many are there now, four?"

"Five," he answered, rolling his eyes. "And do you know, not one of them can do a decent plait."

"How do you know I'm any good? I could be just as bad as they are."

He laughed out loud, eyeing the perfect plait she had just curled into a small bun to sit on the crest of the horse's neck. "Something tells me you're almost as good as I am."

"*Almost*?" She turned to give him the full effect of her scornful look.

He held the reins loose in one hand and had the other on

the cantle of the saddle. Her indignation was lost as she drank in the sight of him. Usually, she would have been drawn to the animal. Her practised gaze would have observed the quality of the coat and musculature, the fineness of its legs, the bone structure. Her eyes would have followed the curve of its neck, back and hind legs. But all she could see were the curves and angles of Ivan Aylward's physique as he sat in the saddle. His position brought to mind the picture of a cavalryman she'd seen in a manual of horsemanship that she devoured as a child. The lines of the soldier's body were so straight, so proper, that it was his photograph she often called to mind when trying to become a better rider herself. Standing in a field on Christmas Day many years later, she could almost have overlaid the image of a uniform on the man before her.

"What?" Ivan asked again.

"Nothing." She answered casually even though her heart was hammering. But she had to give credit where credit was due. "Just thinking you've got an excellent seat. My daddy would have been impressed."

"And from what I've heard, your father was quite the horseman himself. So that's quite a compliment." He paused, looking out across the countryside. "Thank you."

She shrugged. "Anyway, I'd best let you get on." Slowly, she undid the neat plait in the horse's mane. She ran her fingers through the long coarse hair, teasing it out. However, she couldn't seem to stop rubbing the grey's neck. The hints of evergreen and nutty scent of the horse's coat filled her nostrils and she closed her eyes. She missed that smell. She missed the feel of a horse's neck beneath her hands. But this wasn't her horse. And horses … It was a horse's fault, a *grey* horse's fault that … her father … She stared once again into the mare's kind eye.

The force of it hit her in the chest like a physical blow. She felt the burning heat of hot tears gathering in the corners of her eyes. But they weren't tears of grief, they were tears of anger. This animal wasn't to blame for her father accident. *Horses* weren't to blame. *Grey* horses weren't to blame. *She* wasn't to blame. It was something she carried with her always since the accident – *my fault, my fault*. She dropped her forehead onto the grey's neck and hugged her, relishing the warm smooth coat under her palms, breathing in the rich earthy scent that was so unique to horses. Why had she spent so long torturing herself, denying herself the comfort of these creatures? When it was her father who had charted the course of his own fate the day he got up on a horse Estella had told him not to ride. Had she ridden Burt down the lane that evening, she would easily have sat the rear. She would not have pulled back on the reins, effectively overbalancing the horse and pulling him down on top of her. Had her father listened to her, he would probably be spending Christmas Day 1959 looking forward to the St Stephen's Day hunt tomorrow. He would not be interred in a graveyard beside his wife, having killed himself the year before.

His death wasn't the fault of horses. It wasn't Estella's. It was *his*.

She gasped, pressing her face into the mare's strong neck to hide her tears, to hide the sudden outpouring of relief, the pure and unconditional love she harboured for these animals. She was like a mother reunited with her long-lost children.

"Stella …"

She felt a hand on her shoulder but shook her head, tightening her grip on the horse's neck, weaving her fingers through her mane. The animal stood with remarkable forbearance, seeming to sense that, for now, she had to tolerate the person clinging to her. Her carriage was proud, her impressive strength more than enough for both of them. And that's what horses did sometimes: they helped Estella to deal with the problems life had thrown at her. She groomed them, working out her anger with long therapeutic strokes of her brush across their fine coats. She rode out across the fields as if she were running away, feeling a glorious sense of freedom as the wind whipped her face. And sometimes she simply went out to the stable and cried into their necks. True, she had blamed a horse for turning her life upside-down. But that didn't mean she needed to reject the whole species. She had to let it go.

"Stella?"

She loosened her hold on the grey's neck but didn't let go completely. She also kept her face turned away so Ivan wouldn't see her tears. "'M'all right," she mumbled, surreptitiously wiping her cheeks on the sleeve of her coat. Absentmindedly, she hoped it was clean and hadn't left dirty streaks on her face.

"What is it?" His voice was urgent, his hand a gentle but even pressure on her back.

"Nothing," she sniffed.

"That wasn't nothing," he said bluntly. "Tell me what's wrong, Stella."

"Nothing's *wrong*. I just … I realised something is all."

She cleared her throat and wiped her nose. "I realised it wasn't the horse's fault. That it wasn't *my* fault." She gasped and fresh tears flowed down her cheeks. "Daddy wasn't my fault." She raised her eyes to his and, though his face was a little too blurry for her to see clearly, she was sure he could see the relief, the happiness that glowed in hers.

Though he held his horse in one hand, with his free arm Ivan pulled her into his chest and held her tight to him. "You've carried that all this time?"

She nodded against his coat. If she had been in her right mind, she never would have said anything to anyone. But with such an outpouring of repressed emotions she felt free to do and say whatever she wanted. And Ivan was such a solid, reassuring presence, it felt like he was the right person to confess this to. He had not been there to judge her when it happened the way everyone else had. He had no opinions on what she was telling him. He took her at her word.

"How long?" Ivan asked, still not letting go.

"Since the accident."

"When was that?"

"Third of March. Fifty-seven."

"Three years?" He pulled back slightly to look directly at her. "You've been blaming yourself, the horse, for almost *three years*? Why?"

She shrugged feeling a strange weightless calm. "Because … because I thought it was the right thing to do." She had no idea where the explanation came from.

"And did no one ever try to explain to you that it *wasn't* your fault?"

Staring off across the field, she tried to bring to mind such

199

a conversation with her family, Dolly or anyone. But she couldn't remember having any kind of serious discussion with someone who tried to assuage her guilt. People spoke of it being a 'terrible thing' or an 'awful shame'. They neither accused nor acquitted her of her involvement. She had once said to Dolly that she felt responsible for what happened with Reg and Dolly had shouted, *"Of course it's not your fault!"* so quickly and so loudly that it sounded like a lie.

"I suppose people didn't blame me. But I *thought* they did. Even if they *said* they didn't, I probably wouldn't have heard them because I didn't believe it myself."

At that moment, Ivan's bay thrust its head into his shoulder as if to remind both of them that it was standing by quite patiently but would rather be on the move. "Hey!" he admonished. "Don't do that." Yet he gave the horse a pat on the neck nonetheless.

Estella turned back to the grey and ran her hand over her shoulder and across her back. "I haven't touched a horse since," she murmured. "They used to be my life. And then suddenly my life was caring for Daddy and I didn't notice not having them because all my time was spent on him. But when he died –" the word came so easily it shocked her. She paused. "When he died life was just … empty."

"And you never thought of getting yourself a horse to work on, just for something to do?"

It was a simple enough question, yet she had to think about her answer. "No," she said slowly. "Because I thought I didn't *deserve* to have one. That it would somehow be a betrayal of Daddy's memory if I did."

"Surely it's a bigger betrayal to deny yourself the thing

that made you both happy. The thing you shared. Wouldn't having a horse keep his memory alive? The good memories. I'm sure you have lots of them."

As soon as he said it, images began to flicker through her mind.

Reg sitting in the saddle at a hunt, his head thrown back as he roared with laughter on seeing her wade towards him, caked up to the eyeballs in mud having been dumped by her pony. The pride on his face when she won a show jumping class on a horse he bred. The way he patted the neck of a three-year-old Irish Draught mare that won breed reserve champion in Dublin Horse Show. How he had smiled and told everyone who would listen that he had the best Draught mare in the country since he had been beaten by a gelding. He had dined out on it for months locally since Henry Leclerc owned the stallion that had sired her. There had even been a write-up in the local paper about it. And she could even see the happiness on his face when he watched her ride Burt around a field for the first time – only a week after she first sat up on him. "You've done a fine job on him, Stella. He'll make a grand horse one of these days."

The words and images faded. She looked down and her eyes were drawn to her father's trousers hanging loose around her legs. It was all very well to wear his clothes to feel close to him but surely maintaining his life-long passion for horses would be a better way to keep his spirit alive? After all, it was what he had trained her to do.

While the grey was enjoying Estella's attention and was resting a back leg, Ivan's horse was footing about, keen to get going. "Sorry, I should be letting you get on." She

201

fingered the horse's rope. "You get up and I'll hand her to you."

Ivan stayed where he was, unmoving, but with a strange look in his eyes. He cocked his head to the side and stared at her. "I'll swap," he said.

"What?" She hadn't the faintest idea what he was talking about. Then he handed her his horse's reins.

"Swap. You take Bella." He pressed the bay's reins firmly into her hand. "Start as you mean to go on, eh?"

"Ivan … what are you talking about?"

"Well, you've just had some sort of … equine epiphany." He waved his hand in the air and Bella jerked her head back. "Oh! Sorry," he said to her then continued. "So you might as well keep the momentum going, no? If you don't, you're bound to get cold feet. Over-thinking is what got you into this situation. Ride back to the stables with me and you'll have begun."

"I can't ride! I haven't ridden in three years!"

"And what, you think you'll have forgotten how? Get up and your body will remember."

"But I can't ride her! She just took off with you! What if she did the same with me?"

"Are you saying you couldn't sit a horse cantering off? I thought you were meant to be a good rider," he added slyly.

"I was. Not anymore," she answered, narrowing her eyes, knowing he was trying to goad her.

"Look, she might have a bit of a spook at the ditch but nothing you won't manage," he said. "And you're better riding in a saddle anyway. It's more comfortable. I'm trying to be the gentleman here." He passed the lead rope over the grey's neck and tied it on to the far side of the headcollar to form makeshift reins. "You could ride this lady but you'll end up with nothing other than a sore backside going bareback." He grinned.

"And what about your backside?" she blurted out boldly.

His smile widened. "I ride so much it's as much leather as the saddle is. Here," he said, turning around, "have a feel." Estella squealed and went the other side of Bella.

Ivan tittered, poking his head over the saddle. "I'll chase you round the field backwards if it gets you on the horse." His eyes sparkled and she couldn't help but smile back. "Right," he said in a business-like tone. "What length are we putting your stirrups up to?"

With that, the decision was made. Estella extended her arm, undid the buckle on the leather strap and shortened it until the tread of the stirrup was just above her armpit and her fingertips were on the buckle. It was the way everyone was taught to measure stirrups as a child and, though it seemed unorthodox, it worked. "Up seven holes," she told Ivan and heard the rasp of the leather being pulled through. "It's marked," she added, having seen the indentation in the leather.

"Mrs Leclerc rides at that length. Are you sure you don't want them longer? You're surely taller than she is."

Estella shook her head but he couldn't see her. "No, I've always ridden a little short. Or maybe I've got short legs. Mr Leclerc used to tease me about that when he saw the length of my stirrups. Used to say I was 'stumpy'."

"There's nothing wrong with the length of your legs," Ivan assured her as he came around Bella's head, towing his reluctant grey behind him. "Leg up?" he offered, cupping his hands as if to catch her waiting leg.

But Estella kept both feet firmly on the floor, suddenly nervous. "I'm … I don't know. This is a bad idea –"

"Stella, if you don't get up on this damn horse, I'll throw you over her neck and –"

"All right, all right! I'm getting up." She gathered the reins in her hand and grasped the pommel of the saddle. But then she turned back to Ivan. "She really won't do anything, will she?"

"Stella, I wouldn't put you on her if I thought she would do anything. The missus has ridden her and I'm assuming you're just as good if not better than she is."

"I used to be."

"I trust you, Stella. Trust yourself for once."

It was exactly the right thing to say. Taking a deep breath, she lifted her left leg and tightened her grip on the front of the saddle.

"On three," Ivan told her as he cupped her shin in his hands. "One, two, *three!*"

He lifted her with such force that she was almost pitched over the far side of the horse. Luckily, however, Bella stood still. "*Ugh!* Christ …" she grumbled as her stomach full of Christmas dinner flopped onto the seat of the saddle.

"*Very* lady-like," Ivan complimented. He had grabbed hold of her leg to steady her and didn't let go when she swung her right leg over the back of the saddle. "All right?" he asked, loosening his grip slightly as she slid her feet into the stirrups and settled into her seat.

She regathered her reins in both hands and looked out

through Bella's ears which flicked back and forth, clearly wondering who this strange person on her back was. Estella leant forward and gave her a pat. "Good girl." She turned to Ivan. "Good to go, I think. And if I wasn't sitting on a horse, you'd just have got a clip round the ear."

"What for?" he asked indignantly.

"For nearly throwing me clean over the horse! How heavy do you think I am?"

"I'm not used to throwing little bitty women up on horses!"

This time, she really did swing at him but he easily stepped out of the way.

"It's not my fault you weigh nothing. Don't you eat? Or are you one of these people who can't cook?" He hurried around the other side of his mare to be absolutely sure he was out of range.

"Of course I can! And I eat plenty. I just work it all off."

"Well, I'll know not to push so hard next time," he told her as he gathered his makeshift reins.

"How are you getting up –" she began as he squared up to mount his horse. But she needn't have wondered. From a standstill he vaulted onto the grey's back, smoothly swinging his long leg over her rump. He turned, now of a height with her and grinned boyishly.

"Show-off," she muttered, turning Bella towards home. She heard him laugh behind her.

Her body immediately settled into the rhythm of the horse's footsteps. Her movements didn't take any conscious thought. It was as if they had been lying dormant in every muscle, bone and sinew of her body, just waiting patiently to be called upon once again. Every part of her physique knew what to do but her mind took off at a frightening speed, rushing through every worst-case-scenario it could hurl to the front of her consciousness. She had to force herself not to tense since Bella – so attuned to her rider's physical and emotional reactions – would become anxious and likely do something silly like skitter off sideways across the field again. But Estella had sat on many horses much more sensitive than Bella and stayed firmly in the saddle. Anyway, she had to stay in the saddle since she didn't have a riding hat on. And she really would prefer not to come off and land on her head. Back when she was doing it all the time, she sometimes rode the quiet horses without one even though it irritated Reg no end. "Just wear a damn hat, Stella! It does no harm and could do an awful lot of good," was something he told her every time he saw her bareheaded atop a horse. Next time, she thought, I must be sure to wear my riding hat.

Next time!

"Oh good, you finally breathed," Ivan said conversationally as he trotted up beside her and slowed to match her pace.

She ignored his jibe and instead asked, "What's your horse's name?" If she was talking with Ivan her brain might not explode in a heady mixture of fear, adrenaline, worry and joy.

He rolled his eyes. "Dilly."

"*Dilly*?" She gave an incredulous snort and cast her eye over the grey's sturdy form. She looked nothing like a *Dilly*. "Poor you!" She told the horse.

"Apparently one of the old stable lads named her after

Tony Dillon to get in his good graces. She's had it so long, it's stuck."

"*Hmm*, yes, Tony would have loved something like that," she said with distaste. Long before the debacle with the stallions, she had disliked the man who swaggered around Ellendale's stables as if he owned them himself. He was rude to everyone unless they were a man or had money. Estella, therefore, didn't feature at all in his vision of the world. She wouldn't have filled the back of a postage stamp with the civil words he had thrown her over the last decade. But he knew horses and breeding so despite his impudent manner, the Leclercs kept him on.

"Maybe I should call one of next year's crop 'Ivan'. Make my mark, you know? What d'you think?" he asked her seriously.

She chuckled. "I think Dilly's probably a better name for a horse than Ivan."

"What's wrong with my name?" he asked indignantly. He gestured to his mount. "Dillon has a legacy, why shouldn't I?"

"I think you should aim for a better legacy than Tony Dillon's," she said reasonably.

"He set the bar fairly low, all right."

"For instance, Tony wouldn't have been exercising horses on Christmas Day. He'd have disappeared a week ago and not resurfaced until the first week in January."

"Where'd he go?"

"Off to spend some of his cadged fortune, I suppose. Why *are* you riding out horses on Christmas Day?"

"They're going hunting tomorrow with the boss and the

207

missus. I don't like horses doing a full day's hunting after a day stuck in a stable. Don't want them getting stiff or sore or pulling something."

She smiled.

"What?" he asked.

"Daddy always said the same thing. No matter how much we ate at dinner, every year we were out in the afternoon giving the horses a spin, ready for the next day." She reminisced quietly to herself about the afternoon hacks around the headlands of the fields – she and her father chatting incessantly about everything and nothing. They talked most when they were both on horses. As she and Ivan passed over a rough bridge with a torrent of water running beneath it, she noted that the water was high. That would have been the starting point of a conversation that could have lasted for half an hour – about water courses, childhood adventures, aquatic life, weather. She missed such easy conversations.

"That river's very high," Ivan commented.

She smiled across at him. "We used to play in it further downstream as children ..." she began.

Chapter 18

It was getting dark by the time Estella and Ivan hacked the two horses the whole way home. Their chat had flowed so easily, Estella barely noticed she was riding a horse at all. They were simply two people moving through space together to the gentle *clip-clop* of the metal horseshoes on the packed earth and stone of the lane they took back to the stables. They spoke of childhood escapades, their families, horses they had encountered. Though many of the subjects were ones she routinely avoided, somehow discussing them with Ivan felt natural, right. Also, unlike her conversations with Dolly or Rebecca, she spoke as much if not more than Ivan did. And she made him laugh – telling him about the pony who would plod to the end of the lane then break into canter the moment she turned for home, the horse that lay down every time she tried to pick up its feet. Though the first half of her day had been somewhat miserable, the second was turning out to be one of the best Christmas Days she'd had in years. And it wasn't over yet.

When they rode into the yard, they were greeted by several heads protruding from stable doors. There were a few nickers of welcome and nodding heads but otherwise the courtyard was empty of the regular cavalcade of dogs and people it usually hosted.

Ivan slid off his mare. "*Ooo!*" He scrunched up his face and rubbed his backside for effect. "This being the gentleman lark isn't all it's cracked up to be," he complained as he held Bella's rein for Estella to dismount.

"*Aw*, poor you!" she said with faux sympathy. "Good girl," she told Bella, giving her a hearty pat on the neck. She had behaved impeccably throughout their ride. Ivan had joked that the mare only tested her rider if she thought they were good enough to stay on – riders like him. Usually, such cockiness would have irritated Estella but it was delivered with such teasing irreverence that she only smiled and rolled her eyes, knowing he meant nothing by it.

"You could help me rub it better," he said, while continuing to knead his aching bottom.

She snorted. "No, I think you'll manage just fine on your own. Where is everyone?"

As they led the horses to their stables the sound of their hooves echoed off the walls making the place sound emptier than she had ever heard it before.

"Cosied up beside a fire, no doubt. She's in there," he added, directing Estella into a stable adjacent to Dilly's. The side walls were only four-and-a-half feet high so she could easily see Ivan next door as he continued. "Danny Fearon was here early this morning to help clean out the stables but otherwise, I can manage the rest of it myself. It's Christmas, they deserve to spend it with their families."

"And what about you? Don't you want to spend

Christmas with your family?"

He disappeared and returned with a handful of brushes, two of which he passed over to Estella. "Just another day really, isn't it? And my family is always a bit ... sad at Christmas."

"Mine too," she agreed, although she couldn't quite picture a morose Rebecca. She always seemed so cheerful. She untacked Bella as Ivan began brushing his horse.

"Just better to be out of the house, I find." He had his back to her and she heard the once-familiar rasp of bristles on a fine coat. "The horses are always a good excuse. And I like being here when it's quiet. Just me and the horses. And you," he added, smiling over his shoulder.

"I can go if you want." The offer was sincere. But she really hoped he wouldn't take her up on it.

He shook his head. "Unless you have to. You don't have to go home and milk, do you?"

"No. They're all dried off now, ready to calve in the spring. Apart from one. Milk for the table, you know."

"Mind if I put you to work then?" He grinned cheekily over Dilly's rump, having moved to her other side.

She held up the brushes. "Haven't you already?"

While Ivan gave the horses their evening feed of hay, rolled oats and soaked beet pulp, Estella brushed her horse. Bella happily whipped strands of hay from her feeder while Estella worked vigorously on her finely clipped coat. All the hairs were shaved short since horses grew a thick winter coat which was inclined to get sweaty and dirty when they were ridden. When they were damp, it took longer for them to dry and they were also more likely to get chills and saddle

211

rashes if the dirt got into their skin. Not only did clipping look very neat (when done correctly) it also was healthier for the horse as it was easier to keep clean. They did, however, require rugs to keep them warm when they weren't being ridden. Bella, in fact, had two.

"She's a cold soul is poor Bella," Ivan explained as he did up the straps on Dilly's single rug.

"More finely bred than your lady," Estella agreed, nodding her head at the grey. While Dilly was a solid, square-chested and thick-legged creature, Bella was much more delicately built.

"Funny, even though they look different, you couldn't separate them on a hunting field. They're both as clever and brave as each other."

"Have you hunted both of them?" she asked, closing the stable door behind her as she left the mare to her food and rest for the evening.

"No, no. These are the boss's and the missus's horses. I've watched them. Following the hunt, you know? If it's close, sometimes me or one of the lads will ride them there –"

"And then you follow in the car until they're fed up and ride the horses back. Yes, I remember that from when Daddy and I used to be out hunting. Although it was always one of the lads who rode them to the hunt and back. Tony Dillon never did it because he always wanted to hunt himself. Be in the middle of all the important people."

"I'll hunt the youngsters the odd time but mostly I leave it to the others. There's enough to do without spending a day gallivanting through the country. And I like getting to do my own work here. With no one bothering me or wanting to talk rubbish," he finished with a huff. Stuffing his hands in his pockets, he scuffed the ground with the toe of his boot. A lone ginger cat appeared from the barn and slunk across the courtyard, ignoring them completely, yet Ivan's eyes followed it. "Don't get me wrong, I love talking horses. But with someone who isn't talking *at* you and wanting you to agree with everything they say. Because people like that spout a whole load of – of nonsense. And they always seem to want to corner *me* and chew *my* ear off."

Estella suppressed a smile. "You didn't happen to get cornered by The Craven, did you?"

He blinked. "I did, actually. How did you know?"

"Do you know his name is Paul Craven? But everyone calls him The Craven not because he's gutless but because he's always *cravin'* attention."

Shaking his head, Ivan chuckled. "I'd feel sorry for him if he wasn't so irritating."

"Be careful of Paul Craven," she said seriously. "And his mother, Mai. They'd check the pockets of your jacket while you're still wearing it, they're so nosy. And they'll spread stories about anyone. About anything. Doesn't matter if the story's true or not. So just … be careful."

"I'll turn the bugger out next time he shows up here," Ivan muttered mutinously.

"*Don't*. Be civil. Because if you've anything to hide, The Craven will be sure to turn on you and ferret out any secrets you might have. They're dangerous."

"Friends close, enemies closer?"

"That's it." She thought about how it felt like her insides had fallen out of her body when she overheard the rumour that she had killed her own father. *No* – she wouldn't let thoughts like that ruin her day. "Anyway, it's high time I went home."

Darkness was descending quickly and she didn't fancy walking home in the dark. Plus, the air was cooling rapidly now that the weak sunshine had disappeared behind the clouds. Ivan disappeared into the haybarn to get his bike so she waited momentarily to say goodbye. But when he emerged, he gestured to the handlebars upon which he was balancing a sack filled with straw.

"Hop on!"

"*I will not!*" she squawked without hesitation.

She had once sat on the handlebars of Austin's bike as a child in a race against Dolly and her brother. It had ended with the two boys crashing into each other midway down the lane and somehow Estella ended up at the bottom of a pile of four small children and two bikes. She had knocked out two baby teeth and arrived in their mother's kitchen screaming as blood and spittle ran down her chin. Once Prudie had ascertained that there was nothing seriously wrong with the child, she roundly scolded them both. She banished Estella to the back step to hide her tears from Joy since crying always upset her. Feeling rather guilty, Austin had kindly returned to the crash-site and after a considerable amount of searching on his hands and knees, had found both teeth and triumphantly presented them to her as she sat on the step, sobbing dryly while staring out at the chickens pecking in the yard.

When she explained this traumatic incident to Ivan, he stared sceptically at her. "So you're telling me that you can balance on a horse but you can't balance on the handlebars of a bike?"

"It's not about *balance* it's … it's about a bad experience putting me off it altogether."

"Stella?"

"Don't tell me to get on the bike."

Ivan grinned. "I wasn't –"

"You were."

"All right, I was. But if you're not going to ride on it with me, you're taking it home and I'm walking." He thrust the bike towards her.

Knowing he had her cornered, she tutted crossly and folded her arms. She could call his bluff and leave him to walk, she thought. But then he had been kind to her all afternoon and she had truly enjoyed herself. And it really was getting dark. "Fine," she huffed eventually with ill grace. "But if you dump me off the front of this …"

"I know, I know. You'll do me some form of bodily harm."

"That's it."

Nervously, she perched her backside on the bag of straw and turned her face to the road ahead while grasping the handlebars tightly in her fists either side of her hips. She was about to impatiently demand that they move off when two warm, rough-skinned hands slid over hers.

"Relax, Stella." His breath tickled her neck and fanned a light wisp of hair around her ear as he whispered directly into it. "You're safe with me. I promise."

Chapter 19

When she finally crossed the yard to milk their lone cow, the winter night had descended. Ivan had dropped her off at the end of the lane so that he could turn around and head home. The house was completely dark behind her. She had briefly been into the cold, soulless kitchen to stoke up the Aga which was almost completely out but she hadn't even bothered taking off her coat and hat. The whole place was eerily quiet once the sun went down. There were no murmuring chickens, no twittering birds. Even the almost constant sough of the tree boughs that draped their protective arms over the outer reaches of the yard were silent.

The toffee-and-black Jersey stood patiently waiting, her udder swollen with milk. She was the only Jersey they had but her milk was always the best when it came to separating into cream and butter. For as long as Estella remembered, the Fraynes always tried to make sure they had a Jersey cow that calved late in the season so her milk would still be flowing over Christmas. Her father maintained that having the best milk, cream and butter made the holidays that little bit better. And though she had tried to keep up the tradition, no amount of high-quality dairy foodstuffs could save a Frayne family Christmas.

Now that she was home, the unhappiness that had lifted began to press itself upon her shoulders once again. Yet she was determined not to let it grind her into the ground this time. Right in her heart's core, she stoked the beacon which had warmed and lighted a day filled with shadow: Ivan.

On their journey home she found there was hardly enough room on the handlebars for her hands and Ivan's to sit side by side. Slowly, Ivan's fingers had crept underneath hers – or perhaps hers had crept over his and by the time they reached the bottom of her laneway, their chilled fingers had interlocked and stiffened with the cold air rushing over them. Neither spoke as the dusky countryside trundled by – or maybe they trundled by it. It was hard to tell. They seemed to have entered some sort of between-space, floating along, creeping closer and closer to reality. From the moment she had touched the grey mare's neck, she had been transported to another place – a better place, one where there was the potential for happiness. This was the place Ivan Aylward inhabited and its glow warmed her soul in a way she had not known for years. This was what happiness felt like.

She had felt its absence without being able to conjure up remembrances of the feeling that was missing. She knew she had been contented with life once, but could never seem to bring those recollections to mind. Only when the feeling returned did the floodgates open and in poured the life she had loved. It was as if the emotion itself was the key to unlocking years of suppressed memories. Those bright moments in her life had not dared to surface for fear of being tainted by the mire of sadness that overlaid the rest of her thoughts. But once the heat and light had scorched through the darkness, the good times she had supressed bubbled forth, gurgling happily as they played out in her mind's eye. She recalled simple moments of pleasure, the contentment good work brought, her father's often-smiling face, her father walking jauntily on two legs that still worked and horses – horses in the stables, horses in the fields, horses crossing the yard.

Walking through the hushed darkness back to the house, she almost thought her skin glowed slightly, shining in stark contrast to the surrounding black. The yard had once hummed with life and she wanted to hear that vibration once again. Its emptiness was no longer depressing. It echoed with potential, waiting to be filled.

But the kitchen of the house just echoed. Standing in the unlit gloom, she thought about how much she hated that kitchen. Almost twenty years later, it was still her mother's domain. Even before Prudie died, she had sought refuge outdoors, knowing that being under her mother's feet would only result in a scolding. As she flicked on the light, Estella suddenly wondered why she still tried to live by Prudie's rules when her mother had so often pushed her away. She could no longer summon an emotional connection with the woman who had barely connected with her in life, never mind from beyond the grave.

She padded across the tiled floor in her thick socks and sneaked her head in the door of the sitting room. Graeme was fast asleep in his chair, the curtains still open, the fire burnt down to nothing. In the dimness, she could just make out the outline of the whisky bottle. The light from the kitchen drew fine white lines on the wall of the bottle and a halo three-quarters of the way down where it caught the edges of the liquid. At least he hadn't drunk the whole thing, she thought. Even so, there was no point in waking him for supper. He would just tell her he wasn't hungry. He said that so much now. Slowly, she had come to the realisation that it was to do with the amount he drank. Though he tried to hide it, the increase in his alcohol consumption was directly proportional to how little he ate. And though she had tried to ignore it – deny its presence in their lives – she had to admit it. He didn't just have a problem with drink. At the age of thirty-one, Graeme was an alcoholic.

Her consciousness had whispered it to her often but always as a question that she immediately dismissed. Her brother an alcoholic? It didn't bear thinking about. It was just another way she had failed in life. She had failed to save her brother from himself. Austin had levelled that charge at her earlier that day – that she *let* him do it, that she *could* do something to stop him. But what? What could she do? No matter how good her intentions were, nothing she said would change his habits. In fact, any time she did try to intervene it sent him on another binge, each one more prolonged and much messier than the last. Usually, she would find him once he had lost consciousness in a pool of vomit and other fluids. Every time she found him like that, there was always a moment when she thought he might be dead – that he had choked or simply put his body through so much that it shut down permanently. However, when he came around, she was always quietly livid with him for making her worry and leaving her with such a God-awful mess to clear up. It was why she didn't try to stop him anymore. Graeme was just like their father in that sense. Because the more she tried to help, the more he defied her. It was easier for both of them to just not talk about it and allow him to carry on with his functional alcoholism.

Graeme Frayne was an alcoholic.

Austin was not her ally.

Prudie's domestic legacy no longer mattered.

And she wasn't to blame for her father's death.

Today really had been a day of revelations, she thought, as she filled the kettle ready to poach a couple of eggs for her tea. Waiting for the water to boil, she surveyed the debris she had abandoned in the aftermath of their dinner. The turkey was still sitting out on the counter along with the pudding bowl, the tray for the roast potatoes and the saucepan for the sprouts. The dishes were exactly where she had left them too, but the smears of gravy and small bits of food had vanished. Sophie had obviously helped herself to some Christmas lunch. There were probably teeth marks in the turkey as well. The cat wasn't meant to get up on the counter but when it smelt so appetising, who could blame her? Estella sighed. She would tidy once she ate her eggs. She was hungry despite her big lunch. But then fresh air did that. Fresh air and good company.

As soon as her mind brought forth the image of Ivan riding next to her, smiling, chatting, laughing, she felt calmer – *happier*. How did he do that? Although it wasn't just him, she reasoned. It was the fact that she was also in the company of horses. Denying the power horses had over her

220

– their power to bring joy, contentment, peace to her life – was denying half of her as a person. Her connection with the animal was what had made her the person she was. Cutting them out of her life had left her only a shadow of her former self. Living a half-life was no life at all. And it most certainly was not what her father would have wanted.

Food finished, she set to work on tidying up, not even bothering to try and stay quiet. She wasn't scared of aggravating Graeme – just as she didn't fear his temper when standing before him in the pub on market day. That time, she felt brave because Ivan was standing behind her. Now she felt brave because she had the memory of a whole afternoon with Ivan to bolster her. Yet why was it she couldn't feel brave just as herself? Why did she have to cling to the presence of Ivan to feel capable? Slowly, as she scraped and scrubbed at the dishes, she came to the realisation that she did not feel there was any value to her as a person unless someone else gave it to her. She always felt unworthy – that people maintained contact with her out of nothing more than obligation.

"But I'm not worthless."

Standing in the kitchen, late on Christmas Day, she spoke the words aloud. Even as she did, she felt ridiculous. Who was she to give herself value? Surely it was for other people to do that? Anything else was just arrogance. But then neither was it fair to put the expectation on other people to give her confidence. She had to carry her own torch too. Ivan's presence buoyed her more than anyone else's did. However, it was up to her to now take the confidence he gave her and develop it for herself.

As she began to absentmindedly dry and put away dishes, Estella tried to clear her mind of doubt and list all the things she thought – no, *knew* – she was good at. She was a good cook and baker for starters. Despite not having a maternal hand to guide her, she was able to make a recipe turn out as it was supposed to. She was good at farming. All the animals she cared for were healthy and – as far as she could make out – happy. She could calve cows, feed calves, maintain the chickens, fatten the pigs. Then there was all the physical work. She was a physically strong and capable young woman. There was rarely an occasion she had to call on Graeme for his masculine strength. She would always do her best to figure out a way to manage everything alone and – she thought to herself – she therefore showed ingenuity. Of course she had a good, clever brain.

She was good with horses – really good. Little Iris Kellett they called her, after one of the country's top show jumpers. She could say with absolute confidence that she knew what she was doing on a horse. The animals just seemed to trust her, to want to please her, to look after her. It took her much less time to gain the respect and faith of a young horse than it did her father. Often, it was she who was given the task of taming the creatures who came in out of the fields sweating and with bulging eyes. Of course, they would snort and try to get away in the confined space of the stables which they would churn to dung in an hour of fretting. But once she stood calm and firm, talking quietly, soothingly, the fear in their eyes would soften and their heads would drop in submission. They wanted to trust her, they wanted to be near her. The animals knew she was safe, kind, caring – that

222

if they trusted her, they would not be ill-used. She didn't know how they knew, but they did.

She could not – should not – waste her potential.

"Right," she said to the sink. "That can be my New Year's resolution: get back into horses." If she said it out loud, even to inanimate objects, then she would have to do it. Thinking it was no good. She had to *say* it.

"Are you, now?"

She shrieked. Graeme was standing in the doorway groggy-eyed. She hadn't factored in a real person hearing her plans. She hadn't factored in what their comments and judgement might do to her newfound resolve. "Y-yes?" She cursed herself for sounding so weak and unsure. How could she carry out her plan if she couldn't even be confident in telling the first person who questioned her? She swallowed. "Yes," she repeated confidently and clearly.

"Oh. Right." There was a long pause. "You'll still have to do the milking and help out with the lambing and all. Because, you know, I'm too busy to be doing it all myself." Graeme's voice was raspy but he seemed fairly cognisant.

"I know," she said, trying to calm her hammering heart. He hadn't dismissed the idea outright! "I've done it before." She shrugged. "I miss them. The horses."

"Even after what happened?"

She willed her voice not to break. "Even after what happened."

Graeme nodded. "Right then." He glanced around the now-clean kitchen. "Any bread and butter going for tea?"

Chapter 20

On the 29th of December, Estella received a phone call from Barbara Leclerc.

"You absolutely *must* come up to our little New Year's shindig, my dear. I haven't seen you in an *age*. Now, I *won't* take no for an answer. If you're not here by nine o'clock, I'll send my husband up to get you. And you *know* how cross he'd be if I had to do that because he does love to be the *centre* of attention, doesn't he?"

Estella hadn't been to a party at the Leclercs since her father's accident. It seemed most things she thought of these days were things she hadn't done since her life had simply stopped in its tracks after that moment. Only now was she considering how she might make strides to return to the world she had once inhabited.

To that end, she had started with something simple and begun to sort through all the old equestrian equipment that had been scattered around Robin Hill over the last three decades. There were headcollars, a Cavesson lunging collar, lunge lines, training rollers, bits, bridles, girths, four saddles, riding boots, rugs, saddle cloths and dozens of other items to sort through. When she hid it all from her father's gaze, she had simply shoved things unceremoniously into the storage cupboard under the stairs and left everything in the barn hanging where it was. Nothing had been cleaned or sorted which meant much of it still bore the marks of sweat and hair from long-gone horses. The tack outside was covered in dust and every piece of leather was rigidly dry. The items stored inside had fared little better. In the damp of the house, blue, white and green mould had blossomed on the leather, making Estella's nose itch terribly when she disturbed it. But as she washed each piece with warm water and the grey surfaces slowly turned dark, rich brown once again, the task of cleaning the mound of seemingly unsalvageable equipment started to become enjoyable. The smell of leather and saddle soap was gloriously rich. She had missed that smell too. Once everything was clean, she rubbed it thoroughly with Neatsfoot oil to give the leather suppleness and soften it while also stopping it from cracking or snapping when she used it again.

It was in this state of contentment surrounded by horse tack, that Rebecca Aylward found Estella.

"I've been invited to the Leclercs' New Year party!" she said without preamble. "I hope you're coming because if you're not, I don't think I will."

"Hello to you too!" Estella laughed.

"Oh, yes, sorry! Hello! Are you going?"

"Yes, but won't Ivan be going? You'd be fine with him surely?" Estella was going on that possibility alone. But then that seemed a rather disingenuous reason for going when it was the Leclercs who were kind enough to invite her. If Ivan was the only thing that motivated her attendance, then she would be better not going at all.

"Of course Ivan's going. But it was Mrs Leclerc who invited me and Mammy and Mammy said straight off she wouldn't go. She's offered to look after Harry for the evening and everything. I just didn't know if I wanted to go when Ivan was the only person I knew. But if you're there too –" here, she took Estella's hands in hers "– I mightn't feel so out of place."

"I'll feel better knowing you're there too," she smiled, squeezing Rebecca's hands. And she meant it.

Wearing a neat but old dress she was sure she had worn to the same event many years ago, Estella set off on her bike to Ellendale on New Year's Eve. Graeme had already disappeared shortly after he finished his tea and toast so there was no chance she was getting a lift from him to the bottom of the Leclercs' lane. But she didn't really mind. The weather was cool and dry so the only thing she had to worry about was not being run over in the dark if someone happened to be passing. She had attached an old light to the handlebars so she could see where she was going but it had the unfortunate habit of cutting out every time she hit a bump. Only when she blindly thumped into the bottom of the next pothole did it flicker to life once again which made for a particularly bumpy ride. Even though she had given herself ten minutes to get there, she was counting on the road to slow her down enough to not be the first one to arrive. But neither did she want to be so late that they would send out a search party to find her.

She covered the final stretch along the lane at a leisurely pedal. For as long as she could remember, she had adored Ellendale House and as she approached it on the last day of 1959, she drank in the sight of it.

The dozen or so windows in the front blazed with light and warmth that spilled out onto the big-bellied curve of golden stone opening out from the steps up to entrance. A modest portico with a flat roof and corrugated stone columns stood sentinel over the thick oak front door which had been blue when she was a child but was now green to match the fields that extended beyond the gravel sweep. She knew they were there but were swallowed by blackness when the lights of the house could defend against the darkness no more. A spider web of equally black veins clung to the grey façade around the windows which in summer bloomed with green leaves that turned red in the autumn. When they blossomed, the flowers from the ornamental grapevine were always abuzz with insects and released a dense miasma of pollen that almost seemed visible to the naked eye on sunny days.

As she came closer, a number of cars and the odd bike parked in front of and around the side of the house began to take shape. Among others, there were two Fords, a Baby Austin, three Morris Minors and two VW Beetles – one very new, the other very old. By the looks of things, she was far from the first to arrive. Dismounting her bike, she looked closely at the old VW and was relieved to see it was the grey one Ivan drove. At least the Aylwards were there. Propping her bike against the wall, she nervously flattened the front of her coat then realised how pointless the action was since she would take it off as soon as she walked in. Though the windowsills were too high for her to see inside, she knew there were people milling about by the flickering light streaming out. She could also hear the dull rumble of human voices accented by the sharper sounds of music coming from a record player.

Taking a deep breath, she mounted the steps with heavy feet and pulled the bell. She stood in the shadow of the door and waited … and waited. No one answered.

Feeling slightly embarrassed, she swithered about whether to try and get someone's attention through a window but knew she wasn't tall enough. Oh, just be brave, she told herself crossly and, placing her hand on the doorknob, gave it a decisive shove.

"Goodness me! Are you trying to knock me out before the fun's even begun?"

Henry Leclerc had forgone his regular tweed and plus fours. He stood resplendent in a burgundy silk cravat, yellow waistcoat and smoking-style jacket of bottle-green velvet. A broad grin lit his features as he bowed her through the door with his whiskey glass and a cigar in one hand.

"Come in, my dear, come in. Let me take your coat." He took it one-handed and threw it rather unceremoniously onto a settee already overflowing with jackets.

"Thank you," she said as she slipped past him into the bright atrium of the house.

It truly was magnificent. The rich red-brown stairs curved around a large Christmas tree that stood in the centre of its wooden embrace. Tinsel and baubles winked at her and a fat, gaudy angel weighed down its uppermost branch so that the seraph looked as if it had imbibed one too many festive sherries. But before she could observe anything more, she found herself being borne along by Mr Leclerc.

"Now we have whiskey – bit too much for a slip of a thing like you though, eh? – sherry, some God-awful ginger beer but some people seem to like it. There's stout too – no? Not for you? Minerals too which seem to be very popular. I suppose no one wants to be totally squiffy for the midnight service – I take it you'll be going to church, yes? Good, good, we can all go together – bit of a gang, you know." He spotted his wife talking to a man with a salt-and-pepper beard and hailed her. "Barbara! Look who I found on the front step!" Here he caught Estella by the shoulders and held her in front of him to receive his wife's embrace.

"Oh, my *dear*!" Barbara Leclerc was of an age with her husband. Not particularly large though shapely, she was wearing a navy dress with a pleated skirt and large amounts of gold jewellery which somehow didn't look tawdry. She wrapped her elbows around Estella's back, careful not to spill her drink or set fire to her dress with her cigarette while Henry disappeared next door. "It's been *too* long. You've met Bob Lucy before, haven't you?"

And with that she was subsumed into the party.

Conversation washed over her as she stood and listened politely while trying to scan the room. There were several faces she recognised including, surprisingly, the vicar who would be giving the midnight service later on. Estella thought it strange that he was standing in the middle of such decadence and plenty when he often preached temperance in all walks of life. She assumed such men spent their time praying rather than swilling whiskey and eating triangular sandwiches at Ellendale. Of course, there was also the regular horsey set, many of whom wore brooches with equestrian themes just to distinguish themselves from the rest of the crowd. Estella had several such pieces at home but had decided against wearing one since she hadn't been part of that world for a while. Maybe next year, she had said to herself. Instead, the charcoal-grey dress she wore with its print of small soft pink and white flowers was – she hoped – elegant but not altogether noteworthy. Eventually, having completely given up listening to Mrs Leclerc and Bob Lucy's discussion on a family they had known thirty years ago, she spotted Rebecca.

She was holding court at the opposite end of the room, her brown hair shining through the haze of cigarette smoke. It was very clear that Mrs Bruce didn't need help navigating a party. There were five in the group of men and women of which she appeared to be the centre. A sixth young man appeared and handed her a glass which she accepted with a radiant smile. Estella flexed her empty fingers. No one had fetched *her* a drink and she'd surely been there fifteen minutes. She did not begrudge Rebecca the attention she was receiving. On the contrary – she rather admired anyone who could command a group with such apparent ease. Although she did envy Rebecca her effortlessness.

Realising her own companions were now in discussion with someone else, she quietly slipped away, summoned by the presence of food platters and sticky-sweet lemon mineral on a table along the end wall of the room. As she weaved through the clouds of cigarette smoke emanating from various groups, she longed for something to eat to mask the taste of them in her mouth. Approaching the table, she saw large plates with egg, cheese and ham and cucumber sandwiches. There was also a selection of buns, mince pies and chunks of Christmas cake which reminded Estella that they hadn't even started the cake she had at home. Since there was so much sweet food, she forwent the mineral and plumped for a glass of water instead. She poured it and took a sip, still facing the wall. Now that she was there, she wondered how she might leave the table and reintegrate herself into the gathering. Joining a conversation was always so awkward. She felt outside of the whole thing and suddenly longed to be at home on her own. But she was here now. So, despite the lump in her throat, she slowly made her way along the selection of foods and took her time choosing the tastiest-looking dainty on each of the serving platters. She picked at the food she had chosen. She sipped her water. She topped up her glass. She studied the platters once again. She would have to turn around at some point. She should turn around.

"Don't turn around."

Her shadow on the table grew significantly as someone tall stood close behind her. She didn't turn. She didn't need to. She knew it was Ivan.

"Why not?" she asked calmly though her heart seemed to boom in her chest.

His breath touched her ear. "I'm relying on you to save me from Paul Craven."

"He's *here*?" she squawked, turning to look.

"*Don't look!*" he insisted. "I only just got away from him with my ears intact."

She rounded on him. "And what makes you think *I* can protect you from him?" she hissed, quickly scanning the part of the room she could see past Ivan's considerable form.

"He said he doesn't enjoy the conversation of women so I'm hoping if I'm talking to you, he won't want to join in."

"You are joking, aren't you? The Craven *not* talk to someone? As far as I know, I'm a woman and I've been cornered by him plenty of times."

"Ah," Ivan began knowingly, "but this is a new discovery. He's a new man apparently since he began his little men-only plan. He's aiming for more *stimulating* conversations he says and women just don't –"

"Well, *hello* there! Stella Frayne as I live and breathe!"

Despite her irritation, Estella fought the urge to snort with laughter at the look of pure pain on Ivan's face as he hunched his shoulders against the man standing behind him. "Hello, Paul."

"You two know each other then? Or is this a first meeting?"

He was fishing and they both knew it.

Ivan's eyes narrowed and she saw his jaw flex. He turned his shoulder infinitesimally but kept his feet planted squarely, facing Estella. "You know Stella too then, do you?"

"*Ooo! Stella*, is it?" Paul's eyes glittered and his smile became much more genuine.

Ivan rounded on him but Estella beat him to it. "We've met. I call you Paul because it's your name and he calls me Stella because it's mine," she said blandly. "And he's Ivan and his sister is Rebecca." She smiled placidly up into The Craven's cooling gaze. "We're all of an age and I don't see why I wouldn't call them by their Christian names. The

232

names our mothers gave us. The name *your mother* gave you, Paul." Estella's subtle emphasis on his mother was very deliberate. Paul's face blackened at the mention of her. "And how *is* your mother, Paul?" she asked sweetly.

"You could ask her yourself," he began and Estella felt all the blood drain from her face, thinking his mother was suddenly going to pop out from behind him, "but she's killed with the varicose veins. Can barely get around. Mr Leclerc invited the both of us and, only for the veins, she'd be here too."

"That's a pity, Paul. And how are all your sisters? Do you hear from the two in America much? I hear so little about them, you must tell me."

"Oh, they're ... grand, you know ... Oh there's –" he waved across the room to no one in particular "I'll have to say hello to him."

And with that, The Craven was gone.

There was a long pause as two sets of eyes followed his back, making sure he really had gone. Then Ivan gave a low whistle. "Now *that* was masterful."

Estella chuckled quietly. "I learnt that trick from my daddy. If there's one thing auld Paul hates, it's talking about things that aren't to do with himself and his opinions. You're welcome, by the way."

"Yes! Thank you! I must remember that next time he tries to waylay me." He was grinning from ear to ear and suddenly gave a single shout of laughter, shaking his head.

"I wouldn't try the same tack if you're ever unfortunate enough to meet Mrs Craven. If you mention family, it's like one of those wind-up children's toys. Off it'll go and keep

233

going until it … I don't know, falls off the table?"

Ivan's laughter was much more prolonged this time and drew quizzical glances from numerous people. "Oh dear," he sniggered, pinching the bridge of his nose as he continued to giggle into his hand. "Now I've got a picture in my head of a little old fat woman toppling off the table mid-flow."

That set Estella off too. They continued to laugh together quietly, trying not to attract anyone's attention. After a while, however, Estella sobered, frowning as Mai Craven planted herself firmly at the front of her consciousness.

Noticing, Ivan nudged her with his shoulder. "What?" When she shook her head, he frowned too. "Come on, Stella. What?"

"Just thinking of her at Daddy's funeral." It wasn't her only run-in with either of the Cravens but it was the one she thought of now. "I was standing in line, as you do, when people came over to offer their condolences and dear little old Mai Craven came barrelling through everyone – nearly knocked one of Daddy's cousins into the grave – and then she comes up to me and says … she says, 'I'll just stand here beside you and keep the wind off'." She tittered angrily. "As if the bloody wind mattered to me. All she was doing was trying to hear what everyone was saying to me at the graveside." She paused, realising she had crumbled the edge of a mince pie to dust on the edge of her plate. She wiped her fingers. "*Cow*," she muttered eventually.

Ivan was staring at her. "I'm not sure 'cow' is a strong enough word there. What a – a – well – yes. *Hmm*."

"You feel sorry for those varicose veins."

He smiled. "That's it, isn't it? Crikey. So folk down here

are just as bad as they were up home? Worse maybe. Well, that's cheerful, eh?"

"Sorry, I didn't mean to bring the mood down. Just … you know."

"I do. And don't be sorry. You say anything you want to me, Stella. And I'd rather learn what locals are like from you than find out for myself." He picked up the remains of mince pie she had crushed and popped it into his mouth, chewing thoughtfully. "I'll come away from this evening much better informed, thanks to you," he assured her as he swallowed. "Not only do I now know how to get rid of Paul, I also know to avoid his mother like the bloody plague."

At that moment, Henry Leclerc appeared, apparently having been spat out of the other room at great speed since he was half running towards them. "Ivan! Ivan – oh and Stella too! Excellent! We're in the middle of a discussion next door about crossbreeding the Irish Draught and I'd like your opinions to back me up!" He grabbed both of them by the elbows and neatly slid Estella's arm through his, patting her hand. "I really don't know why I invited so many people to our party who don't agree with me …"

Ivan grinned over his employer's head at her. Estella looked away and bit her lip.

The conversation between Henry Leclerc and his friends turned out to be quite enjoyable. She was glad to discover she wasn't the only woman in the group though she and Ivan were the youngest by quite a distance. The talk was familiar, easy, playful and though she said little, the others listened when she did speak. Mr Leclerc's eyes shone with whiskey and pride as he nodded enthusiastically while she spoke. "*You're right! Isn't she right?*" he boomed, making her cheeks glow with a mixture of pleasure and embarrassment. Had it not been for the fact that Jacqueline Hawes – a woman in her mid-fifties who was contorted by many falls from many horses over the years – and Ivan nodded in agreement with her opinions, she would have thought it was simply alcohol that gave Mr Leclerc such confidence in her views. Mostly, however, she was glad to find all her knowledge still intact, waiting to be recalled – from breeding to training, to hoof care and diet. And while part of her felt that this was an evening her father would have relished, the thought made her happy rather that upset at his absence. Because it wasn't just Reg's favourite subject they discussed. It was hers too – something she owned in her own right rather than something that belonged only to him.

By the time a number of the company were slightly red-faced and sleepy, the summons to midnight service rippled through the various enclaves of the house.

Ivan, after making several voluntary trips to fetch people food and drinks, had eventually come to sit on the armrest of the sofa beside her. She had been acutely aware of his thigh touching her elbow and his long arm extended behind her to where his hand rested on the back of the seat. When everyone began to heave themselves from their seats, his fingertips touched her right shoulder and she felt the slight pressure of his forearm across her back.

"Is someone coming to collect you or do you want a lift to church?"

"I have my bike," she told him uncertainly, not really

wanting to ride it in the dark so late at night with her dodgy light.

He stood swiftly and proffered his hand to pull her out of the depths of the sofa. It seemed to have swallowed her backside and she was struggling to reclaim the lower half of her body from it. "Up we come!" he said with a grunt then added, "You look lovely, by the way." He cast his eyes admiringly up and down her figure.

She chuckled a little to hide her embarrassment. "And you only noticed that now?"

"No," he answered, inclining his head towards her. "I was just so delighted by your company it went clean out of my head."

She flicked her hand at his arm and he dodged out of her reach. "Rubbish! You were just relieved I got rid of Paul."

"I was," he agreed. "But I really did enjoy your company. I *do*. And you *do* look lovely."

"Absolutely!" piped up Mr Leclerc as he waded past. "Best-looking girl here. Apart from my good lady wife, that is. And your sister, Aylward, looks quite lovely too. We're lucky to have three of the best-looking girls in the county with us tonight!"

They watched him steam into the melee of coat-collection and begin to organise lifts for all the various people to their various masses and services. "He started off well," Ivan commented. "But I think he faded a bit near the end of the 'Complimenting Stella Stakes'."

"I didn't notice you having a particularly big finish either then," she replied as they entered the scrummage for coats and she plucked hers out.

Ivan took it from her and held it out.

"Well, I think you're definitely the best-looking girl in the room. No contest," he whispered as he helped her on with her coat.

"Stella! Goodness, I haven't seen you all night! I wasn't sure you were here. Oh, doesn't she look lovely, Ivan?" Rebecca hugged her. "I like your dress. We scrub up well, don't we? Ivan, can you get my coat?"

Before she could reply to anything, Estella found her arm linked in Rebecca's as she was borne down the front steps to Ivan's car.

"*Brrr*, it's cold!" Rebecca said, hopping up and down, jostling Estella.

"Here." Estella opened her coat and, giggling, Rebecca cuddled in close, the cold of her white blouse something of a shock against Estella's ribs. "Gosh, no wonder you're cold, there's nothing to that shirt!"

"You sound like my mother! 'Is that skirt not a bit short and flimsy for going out of a winter's night?'" she said, doing an excellent imitation of her mother's voice. She plucked at the maroon fabric which came to just below her knee and was billowing slightly in the breeze. It matched her dark-red lipstick. "Although she might have had a point," she reasoned as Ivan walked up, holding her coat in his fist.

"Oh, you've found a coat, have you?" He eyed the two of them trying to stand in the one garment.

"Give it here," Rebecca answered, reaching for her coat and putting it on. She shivered. "I'm not sure her coat suits me as well as it suits Stella."

"Well, I can tell you for nothing it doesn't *fit* you *as well*

238

as Stella. That's a one-man coat there."

"It's a one-woman coat, actually," Estella chipped in, cheekily.

"True. Mine's more of a two-man jobbie," he said, opening the front panels wide. "Step in here, Stella, and I'll show you."

He grinned, daring her to step into his arms.

She rolled her eyes. "Come on or we'll be late. And I don't want to be the one the vicar stops his whole sermon for."

"Oh, yes, isn't it *awful*!" Rebecca agreed. "Waiting for people to take their seat and the whole congregation watching them do it. Come on, Ivan. Chop, chop! Oh, but ..."

Estella noticed the man she saw bringing Rebecca a drink earlier. Howard, she thought, finally recognising him from the days back when she was riding horses. He was footing nervously a few yards away, his eyes on Ivan's sister. Around Ivan's age, he was thin, angular, of medium height and had dark hair.

"I said we might be able to give Howard – Mr Anstruther – a lift to church," Rebecca said. "Would that be all right?"

In the faint light of the windows, Estella was sure she saw her blush.

Howard Anstruther stepped forward cautiously, glanced up momentarily then cast his eyes down once more, not daring to meet Ivan's gaze.

Viewing him suspiciously, Ivan briefly drummed his fingertips on the roof his car. "All right. In you get." Then he got in himself and reached across to open the passenger door.

Howard somehow managed to fold his gangly legs into

the back of the car alongside Rebecca. Estella hopped into the front and Ivan gunned the engine to join the cavalcade trundling down the driveway.

Once they reached Glencoyle village, the cars separated, some heading to the Catholic chapel that sat a field behind Nelly Sweeney's and others to Church of Ireland church at the far end of the main thoroughfare.

Stepping out of the car into the cool night air, the windows of the church glowed gold in the blackness. They rushed towards the swelling sound of the organ playing inside, hurrying for fear that the gathered crowd would begin to sing before they got to their pews. However, they needn't have worried since there were several family pews empty once they ducked into the light and mild warmth of the nave. Estella scanned the crowd for her own family members but, seeing no one, she simply allowed herself to be led, to sit with the Aylwards who had a pew near the back. Howard Anstruther joined them too, sitting closest to the aisle. However, once the service began, he was shoved further and further in as latecomers ducked into the final few pews rather than bear the shame of walking down the length of the church under the disapproving gaze of the zealots with prayer books dutifully held close to their faces.

As Estella sang the second hymn, the shuffling gait and dark hair of her brother caught her eye. Graeme slid into the last pew on the opposite side and leaned into the man next to him, indicating that he needed to share a prayer book. Of course he had forgotten his own, she thought.

In her own row, while there had been much fumbling in pockets and bags, everyone managed to produce their own.

Just. She had to fight down giggles when Ivan had wrestled his from the depths of his jacket pocket only for the much-sellotaped front cover to come off as he freed it. It tickled her to see the words *'Ivan William Aylward'* written in childish script on the first page along with the date '3rd June 1931' which she presumed was his date of birth. So he would turn twenty-nine a month after her twenty-sixth birthday. That pleased her, though she didn't really know why. And it wasn't something she should be bothering about when she was in the middle of church.

The organist and the vicar mistimed the service somewhat so that they were in the middle of singing the final hymn when the clock struck twelve. The voices of the congregation faltered momentarily but swelled once more. When they finished, there was a flurry of activity as people shook hands with everyone around them and wished them a happy New Year.

Being amongst the last few seats and caught behind the latecomers, Estella stood impatiently in the pew, waiting to get out and find Graeme to get a lift home. She knew she could ask Ivan again but she didn't want him to go out of his way even if it was only a few minutes.

"Ants in your pants?" Ivan asked as he stood behind her, noting her restlessness.

"No," she answered defensively and made to turn to him but instead found his chin almost on her shoulder. As she craned her neck back to look at him, she was suddenly aware of the shape of his face. She liked the way his smiling cheeks bulged and swelled over the protrusion of his cheekbones. This late at night, the stubble on his cheeks was

241

much darker than she had seen it before. And being so close, she could also see the individual pitted acne scars that speckled his cheeks. Yet these blemishes added to his rugged handsomeness rather than detracted from the sun-browned skin. He looked down at her and a thick wave of dark brown hair flopped over the large expanse of his forehead. Her fingers itched with the urge to push it back into place.

"On you go then."

Estella blinked. She had been staring at him and was completely unaware that the pew in front of her had cleared. She almost collided with Rebecca in her hurry to catch up. Trickling out onto the gravel, they all shook the vicar's hand but Estella barely heard his hope that she would have a happy and prosperous year. She was searching the chatting groups for Graeme. Surely he had seen her and was waiting somewhere? She drifted between the gathered people, trying to see faces in the weak light of the church. But she couldn't even find Graeme's car, never mind him.

"*Stella? What are you doing? Come on!*" Ivan stood in front of his car, swinging the key around his finger.

She walked towards him, still scanning the parked cars. "Looking for Graeme to bring me home. Have you seen him?"

"I'll bring you home," Ivan answered promptly.

"But –"

"*Stella! Ivan! You are coming back, aren't you?*"

Barbara Leclerc came clacking across the road in her court shoes while her husband sauntered behind in the middle of a posse of partygoers.

"Yes, yes, do follow us over," he said enthusiastically.

242

"The night's only begun! Anstruther's coming, aren't you, man?"

Ivan glanced at her but she kept her face neutral, not wanting to sway him either way.

Rebecca, on the other hand, piped up, "Oh come on, Ivan! We never get to go anywhere! Let's enjoy it while it lasts."

He was silent for a moment, kicking some loose chippings. "We'll see you over there in a minute, Barbara. Are you wanting a lift again, Anstruther?"

Rebecca clapped and wrenched open the passenger door of the car which screamed a rusty protest. Anstruther meekly folded long legs into the back with Rebecca but Ivan crossed to Estella. "Do you want to go home?" he asked quietly. "I can drop you off no problem."

"I –" It felt like he was trying to get rid of her.

"I'm not trying to get rid of you. I'd be happy if you came. Delighted. But if you don't want to, don't feel you have to."

"I'll come."

Chapter 21

The group that returned to Ellendale was somewhat smaller than the one that had left it an hour previously. Estella was glad to see that Paul Craven was not among the fifteen or so people who adjourned to the much cosier drawing room at the back of the house. The remaining food and drink had been piled high on a few plates and carried in to sit on a coffee table in front of the fire. There was a little back and forth as extra glasses and empty plates were fetched but eventually everyone settled down with drink in hand and whatever food they had scavenged. Conversation struggled a little at first but once the record player was brought in under the instruction of Mrs Leclerc, the ambient noise seemed to encourage talk and swapping of places.

"Budge up."

Ivan flumped down on the seat beside Estella that Rebecca had just vacated to join Howard Anstruther. He and Ivan had been picked as the two, strong, steady young men to bring in the record player and once they moved it had given everyone else licence to do the same. The loveseat they were sitting on had barely been big enough for the two women, never mind someone as large as him which meant that no matter how much she budged, they were stuck close together. With the warmth of the fire and many bodies, Ivan had removed his jacket and she was shocked somewhat by the heat emanating from his body. The thin fabrics between them meant that the side of her left arm warmed immediately but the rest of her body suddenly felt cold.

"Any resolutions for the coming year?" he asked.

"Oh, you know, trying to be kinder, not get cross with people who can't help the way they are." She sipped her drink and observed the room.

"That's not your resolution."

She turned and found his face close to hers. But this time, she looked away. "What makes you say that?"

"Because I know it's not true."

She scowled. "Awfully sure of yourself, aren't you?"

"Can you tell me I'm wrong?"

"Yes." She twisted the stem of the glass between her fingers. She didn't really like sherry but had taken the glass Henry Leclerc had given her anyway. "No."

"Yes or no?"

"I want … I want to be braver this year. I want to stand up to Graeme, to make myself go places and do things. I've been … stuck in the same rut doing the same things over and over again for too long. And … and I want to ride again and go to shows and train horses and …" Her speech died on her lips. It felt wrong to have said all of this aloud. She was supposed to do something charitable or better herself with a resolution, not list her ambitions. "Sorry."

"You should add not saying 'sorry' so much."

She was surprised to see he was smiling at her and despite herself she smiled back. "How'd you do that?"

"What?"

"Well, I shouldn't have said any of that. About Graeme. Horses."

He shrugged, jostling their shoulders. "Maybe you just wanted to tell someone. And I asked. Sometimes all you need is someone to listen." He paused, swilling his stout bottle. "And it's not good to hold on to things. I think you realised that not so long ago."

She thought back to Christmas Day and how she had broken down in front of him, clinging to the grey horse's neck. "You shouldn't have seen that."

"Sometimes we all just need to have a good cry. And horses are good listeners."

"Yeah," she agreed.

"Although, they're not great at hugging."

She chuckled. "No."

"People are much better for that."

She knew he was looking at her. "What's your resolution then?"

"Oh, y'know, be kind or something – *ow*! You've got very pointy elbows." He took a swig from his bottle. "I want to get to know some people better. Make … friends. Instead of just working. Except Paul Craven. He can stay exactly where he is."

"Agreed!" She clinked her glass with his bottle and downed the remainder of her sherry, just to get it over and done with. Her eyes stung and she shuddered.

"Want another?"

"*No!*" she choked, making him grin.

"Sherry's not your drink?"

"Definitely not."

"What is then?"

She thought for a moment. "I used to like hot ports out with Daddy, especially when we were hunting. But mostly I just drink tea."

Ivan closed one eye and stared into the depths of his stout bottle. "Tea sounds like a good plan right about now."

He put down his bottle, hauled himself up out of the seat and made a beeline for Mrs Leclerc. Estella watched as he spoke in her ear, saw her nod and smile then pat him on the arm.

He returned and proffered a hand. "Tea, m'lady?"

"You didn't ask her for tea, did you?" It seemed like a highly irregular thing to do at a party where there were bottles and glasses everywhere. Nonetheless, she took his hand and allowed herself to be pulled upright again.

"Course I did. Come on."

He led her back out into the hall and through a door behind the Christmas tree that she had never used. At the far side was a long, worn set of unvarnished stairs, grey-white with age which were plunged into dusk as soon as the door closed behind them. It didn't belong in the same world as the burnished red-brown stairs above it. Ivan had to cock his head to the side at an uncomfortable looking angle to avoid cracking it off the low curved ceiling that cocooned them. Estella, however, was more concerned about falling head first into his back since the light was poor and there were no handrails to hold on to. Instead, she pressed her palms against the cold uneven surface of the walls, hoping they might steady her. In the dark, the descent seemed much longer than it should have. As children, she and Austin had sometimes been brought up to the kitchen from the stables to see Barbara while their father worked on the horses. And, of course, she had been to a few parties upstairs over the years. But she had never moved between the two spaces and hadn't realised how deep the basement went. It seemed to have been cut into the bowls of the earth.

The kitchen was just as she remembered it. Terracotta tiles covered the entire floor – most of which was, in turn, obscured by a gargantuan oak table – the older brother to the slightly smaller one that sat in her own kitchen. The ceiling was high and studded with ancient hooks and pulley wheels from its days as the bustling kitchen of a grand house. The walls were adorned with various cooking accoutrements – jars of ingredients, bags, baskets, bowls, utensils, pots and pans. Onions and garlic hung in vertical strings attached to a washing line on a pulley. However, the pervading smell was of damp dog and, as Ivan crossed the space, he was greeted by a choir of sleepy *'woofs!'* from a large alcove beside the chimney breast.

"Hello, chaps," Ivan said quietly as a fat Labrador extracted herself from the pile and shuffled over for a rub. Once he had filled the kettle and set it on the gas hob, the dog sat with a grunt, leaning up against his knee.

"Friend of yours?" Estella was perched on the edge of the table, feeling distinctly out of place, wearing her good clothes in the Leclercs' kitchen with none other than Ivan Aylward.

He rubbed the dog's ear and she groaned appreciatively. "Jojo and I are the *best* of friends. Aren't we, Jojo?"

The end of Jojo's tail gave one, two dull thuds on the floor.

Ivan frowned critically. "Well that's hardly a ringing endorsement, Jo," he admonished mildly. The dog's tail twitched. "When I first came here, all they did was bark at me. I'd come out of a stable and one would start and all the others'd join in. I thought I'd never be able to make friends with them. Now they follow me around like I'm the boss."

"You must have done something right."

"Bringing them fat off a lump of bacon Mammy cooked might have helped."

She laughed. "Bribery always works. No wonder they follow you round! They keep thinking you're going to feed them!"

The kettle behind him began to rumble ominously. "I wonder would bribery work in the same way with people."

She considered. "I suppose it depends on the person. And what you bribe them with. And what you want in return."

"What would it take to bribe you?"

She blinked. "Why would you want to bribe me?"

"Oh, I don't know." He looked away. "Maybe I could … if you … Maybe get you to spend time … with … me." He chanced a glance at her but quickly turned to the kettle which was now singing on the hob. Unerringly, he reached for teapot, tea, sugar and fetched milk from the fridge with one hand while unhooking mugs from a tree on the counter.

"You seem to know your way round." She tried to sound teasing but it didn't quite come out right. She was still trying to make sense of what he had said.

"Oh, y'know, they have me up here a good bit for tea or lunch. Or breakfast sometimes if I'm out early."

She nodded even though he wasn't looking at her.

"Milk and sugar?"

"Please. Half a teaspoon. Leave it to thicken a bit though. The tea," she explained, "I like it good and strong."

"Proper tea."

"That's it."

He brewed the tea in silence then poured the rich brown liquid into two mugs before adding milk and sugar to both.

Estella stepped forward as he turned to hand her the mug. "Thank you."

She took a sip and closed her eyes.

"Is it good?"

"Perfect."

"Who knew tea was the way to your heart?"

Together, they leant against the counter and drank. It just didn't seem appropriate to sit at the Leclercs' table. With her head cast down, she realised their positions mimicked each other perfectly. Both held their mugs in two hands and had crossed their left leg at the ankle, leaving all the weight on their right. There were only a few inches of space between them and, slowly, Estella allowed herself to glide along the edge of the counter, closing the gap until her shoulder gently bumped into his arm. He untangled his legs and placed his feet firmly on the ground as he took her weight.

Dropping her head into his shoulder, she sighed quietly.

"You don't have to bribe me, you know. If you want to spend time with me, I want to spend time with you."

He slid his arm out from beneath her head and wrapped

it around her shoulder, pulling her close. She could feel the line of his collarbone against her temple and smell the scent of Lux soap. She used the same at home but somehow the heat of his body made the fragrance stronger. Without conscious thought, she put her arm around his waist. It was simply the natural thing to do.

He spoke into her hair. "Come back tomorrow, will you? Mid-morning. To the yard. There's something I want to show you."

"All right."

"Good," he answered, kissing her head. "Good," he repeated and put his tea on the counter.

Estella watched his empty hand flex hesitantly for a moment before he lifted it to her cheek. His palm was hot having been wrapped around the mug. She smiled softly, surprisingly comfortable with the feeling of his skin against hers and closed her eyes, tilting into his touch. The pad of his thumb caressed her cheekbone and his little finger curled, drawing her face upwards until her gaze met his. His warm brown eyes studied her cheeks, her nose, her brows, her lips.

"You have the most beautiful blue eyes," he murmured. Then he leaned down and kissed her. His lips were warm – soft yet unyielding. He teased her bottom lip and she responded, moving her mouth against his, feeling the heat of their connection through every bone, muscle and sinew in her body. But just as she was about abandon her own mug and push off the counter to deepen their kiss, Ivan broke off.

The eyes that darted back and forth examining her face for a reaction shone with mischief and undisguised glee. His

251

lips – the lips that had been pressed against hers only moments before – quirked into a smile. He hummed with pleasure and leant back against the counter, pulling her against his shoulder once more, giving her a squeeze. She squeezed his waist back.

They finished their tea still holding on to one another. Once the last drops had been drained, Ivan took the mugs to the sink and washed them while Estella dried. Each moved about the kitchen with a familiar kind of domestic ease as they replaced every item they had used. As they left, Ivan turned to check the room was set to rights then turned out the light.

It was as if they had never been there at all.

Chapter 22

Ten o'clock next morning found Estella cycling up the potholed lane to Ellendale's stables. She was grateful Ivan had possessed the foresight to somehow cram her bike into the back of his car, saving her the walk back to collect it. As usual, she was greeted by several very loud, hairy balls of protective, curious energy the moment she peddled through the gate. Small dogs flew at her while Jojo clambered to her feet, stood exactly where she was and boomed out several powerful '*woofs*!' while wagging her tail enthusiastically. Numerous voices coming from disparate directions roared out orders to be quiet which only a few of the animals listened to. Estella saw Jojo give one more bark then slump back down into the middle of the horse rug she had commandeered. Two other dogs trotted back to join her, padded the woven fabric like seagulls looking for worms then curled up close to the warmth of the Labrador. However, there were three terriers of various sizes who remained vigilant and followed Estella as she wheeled her bike across the yard, one of whom continued to yap in an irritating fashion.

"*Shut up, Percy!*"

Ivan appeared from the gate at the far end of the courtyard, a saddled horse preceding him at a distance of several yards. He held two long-reins, one in each hand, attached to the bit with which he was steering the horse. He drove the horse in a neat circle around the pump at the centre of the yard then with a calm, "*Woah*," halted it placidly a few feet away from Estella. He dropped the right rein on the floor and the horse stood as he gathered the left and walked up to its head.

"You've got that one going lovely," she complimented him. "Daddy always said you'd never know the true feel of a horse in your hands until you long-reined it."

"And you agree?" he asked, undoing the right rein from the bit. "Good boy!" He patted the horse's neck.

"Of course. You can teach them so much from the ground without them having to worry about some strange heavy lump sitting on their back."

"You're hardly a heavy lump," he reasoned.

"But you are," she countered. "I'm sure horses get quite a shock when you suddenly land on their backs. But if you long-rein them first, they learn to balance themselves and listen to your voice and to steer. And you don't even have to worry about them exploding and bucking you off if they're not keen on the whole breaking idea. And you get to know what to expect when you do eventually get up on them."

"I take it you've long-reined a few in your time?"

"A few." She gave him a small smile and fell into step with him as he led the horse to its stable. They walked shoulder to shoulder and Estella could almost feel the pressure of his arm around her the night before, of her cheek against his chest, his kiss on her head.

"I have a question," he said hesitantly as he undid the girth on the saddle.

Automatically, Estella began undoing the buckles on the bridle. She didn't like standing idle. "Go on."

"Well, you think long-reining is beneficial, yes?"

"Yes."

"Then why didn't you say that? I'm not trying to criticise – it's just something I noticed. Last night especially. Whenever you gave your opinion to any of the boss's questions, you nearly always gave it as your father's opinion. "Daddy used to say …""

The end of his sentence hung in the air or, rather, it was as if it sucked all the air out of the dark little stable. She couldn't breathe. A weight crushed her lungs. She opened her mouth to speak but couldn't get any words out. How did he do it? How did Ivan Aylward manage to turn a casual conversation about training horses into something that left her lightheaded and inarticulate. And ashamed – embarrassed even. How was it that he got to the heart of her weaknesses without even appearing to try? She felt her bottom lip tremble and clamped it shut. Willing herself not to break down in front of him yet again, she screwed her eyes tight shut and bowed her head. She sensed Ivan moving beside her, dragged in a deep, ragged breath and opened her eyes.

"Stella, I didn't mean –"

"No." She cut him off. "No, it's fine. You're right. You're –" she stopped to clear her throat. "You're completely right. It's just … no one's ever pointed it out to me."

"I didn't mean to upset you," he said as he removed the saddle. "I just wondered why you did it."

"I don't know why. I just do." She guided the horse's head down and slid the bridle off over its ears.

"I think maybe we offer other people's opinions because we don't have confidence in our own." He wasn't looking at her. Instead, he began absentmindedly rubbing at the rumpled hair on the horse's flank. "I used to do it all the time. Quote my uncle because he knew more than I did. Still does, probably. But then I was selling this gelding to an Englishwoman and she asked what I thought of him. So I told her what my uncle thought about him. And she just said to me, "I asked what *you* thought, not your uncle". I didn't know what to say to her. I think – I think we need to learn that our opinion is actually worth something, even if whoever we're talking to knows more than we do."

"It's just nearly everything I know, I know from Daddy."

"But then you know it too. And if you agree with it, can't it be your opinion too?"

She thought for a moment, scratching underneath the horse's forelock.

"Yes. Yes, it can. It's just I got so used to deferring to him that I never really thought for myself. And people always wanted to know what Daddy had to say, not me."

Ivan's frowned. "Well, harsh as it might sound, he doesn't have a voice anymore. You do. And it's a good one. You should use it." With that, he adjusted the saddle he was holding against his hip, took the bridle from her and walked out of the stable, calling, "Can you put his rug on for me? It's in the corner of the stable. I just want to go and get Mr Leclerc."

Estella did as she was bid and had just finished fastening the straps when she heard Henry Leclerc's resonant voice fill the courtyard. Emerging from the dimness of the stable, she was met by the canary-yellow waistcoat of the proprietor of Ellendale, with Ivan at his shoulder.

"Here she is! Little Iris Kellett herself! Well, Stella dear, did you enjoy last night? It was very good, wasn't it?" He put his arm around her shoulder and though she began to speak, he cut her off, apparently too excited to listen. "We have something to show you. I'll admit I was a little surprised when Ivan suggested it. *Delighted* though. *Abso-bloody-lutely* delighted when he asked. And about time too."

While he spoke, he steered her across the yard towards the gate and a second block of stables which she knew was behind the main courtyard.

"It's Ivan, of course, who's done all the work. All I did was tell him which one — because I remember your favourites. And I did hold her while he was operating the clipping machine. That was my contribution. So she's got a nice clipped coat rather than looking like a hairy molly. Ha! Scrubbed up nicely, you wait and see! Wait, wait!" They stopped halfway down the block and he gripped her by both arms, positively vibrating with excitement. "You just stand here with me. And Ivan, you go on in and bring her out."

Ivan grinned and winked at her as he sauntered past, whipping a headcollar and rope off a hook as he approached the last stable. "Give me a minute. I have to take her rug off."

"Do hurry up!" Henry Leclerc told him with giddy impatience.

"What's going on?" Estella was beginning to think she knew but didn't dare hope.

"You'll see, you'll see!"

She had to hand it to Ivan – he moved fast. In less than a minute, he was walking out of the stable leading a mare not unlike Dilly in colouring but with much finer bones and a streamlined body. And, though she hated to admit it, the animal also looked like Burt – the horse that changed her father's life. But she knew it wasn't Burt. The night before, when she came back from the kitchen with Ivan, she'd overhead Mr Leclerc telling Jacqueline Hawes that Burt had been sold up the country, "A *long* way up the country."

His full sister was, however, standing on the cobbles in front of her. A single wisp of hay hung from the horse's mouth, indicating why she had not popped her head over the door to greet them. Estella knew that had she not been munching on her breakfast, this beautiful creature would have had her head out, keeping an eye on all the goings-on. The mare stood proud, with ears pricked and eyes bright, observing keenly now there wasn't the distraction of food. Ivan, unusually, didn't look that tall standing beside her. She was a good hand higher than any of the horses Estella had seen him handle before and yet he was not overpowered by her. Despite her size, a child could have handled her. That was her nature. She was kind, athletic and striking. She was –

"Hedy?"

The hairs on Estella's arms rose as the mare suddenly focused on her alone. Hedy's nostrils flared. She dropped her head then raising it again, nodding almost in acknowledgment. Estella's feet moved before she was

258

conscious of telling them to. With half a dozen strides, she had her hands on the horse – the horse her father had bred from his favourite mare eight years ago. Estella had been there at her birth when she slithered onto the straw – a slimy black creature with ridiculous long legs and ears. Over time, she had grown into both as her black coat faded to grey. In the eight years since her birth, only the steel colour of her legs and a few stray streaks in her mane and tail hinted at her original darkness. The rest of her was almost pure white. One day, Estella knew the remaining colour would drain from her limbs as if it had been leaking out through her feet as she aged. But that was a few years off. Standing with her shoulder under the animal's throat and her hands either side of her neck, she knew that Hedy was entering the prime of her life. All she needed now was someone to ride her.

"Boss says she was your favourite," Ivan said quietly. "I only got her out of the field on Stephen's Day so I've not done much with her. Ridden her four or five times just to make sure she remembers what she's doing. She's been a lady. Lovely to ride."

"She always was," Estella said quietly, running her hands over the curves of the mare's body. She was a little on the plump side and her chest was slack instead of bulging with muscle but otherwise she looked wonderful and the soft hairs left behind after her shaggy winter coat had been shaved off begged to be stroked.

Walking around the horse's backside, running her hands over her all the while, Estella came face to face with Ivan. "You did this? For me?"

He shrugged.

259

"He came up to me first thing on Stephen's Day and asked could he get one of the Frayne horses in out of the field," Leclerc boasted, beaming at his farm manager.

Ivan coloured under his proud gaze.

"Honestly, I could have kissed him I was so pleased to discover you wanted to ride again."

"Why did you keep some of them?" she asked. It was something she had wondered about ever since Ivan told her some of Reg's horses were still at Ellendale.

Henry Leclerc's face became sombre. "Because, my dear, I couldn't let go of a stable of horses your father spent almost thirty years creating. I owed that much to Reg. He was –" his voice cracked and he cleared his throat. "He was my best friend. I loved him like a brother. Selfishly, I wanted to keep some of them close to remember him by."

Estella fought the lump rising in her throat.

"It was a joy to think I was continuing his legacy. And," he reached out and placed his hands on her shoulders then her cheeks, "I knew you'd always come back to it. It's in your blood, Stella. You never could have lived your entire life without it. I was keeping them safe until the love came back to you. But now it's time I returned them. They're yours. Stella. All yours. Whenever you want them."

"Thank you," she choked. "Both of you. You don't, you can't know what this means –" She dropped her head and shut her eyes tight, willing herself not to cry. Next moment, she was being crushed to the canary-coloured felt of Henry Leclerc's chest.

"Anything for Reg's little girl," he murmured. He released her. "Anything, you hear? You come to me."

She was about to reply when, without warning, he slapped his forehead.

His eyes suddenly focused on the horse behind her. "A lone grey horse!"

She turned to look at Hedy who cast a wary eye over the man in the yellow waistcoat. "What?"

Ivan looked equally nonplussed.

"A lone grey horse!" Leclerc repeated, glancing back and forth between them. "It's bad luck to see a lone grey when embarking on a new venture! You have to see a pair. Two bring you good luck."

There was silence for a moment then Ivan and Estella's eyes met. They couldn't help it. They burst into laughter.

"Come off it, Boss! You don't believe that, do you?" Ivan spluttered.

"You can never be too careful with horses," Leclerc answered haughtily though Estella could see he was fighting a sheepish smile.

Ivan wrapped an arm around her shoulders, pulling her close. "I think Stella here will be all right," he said confidently, looking down at her.

She slipped a hand around his waist. "Are you sure?" she asked in mock seriousness. "We don't need to go and get Dilly, do we?" It gave her a thrill to watch him titter in return. Reaching past him with her free hand to rub Hedy's nose, she gave his waist a little squeeze. "I can't believe you've done all this for me. Thank you. *Thank you*."

"You're welcome, Stella."

"Do you know," Mr Leclerc piped up, "I've just remembered there's a second part to that superstition."

261

"Oh?" Ivan grinned.

Leclerc nodded. "A lone light grey *is* bad luck at the beginning of a new venture. Unless ..." He clasped his hands behind him and rocked back and forth on his heels, pausing for effect. "*Unless*, that is, you see this lone grey with your ... lover."

Estella felt her skin flame. She glanced at Ivan. His face had gone red too. But he didn't let go of her shoulder.

"I think Dilly can stay in her stable," Mr Leclerc said dryly.

Chapter 23

It was agreed by everyone that Hedy would remain at Ellendale for the foreseeable future. Estella thought it unfair to take the mare away from all the other horses when she had spent years as part of a herd. Also, while she trusted the horse, she still wasn't quite sure of herself and it felt safer to have other people around to keep an eye. And, of course, it meant she got to see Ivan.

Every day, once she finished the jobs in the yard at home, she cycled over to the stables and found Ivan who was always ready with a hug or kiss of greeting. They would then tack up Hedy and whatever other horse Ivan wanted to exercise before heading out to ride around the headlands of the fields or hack along the roads. There was also a large area of woodland on the Ellendale estate which they often found their way to. Shrouded by hundreds of evergreens, the sound of their hoofbeats was muffled by the spongy detritus of rotting vegetation. Yet their voices were loud which often led them to talk quietly, unwilling to disturb the hush. They were entering a different world of which they were not the masters. It was the creatures who belonged to the woods – the crows, the pigeons and the songbirds – that had the right to make their voices heard. Sometimes, the humans simply rode in silence, listening to the chatter of unhuman utterances that swelled above them unseen. However, as they rode – sometimes side by side, more often in single file – there was always one sound that drew them onwards. The susurration of water flowing over rocks and between muddy banks drew them onwards like the beguiling melodies of the Pied Piper. On still days, they could hear the soft hiss of the flood from the moment they ducked under the canopy. Or perhaps it was just the sough of tree branches moving ceaselessly that lured them into the depths. Either way, it was the river they always sought out, despite the apparent aimlessness of their rides. Sometimes they rode along the bank but frequently they either jumped over or walked through it depending on how wide or deep it was at that particular point. Other occasions saw them ride along the riverbed – splashing one another, laughing, shouting. It was really the only time they allowed themselves the freedom to break the cloister-like hush that habitually shrouded them.

January transitioned smoothly into February and, with the changing of the months, Estella realised that she was changing too. She woke up looking forward to the day ahead since each was filled with potential instead of monotony. When she opened her curtains, the weather appeared to be better even though it was still generally quite cool and wet. Her whole body felt physically lighter and the jobs around the farm became easier. She suddenly had twice the energy she was used to having and, though she was working harder to fit in her visits to Ellendale, she wasn't half as tired. It was as if her system was suddenly flooded with strength and vitality. But when she paused to think about it, she couldn't decide whether it was her return to riding or the connection she was forging with Ivan that was the source of her newfound happiness.

Yet, despite this lightness, there were other aspects of her life which were still the same, if not markedly worse. For starters, Graeme, continued to drink. The politeness and restraint he had shown at Christmas was an anomaly rather than the turning over of a new leaf. Once the first month arrived, he returned to the pub and stayed there. The siblings' interaction was again limited to a few shared meals a week – of which Graeme ate very little – and one passing the other on their way in or out. And there was no point in trying to start a conversation with him since he inevitably turned snappish and defensive.

With Austin, on the other hand, she would have been pleased if things had gone back to the way they were. But they didn't. Since the disastrous end to their shared dinner, she had heard nothing from him. He didn't even return to table tennis after the winter break. It was Marion Ward, the practice secretary, who rang to apologetically deliver the news to Estella that her brother wouldn't be able to bring her to training.

"He'd ring you himself but he's that busy what with Mr Shannon being off he just doesn't have time."

It was the first Estella had heard of the practice's head vet not working. "Has he been off long?" she asked. She had

265

known Tommy Shannon for as long as she could remember and even as a child he had seemed like an old man. When her father co-owned the practice, it was Tommy who had been the senior partner. He was definitely getting on but he seemed to take everything at such a measured pace he had never needed to slow down. Until now, apparently.

"You mean you haven't heard? He hasn't worked since the start of December. He'd had a lump on the side of his neck for a few months that I kept telling him to get seen to but it wasn't until he couldn't do up his shirt collars that he went to the doctor. Been in and out of hospital ever since. Had the lump removed, of course. But he's still not right. I'm surprised Austin didn't tell you."

Estella was too. She was, in fact, quite hurt by the omission. Austin always told her so much about his work – the calvings, the stitching, the injections and infections. He relished the details of each case and exulted in the retelling. So why had he kept silent on the illness of his closest work colleague and their father's friend? She couldn't understand it.

It was Rebecca Aylward who offered a credible explanation.

"Well, maybe telling you would just make it too real," she said at table tennis when Estella told her about Austin's silence. "Maybe he sees Mr Shannon as a kind of father figure and, having lost one, perhaps it's just easier for him to pretend that everything's all right so he doesn't have to think about Mr Shannon being ill."

Estella could see her point. She had done the same thing herself up until recently by not talking about Reg. Every time she did, it hurt and brought his death back to her with visceral clarity. Only now was she capable of speaking his name and not having to swallow a lump in her throat.

Edgar Chapman was, of course, devastated to lose the club's best player. He couldn't seem to understand that the animals really did require the ministrations of a vet and wouldn't just 'manage' without Austin's attentions. For the first few weeks, he badgered Estella, begging her to speak to her brother. Though Estella laughed it off at first then got angry with Edgar's constant pestering, it wasn't until Ivan very abruptly told Chapman to leave her alone that he eventually desisted. And though she was grateful for Ivan's intervention, she was irritated that it had taken his involvement to silence Edgar. If she wanted to be braver, she had to defend herself.

However, she did enjoy having Ivan there to stand up for her. She enjoyed lots of things now she had Ivan there to share them with. The more time she spent with him, the more she struggled to fathom how he was almost twenty-nine yet still unmarried. And why was it that *she* was the one he held hands with? Why did he now steal kisses from *her*? Because they kissed – daily – and she glowed with pleasure at the remembrance of each and every one. How he whispered compliments to her lips and marvelled over the striking combination of her 'bay' hair and blue eyes. But why had he taken a shine to her? Why not the likes of Dolly Greer?

Again, it was Rebecca who offered an answer when a red-faced Estella stutteringly wondered aloud at his bachelorhood.

"Well, he's never met a girl whose interests are so similar to his own. How many girls your age do you know that can talk about riding and breeding and caring for horses?

Honestly, Stella, I've never seen him talk so much to a girl in his entire life. He doesn't even talk to me as much as he talks to you. And, of course, he got plenty of attention back home but he was never that interested in the girls that liked him. He always got bored and ended up breaking their hearts. Not that he's going to do that to you!" she said quickly, seeing the sudden panic on her friend's face. "He won't do that, Stella. Honestly. With you it's different. And besides, if he *did* do anything wrong – which he won't! – he'd have me to deal with." She put her hands on her hips and reshaped her features into what was no doubt meant to be a severe mien.

All her expression did was make Estella laugh. But she did feel more secure in the relationship after Rebecca's reassurances.

However, all the reassurance in the world would not have given her the courage to face her next challenge: Sunday lunch with Edna Aylward.

When Ivan invited her, the look on her face made him guffaw. "It's only my mother," he snorted, "not the hangman."

She had tried to laugh off his teasing. But deep down, the memory of the cold disapproving aura that emanated from Mrs Aylward on the occasions Estella had met her was enough to make her fearful. It didn't matter that she would have the support of both Ivan and Rebecca. If their mother took against her, she didn't know what she would do. She didn't want to cause tension between the family but, on a much more basic level, she just wanted to be liked. Mrs Aylward had raised two of Estella's favourite people and she wanted her approval. Plus, she was already secretly hoping that she might one day be able think of herself as a member of their family. And the last thing she wanted to do was swap one family suffused with hostility for another.

It was Dolly she turned to for advice on this occasion since Ivan and Rebecca were predisposed to laugh off the apparent standoffishness of their mother. They just couldn't see the situation from the perspective of an outsider. Dolly could. And knew exactly how to respond appropriately.

"Edna Aylward!" she squawked. "You've got to go to her house and share her kitchen and ... *Edna Aylward*! Lord help you, Stell." She shook her head and patted her friend sympathetically on the shoulder.

"I know." Estella grimaced. "Any advice?"

"Don't do anything stupid?"

"Really, Doll, I think I'd worked out that much myself, thanks. Come on! You've met a few mammies in your time. What should I do?"

"You make me sound promiscuous," Dolly answered, affronted. "I've only met three mammies in my time."

"Three more than me then. So I'll bow to your superior knowledge."

"Right. How to make a good impression on a prospective mother-in-law. *Hmm* ... Dress well for starters," she said, glancing up and down at Estella's trouser-clad legs. "First impressions, you know. And are you going to bring her something?"

"I don't know." Estella chewed her lip. "I was wondering should I buy her a present or bake something or give her some jam or ...? I don't know!"

Dolly cocked her head, thinking. "Don't buy anything.

That's too extravagant. You don't want to look like you're trying too hard because then she'll wonder what you're trying to hide –"

"Dolly!"

"What? It's true. I'd wonder what you were trying to compensate for if you gave me something really expensive. *Anyway*," she said loudly, talking over Estella's attempted protest, "I'm not sure I'd bring her baking. I've heard she's a very good baker herself so it might be hard to impress her that way. I'd say bring her some of your jam. You make good jam and it's a practical gift and you won't be going in empty-handed. And," she added, "it'll show you can cook so if you end up looking after her son, at least he won't starve."

"He won't starve because I can make jam?" Estella said sceptically. "I've heard of man not being able to survive on bread alone – but jam alone?"

"True," Dolly agreed. "But if you can make jam, that shows you know how a stove works so that'd suggest to me that you might just – *just* – be able to cook."

"Just."

"That's the spirit," Dolly said cheerfully. "Make sure she knows you'll make a good wife."

Estella looked glum. "I'm not sure I'll ever be able to convince her of that."

"Rather you than me," Dolly replied, not without sympathy. "Gosh, I'm glad my Roy's mother is over the water in England. I likely won't have to worry about any of this stuff. By the time I meet her, it'll be too late for her to change his mind."

"Aren't you lucky," Estella muttered.

Chapter 24

Though she always took care to look neat and presentable for church, Estella dressed with exceeding precision on this particular Sunday in late February since she was going to the Aylwards straight afterwards. Dolly had helped her choose a burgundy dress that was pretty but not too fancy and not too new-looking either – 'We don't want her to think you set too much store by clothes, after all.' There were three jars of jam – blackberry, raspberry and plum – filling the bottom of her handbag so that there was hardly room for her prayer book, hanky and purse.

By the time she wanted to leave for church, Graeme still hadn't surfaced. It was an increasingly frequent occurrence. His waking hours seemed to be travelling further and further around the face of the clock as he arrived home in the early hours and slept late. She had hoped he would give her a lift to the village to save her good clothes from the wet spatters of bike wheels. Standing in the kitchen with the strap of her handbag digging into her shoulder, she swithered about borrowing his car. But he didn't like her taking it in case he 'had need of it'. Also, she supposed Mrs

Aylward might think her hoity-toity if she turned up to their house in her own car. And that wouldn't do at all. Bike it was, then.

Estella sat with Dolly and her family for the service. When she had walked in, Dolly had surveyed her from head to foot then offered an approving nod. And once the last note of the last hymn had been sung, she had squeezed her friend's hand, whispered 'Good luck!' and winked. Though grateful, Estella was so nervous she barely acknowledged her kindness.

When everyone stood up to leave, she allowed herself to turn and search the congregation for Ivan. She worried that he would leave without saying anything to her. She didn't know why she wanted him to say anything since all the arrangements for lunch had already been made. But she still ached for his reassurance – a look, a smile, a nod, anything. So much for being brave. However, as she stepped out of the church into the grey day to shake the vicar's hand, her eyes sought and found him.

Ivan had managed to find the only shaft of sunlight in the entire graveyard. Standing in front of a youthful evergreen, he squinted in the brightness that chose him above all the other apparently pious souls who trod the path away from the churchyard. How was it he had chosen her, she wondered. With his strong shoulders, notable height and athletic physique, there was hardly anyone immune to his looks. And he was hers! She marvelled at the unruly brown hair curled in waves over his head and shot through with chestnut streaks. She glanced across the graveyard to follow his distant gaze but could see nothing of note. He seemed to

272

be lost in thought with his hands clamped on his cloth cap and his feet planted firmly on the gravel walkway. Was he thinking about her? No, she thought, he wasn't that shallow. There was no way she was his ending and beginning. There was no way she filled his thoughts as much as he filled hers.

"Lost?" she asked, walking up to him.

"*Hmm?*" Though he turned his head, he looked through her.

"In thought," she clarified.

"Oh!" His face suddenly split into a luminous, wide grin. "Sorry," he added as he discreetly took her hand in his and threaded their fingers together. "All set?"

She nodded.

"Right. Come on then."

They climbed the path up to the gate where she found Ivan's bicycle propped against the wall beside her own. "You cycled?" He usually drove the car with his mother and sister.

"Foal born over at Ellendale last night. It's early and not too bright. Couldn't figure out how to suckle by itself." He rubbed his face and, now that he was out of the direct sunlight, she saw the shadows under his eyes. "I've been with it all night and morning. Wasn't even sure I'd make it to church. But," he grinned, "Mammy insisted I bring my good clothes with me so that I could change and come straight to the service. No excuses, eh?"

Estella was secretly quite glad of his mother's intervention. "How's the foal?"

"Better. Sucked at least. Left Danny Fearon to keep an eye. Anyway, being late means I can cycle back home with you."

273

She relaxed a little then. He was going to the house with her. She wouldn't have to ride there alone. She wouldn't have to turn into the driveway or approach the door alone. It all seemed so much more achievable when she had him beside her. In the same way she was now able to ride some more of the horses at Ellendale and not just Hedy – because he encouraged her, had faith in her. Though she was uncomfortable with her dependence, she knew that, right now, she needed him.

There was no knocking on the door when they arrived. Ivan walked straight into the kitchen and they were hit by the smell of cooked meat and another sweetness that Estella couldn't quite pinpoint. Edna was there with an apron around her waist and Rebecca was helping Harry set the table as the little boy counted all the pieces of cutlery clutched like a shiny metal bouquet in his pudgy fist. It all seemed so warm, comforting, domestic. The cosiness of the kitchen helped with its dark wooden cupboards and welcoming heat.

However, standing just inside the door, Estella did feel panic rise in her chest as Mrs Aylward approached. It was all she could do not to back away. But then she felt Ivan's hand spread wide on her spine and it was as if the strength in his body leaked through his fingertips into hers. She stood taller, more confident, and met his mother with a smile and a proffered hand.

"Hello, Stella." Mrs Aylward's hand was damp from washing as she shook Estella's. She smiled but struggled to hold eye-contact.

Wondering if her smile was too bright, too forceful, too

much, Estella faltered. "Hello, Mrs Aylward. *Um ... um* this ... there's a lovely smell. Really lovely."

"Oh, it's just the usual roast." Mrs Aylward turned and began laying out plates on the end of the table, still not looking up. "Nothing fancy. Take off your coat and sit down there. It'll be ready in a minute."

Ivan silently took the shoulders of her jacket and she stepped out of it. But as she did so, she heard a faint glassy clink in her handbag. "*Oh!*" Her shrill exclamation made everyone look up. She had forgotten the jam and now that she remembered she wondered how one handed over such gifts. "I brought ..." She hastily removed the pots from her bag and awkwardly placed them on the table since Mrs Aylward now had a roasting dish in her hands. "I brought these. I ... thought you might – blackberry, raspberry and plum. Maybe you'd like them. I don't know."

Mrs Aylward looked directly at her. Seeming to sense Estella's desperate need for approval, her lips tightened in a smile. "That's very kind of you, Stella. But you didn't have to do that. Not at all. But thank you. I don't get plum jam very often and it's one of my favourites."

"We have loads. We've a plum tree in the garden and I always use them for jam otherwise the wasps get them."

And with that, they stumbled into the relatively safe territory of jam-making and preserving fruit and vegetables for the winter. Soon Estella realised that Edna Aylward wasn't expressing disapproval when she looked away. She was, in fact, very shy. She preferred to listen to the conversation of her children rather than offer comments herself. It seemed strange that such a taciturn woman would have two such verbose children. Yet, when they did get her to join the conversation, she did so willingly. It turned out she knew a great deal about the Leclercs' horses even though it appeared she had never seen any of them.

"Ivan tells me all about his day every evening when he comes home," she explained to Estella. "So I feel like I know all the animals and the people too. And lately I've been hearing everything about your ride-outs together too."

Estella felt the heat rise in her face. She hoped Mrs Aylward didn't hear *everything*. Glancing sideways at Ivan, she saw him biting the inside of his lip, eyes glittering. She looked away but suddenly felt the pressure of his hand on her thigh. Instinctively, she kicked out at him and felt her foot connect. There was an almighty bang. All of them jumped except Ivan who pitched forward, having walloped his knee on the underside of the table.

"Are you all right?" his mother asked concerned.

"Fine," he said through gritted teeth. "Just got a sudden pain in my ankle. Like I'd been kicked. Very strange."

Estella didn't dare catch anyone's eye though she could feel the burn of Rebecca's bright orbs on the crown of her head. "This trifle is lovely, Mrs Aylward," she said loudly. "Best I've ever tasted."

"Thank you, dear," she answered as under the table her son carefully stood on Estella's foot.

Chapter 25

Estella insisted on helping to clear up after the lunch was over, despite Mrs Aylward's protestations that she was their guest. However, Estella held firm and was rewarded for her resolve with a warm though tight-lipped smile and some leftover trifle to take home in a jam jar. They all migrated to the sitting room after that, where Estella sat on the rug in front of an open fire with Rebecca and Harry. He had shyly requested that she help him with a jigsaw and she had, of course, readily agreed. She had very little experience with small children but if all children were as well-mannered and sweet as he was, she might quite like them. Sitting on his mother's crossed legs, he carefully sorted through the pieces in considered silence. He turned them all the right way up and separated the edges onto another section of the rug so that what initially looked like quite a complicated jigsaw for a five-year-old, now looked to be well within his capabilities. In fact, Estella wondered why she had been asked to help in the first place since he seemed to have it all under control.

"Will we make the edges?" he asked, clearly keen to have her opinion on the matter.

"That's an excellent idea."

He nodded and set to work, apologising politely when his hands collided with hers as they sought out the individual pieces. She really was very impressed by the speed with which the puzzle took shape. At one point, she raised her eyebrows to Rebecca who shrugged and rubbed her son's arm lovingly. This was a version of Ivan's sister that she didn't often see: the mother. Of course Rebecca glowed with pride whenever his name was mentioned but Estella hardly ever saw them together. It was heartening to bear witness to such a loving bond.

Periodically, Estella glanced at Mrs Aylward and Ivan who were sitting in armchairs reading the Sunday papers. A few times when she glanced up, she caught Ivan staring at her. He would wink or smile then shake out his paper and begin to read again. However, after about half an hour, when she looked up, she found both Ivan and his mother were fast asleep. Catching Rebecca's eye, Estella jerked her head in the others' direction.

Rebecca rolled her eyes. "Regular occurrence," she said quietly.

They were silent for a while, watching Harry painstakingly fill in the blank picture.

"Have you ever been to a Hunt Ball?" Rebecca suddenly asked in a low voice.

Estella glanced up. There was a slight flush in her friend's cheeks.

"Howard Anstruther's asked me to go with him." The pink blush intensified.

Estella grinned. She knew that Anstruther had been *very*

attentive at New Year. But since then, his interest had continued. He had visited Rebecca at home once and also telephoned the house to speak to her on a number of occasions. However, Rebecca confided that her mother was very unhappy with Howard's persistence. She simply didn't trust his good intentions. "Mammy doesn't trust anyone," Rebecca said crossly, one evening at table tennis. "Not after —" She had stopped short, then muttered, "If anyone should be suspicious of a man, it's me," but it seemed to be directed more to herself than anyone listening.

"That's very good of him. The Hunt Ball's always good fun," Estella said mildly, knowing what was coming next.

"Do you think I should go?"

"It's a good night out. Very posh."

"That's not what I'm asking."

"I know it's not what you're asking."

"Stella ..."

"Rebecca ..."

Rebecca, narrowed her eyes and pouted.

Estella did the same, trying to mirror her friend's irritated expression.

Despite herself, Rebecca's lips quirked. "Do you think I should go?" she asked again, bluntly.

Estella sighed. "That's up to you. I can't decide for you."

"I want to go. But I don't want people to start talking."

It seemed an odd thing to worry about. But then there was something Rebecca wasn't telling her – Estella was sure of that. "People will always talk. And if there's nothing to talk about, they'll make something up."

Frowning, Rebecca idly stroked her son's blond hair. "I

wish they wouldn't. If it were you, would you go?"

"I am going." The previous week, Henry Leclerc had come striding across to where she and Ivan were dismounting two Ellendale horses and declared both of them would be coming to the Hunt Ball next month. He had bought a whole table-worth of tickets and they were the first guests he invited to fill it. "Mr Leclerc wasn't to be argued with."

Rebecca nodded and carefully glanced at her mother. "Howard's been invited by Mr Leclerc too. So, to keep the numbers even, Howard asked me."

"To keep the numbers even?" That didn't sound particularly romantic at all. But maybe that was Howard's way of encouraging Rebecca to come without apparent amorous intentions. "Sounds safe enough. And you'll be on the table with Ivan and me. People might talk but they probably won't say very much if you're with your brother."

"I thought that too. But then I didn't know if Ivan was going because, well, I didn't want to mention it." She glanced at her mother again. "I don't want Mammy to get angry or upset over it. Her attitude is just 'keep your head down and get on with it'. But I ... I don't want to live the rest of my life like that. Alone with Harry. I want to *live* a little. And I do love a good party," she added with a mischievous grin.

"I think you've already made up your mind."

"But if you thought I shouldn't go, then I wouldn't."

Estella snorted. "You know I won't tell you not to go. It'd be lovely if you were there. But I'm not going to say you should go. That's your decision."

"You just don't want to say yay or nay in case Mammy

hears," Rebecca hissed. "Not after getting in her good books."

"No, that's not it." Though it was a little. "It wouldn't really make her *that* angry, would it?"

Again, Rebecca checked her mother was still sleeping. "I think ... she'd be disappointed more than angry. I know she's only trying to protect me. And Harry. But sometimes there's a fine line between protecting and smothering someone, you know?"

Estella didn't know. The only person protecting her was herself. It was she who had asphyxiated her own mind and body for the last number of years. She found it thrilling – invigorating even – to finally have someone like Ivan who could help her snap the choking bands of her restraints. She had cloistered herself for too long and now it was like the world was expanding exponentially before her. A future seemed possible. But it seemed Rebecca was still in the midst of her insulated existence. She was yet to break free.

Unbidden, the illustration from a long-forgotten children's book flashed into the forefront of Estella's mind. It was the picture of a beautiful brunette sitting in the window of an impossibly high tower, her plaited hair hanging down the rough stones of the outer wall. Below stood a liveried knight. She couldn't remember the exact details but she knew that the knight – she always liked the idea of knights because they rode horses – had rescued the maiden but, in the process, had fallen from the tower and been blinded by thorns. Were Ivan and Howard their rescuing knights? Both men rode horses, at least. And she and Rebecca lived lives of seclusion. But what would be the consequences of these rescue missions for the men, she wondered. Would some great tragedy befall them as it did the knight from the story? Would they suffer for their good deeds? Was something bad going to happen to Ivan because of her? After all, something bad had happened to many of the people she loved.

Stop it, she told herself sternly. Comparing her own life to that of knights and maidens in fairy tales was utterly stupid. Reality was not black and white, good and evil. And she and Rebecca had much more agency than some poor girl marooned at the zenith of a bloody great tower. They made their own decisions. And nothing was going to happen to Ivan. Or Howard. Estella was not cursed. She had just been deeply unlucky in her life. And besides, there was that superstition Henry Leclerc had told them – about seeing a grey horse with your lover being a good omen. Yes, she would focus on *that* rather than some silly story about distressed damsels saved by gaily dressed nobles.

Both Mrs Aylward and Ivan woke for tea at four o'clock. Though she was invited to stay for the rest of the evening, Estella declined. There were jobs that needed doing around the yard at home. Once she had a cup of tea and an iced bun, she said her goodbyes to three-quarters of the family (while receiving an invitation to visit again) and left with Ivan who was going to check on the foal.

The evening air had turned chilly so, rather than cycle, they took his car which wasn't really much better since the air whistled up through the gaps in the floor. It was even colder when they arrived in the yard at Ellendale with the wind swirling around the enclosed square. Ivan shivered as he stepped out of the car.

"Should've changed at home," he said as he crossed to the tack room. Estella automatically followed him into the shelter. "Coming to watch?" he asked as he grabbed his freezing yard clothes from on top of a saddle and turned to find her just behind him.

"*Oh!*" she squealed, pirouetting on the spot as she covered her eyes. "Sorry!"

He sniggered behind her. "You *can* watch, you know. I don't mind."

"*Um ...*" Politeness made her keep her back turned. But then something stirred in the pit of her stomach. It felt like butterflies. She shifted from foot to foot. She wanted to look. She wanted to see him – to see all of him. Her shoulders turned involuntarily – almost. No. She couldn't look.

"It's just skin, Stell."

She turned. He had paused in the process of donning his work trousers. Beneath the tails of his shirt were two elongated shanks, lumpy with jutting bones and protruding muscles. Hair darker than that of his head smattered the white and blue-veined skin. They were an athlete's legs. She managed to take all of this in during the brief moment when he hopped on one foot to whip his trouser-leg on. Seeing him fully clothed, she felt a sudden surge of disappointment which turned to a fluttering thrill when he took hold of the back of his shirt and jumper and stripped both off in one go. Her stomach dropped as she drank in his pale torso with a dusting of dark hair over his chest. Her eyes swept up the length of his brown, freckled arms to the point just above his elbow where tanned skin faded to white. She had similar lines on her own arms. Gliding further up over the curving

283

lines of his broad shoulders, she saw they were knotted with strength and stippled with goose bumps. The muscles of his chest were lightly shadowed but not bulging. They clung to his ribcage – flat, hard and slightly ridged where they met his breastbone. And then it was all gone as he dived into his shirt and work jumper.

"*Ugh!* That's c-c-cold," he chattered, performing a funny kind of loose-limbed shiver as he hopped from foot to foot and threw on a coat. He looked ridiculous.

Estella burst into a fit of giggles. "If you dance like that at the Hunt Ball, they'll throw you out!"

"And you'd be coming with me," he said as he rushed towards her and swept her into his arms.

With her feet suddenly several inches from the ground, he carried her out the door as she squealed and smacked his shoulders. "Don't! You'll ruin my good jacket!" she cried.

But he didn't let go. Instead, he put her down and kissed her hard on the mouth.

Her eyes flew wide open. Before, their kisses had always been chaste, sometimes slightly awkward pecks. Nothing worthy of note to anyone except Estella who had counted and cherished all of them over nearly two months. After each one, she had glowed with childish happiness and smiled stupidly. But this one didn't make her smile. When he pulled away, her face was white with shock – apart from her lips. Her lips were a deep, lusty red. However, as soon as their gazes met, the colour from her lips began to leak into her cheeks. His eyes shone black, his pupils dilated. She was shocked, exhilarated, jittery. She had stopped hitting him and her hands were now pressed flat against his shoulders. He

284

kissed her again – hungrily, insistently – and this time she kissed him back, stretching up on her tiptoes to reach him.

He broke away, breathing fast. She was breathless too but when she looked into his face, she realised he wasn't concentrating on her at all. Instead, his focus was over her shoulder. She turned to see Danny Fearon crossing the yard with a much too studied air of oblivion.

"He didn't …" She couldn't finish the sentence. She was too mortified at the thought that the old hand had seen their embrace.

"I'm sure he did," Ivan said nonchalantly, leaning up against the doorframe of the tack room. "Don't think Danny'll mind though. Probably livened up his day a bit."

She slapped him in the chest and he cringed away, bring his arms up to protect himself from further attack. *"Don't!"* she hissed. "It's embarrassing!" She glanced over her shoulder to find Danny had disappeared into a stable.

"Why? It's not like everyone doesn't know we're courting. Am I not allowed to give you a kiss every now and again?"

"It's not *that*. It's just … I don't want people seeing is all."

"Are you ashamed about kissing me?"

"No! Don't be stupid! It's just … it's just … *private.*"

"So you don't mind kissing in private?"

"No."

He leaned down to her so that she could feel the tickle of his breath on her cheek. "Then we'll have to find somewhere private."

She stretched up, placing one hand on his chest and the other on his arm. Her lips grazed his ear. "Maybe," she whispered. Their eyes flashed with unspoken promise for a moment before she turned away and headed towards the foaling box. "Come on. Let's have a look at this gangly-legged wee baby."

When she looked over the half door, she was met by the wary scrutiny of a chestnut mare with a white flash down her nose and three white socks. A tiny foal with three matching white socks was half hidden under its mother's distended belly. Estella grinned as she heard the even rhythm of voracious sucking. Ivan stood close, one hand either side of her as he rested them on the top of the door, encasing her between his arms.

"Looks to be doing well," she commented, leaning back against his chest. She had given up protecting her good coat by now. Besides, his chest wasn't particularly dirty. It was the cuffs of his clothing that seemed to collect most of the muck.

"You wouldn't have said that last night," he muttered. "Weak as a kitten. Amazing how they can pick up so quick. But we're not out of the woods yet."

"I know. Daddy always said he had a love-hate relationship with foals. He loved his own but any time he saw someone else's it usually meant they were sick."

Ivan shifted, placing his hands over hers and resting his chin on her head. She felt it move as he spoke. "Do you know that's the first time you've mentioned something your father said all day. When you were talking at lunch, you weren't relying on his opinions. You had your own."

She shrugged. "I've been trying ever since you said it to me. To be ... braver when I'm talking to folk. Anyway – I don't suppose your mammy would be that interested in

Daddy's opinions on treating scabies in sheep or such like." Ivan laughed. "True! Come on," he said, kissing her hair. "The sooner I get done here, the sooner we get in out of this cold. Although I think Danny might have beaten me to most of the jobs."

"If you're not careful, he'll have your job," she teased.

"No chance," he scoffed, adding confidently, "I'm irreplaceable."

"I'll *replace* you in a minute, ye cocky whatsit," she muttered, pushing past him as he guffawed at her reply.

Ivan spent the next ten minutes drifting around the yard from stable to stable, checking everything was as it should be before declaring that Danny had, indeed, beaten him to almost every one of the evening's tasks. Estella followed him around the yard talking about nothing other than horses – as was their wont – and it wasn't until they were heading back to the car that Danny miraculously reappeared to tip his cap to both of them as he pushed off down the lane on his bike.

It was dusk when Ivan's headlights swept the walls of Robin Hill. The darkness and silence of the small square of cobblestones told Estella that there was no one there. It wasn't until she had climbed out of the car and slammed the door shut that an accusatory bray from Beryl told Estella how neglected the animals felt.

"*I know, I know!*" she called.

"What can I do?" Ivan asked, standing by the car as she hurried to the house to change.

"Feed Beryl before she throws a tantrum."

When she came back out in yard clothes, she found Ivan

287

scratching the donkey's poll. "Tantrum averted," he grinned. "What now?"

"Would you mind doing the pigs? There's a bucket of slops in the barn. And close in the chickens. Actually, could you collect the eggs while you're at it?"

She was almost finished milking the lone cow when Ivan arrived with a bucketful of eggs. Estella took one look at his shining, happy face and turned away, hiding her grin in the cow's flank. "You'd think you'd laid them yourself, you're so chuffed."

"I got pecked twice collecting them!" he told her gleefully – a little boy once again. "They're vicious little beggars." There was a pause. "I expect a kiss for my efforts, by the way."

She screwed her head around and viewed him critically. "*Do you* now?" She finished milking the cow and removed the pail from beneath her feet.

Standing, she stretched up on her toes to plant a slow seductive kiss on his lips. When she pulled away, he followed her down and stole a second kiss.

"*Oi!*" she admonished. "No overcharging!"

He grinned impishly but didn't reply.

"Come on then," she sighed, "let's go inside out of the cold and wash your eggs."

Picking up her bucket of milk, she turned out the light and they were momentarily plunged into total darkness until their eyes adjusted and they were able to pick out the black and grey lines of the yard in the shadowy light. As they stepped outside, Estella noted how everything was washed of its cleanliness and warm colours by the dusk, but she was still able to see the corners of the square and make sure Ivan had closed all the doors he was supposed to.

"Checking up on me, are you?"

"I do the same every night myself, just making sure I've done everything. It wouldn't do for Beryl to get into the feed shed and gorge herself. Not only would it make her sick, it'd be a terrible waste of food."

"Practical to the last, you are," Ivan replied, bumping his hip against hers. "You'll make someone a right good wife someday."

Though her stomach somersaulted, her steps didn't falter. "Will I now?" she said lightly. "I suppose he'll be a right lucky fella then, won't he?"

"Oh, aye …" he said with equal casualness but she could see he was fighting a smile.

She was already removing her coat and hat as she opened the back door, realising she hadn't stoked the Aga or turned on the light before doing the milking. She had been too eager to get back out to Ivan. Her boots were also removed in short order and she had just turned on the light when she stopped dead.

The throaty gasp she made didn't reach Ivan who was still unlacing his boots. However, when she heard his footsteps, she turned and blocked the doorway, her hand held aloft to prevent him coming any further.

"What?" he asked, smile fading as he took in the sudden wild look in her eyes. "*What*?" He stepped forward but her rigid hand was solid against his chest.

"Don't."

"Stella, what is it?"

There was a brief pause. "Graeme's in there." She spoke

through tight lips. His car must still be outside the pub, she thought.

"And, what, I can't come in if he's here?" Ivan tried to maintain a blithe tone but Estella knew him well enough to hear his annoyance.

"It's not that. He's ... he's in no fit state to be seen." She dropped her gaze, ashamed.

"Let me see."

"No! Ivan –"

He pushed past her into the cool kitchen and stopped, surveying the picture before him.

His face was completely neutral as his gaze roved from the shattered plate on the floor and the sad fragments of food that had congealed on the tiles to the man at the table. His upper body stretched the width of the long, narrow table, his arms reaching towards something that was not there. His head had disappeared behind his shoulder, his face turned towards the Aga at the other end of the room. And, standing sentinel over the entire tableau was an empty whiskey bottle, a foot away from Graeme's right hand and ready to roll off the edge of the table if it was given the slightest push.

"Sorry."

Ivan dragged his eyes away from the eldest Frayne to look at the youngest who stood beside him, grim-faced. "What?"

"I'm sorry. You shouldn't have to see this. I'll – here, give me those eggs. You go on home. I'll ... I'll deal with him. This." She reached blindly for his bucket but he pulled it beyond her grasp.

"I'm not leaving you here with him," he answered bluntly and a little too loudly.

Her head snapped up, panic unmistakeable in her eyes.

He took a breath, clearly attempting to quell his anger. "You're not dealing with this on your own." He stood firm, plainly not going anywhere. "And there's absolutely no need for you to apologise. Not for him. This isn't your doing, Stella. It's his." He threw a look of pure loathing at the body slumped across the kitchen table. "All his."

"Well … actually, I was just going to clean up around him. Leave him where he is. I find that's the best way to deal with him. He usually wakes up at some point and either heads out or goes up to bed, depending on the time."

"Usually? How often does this happen?"

It was several seconds before she carefully answered, "More often lately."

"Has something happened?"

"Not that I know of," she said. "Mind you … if something had happened, he'd never say anything to me."

Ivan nodded then headed over to the sink with his bucket of eggs. "Do you want to wash these? I'll clean up around Sleeping Beauty."

Estella tittered. It was either that or she cried. "No, you do the eggs. I'll have this tidied in no time."

However, the first thing she did was go over and stoke the Aga. Dominated as it was by Graeme's prostrate form, the room was oppressive enough without the physical chill. Once that was roaring nicely, she filled a basin with tepid water and set about cleaning the floor. She did all of it as quietly as she could and was pleased that Ivan wasn't disturbing the peace either. His presence gave her a sense of true calm in what was usually quite a tense situation. She had an ally if Graeme woke and it made her fell immeasurably safer. She didn't *think* her brother would do anything to her. He never had in the past. But there was no telling what state he would be in once he regained consciousness. And an addled brain could do all sorts of things to a person. Even so, with or without Ivan, it was better to tread lightly.

As she scraped up the remains of his Sunday dinner – peas, potatoes and gravy – she snorted. "Doesn't say much for what he thinks of my cooking when this is where it ends up."

Ivan turned to see her crouched on the floor with her cloth and basin, smiling up at him. His look of concern turned into one of mock seriousness. He sucked air in through his teeth. "*Hmm.* I may have to rethink my assessment of you making a good wifey if that's the standard of the food. Some poor fella might starve."

Estella covered her mouth with the back of her hand to stifle her chuckle. However, she glanced up at the motionless form above her. She might feel safe, but she still didn't want to wake him. Finished cleaning, she stood and carefully backed away. She would have to buy some new crockery next time she was in town. There had been several breakages – whether accidental or intentional – over the last year. Enough to mean that if he broke one more plate, they would have to take it in turns to eat their dinner.

"Am I going to get one of these eggs for my supper, then?" Ivan stood expectantly by the draining board, leaning over his eggs with the covetous pride of a thieving fox.

"Maybe a boiled egg and some toast?"

"You don't boil fresh eggs," she told him. "They don't separate that well from the inner membrane of the shell. You're better with slightly older ones for that job."

"But I want *my* eggs," he whinged playfully.

"Come back in a few days and you can have one of yours," she replied, standing on tiptoe once again and kissing his cheek.

Just as swiftly, he wrapped one arm around her waist and kissed her on the lips with a smile. She could get used to this, she thought. The warmth of him, the strength of his body pressed up against hers. The slight bristliness of his stubbly chin and cheeks. The gentle yet insistent press of his soft lips against hers. It consumed her, made her fingertips tingle. Her body flooded with heat as if his affection became liquid where their mouths touched and trickled down through every artery and vein in her system. When he eventually pulled away with a little groan, she saw the jewel-bright shine in his eyes once again.

Returning to the room, both glanced guiltily at Graeme. But he remained oblivious.

"So I've got to come *back* if I want one of *my* eggs?" Ivan murmured.

"They're actually *my* eggs. Or my hens, at least."

He shook his head. "Finders keepers. Anyway – are you sure this isn't some sort of ploy to keep me coming? Promising to feed me *my* eggs if I come back."

"Of course it is," she replied blandly. "Because clearly there's nothing else here worth coming back f–" she squealed as he poked her in the waist *"Don't!"*

293

They frantically shushed one another as Graeme shifted and grumbled but mercifully remained asleep.

Estella extended her arm, pointing to the hall door. "Go into the sitting room on the right before you get us both in trouble," she hissed while fighting a smile. "You can light the fire to keep us warm."

Ivan leaned into her. "I can think of another way of keeping us warm."

Her breath caught in her throat. She knew what he meant. And she knew there was no way she would allow it to happen. She narrowed her eyes and shoved him away. "No chance," she said determinedly. She wasn't going to admit to him that the idea was tempting. One of them at least had to remain sensible. She just wished it wasn't her. She was scared she wasn't strong enough to be the responsible one.

However, he seemed to sense her unease. Wordlessly, he wrapped his arms around her shoulders, kissed her hair then stepped away.

"I'll light the fire," he told her before disappearing into the sitting room.

By the time Estella had boiled the eggs and buttered the bread for supper, Ivan had the fire going. However, there was still a damp chill to the room so she laid out their modest spread on the hearthrug. For the second time that day, she sat in front of a fire with an Aylward, speaking in quiet tones and enjoying the apparent familiarity of the situation. In the presence of nothing other than the cheerful crackle of the fire, she allowed herself the simple pleasure of observing Ivan without having to concentrate or worry about anything else.

She watched as his eyes roved around the room and finally settled on the small group of framed family photographs on a shelf in the corner. He stood, drawn towards the most populated of the neat, black-and-white images.

"What age were you here?"

"Eight. The year before Mammy died."

"You look like such a baby. So small."

"I was tiny until I was about fourteen and then my body suddenly realised it was supposed to grow and I just shot up."

"I was the same. A proper wee fart until I was fifteen and grew a foot one summer." He turned back to the photo, leaning in. "So this is the famous Reg Frayne. Austin's very like him. And Graeme not at all."

"He's like my mother's side of the family. The Austins. She was Prudie Austin before she married Daddy."

He nodded, understanding. "And that's Joy beside your mother."

"She was always beside my mother." Estella got up to stand with him. "I haven't looked at this in years. Mammy had an awful time trying to keep Joy quiet in the photographer's studio. She always got upset going somewhere unfamiliar. Mammy was so angry with Daddy for organising it. Said it would upset Joy too much. Daddy just said he wanted a picture of the whole family together. Usually he would give in when Mammy got cross. But not that time. He was adamant." She reached out to the glass, touching her child-self. "I was so upset when it was taken. We all were."

"You don't look very happy all right."

"That was the fashion. You were supposed to look serious. Dignified, I suppose. Anyway, he couldn't have got us to smile even if he tried. A few seconds after the photographer took it, Joy kicked off. Daddy almost forgot to pay he was in such a rush to get out. I almost think the photographer would have let him too, just to get rid of us."

"You don't look like anyone," he added, stroking the hair of the child in the photo with his fingertip.

"Do you think so? People used to always say Austin and I were very alike when we were little."

"No!"

"Maybe it was just because we were inseparable. We almost … became the same person. You couldn't have one without the other."

"What went wrong, eh?"

She had told Ivan about her falling out with Austin on Christmas Day. "Everything, I suppose. Or maybe we just grew up and became different people."

"Do you know, when I first met you, I thought you were Austin's wife."

Estella looked aghast. "No! How?"

"Because Mr Leclerc just said here's Austin and here's Stella. He never mentioned the fact that you were brother and sister. Similar age, both Fraynes. So I just assumed because you looked so different."

She shuddered but then caught her own hypocrisy. "Actually, I thought the same about you and Rebecca when you first arrived. I think most people did."

Ivan winced and looked at his feet. "Yeah, there were quite a few people who thought that. And Mammy didn't exactly do anything to correct them."

"Why not?"

Ivan turned and walked away from her. He seemed to be fascinated by every part of the room she wasn't occupying. Eventually, he turned to her. "Just ... Mammy thought the less people definitely knew about us, the better."

"Why?" Something was off. He couldn't even make eye contact.

"I – I can't. It's not for me to say. I trust you. Of course I do! But if Mammy knew I'd told you, she'd be angry with both of us."

"Angry about what?" He was scaring her with his ambiguity. "What did you do?"

"*Me?* Why'd you assume *I* did anything?"

Estella waved her hands frantically to quieten him, glancing nervously at the door to the kitchen.

"I didn't do anything," he said, striding over to her. "The whole thing's got nothing to do with me."

She saw the truth in his eyes. And her sudden panic evaporated. The fire popped and spat as they stared at one another, Ivan still on his guard.

"Okay. I believe you," she said calmly.

His shoulders slumped.

"But promise me one thing?"

"Oh?"

"That you'll tell me what's going on eventually."

"Stella, it's not –"

"For you to say. I know. But ... I'd like you to trust me enough to tell me. Eventually." He frowned and opened his mouth as if to say something but she placed two fingers on his lips to silence him. "Let's talk about something else."

They sat in front of the fire for another hour until Ivan

thought it best to go home. His mother would worry since he hadn't told her of any plans to stay out past suppertime. Also, the longer he remained at Robin Hill the more likely it was that Graeme would wake and – though Estella felt safer, calmer – there was no telling how he might react on finding another man in the house. He could be quite affable. Or he could throw something at Ivan's head. And Estella rather liked Ivan's head. So it was with theatrically exaggerated silent footsteps that they crossed back through the kitchen to the door, trying not to giggle.

"See you tomorrow?" Ivan said quietly as a blast of cold air from the yard enveloped them.

Estella threw her arms around his neck, seeking his warmth as much as his affection. "Course you will. Bye." She kissed him on the mouth. She had kissed him more today than she had any other day. Their intimacy felt easy now rather than worrying.

"Bye," he whispered, kissing her back.

Then, with a cheery wave, he was in his car and gone.

Closing the door softly, she left all their dinner things to be washed in the morning. The only concession to noise she made was opening the Aga to stoke it once again in the hope that it would stay warm all night. Then, it was simply a case of mounting the stairs and heading to bed. She moved about soundlessly, always keeping her ear cocked for any sign of movement below. However, it wasn't until much later that she was awoken by the tell-tale thuds of her brother's heavy feet on the stairs. She looked at the luminous hands of her bedside clock.

It was twenty-past three in the morning.

Chapter 26

On Monday morning, after riding at Ellendale, Estella set about cleaning out the hen house. As she scraped up droppings with a spade and swept up the straw, she smiled to herself, imagining Ivan stooping under the sloped roof as he carefully searched each corner of the dark coop for eggs. While she brushed, two hens sat in state in their boxes, one a Rhode Island red, the other a speckled Barred Rock. The red hen had a habit of finding a box with a few eggs in it and sitting to incubate them. She didn't seem to realise that was an impossibility since they didn't have a cockerel. Yet, it was better for the hen to be outside picking with the others rather than confined inside so, more often than not, Estella had to poke her with the bristly end of the sweeping brush to get her out. It was that or have her hand pecked bloody by the would-be mother.

She was just squaring up with her brush to oust the hen when she heard the cheerful ring of a bicycle bell and a '*Cooey!*' However, having committed to dislodging the chicken, she continued to slide the brush up beside the bird and hoosh her out. The hen pecked, flapped and squawked as the brush connected with her proprietary little body but Estella managed to shove her off a clutch of five eggs. She tumbled out onto the freshly cleaned floor with a particularly affronted cluck, then righted her feathers and stalked out through the hatch in as dignified a manner as she could muster. The speckled hen looked on distrustfully.

"It's all right, honey," Estella told her. "You can stay where you are."

"Are you dispatching a chicken in there or can I come in?" Dolly stood on the threshold of the coop. Monday was her day off since she worked weekends at the post office telephone exchange. Estella fought the urge to laugh when she saw the look of trepidation on her friend's face. For someone brought up on a farm, she was incredibly squeamish.

"No, just finishing up." She came out and closed the door behind her. "Come on into the house. How are you keeping?"

"Good. How was Sunday lunch?"

Estella smiled.

Dolly grinned back. "That good, eh? I was worried you'd be curled up in a ball rocking back and forth if it'd gone badly. Thought I'd come and check, you know?"

"Well, I think it was quite successful. Aside from the fact Mrs Aylward fell asleep."

"You sent her to sleep?" Dolly looked horrified. "*How?*"

"*I* didn't *send* her to sleep. We ate and then she *fell* asleep. So did Ivan."

Dolly frowned as they stopped to remove their footwear. "Bit rude, no?"

She shrugged. "Didn't mind. I spent most of the afternoon

300

talking to his sister. Howard Anstruther seems quite taken with her."

"Howard? He's too quiet," Dolly said with a swipe of her hand, dismissing him. But then her eyes took on a dreamy sheen. "Not like my Roy."

Estella turned away to role hers. "That must be a record."

"What?"

"The amount of time you've spent here without mentioning the *divine*, the *glorious* Roy Oaks. What's it been, more or less than a minute. Better than last week when you arrived and practically screamed at me '*Roy's asked me to the Hunt Ball!*' before even saying hello."

"I was excited." Dolly huffed and pouted. "I've never been before. You have. It's not something special for you. It's just … the done thing."

It was rare that Dolly brought up the difference in their situations. While her family wasn't poor, neither were they as wealthy or widely known as the Fraynes. Reg's job had given them both money and the freedom to mix with all echelons of society. It wasn't every young woman who, like Estella, got invited to Henry Leclerc's personal table at the Hunt Ball.

"I was only teasing," Estella answered rather defensively as she put the kettle on. But then she softened. "And besides, it *will* be special this year. Because you and I'll both be going."

"Ivan asked you. Knew he would."

"Actually, Mr Leclerc just shouted at us that we were both going and that was the end of it. But he shouted in a *polite* way."

Dolly laughed. "As long as you're going. I don't know that I'd be brave enough to go without you being there too."

Estella snorted in response.

"All right, I would because Roy would be there. But it'll just be so much better with you there. *And* you can help me with my dress. In fact, we can help each other. Just like old times."

In previous years, Dolly had helped Estella to make her ball dress since she was the more accomplished seamstress.

A smile began to widen across Estella's face. "Sounds like a plan."

"What about making a day of it?" Dolly suggested, already vibrating with excitement. "Go up to Dublin and have a look in Cleary's or Arnott's for some fabric. A girls' day out. How long is it since we've had one of them?"

"Long time. I haven't been in Dublin since Daddy was in hospital. 'Bout time I grow a spine and go back, I suppose," she said cheerlessly then gave herself a little shake and forced a smile. "It'll be fun, just us two … or …"

"Or? You don't want to bring Ivan, do you?" Dolly asked with a titter.

"*No*. I'm wondering …"

"*What*?"

"Well, Ivan's sister, Rebecca –"

"She's so pretty!"

"That's her. I think she's going too. Howard asked her. I wonder should we see if she'd like to come with us? It's up to you, of course. If you want it to be just us two –"

"No! Of course not! Invite her. The more the merrier!" She gave a shout of laughter. "Can you imagine all the heads

302

turning with the three of us striding along under Nelson's Pillar? We'll have all the Dubliners convinced that the countryside's filled with good-looking women."

Estella huffed. "If everyone's going to be staring at us, I think I'll stay at home."

"Oh, stop it, you!" Dolly admonished. "Even if you won't admit it or can't see it, everyone else can."

"I've a wonky nose. And freckles and marks and –"

Dolly got up and stood six inches from her face. "All I can see is my best friend. And she's just lovely. End of." She sat again and folded her arms decisively, chin out in defiance.

Estella couldn't hide her blush. "Thank you," she mumbled eventually, scuffing her heel on the tiled floor. "You're lovely too."

"Thank you," Dolly said graciously. "Now make that tea. We've got some serious planning to do."

Chapter 27

That afternoon, Estella cycled to the Aylwards to invite Rebecca on their little expedition. Though she was worried she might incur the wrath of Mrs Aylward and undo the good impression she had made, to her surprise, Ivan's mother didn't react at all when Estella hesitantly asked if Rebecca would like to join her and Dolly on their trip to Dublin. Both younger women threw covert glances at the older, but she stoically continued to batter sugar and butter in a mixing bowl as if there was no one else there.

"I don't know," Rebecca answered, rubbing her fingers through Harry's hair as he sat at the table writing out sentences. "No, lovie, your 'd' is backwards. 'Daffodils' not 'baffodils'."

"Well, I just said I'd offer. You're welcome to come with us, even for a day out. Or if you wanted to just do some general shopping."

"If you went," Mrs Aylward suddenly joined in, immediately drawing their attention, "you could get me some good sturdy material for trousers and skirts."

Rebecca laughed. "Between Ivan and Harry, I'm not sure

which one goes through trousers or shorts quicker," she told Estella.

"And maybe some decent Aran wool. That stuff locally is just not up to scratch for the price of it. And some buttons. I'll maybe make a list."

"Can I come?" Harry piped up.

"No, sweetheart, you've got school," his mother said gently.

"We'll have to look after ourselves for the day, won't we, pet?" said his granny. "Or maybe you won't need looking after at all. But I know I will. And aren't you the man for the job?" She then turned and looked directly into her daughter's eyes. "You go on and have a day out."

Having gained Mrs Aylward's approval, the three women set out early on Thursday morning to get the bus up to the capital. Ivan offered to drive them into town since he needed to buy some tack at the saddlery shop just off the market square.

The excitement at their impending journey was like being back at school, Estella thought. When they enjoyed clandestine little parties after-hours on the dorms right under the noses of the hall monitors. A kind of childish giddiness seemed to transmit from one woman to the next as they each sat into the car and squealed with delight as Ivan hunched over the steering wheel, wincing with a longsuffering air. The electricity that fizzed around the three girls, flowing between them every time they touched – which they did often – reaching for one another as if checking they were still there. Had they thought about it, they would have laughed at their own ridiculousness. But they didn't think about it. For once, they simply relished the freedom to be young, silly women.

Though he grumbled and made several allusions to his gladness at not having to drive them the whole way to Dublin, Estella could see Ivan was, in fact, enjoying their youthful daftness and relishing his role as the only aloof, sensible one among them. When he dropped them off, he made such a to-do about his relief at finally being free of them that, on impulse, Estella leaned through his window and planted a big wet kiss on his mouth, arresting him mid-flow. He subsided after that with a large, foolish grin on his face and gave an enthusiastic wave and toot of the horn as he drove off to the sound of Dolly and Rebecca's vociferous teasing.

An old lady in a knitted grey coat and black felt hat stood at the bus stop viewing them with obvious disapproval. "Young'uns," she muttered, shaking her head.

It was enough to send them all into another volley of giggles.

Once they were on the bus and surrounded by other travellers, they settled into a more serious discussion of where they were going and what they planned to buy since it seemed Mrs Aylward wasn't the only one who'd written her daughter a list.

"You should see all the stuff Mammy wants me to get," Dolly moaned. "I'll need to hire a porter to carry it all. And I can't afford a porter."

"Smile at him and he might do it for nothing," Rebecca suggested, grinning cheekily.

"I couldn't! It'd be like I was betraying Roy, flirting with another man."

"Stella'll flirt with him for you then."

"I will not! I'll carry your shopping myself before I'd do that."

"Excellent," Dolly replied, perking up immediately. "Problem solved."

Estella scowled at her but was resolutely ignored.

"So, what are we planning for our dresses?" Dolly asked. "Any ideas, patterns, colours? I like one of the ones in here but I don't know if it'd suit." From her handbag she pulled two well-thumbed copies of *Woman's Own* which her aunt had no doubt sent over from England. She flicked through one feverishly. "This. What do you think? Or this."

The other two made approving sounds as they viewed dress after dress and tried to decide which would best suit each of them. They discussed fabric, flattering cuts, the most fashionable prints and the shades or hues that would flatter skin tone, eye and hair colour. They even covered accessories and footwear.

"With all three of us going with our handsome men – mine being the handsomest, of course – those posh folk won't know what's hit them when we arrive in our lovely frocks. We'll turn every head in the place," Dolly assured them as they disembarked after several bone-shaking hours on the bus.

"I'd rather we didn't do that," Estella muttered, dipping her head as if there was a crowd ogling her at that very moment.

Rebecca linked arms with her as Dolly preceded them up

307

the street, taking charge. "It's difficult not to see the worst in ourselves," she said quietly. "We all think everyone stares because they see faults in us. Except Dolly Greer perhaps," she amended with a knowing grin as they watched her stride self-assuredly up the pavement. "But what we – you – have to realise is that people just look. Sometimes they approve, sometimes they disapprove. The one thing you have to think about is whether you and the people *you* care about approve, no one else. Strangers' opinions don't matter. Believe me when I tell you – you are a kind, caring, clever, *beautiful* young woman. *That* is what you need to remember every time you walk into a room. You deserve to be there. You *belong* there." She finished with a sincere, reassuring smile and nod.

Estella, on the other hand, glowed with embarrassment. "Thanks," she mumbled. Not managing to make eye-contact.

But Rebecca seemed satisfied or, at the very least, knew her friend well enough to be sure that was all the response she was going to get. "Right. Let's hurry and catch Miss Greer before she gets herself lost with all the excitement."

The shopfloor of Cleary's department store was heaving with people – mostly women – in the late morning rush. The hubbub of voices and the rumble of heels on the wood-panelled floor washed over the three girls as they pushed though the main doors, hurrying to escape the cutting wind that whistled up O'Connell Street from the Liffey river. Dolly led them through the sea of moving fur, wool and tweed coats, past shelves full of men's shirts, racks of overcoats and ornamental hat-stands bedecked with every type of headwear imaginable.

Estella viewed a tottering pile of shoeboxes behind a harried shopgirl with some trepidation. One inopportune movement and the youngster was sure to be buried under a cascade of 'Finest Ladies' Footwear'. Ahead, a towering stack of white cartons seemed to be weaving its way through the shoppers of its own accord until she spotted a pair of black-clad legs shuffling beneath it.

Had it not been for Dolly's magenta hat, they would have struggled to recognise her in the ebb and flow of people. Without the slightest deviation, she led them to the appropriate counters for dress patterns and was already flicking through the first thick volume of Simplicity dresses by the time Rebecca and Estella reached her. Without pausing, she indicated that they should also take a book apiece. "You take Vogue and Stella can take the Butterick ones. Just remember Butterick's always a size too big so if you chose one of theirs, go for a smaller measurement."

Estella was inclined to listen since Dolly had been a domestic-science whizz in school and had helped almost every woman in the village with their dressmaking – whether it was something for a day out at the beach or their wedding dress. Many people, including Estella, assured her that it was something she could make a living out of but she always laughed them off, saying she couldn't possibly leave her job at the telephone exchange. If she did that, where would she get all her gossip from?

They spent half an hour rifling through multiple pattern books until each of them had chosen a dress they thought would flatter their figure and that they were also capable of making. There was a tense wait when they handed over their slip of paper with the pattern codes to the lady behind a counter of dark-wood panels, glass and green baize. Estella fought the urge to reach out and smudge the polished surface. If they didn't have the pattern she wanted, she thought she might just mucky the glass with her fingers in annoyance. But she and the glass were both in luck since the lady returned to them with a smile and three pattern envelopes in her hand.

Their next task – which took them an equally long time – was finding just the right shade and weight of material to make turning the pattern into an actual garment as easy as possible. And though Estella had an idea that she might like to try and make a velvet dress, Dolly was quick to dissuade her. "If you get the nap wrong on velvet, it looks awful," she warned. "It'll look like you're wearing two different colours of fabric."

Rebecca found hers first – a simple rich burgundy which they all agreed did wonders for her complexion and accentuated the reddish tones in her brunette hair. Dolly chose a loud, complicated material with a black background and orange, white and bright pink, big, blousy flowers. "It'll be hell to join up the pattern," she informed them excitedly, her eyes glowing with maniacal relish at the prospect. "But I love a challenge!"

Estella proved trickier. Choosing to follow Dolly's advice, she forwent the velvet and opted for a charcoal grey which she thought was a bit like the background colour of the dress she'd worn on New Year's Eve. It was unfussy and elegant, she thought, until Dolly yelled at her to put it down.

"Why, what's wrong with it?" Estella asked, still holding it.

"*Wrong*? There's nothing right with it. It's just *blugh!*" The sound was one of absolute disapproval. "It's so *boring*."

"Well, I don't want to stand out like a sore thumb!"

"Like me?" Dolly asked, eyes flashing.

"*No!* You'll look fabulous because you're confident enough to wear bold patterns. I'd rather just …"

"Not be seen at all?" Rebecca chipped in.

Estella fought the urge to say, 'Yes! Exactly!' But that probably wasn't the response her friends were looking for.

Dolly stood and considered for a moment, hands on hips. "Tell you what, Rebecca and I are going to choose the fabric for you because you clearly have no taste." Estella tried to speak but Dolly ploughed on regardless. "And we don't want you turning up dressed in a nun's habit. Although if you *did* do that, you'd definitely stand out."

"Dolly –"

"No! We're choosing for you. *End of*." She walked off with an air of great importance.

Rebecca smiled sympathetically and squeezed Estella's arm. "Don't worry, I won't let her go completely mad," then followed Dolly.

Left alone, Estella wandered over to the haberdashery section and bought some buttons to replace the ones Graeme kept pulling off his shirts and coats. She also wanted wool for knitting as, like Mrs Aylward, she believed the quality and price was better in the city when you wanted to make clothes for good-wear. However, she barely had the buttons in her handbag when Dolly came hurrying over with Rebecca trailing behind, a bale of fabric in her arms.

"This is the one," Dolly gushed, fingering the fabric lovingly.

Estella's fear of Dolly choosing something completely incongruous had been unfounded. Her friends knew her well. There was no pattern, just block colour royal blue. It was beautifully soft to the touch – almost velvety. She wanted to lean down and rub it against her cheek. Stylish and not too flashy. "It's perfect. Thank you!" She hugged both of them but was careful not to crush the fabric.

Over their shoulders, she spotted a shopgirl viewing them suspiciously.

"Right!" Rebecca said, turning them all around. "Now let's bring this back before the lady behind the counter gets cross with us!"

With the final purchase of several yards of fabric for Estella's dress, the bulk of their shopping was complete. Of course there were buttons, zips and threads of the appropriate colours to add but once they had done that, they were contented enough to head for lunch. All that remained for the afternoon was what they had been asked to buy for other family members. But there was little stress involved in buying shirts and wool. They enjoyed the cool air of the streets, the hustle, the piercing cries of the street-hawkers and the brightly-coloured window displays. They were young, free of cares and thoroughly enjoyed each other's company. As she walked shoulder to shoulder with her friends, Estella could not help but smile constantly. This is what happiness is, she thought to herself. This is what it feels like.

And it was glorious.

Chapter 28

The following week, Estella spent every evening at Dolly's wrangling her dress into some semblance of … a dress. The three of them had spent the hours carefully planning how best to lay out their dress patterns, pin, cut, tack and what order to sew each of the pieces together. Though there was some stress involved in the making of one's own dress for such an occasion, Estella found having company made the job so much more fun and seem more manageable. Of course, Ivan and Roy both complained about the considerable amount of time that was going into the production of something as silly as a dress. They begged, they sulked and they teased. They whinged about having to spend their evenings alone when they could have been having fun with their girls. Then Ivan tried flattery.

"You could go in a hessian sack and you'd still be the prettiest girl in the room."

"I wouldn't be the prettiest girl in the room because I wouldn't be allowed *into* the room." Estella knew there was a strict dress code that couldn't be flouted.

"Thank goodness Howard isn't familiar enough to whine

at me for my absence," Rebecca muttered.

"Just you wait," Estella replied.

Her familiarity with Ivan increased with every hour they spent together. Every evening he would collect her and his sister from Dolly's to save them cycling home in the dark. He would drop Rebecca off then continue on to Estella's where he would frequently come in for a cup of tea. But the tea often remained untouched, cooling on the table while they sat in one armchair, arms wrapped around each other as she cuddled into his chest, her legs dangling out over the armrest while Sophie eyed them haughtily from another seat. They didn't worry about being seen by anyone else. Graeme was out every night the pubs were open and was never home before Estella went to bed.

Though she naturally worried about her brother, there was nothing she could do. When she'd casually ask where he'd been the previous night earlier in the year, he had flared immediately and accused her of spying on him. Now, despite living in the same house, her relationship with Graeme was about as verbose as the one she had with Austin and she hadn't spoken to him since Christmas. She, therefore, thought nothing of going to bed in an empty house on a Friday night in March – not long after the second anniversary of her father's death – because it was what she had been doing for months.

However, when she woke on the Saturday morning with the sun tickling the edge of the curtains, she immediately felt something was wrong. For a moment, her sleep-fuddled brain couldn't work out why such a presentiment chilled her empty stomach. Then she realised what it was. Graeme wasn't home. She knew it instinctively. There was no way she would be unaware of his presence in the house. He couldn't have stayed quiet if his life depended on it.

Still in her nightie, she threw on her dressing gown. The light streamed through the window of Graeme's room, warming the cover of the empty bed. She crossed the floor and looked out at the yard, wondering if her brother had perhaps fallen asleep in his car. But the cobblestones were as empty as the bed behind her. He never made it home. She stood bracing against the windowsill. Maybe he was so drunk someone had taken pity on him and brought him home. However, she knew that would never happen. A drunk Graeme could never provoke kindness or pity. It was more likely someone had driven *over* him rather than driven him home. The thought made her stomach drop. No, there was bound to be a reasonable explanation. He had fallen asleep at Sweeney's and, rather than risk his ire by waking him, they left him to sleep it off. That was it.

However, she couldn't spend her time worrying. She had work to do. The newly calved cows needed milking and the calves needed to be fed. And then the other animals needed feeding too. So she got on with it.

She was still out in the sheds when she finally heard a car trundling up the drive. Holding her breath, she peeked out. Graeme's car swung into the yard and halted violently. She heard the handbrake screech as he yanked it. He was clearly in a foul mood. For a moment, she considered hiding in the shed, but curiosity got the better of her. Besides, if he was really insufferable, she could just leave since she was due to ride out three horses that day over at Ellendale. Confidently, she strode across the yard and came to a halt half a dozen feet from her brother. He was sitting in the car with the door open, feet planted on the ground as if preparing to heave himself out but had yet to muster the energy to do so.

"What happened to you last night?" Estella asked bluntly.

He lifted his head to look at her and she stifled a gasp. His skin was waxy and discoloured – the pallor of a corpse. However, his eyes were wide and shiny, rimmed in angry red. And the whites – which she knew had been the wrong colour for months now – were flaxen rather than clear white. He just looked … *yellow*. In the unforgiving grey light of the morning, she really saw her brother. He was sick. Sick because he was lonely, sick because he had a chip on his shoulder that had no business being there. Sick because of the alcohol. He had been gifted a good life – an excellent farm, animals and the money to run it comfortably. Instead, he was frittering every advantage away for the sake of pouring poison down his throat night after night. Because it *was* poisoning him. He was now well on the way to killing himself – slowly dying with every mouthful of whiskey or stout he swallowed. And there wasn't a thing she could do to stop him. Graeme was sitting in front of her, staring at her and he was dying.

"What do you care where I was?"

She blinked, ignoring the question. "Are you all right?"

"Why wouldn't I be? Life's all roses. Didn't you know?" He tittered angrily.

"No, it's not. Quite often it's horrid."

He glanced at her then looked away. Still standing before

316

him, Estella watched her brother's face slowly crumple. But she didn't go to him. She knew if she did that, he would just push her away. He looked so ugly, she thought, as he fought to contain the bitterness, the anger, the disappointment that was writ large on his face.

"I've had to sell it."

"Sell what?" she asked, confused.

"The rest of the wood," he eventually spat out.

She stared for a moment. "What wood?"

He threw a scornful look at her which, only a few short months ago, would have frightened her away. But now she held his gaze.

"The wood down the other end of the farm," he snapped, walloping the steering wheel with the ball of his hand.

She knew where he was talking about. She had known before she asked the question. But she clung to the momentary hope that she was wrong. The vivid remembrance of felled trees and pale stumps she had seen when walking past on the day she met Ivan and rode again – Christmas Day – flooded her mind. She hadn't thought about it since. The woods were nothing to do with her. But they weren't anything to do with Graeme either.

"Graeme, Austin owns the woods."

Her eldest brother snorted. "No, he doesn't. They're mine. Or they were until last night."

"But … have you handed over the title deeds?"

"*No*," he scoffed. "I've sold the *wood* off it. Not the land itself. And it was worth a fair bit." His yellowed eyes widened in surprise at his apparent good fortune. "And, sure, once I have a bit of money again, I can re-sow it or clear the land or … *what*?" He narrowed his eyes at his sister, sudden buoyancy lost to irritation.

"Graeme, I'm telling you, Daddy left the woods to Austin. The trees, the land – it's not yours to do anything with."

He was shaking his head before she even finished. "You're wrong." Hauling himself out of the car, he swept past her into the house without a backwards glance.

The hair at the back of her neck began to prickle. Her stomach felt cold. She almost ran to the back door, arriving in time to see her brother abandon his boots in the middle of the porch. "Graeme –"

"Oh, would you ever just *go away*, Stella!" he shouted, rounding on her. "Always picking his bloody side!"

"Graeme, this isn't me picking sides! This is me not wanting you to get in trouble. If the land was yours, I wouldn't say a thing. You can do whatever you like with it –"

"*Yes*, I can –"

"But it's *not* yours and … and I can prove it."

His stare was murderous but she didn't back down.

"Go on then."

She walked calmly past. She would not panic even though that was exactly what she wanted to do. Her brothers hated one another enough as it was. Things didn't need to get worse. And if she was right – she *was* right – they would. Yet her steps unwaveringly carried her. Her knees bent so that she was kneeling in front of the cupboard below the family photos in the sitting room. She glanced up at the serious faces of her family and said a small prayer to her parents, then opened the cupboard door.

Graeme was sitting in the kitchen, his forearms spread wide and resting on the edge of the table and a whiskey bottle in pride of place before him when she re-entered. He looked up, still chewing with deliberate slowness on bread and butter, but his gaze never reached her face. He was looking at the piece of paper clutched in her hand. She had read through it twice before she was sure she could bring it to him. Wordlessly she placed it in front of him. He continued to eat, ignoring it.

"What's that?" he snapped eventually.

She didn't answer. Instead, she pulled out a chair and sat, marvelling at her brother's absolute refusal to engage with what was staring him in the face. Perhaps he thought if he didn't open up the folds of thick, cream-coloured paper inked with rows of black letters that the words they spelt out would not be real. But the words were real.

She reached across, flattened the sheet on the table and directed him to a paragraph halfway down the page. She remembered it from the reading of the will a short while after her father's funeral. The details had been so specific: '*To my son, Austin, I leave the remaining eighty-three acres east of the main lane as well as the six acres of woodland to the west of the aforementioned laneway's termination. I suggest that, should Austin ever need to purchase his own veterinary practice or buy out Tommy Shannon's share of our partnership, that he sells the six acres of mature trees and the plot of ground separately to raise sufficient capital without losing prime farmland.*'

Sitting opposite Graeme as he read their father's words, Estella's whole body ached. She watched as the righteous anger slid from his face and the cool, arrogant gaze

319

shattered. His eyes roved the pages, reading from the start but coming to a halt in the same place. Slowly, his head began to shake and his lips mouthed one word over and over: *no, no, no*. He really hadn't known. She wondered whether he had been so angry with Reg for dividing the farm in two that he had simply stopped listening once he discovered all the land would not be his. Suddenly, she felt a wave of fury wash over her and it was all directed towards her father. How could he have done this to Graeme, knowing the animosity that existed between the brothers in the first place? Austin didn't need land. He had a good job that paid well and he loved being a vet. He had no intention of being a farmer. Graeme was the one who wanted – *needed* – the land. But their father had instead gifted half of it to his favourite son. Even now, from beyond the grave, Reg Frayne was still showing them which of his children he loved the most.

"How … *how*? I need it to pay off –" Though he could barely give voice to his words, they seemed far too loud for the crushing silence of the room.

Graeme raked a shaking hand through his hair making it stand on end, adding to his look of wide-eyed wildness. Estella could see he was on the verge of explosion – or perhaps an implosion. He seemed undecided himself. Instinctively, she reached a hand across the table but he withdrew his, hiding it under the table.

"We can work it out," she told him. She had no idea what he needed the money for. As far as she knew the farm wasn't making a loss. "We can fix this. I have some money saved –" he shook his head *"No*, Graeme, listen to me! I can lend you the money and you pay me back when everything comes

320

right again. *Come on*, Graeme! Let me help you."

"*No.*" The stubborn, arrogant set to his jaw was back. He looked off into the middle distance. "Why is it I can never do anything right?" he said to himself, then without warning, and with a show of strength she had no idea he possessed, he lifted the lip of the table and crashed it back down in utter frustration, making everything on it leap in surprise. Indeed, the bottle of whiskey plain keeled over, depositing its contents across the scrubbed surface as if vomiting from the shock of such a sudden outburst. Crying out in disgust, Graeme leaped to his feet and stormed out of the house.

Estella remained pinned to her seat, hands flat on the table as she tried to steady the world around her. It didn't work. She heard the scream as the car engine revved and the patter of stones as they were thrown across the yard by spinning tyres. The quiet that followed was punctuated by the *drip-drip-drip* of spilt alcohol onto the floor. It was this that eventually brought movement back to her limbs.

Getting to her feet, she felt much older than she was. Why did everything in her family have to go so wrong? Were they cursed? It certainly felt like it. Finding a cloth to mop up the strong-smelling spirit, she wondered whether the Frayne family curse would spread to the next generation – to the children she and her siblings might one day beget. Sitting back on her heels, she watched absently as Sophie stalked around the outer edge of the kitchen, hopped up on one of the armchairs and viewed the scene with distaste. Children. Could she see herself or her brothers as parents? Not really. Children were a foreign concept to a family forced to grow up quickly. Estella could hardly remember anything but a few flashes of her own childishness. She had little contact with the younger generation and never sought out children or babies. She was too enamoured with animals – with horses.

Her mind inevitably drifted to Ivan. What were his thoughts on children? Did he like them? She supposed he must since he was so fond of Harry. What if they had children in the future? Could she break the curse of her own family's bloodline? If anyone could save her and her potential offspring from ill-fortune, it was Ivan. In the short time she had known him, the light and happiness he brought to her life had given her hope that there were better times ahead. She was shaking off the past and beginning afresh.

But the past wouldn't let the Frayne children go. No matter how hard they tried to escape it, the past always clasped them with a firm hand and held them back.

Chapter 29

Thoughts of her brother's predicament consumed Estella over the subsequent days. However, she was not allowed to wallow completely. She was now riding Hedy as well as several of the young horses at Ellendale. Gymkhana season was fast approaching and the Leclerc horses were being trained to show jump. Little Iris Kellett was, therefore, called upon to rediscover her affinity for the sport and, between herself and Ivan, they were schooling up to ten horses a day over a course of coloured and rustic poles that had been set out in a flat, grassy field beside the yard. Regaining the skills that lay dormant and cobwebbed within her took all of her concentration. It was exactly what she needed. For a few hours every day, she was taken out of herself, away from the gnawing worry of the imminent implosion of her family. Jumping the horses required both her brain and her body. The practice consumed her just as her unhappiness would have if she had not had the obligation to turn up at Ellendale every day and earn her keep.

Sensing her need for this escape, Ivan encouraged her, pushed her to achieve something – no matter how small –

with every practice. Of course, he had asked her what was wrong. But her answer was vague. The problem was someone else's and not hers to divulge. And though Ivan could have forced a reply, he didn't. She was allowed to have her own thoughts or worries. She was allowed to keep them from him. When the time came for her to speak, she knew he would listen.

With so much of her time taken up at Ellendale, it was understandable perhaps that she had seen very little of Graeme. But Estella also wondered whether her eldest brother, like Austin, was avoiding her. What she did see of him did nothing to ease her concern.

While his eyes were an even more alarming shade of pale yellow, his skin now looked like rotting oatmeal flecked with vivid threads of crimson red. It was both pasty and grey. Around his nose, the veins were breaking, his life-force finding weak spots in his body through which to seep. And on the two occasions he had carried things across the kitchen, she had noted the rattle of cutlery on crockery. Unless his hands were stuffed in his pockets, they shook constantly.

With this unhappy burden eating at her conscience, even the promise of the Hunt Ball couldn't completely buoy her spirits. Frenzied as her friends were with preparations, they barely registered Estella's long silences when they gathered in the evenings to talk over one another excitedly. Their giddiness was so alien to her, she even considered not going to the ball at all. But there was no way she would abandon Ivan. She needed him. Without him and his inclusion of her in all aspects of training the horses at Ellendale, she likely would have sunk back into the despondency that she had wallowed in for so many of the previous years.

It was, therefore, with a feeling of duty and forced jollity that she dressed with Rebecca at Dolly's house on the evening of the ball, repeating the phrase, 'That looks nice,' too many times. However, there were moments when ripples of real happiness washed through her. The sight of Rebecca twisting locks of Dolly's silky blonde hair into elegant swirls at the back of her head. The dainty point of Rebecca's toes as she stretched out a leg to see how her dress moved. Her own reflection when Dolly stood her in front of the mirror, a beaming smile radiating over her shoulder as they viewed the beautiful blue dress they had created.

"I told you it would suit you," she said.

Eventually the last of their faffing concluded as they smoothed down their dresses and were lured downstairs by the increasingly impatient calls of Ivan below.

"I swear, if you're not down within the next *two minutes* I'm going and you can *walk* there in your posh frocks!"

Descending to see him pacing the hall in his evening suit gave Estella another little thrill. Though his hair was madly tousled by the disturbance of restless fingers, he knew how to stand tall and proud in his black suit and crisp white shirt.

"Aren't you handsome!" his sister grinned, making him scowl. But Estella thought it might have been to hide the gratified blush colouring his cheeks.

Rebecca reached up to straighten his bow tie but he batted her hands away. "Don't. Mammy did it for me and if it gets any tighter, I'll either choke or tear it off and stamp on it. And I can't do that. It's got to go back to the hire place tomorrow."

"But it's crooked!" she admonished, reaching up again.

"*Don't!*" he yelped, swiping at her.

She swiped back and for a moment they fought childishly, slapping ineffectually at one another until Estella stepped in, pushing them apart.

"*All right!*" She laughed as Rebecca ducked under her arm to poke her brother in the ribs and Ivan reached over her shoulder. "That's enough! Leave her *alone*, Ivan."

"*Me* leave *her* alone? She started it! Why'd you take her side?" he huffed.

The smile slid from Estella's face immediately. She turned away but Ivan grabbed her wrist.

"Come on, girls! Carl's brought his camera especially so you're not going anywhere till we get a picture!" Dolly's mother appeared, towing her eldest son by the strap of his camera case. "Let's get one in front of the white wall of the house before the light goes completely."

She marched straight out, continuing to haul Carl as he gibbered about the likelihood of her snapping the strap. The others – including Dolly's four younger siblings – all skipped out, leaving Ivan and Estella last.

"I didn't mean it," he said without preamble. "You know I didn't."

"I know. Just …"

"I shouldn't have said it." He knew about her being caught between her brothers. "Stella, forget about them. I know it's not in your nature to do that but try to live in the moment, just for tonight. This night is for you, not them.

326

Enjoy it." He clasped her shoulders, leant down and kissed her softly on the lips. "Because you look too beautiful to waste tonight on worry."

She smiled up at him. "Your bow tie *is* crooked, you know."

"Oh sod off," he muttered just as Dolly's voice reached them from the yard.

"Hurry up, you two! It's bloomin' freezing out here!"

Chapter 30

They met Howard Anstruther and Roy Oaks outside the hotel where the ball was being held.

Though both men cut decent figures, with a hint of pride, Estella still thought Ivan was the most handsome of their trio. However, she was afforded little opportunity to admire him before they were swallowed by the throng of folk dressed in their finest apparel for the night ahead.

Henry Leclerc was easy to spot propping up the far end of the bar in his siren-red waistcoat as he halloed everyone within thirty feet. It also seemed he was standing half the room drinks to the increasing annoyance of the bar staff who were harried enough as it was without keeping an eye on his tab. Jacqueline Hawes, dressed in her accustomed tweed, bowed gracefully to them as they approached, clinging to a fox fur draped around her neck. She stroked it absentmindedly as she chatted to Barbara Leclerc who waved at Estella when she spotted her.

"Oh God, there's that awful Craven man," Rebecca groaned. "Hide me!"

"Why?" Estella asked, obligingly moving in front of her.

"Because he wouldn't leave me alone at that New Year party while you and Ivan were in the other room talking horses. Stuck to me like a limpet to a rock until I told him in front of everyone that I wasn't bloody interested."

"You didn't say it like *that*, did you? Not in front of *everyone*?"

"Um ..."

"*Rebecca*!" Estella hissed. "*Why*? Don't you know what he's like?"

"Well, I didn't *then*. I do now because Ivan told me. I just wanted to get rid of him."

Estella cringed. She hoped The Craven didn't remember what Rebecca had said. Because if he did, he would go out of his way to say something nasty or embarrassing to her in retribution.

"This is like being in a Jane Austen novel," Dolly piped up, having missed the others' whispered conversation.

"Except none of us are looking for husbands," Rebecca answered airily, shaking off thoughts of Paul Craven.

"Speak for yourself," Dolly huffed. "I'm always on the lookout."

"So are they," Estella countered. "So they can see you coming a mile off."

Dolly scowled as Rebecca fought to turn her laughter into a cough. She had considerable success since, in stifling her laugh, she choked and genuinely did succumb to a coughing fit.

"Are you all right?" Howard Anstruther's low, earnest voice asked as he appeared beside them.

"Oh she's *fine*," Dolly answered. "Just choking on *darling* Stella's fine wit. At *my* expense."

329

Estella bit her lip. "In fairness, Doll, you do set yourself up for a fall."

"And if you fall, I'll catch you!" Roy answered, swooping in to catch her around the waist, making his beloved squeal with indignation and delight.

While all eyes were on them, Estella felt familiar, strong arms wrap around her own middle. "All right?" Ivan whispered in her ear.

She enfolded his hands in her own and leaned her head back against his chest. "All good." She smiled and tried to look into his face but the angle was all wrong. Besides, his attention seemed to have shifted. She felt him tense behind her and followed the direction of his body to the far side of the room where she saw ...

"You never said your brother was coming," Roy commented, noting the group's change of focus. "He did a cracking job fixing up one of the hound's paws for us last week. Darn good vet, he is." The huntsman didn't register the effect Austin's appearance had on the other Frayne beside him as he threw a hand in the air. "*Hoy! Austin!*"

"*Roy!*" Dolly hissed, grabbing his arm.

But it was too late. Austin was already making his way over before he noticed the rest of the huntsman's company. His footsteps faltered. He locked eyes with the sister he hadn't spoken to for three months. Estella shrank back into Ivan's torso, wishing that his bulk would swallow her whole. It seemed her immobile feet weren't even capable of turning and walking away. Yet her brother continued to move reluctantly closer, dragged onwards by a woman on his arm.

"Is that Marion Ward?"

Dolly's question caught Estella's attention. Her gaze slid away from Austin to his companion. The veterinary practice secretary was perhaps slightly paler and less jovial-looking than usual. Yet her chin was held high and there was a determined set to her jaw as she clung to Austin's arm in a possessive fashion. As she cut through the crowd, Marion was making it clear to everyone that she wasn't just there as a handy plus-one. She was there to show off.

Estella's fury and indignation at the sight of her brother was instantly swamped by a cascade of garbled, shocked realisations.

Austin and Marion?

No. It wasn't possible. The year before last, Estella had baked Marion a cake for her fortieth birthday. And Austin had only turned twenty-seven the month before. Yes, she was a very popular woman. All the farmers who came in to collect medicine or bring in a sick animal thought very highly of her. She always had a perfectly made-up face – from mascara to impeccably neat lipstick. She dressed in a way that flattered her curvaceous figure – though the shiny mauve frock caught under the bust and dropping to the floor didn't really show it off. But she wasn't pretty. Her face was square, her hair mousy. In her heels, she was even slightly taller than Austin. She was not petite and radiant like Rebecca Aylward. She wasn't Dolly Greer either. It was impossible for a man not to admire either of them. Yet it appeared Austin had chosen a woman who was more than a decade older than him. And they had known Marion since she became the practice's secretary twenty years before.

331

Marion first met Austin when she was a grown woman and he was still a little boy. Estella was even sure of more than one occasion where both she and her brother had sat on Marion's knee while they waited for their father to finish his work.

Austin and Marion?

They arrived just as the gears in Estella's brain ground to a screeching, creaking halt. She couldn't move her tongue, open her mouth – nothing.

"Hello, everyone," Marion said smoothly.

"How are you, Marion?" Ivan asked, clearing his throat at the end of the question.

He had moved from behind Estella to stand beside her, a protective arm firmly clamped around her waist. She wondered if he was protecting her from Austin or Austin from her. No doubt he could feel her expanding beneath his fingers like a threatened cat. He gently but firmly gripped her. *Calm down*, his touch urged.

"Oh, I'm grand, grand. You? I have to say, you're all looking lovely, girls. And the men too, of course. *Ve-ry* handsome!"

She stepped forward, sliding her arm out of Austin's grip and reached out to run her fingers down the lapel of Ivan's jacket. That was the other thing about Marion: she was more of a flirt than Dolly – and that was saying something. Estella bristled afresh. She felt like telling Marion not to touch him. But then Marion stepped back and linked arms with Austin once more and Estella felt like telling her not to touch him either. He looked like a lost little boy clinging to the wrist of the kindly woman who found him. Maybe that was exactly what he was. There was always something a little childish about him despite his grown-up lifestyle and occupation.

"Hullo, Stella."

Austin was staring right at her. But then she had been staring at him, trying to fathom what he was doing standing in front of her, never mind having Marion with him.

"Austin." Her voice was clipped, cold.

It was all she could manage. If she started to talk, there was no telling what subject she might berate him on, what truths she might reveal. Everyone around them seemed to be holding their breath as they looked from brother to sister. She had to think of her friends, of Ivan. She would not make a scene. There was, therefore, an audible sigh of relief when the gong for dinner sounded. Without a backward glance, Estella walked away from her brother, leaving the rest of the company to trail in her wake.

"Well," Ivan muttered, catching up with her, "at least that first meeting's over and done with."

"Yes."

"Congratulations, by the way."

"What for?"

"Not punching him square in the nose," he answered, pulling her out of the onward press of bodies so that they were standing to the side of the door rather than going through it. "I think I would have been sorely tempted."

"So was I," she admitted. "But seeing him with Marion Ward took the wind out of my sails a bit."

"Turn-up for the books that. I never would have guessed it."

"I've known them for twenty years and *I* didn't see it

coming," she answered, shaking her head as if she had water in her ear. An image of her brother and the secretary arm in arm had just blazed before her eyes. "What is he *thinking*? She must be fifteen years older than him."

"Yeah, it does seem a little … irregular. But … if they're happy …" He shrugged.

She shuddered in response. "It's just not right. Not normal."

"My auntie married a fella who was eighteen years older than her. And they were happy enough."

"But that's *different*. It's normal for the man to be older. Even the woman can sometimes be a little bit older. But not … nearly old enough to be his *mammy!*" she hissed.

Ivan lifted his hands then slapped them back down on the legs of his trousers. This subject was clearly not one he felt qualified to discuss. "Just, I don't know, let them on, I suppose. It'll hardly effect you that much, will it? If they're happy," he repeated, "what harm?"

"It's just … *embarrassing*," she said quietly, an earnest appeal for sympathy on her face as she looked up into his.

He bit his lip, fighting to maintain an understanding expression. But he couldn't. "You look like you've got toothache," he snorted and then covered his mouth. It was no use. A deep rumbling laugh swelled from his chest and escaped through his fingers.

Estella – completely put out – took a swing at him and smacked him hard on the shoulder.

"*Ow!*" he yelped, hunching into himself and drawing a knee up as if he was going to kick her. "*Don't* hit me! Hit your sodding brother!"

334

"You're closer," she said, taking aim again.

"I'll go and get him for you." He danced out of her range. "Just *don't* hit *me!*"

"Don't bother. He's not worth it." She stood for a moment then sighed and turned to join the final stragglers as they entered the dining room.

In a moment, Ivan's arm had snaked around her. "You know, aside from the violence, I much prefer this feisty Stella to the mopey one."

She rolled her eyes but smiled secretly to herself. She hadn't felt this invigorated for a while. It was just the sort of distraction she needed to force her not to care about what was going on at home. Mutely, she allowed Ivan to guide her to their table without really paying attention to where he was taking her.

"Oh, for the love of –"

The table twenty feet away had two empty places. She followed Ivan's gaze, expecting to see her brother. But instead she saw –

"The Craven." She groaned. Aside from Austin, he was the last person she wanted to see.

Paul Craven sat with the self-satisfied smug grin of someone who couldn't quite believe his luck but teetered on the edge of thinking he was exactly where he was supposed to be. By the colour of his cheeks, he had already taken full advantage of Henry Leclerc's bar tab. And the eyes which alighted on Estella were shining with greedy expectation of what was to come. She shuddered as he patted the empty seat beside him.

"Rebecca hates him," Ivan told her in a low voice. "Why's he here?"

"Mr Leclerc thinks he's *entertaining*. There must have been a spare seat at the table."

"And what, Tony Dillon wasn't available?"

Estella shushed him discreetly and turned to face him on the pretence of wiping a mark off his suit jacket. "Be careful saying that name in here. He swindled most of the room. And while bygones might be bygones of an ordinary day, when there's drink taken –"

"It could be a different story." He nodded, looking over her head. "Understood. I just wish that silly bugger wasn't at our table. Look at Bec."

She waited a moment then turned airily and allowed her gaze to rove over the table as she approached. Rebecca appeared quite glum. Willing her to look up, Estella was met with a dull stare from her friend. Trying to draw a smile from Rebecca's unhappy face, she stuck out her tongue. It worked. Rebecca ginned but then cast her eyes in Paul's direction. Estella rolled hers in response then winked. Keen to show both Aylwards that she wasn't going to let him ruin their night, she did something she would never have willingly done before: she took the seat beside The Craven.

"*Ooo! Two* beauties at my table," Paul cackled as she settled herself into her chair.

She didn't bother to respond to the fact he had said 'my' table as if it was at his pleasure that they were offered a seat close to his person. But when he placed an overfamiliar hand on her forearm, she slowly and very deliberately pulled it away.

"And both of us are here in the company of other men. So you can look, but no touching, Paul, there's a good chap."

She offered him a radiant smile that never heated the

336

glacial blue of her eyes. At that moment all she wanted was for Rebecca to have a good time. That was her motivation for saying anything at all. It wouldn't do for her first ball to be ruined by The Craven. Holding Paul's malevolent, piggy gaze, she felt Ivan's heavy, possessive, protective arm drape across her shoulders. Before, she would have sat mute, shrinking away from the likes of Paul Craven. Yet, in Ivan's presence, the words came easily. She had wanted to wipe the arrogant, deprecating leer off Paul's face for years. And now, it slid from his cheeks and chin like a gobbet of spit down a window. The triumph sent a thrill though Estella's body.

Had Reg been sitting with her, she would have feared his disapproval. No matter how much he disliked someone, her father always tried to maintain civility. But then, Reg Frayne was a man so he could do that and still command respect. Estella had thought that if she stayed respectfully quiet, respect from others eventually followed. But there were some people who would never respect her. And if that was the case then it wasn't worth being polite to them. The scales fell and she saw the power of such forthrightness. It was what she needed more of in her life, she thought. It was the way forward with both of her brothers. And she had Ivan at her back. The touch of his hand made her body sing with confidence.

She focused her attention on Paul again. Best to get the killer blow in early and ward him off for the rest of the evening.

"You never told me last time – how are your sisters, Paul?" she asked sweetly.

Ivan's fingers dug into her flesh. Yes – if Estella had any say, tonight would be a good night.

Chapter 31

For a man with the most coordinated, gentle movements when he sat astride a horse, Ivan – Estella discovered – was not a natural dancer. She was reminded of the first night she had seen him at table tennis, galumphing up the hall like an energetic puppy, as he whirled her around the dancefloor at great speed but with little grace. Dolly fared little better with Roy whose preferred style of dance seemed to involve spinning his partner in dizzying circles until she was squealing for him to stop. Indeed, their partners left so much to be desired, Estella and Dolly shirked their menfolk and took to the floor together, taking it in turns to play the gentleman.

"This is like dance lessons back in school!" Dolly giggled as Estella dropped her in a graceful dip. "Although back then, you and I were the country dunces at the back of the class. Now look at us!"

They cut across the floor in tango fashion, sweeping the two-steppers aside.

"Hullo, Becca!" they called, passing Rebecca and Howard who were managing a half-decent waltz.

Surprisingly, the next couple they met was Austin and

338

Marion Ward. Casting surreptitious glances in their direction, Estella saw the triumphant look on the older woman's face as Austin whirled her in a circle. It was a wonder he was on the floor at all since he usually sat in a corner talking horses with the rest of the reluctant male dancers. Like Roy and Ivan. It was a pity, she thought, that more men weren't similarly ensconced – one man in particular.

As they swept by, Estella's eyes rested on the edge of the dancefloor. "*Go left!*" she hissed to Dolly who promptly went right. "Not *your* left, *mine!*" she said, hauling her friend away from a swaying Paul Craven. He had asked both of them to dance during the course of the evening but they had each come up with convenient excuses. Estella couldn't help but feel there was something quite sad about his frequent traipse to the bar. But then she remembered the way he looked at her, spoke to her and her sympathies waned. She was careful, therefore, to continue steering herself and Dolly as far away from him as possible. Poor Rebecca, however, was not so lucky.

Estella wasn't sure what happened. She only just registered Howard wending his way through the tables but thought nothing of where Rebecca was. The song playing was particularly fast so she and Dolly were paying particular attention to their feet. Both were wearing higher heels than they were used to and weren't keen on toppling over in the middle of the floor in front of the great and good of the county. However, as the song ended and the band seamlessly transitioned into a much slower number, Dolly's attention suddenly shifted.

"Oh …" she murmured. "Oh!" her tone was sharper. "Oh … *Oh! Uh-oh!*"

Estella was alone. Dolly had been in her arms and then she wasn't. Turning, disorientated, she saw the swish of Dolly's frock as she scrabbled through a distracted crowd. The room suddenly seemed to be focused on a knot at the other side of the dancefloor. Even the musicians were losing time as they craned their necks to see what was happening. Shouldering her way through the gathering group, she almost knocked Dolly into the centre of an empty space that had formed around four people. Marion seemed to be supporting Rebecca Aylward while Austin appeared to be rendering a similar service to The Craven whose face was a frightening shade of magenta, a sheen of sweat on his brow. A protective hand hovered over his privates – a precaution taken too late, apparently. He eyed Rebecca with furious malevolence but she stood her ground, straightening her back as more party-goers formed up around them.

"*Silly cow!*" Paul wheezed. Several people clucked their disapproval but he continued. "All I wanted was a dance. You didn't have to go and do *that!*" He indicated his injured manhood.

A drunken titter burbled from the watchers.

"You don't ask a woman to dance by grabbing her backside and shoving your *thing* in her front." Rebecca's voice was cold with fury but strong enough to carry.

Austin let go of his charge with alacrity. "Ah now, Paul, you can't be doing that."

"I did *not!*" he answered hotly.

"You did," Marion piped up. "I saw it."

"So did I," added Dolly. "From all the way over there."

Paul rounded on Dolly. "Oh well, *you'd* know, wouldn't

340

you? Handled enough of them from what I've heard!"

Dolly sputtered and squeaked, incapable of forming a reply to such an accusation. Yes, she was a flirt, but she was an innocent flirt.

Estella grabbed her arm just as she spotted Ivan and Roy shoving to the front of the gathering. "Pay him no mind, Dolly. *He's drunk!*" She spat the words at Paul, hoping they would make him recoil. They didn't.

"Oh, you'd know about drunks, wouldn't you, Little Miss Frigid? With that brother of yours!"

"*Hey!*"

Why Austin thought this was the moment to defend his brother when he had called Graeme a drunk to his face, Estella barely had time to consider as Paul barrelled onwards.

"Right company Reg Frayne's little lady keeps, ha? Drunks and hoors, is it?" He threw the last word at Rebecca. "Cos I know all about you, missy!" He stabbed a finger at her. "Oh yes, my mother found out all about you and your *past*! That fake husband of yours and your bastard babby boy!"

The rest happened very quickly. Rebecca seemed to crumple in Marion's arms. Estella's scream of rage was drowned by the animal roar of Ivan who dived for Paul. Roy Oaks threw himself on Ivan's back, slowing him enough to prevent the white-knuckled swing of a fist connect with The Craven's fleshy jaw. Ivan's lunging assault sailed within an inch of his quarry's nose and he stumbled, carried by the momentum of his punch and also the weight of Roy – solid as his name – doggedly clinging on. However, as Ivan struggled against the well-meaning hindrance that was his friend, another figure sliced through the gathering, hands outstretched. Howard Anstruther's fingers closed on the lapels of Paul's jacket. Before anyone really realised he was there, the force of his approach had carried The Craven backwards until his feet fell away beneath him and he slammed into the floor. Howard somehow managed to keep his balance but he didn't let go.

"*You will apologise!*" he snarled, leaning down as he lifted Paul's flailing body from the floor.

The room fell deathly silent. The two men were virtually nose to nose as the crowd looked on aghast. It seemed they were more shocked by Howard's behaviour than they were by the cause of it. Almost everyone knew The Craven was trouble. They expected it, even looked forward to his rudeness and misbehaviour livening up dull occasions. But what they did not expect – or ever countenance the possibility of – was the arrival of Howard Anstruther into the middle of such a volatile situation. He was reserved, silent, barely noticeable. He was impossibly gangly, walked with bowed head, hunched shoulders and was so thin the joke was that you missed him if he turned sideways. Up until that point, he had apparently spent much of his life sideways since no one ever really saw him at all.

But they all saw him now. White with fury, his teeth bared, he shook Paul Craven as if he weighed nothing. Horsey men, Estella thought. They were deceptively strong. Danny Fearon at Ellendale was a prime example – seventy if he was a day and strong as any young lad. Looking at Howard, she knew he was all muscle stretched tautly over powerful, angular bones. Beneath the scrawny exterior, the clothes that never seemed to fit despite being of the best quality, Howard was strong as an ox – strong as a horse. And beneath his shyness and mild manners, there was a person who stood up to be counted when it mattered. He was defending her friend like a brother, a lover. And for that, Estella could not think more highly of him.

Paul's scrabbling hands eventually found his assailant's wrists as he tried to pry Anstruther's fingers from his clothing. But Howard wouldn't budge. Red-faced and helpless, Paul gibbered nonsensically.

"*Apologise!*" Howard spat, hauling the rag-doll figure in his hands upright as if The Craven weighed nothing.

Paul began to keen, tears welling from his eyes. Moments before, he had been drunk and bullish. Now he was simply drunk and frightened. Estella wondered if he might soil himself in front of everyone since the rest of his faculties seemed to have deserted him. She glanced at the lower half of his body and was surprised to see his tiptoes barely had purchase on the floor. How humiliating, she thought. She felt a grim sense of satisfaction seeing him dangle and squirm like a worm between a child's fingers.

The tension was broken by the appearance of Mr Leclerc who chuffed into the centre of the group with the words, "What's all this, what's all this? *Oh!* Anstruther! Good Lord! What the –"

Confidence vanishing at the sight of the furious young man gripping his favourite jester, Leclerc's face fell. Suddenly, his bluster was replaced by a weak chin and swinging hands. Estella thought that, if he could have, the owner of Ellendale would have happily shrunk back into the crowd and let things carry on. But he had committed in front

343

of everyone so there was no turning back. Appraising the situation, he appeared to come to a conclusion. The slightly glassy expression cleared and he hitched up the waistband of his trousers.

"Put the man down now, Anstruther, there's a good chap. He's not that –"

"*He is!*" Howard snapped. "He's a disgusting little man! And he's not going anywhere until he apologises to Rebecca."

All eyes in the room seemed to swivel to Rebecca. Estella saw the panic in her eyes but she stood as tall as her small frame allowed. She wasn't cowed by Paul Craven's accusations.

Voices. Several of them sounded in the silence.

"He's right. He shouldn't be saying the likes of that."

"Aye, she's due an apology."

"Has to say sorry, he does."

"He'd be sorry if he said that to *my* woman."

Murmurs of approval and acquiescence. No one spoke up for Paul. All of them, without exception, sided with Rebecca.

She grew taller still, the support around the room buoying her. And her staunchest defender was still holding firm to her accuser.

"I was married before," she began calmly.

"*Rebecca, don't!*" Ivan warned, still struggling against Roy.

She ignored him. Her eyes were fixed on Howard Anstruther who had turned to look as soon as he heard her voice.

"I was married to a man I loved and I believed loved me.

It was only after we lived together for more than two years, had a child together, that he left me." She paused for a fraction of a moment. "He left me to go back to his first wife." There was a gasp but Howard held her gaze. "I didn't know he was already married. No one did."

"So your little boy *is* –" Paul Craven's triumphant wheeze was cut off by one word.

"Perfect," Rebecca answered succinctly.

"And will grow to be a better man than you could ever dream of being." Anstruther shook Paul as he spoke. "So you're going to apologise to this good, kind, loving woman and then leave."

The Craven cast his head from side to side, looking for someone – anyone – to step in and defend him. But no one did. Not even Mr Leclerc. His enabler finally saw the man before him for what he really was. The look of disappointment on his face was that of a child whose favourite toy lay broken at his feet.

"Apologise to the lady, Paul," he said quietly, eyes downcast.

It was as if the bubble had been burst. He sagged in Anstruther's grasp and stared at the floor. Eventually, he looked up, meeting Rebecca's defiant gaze. "I'm sorry," he said tightly. "I shouldn't have done … Said those things about … about you. Or the boy." He turned his face back to Anstruther. "Satisfied?"

Disgusted, Howard released him, shoving him in the chest to force as much distance between them as possible. "Get him out of here," he said to Austin. "If I see him again, he'll have both Ivan and me to deal with. And Oaks won't be holding him back next time."

"I can help if you like," Roy said with a cheerful leer in Paul's direction.

Taking a firm hold of his arm, despite Paul's attempts to pull away, Austin steered him though the parting crowd. Estella didn't bother to watch them go. Ivan had wrenched himself from Roy's grasp, popping a button on his suit jacket in the process, and was heading towards his sister. But Howard got there first. Marion stepped back and was swallowed by the dresses and suits behind her as he clasped Rebecca lightly by the shoulders. He bent his knees so they were nose to nose just as he had been with The Craven a moment before. Now, however, there was nothing but kindness, warmth and concern in his face. Gently, he rested his palm against her cheek, his thumb catching the moisture that had gathered beneath her left eye.

"He's gone. It's all right. You'll be all right, won't you?"

She reached her small hand up to his and kissed the ball of his palm. "Yes. Yes, I'm fine."

Estella looked away. It was a private moment that was not meant for prying eyes. She shifted her gaze to Ivan who stood looking slightly lost as the crowd around them dispersed and the band swung into action once more.

"You've lost a button from your suit," she admonished gently once he was within reach. Placing her hands on his chest, she felt him heave a great sigh as they began to sway to the music.

"I've lost three. They'll never let me hire a suit again."

"Here's one!" Dolly said, stooping to pick up a beetle-like button from the floor and almost causing Roy to topple over her.

346

"Mammy's going to kill me," he muttered glumly, rolling the offending article in his palm.

"Surely you can sew on a few buttons?" Estella cocked a worried eyebrow. He wasn't totally useless, was he?

"Of course I can! But you know Mammy. She'll nearly be standing in the doorway waiting for us to come home. And if she sees this –" he indicated the bulging front of his jacket "she'll eat me."

"She'd want a healthy appetite to manage all of you, mate," Roy said reasonably. "Maybe only a bit of shoulder or rump to start. And I don't suppose you'd be that tasty. You're all sinew like Anstruther over there."

They all turned to look at Rebecca and Howard pressed close as they moved to the music.

"Who'd have thought it, eh?" Dolly said with wonder. "Quiet chap like him."

"Always watch out for the quiet ones," Roy answered sagely.

"So we needn't bother watching out for Dolly then?" Ivan asked innocently.

They laughed as Dolly scowled at them. "I was going to be nice and tell you there's another button over there, but now I'm not sure I will," she huffed.

Estella steered them over to where Dolly indicated and, bending to pick it up, she heard Howard Anstruther's voice.

"I'm taking your sister home. Is that all right?"

Estella straightened to find Howard and Rebecca standing close, holding hands.

"Yeah, fine," Ivan shrugged. "You're happy to go home with him, Bec?"

347

"Yes."

Estella noted how she squeezed Howard's hand as Ivan asked, "You sure you're all right?"

She lifted one shoulder then dropped it. "Could be better. Could be worse too. I'll live."

Then, without warning, Ivan threw his arms around his sister, engulfing her small frame in a bone-crushing hug. "You know I love you, Bec? No matter what. You and Harry."

"Goodness!" she gasped, laughing as she extricated herself. "Nobody died! We're all fine. And yes," she added, reaching up on tiptoe to kiss him on the cheek, "I know you love us."

Estella and Ivan watched Howard's retreating back meander through the crowd before he disappeared through the far door, Rebecca presumably at his side. They stood still in the middle of the floor, oblivious to everything around them until Dolly's excited voice called them back.

"Found another one!" she shouted gleefully, waving a shiny black dot above her head.

Chapter 32

Once the adrenalin rush of the confrontation with Paul had subsided, Estella and Ivan's interest in the party waned significantly.

"Home?" he asked.

"What about Dolly?"

"I'm not leaving yet!" she squawked when they found her steering a still-reluctant Roy around the dancefloor. "I put a lot of effort into this dress so I want to get plenty of wear out of it."

"I'll dr-drive her home," Roy offered, slurring the word slightly.

Dolly looked at him sharply. "You will not. It's me who'll be driving you home before we end up in a ditch."

"Fair enough," he shrugged heavily.

"Might be an idea," Ivan said as they left. He fished his keys out of his breast pocket and dropped them into Estella's hand.

"You don't seem drunk. And I should know what one looks like."

"I hold it well. And I don't drink as much as either Roy

or Graeme. Nowhere near." He stroked the puckered front of his jacket. "Mammy's going to kill me," he repeated mournfully.

"Oh for goodness' sake! *I'll* sew on the bloody buttons when we get home and then you can appear presentably before your mother."

He grinned over the roof of the car as they got in. It was a slightly vacant smile. Over his shoulder she spotted Austin handing Marion into the passenger seat of his car. He seemed to sense her eyes and looked up. Estella nodded. He nodded back then they both silently got into their cars and drove away.

The yard was empty and the house silent when they got back well after midnight. Without turning on the light in the porch, Estella bent to undo the straps on her shoes. A bleary-eyed Ivan, who had shuffled in behind her having fallen asleep on the journey home, promptly collided with her. She yelped and threw out her hands to steady herself as Ivan grabbed at her. He found purchase on the material at her hips and pulled her back against his front.

"*Oof!*"

He cringed as she over-balanced and fell into him with much more force than either intended. Then he froze. They both froze. He exhaled and she felt the warmth of his breath on the back of her neck. It tickled. Slowly, cautiously he released the fabric of her dress finger by finger then crept his hands forward to her stomach. His large hands splayed luxuriously, thumbs grazing the bottom of her breasts, pinkies dipping into the hollows beside her hipbones. She seemed to grow taller, stretching her neck, throwing her head back against his shoulder, closing her eyes. Moist lips brushed the skin beneath her ear, his palms pressed firmly against her belly, fingertips twitching with the desire to move, to explore.

Estella became aware of how hot she suddenly felt. Her cheeks burned, her back, her legs, her stomach. Yet her feet – scalded from hours in uncomfortable shoes – now stung sharply on the cold tiled floor. Liquid warmth slid through her veins in waves as her brain tried to process the wild emotions and exquisite sensation of Ivan pressed up behind her.

"*Oh!*" she murmured.

"*Oh ...*" he murmured back.

Estella felt something soft brush against her ankle and yelped again. But it was only Sophie who had come to weave herself around their legs – half welcome, half admonishment.

Thrilled and mortified by his closeness, Estella disentangled herself from him.

"Damn cat," she heard Ivan mutter as she scampered across the kitchen to fetch her sewing box from the other room. When she returned, the glow in her cheeks had become patchy but the rest of her body still felt unaccountably warm. Ivan stood awkwardly in the centre of the kitchen, jacket in his hands. He tried to catch her eye, but she wouldn't look at him.

"I can sew the buttons on."

He reached for the sewing box, but she held it out of his reach. His great paws looked far too clumsy to handle the delicately embroidered box, never mind its fiddly contents.

351

Those hands had been wrapped around her moments before. She felt her skin flame again.

"No, I'll do it. I don't trust you." She still couldn't look at him. She grabbed the jacket and walked over to stand below the light under the pretence of getting a better look at the garment. But really, she just needed to distance herself from him. If she continued to stand close to him, she wasn't sure what either of them would do. She was even careful not to glance in his direction when he walked over and threw himself down in her seat by the Aga.

"That's where I sit," she chided lightly.

He patted his knee. "Welcome to sit here if you want," he grinned, finally catching her eye. He winked. She shook her head furiously. However, the cat apparently had fewer scruples and happily hopped up on his proffered knee. "*Oi! Not you!*" he told her and attempted to lift her off. With lazy efficiency, Sophie sank her claws into the legs of his trousers. "*Oi! Ow!* Not the trousers!" He gave up trying to remove her. "Bloody cat," he grumbled.

Estella cackled. "Good girl, Sophie. You tell him."

"Witch!"

It took her no time to reattach the buttons. Ivan sat watching, stroking the cat absentmindedly. The silence was comfortable. Estella found herself wondering if they would always be like this – if there was to be an 'always'. Of course there would be. She and Ivan were made for one another. They loved each other. But then Rebecca had said she loved her husband. And he had duped her in the most abominable of ways.

"Rebecca …" he said.

"*Hmmm?*"

"Her ... she was ... married."

"*Mmm.*"

Ivan sighed heavily, rubbing the purring cat's ears. "I wish she hadn't told everyone. Mammy'll be livid."

"Why?"

"Because it's no one else's business but hers. And now it's all people will see when they look at her. Treat her like she's – I don't know – a *fallen woman* – when it wasn't her fault. He was a posh-sounding lad over from England. Ten years older than her. All charm. Even Mammy liked him."

"Did you?"

He shrugged. "Thought he was full of himself but Bec seemed happy so ... I wasn't going to interfere in *that*. But it was only afterwards that we realised no one really knew anything about him. He was back and forth to England a lot. For work, he said. Or visiting family. Wasn't until he wrote to Bec to say he was staying with his wife and children that we realised what he meant by *his family*. Harry's lucky – he doesn't remember him. It was Rebecca he hurt the most. Because no one could look at her anymore. People we'd known since we were toddlers and they wouldn't even speak to her. So she left."

"Left?"

"Ran away, I suppose. Left Harry with Mammy and went to work in a linen factory up round Belfast."

"I didn't know that."

"No one was supposed to know any of it. That was the whole point of her coming down here with us. New start for all of us. And she hated it in Belfast and being away from

Harry. It was all going so well too. But then that – that *bastard* – Craven had to come along."

"Suppose that's why she told everyone. It was better for her to tell everyone on her own terms rather than on his."

He huffed. "Suppose. Still … I wanted to hurt him so badly." His voice was hollow, ashamed. Yet his gaze was defiant.

"If there hadn't been anyone else there, I probably would have stood by egging you on. His comeuppance was long overdue." Words she had never said to another living soul were suddenly spilling out of her mouth "He and his mother spread a rumour that I'd killed Daddy."

Ivan was abruptly on his feet, cat in hand, red with fury. "*What?*"

She didn't reply. There was no need. She had said all she was going to say on the subject. Slowly, abstractedly, Ivan began to stroke the cat in his arms. "And Mr Leclerc *still* invites him to things."

"I suppose because he gave no credence to the rumour. It never went far so not many people heard it. But I heard it. And just because Mr Leclerc didn't believe it, didn't mean some people who heard it didn't look at me funny down the shops and … wonder."

Still holding the cat with one hand, Ivan walked over to her and awkwardly hugged her head to his chest. Sophie began to purr, radiating warmth and contentment. Estella could feel the heat of Ivan's skin on her cheek. His large hand seemed to cover most of her skull. How was it that life often felt so heavy yet when he touched her everything seemed softer, lighter? His touch offered her a relief that no other human contact gave her – except maybe Dolly's. This must be what it's like to find *your person*, she thought. To find someone who didn't need to make grand gestures, who didn't need to do anything lewd or erotic to make her feel his love. He simply held her to his body and she felt the love pour from his chest and wash over her.

"I should go," he said.

"Yes."

Neither of them moved. The cat continued to purr.

"Or I could ... stay ..."

"Stay?"

"For a while. If you want. I don't know." He began to pull away but she grabbed a fistful of his shirt. "Careful!" he sniggered. "Or I'll need more buttons sewn on."

"I can do that."

"I know." He gave her shoulder a squeeze. "You'll make me a good little wifey."

She stood and took the cat from him. "You really like me enough to make me your wifey?" she asked, turning away.

"Of course," he laughed. "Why'd you ask?"

"Why do you even *like* me?" she countered, rounding on him with a shrewd eye.

He looked taken aback. "I ... well ... because you're you. We just ... I don't know. I've never really known someone I could talk to so easily. Who doesn't resent the fact that I live and breathe horses every day of the week. Who's there *with* me." He took her hand. "Stella, I've met plenty of girls over the years but not one, *not one*, understood what I do – who I *am* – the way you do. You're the only girl I've ever been able to picture growing old with, having a family. We are ... we just work." He ended with feeble shrug.

Mollified, Estella glowed. She hadn't really expected an answer when the words passed her lips. She had been shocked they even got that far. But she was tired and they just slipped out. Now, she was glad they had. She bent and dropped Sophie on the floor then, in two strides collided with Ivan's chest and wrapped her arms around his back. He reciprocated, squeezing her tight, lifting her up on her tiptoes.

"Oh, clothes," Ivan murmured to himself.

"What?"

"I was wondering why you felt smaller than usual. No big coat or woolly jumper. Only the dress. You just … felt different."

"Know me that well, do you?" She smiled into his chest.

"I know exactly how you feel. I'd know in the dark," he said confidently. But then she felt a rumble building in his chest. "Oh …"

"Yes," she answered dryly. "*Oh*." They stood together for a long time until Estella's eyes began to feel heavy. "I'm going up to bed." She disentangled herself from his arms but stood before him. "Coming?"

He cocked an eyebrow.

"Not for that," she told him firmly.

"No," he agreed, but she couldn't help but see his slight disappointment.

"I'll set Sophie on you if you misbehave," she threatened as the cat's bushy tail preceded them along the hall and disappeared up the stairs.

"Bloody cat," she heard him mutter.

* * *

After he had been to the bathroom, Estella – determined not to lose her nerve – showed Ivan into her room. She cringed a little at the plethora of childish objects dotted on every flat surface – from plaster ornaments to china dolls. The wall above Joy's old bed – on which Sophie sat in state – was also covered with photos, newspaper clippings and rosettes from past equestrian triumphs. It was this display that Ivan was immediately drawn to as she fished her pyjamas from under the pillow and scampered out muttering, "Bathroom."

Once she was in there, she snapped the door shut and leant her head against the wood. Ivan was in her bedroom! What were they thinking! She laughed quietly to herself and shook her head. If anyone were to find out! But they wouldn't. No one would know about this. She trusted Ivan's discretion and she certainly wasn't going to tell anyone – not even Dolly. She stood and watched herself in the mirror. The perfect make-up and hair from earlier in the night was now somewhat … crushed. Around her eyes especially looked smudged. Why was there a man waiting in her room for this crumpled mess? She began pulling the pins from her hair to allow the stiff tresses to slowly uncoil from the complicated up-do Rebecca had knotted them in. She ran her fingers through to loosen each of the tails but they had no effect. Giving up on her hair, she reached to the nape of her neck and undid the hook and eye above the zip. She reached for the zip … and reached … and reached. She *couldn't* reach. Her reflection sized her up.

"Well, you're going to have to get out of it somehow," she told herself.

Squaring her shoulders, she marched back to her room where Ivan was still perusing her wall of achievements. He opened his mouth to speak but she beat him to it.

"Can you unzip my dress, please?" she blurted out, turning her back to him before she saw his reaction.

It was a moment before his warm fingers brushed the bare skin just above the dress. She resisted the urge to shiver. With deliberate slowness, he pulled the zip, trailing a solitary fingertip down her spine. However, before he got too far, Estella jumped forward.

"That's fine! I can do the rest." She clutched the dress to her front.

"How were you going to get out of it on your own?" he asked curiously.

"I never really thought about it," she admitted. "Or maybe I did and that's the only reason you're here. You can go now." She grinned.

"No, I think I'll stay." To make his point, he threw himself down on her bed.

It took Estella all of five minutes to run back to the bathroom, change and hurry through her nightly routine. Even though it was heading for two o'clock in the morning, she still brushed her teeth and washed her face. However, as she passed the door to Graeme's empty room, she hesitated, wondering where he was. Carefully, she firmly pressed down the rising worry that threatened to overtake her good mood. The fact was that Graeme was determinedly paddling his own canoe. Better to simply carry on to the room in which there was a man waiting for her.

Ivan lay across the bed, his head propped against the wall,

his legs stretched an impossible distance over the floor. It looked deeply uncomfortable. Estella held her dress protectively to her chest, wanting to put it away but also to cover herself with it. She hung it on the front of the wardrobe.

"Budge up," she ordered, shooing Ivan out of the way.

He drew his legs up onto the covers, plastering himself against the wall so that she could get in and lie beside him. He took up so much room, she wondered if the queen-size mattress was large enough to accommodate both of them. But she found they fitted quite cosily – her under the covers, he on top of them. As she snuggled into his bulk, he threw an arm over her, pulling her close so they lay back to chest. She felt the warm moisture of his breath on her shoulder. He kissed her hair, brushing it out of the way before he kissed the shell of her ear. She, therefore, got quite a shock when he yawned noisily directly over her ear.

"Boring you, am I?"

"I'm not bored right now, no," he assured her, burrowing into her neck until she wriggled and squeaked beneath him.

They were both slightly breathless by the time his teasing subsided. She held his arm tight to her but noticed he was, for once, slightly cold. "Here." She threw one of the layered blankets over him. He tucked it under his arm and settled around her again.

"Light off?" she asked eventually.

"Think so."

She switched off the bedside lamp. "Night."

"Night," he whispered. Then, giving her a final squeeze, "I'd know how you feel in the dark …"

Chapter 33

Ivan left early in the morning – or perhaps later in the morning since they had gone to bed in the wee small hours. He murmured something unintelligible, kissed her forehead and snuck out. She probably should have made more of an effort to say goodbye but he had barely left the room before she was asleep again. When she woke, it was to the shrill ringing of her alarm. There was a weak sun shining through her curtains, promising a damp but sunny day. She breathed deeply and could still smell the masculine scent of Ivan on her bedding. She turned over, burying her head in the covers, giggling like a schoolgirl. What a thing it would be to wake up to that smell every day!

As she rose, stretching her limbs, she thought – rather guiltily – about how lucky she was to have no one who would interfere in her relationship with Ivan. Really, they could do anything they liked. Her brothers didn't care and she had no mother or father to scandalise. Not one of her friends would know how it felt to share a bed with a man and have no fear of being found out. Of course, nothing had really happened. They had kissed and cuddled and touched with curious, cautious fingers but it hadn't gone any further. Had she wanted it to, it would have. But for some reason, she couldn't quite bring herself to turn the page and invite the next phase of her life to begin. There was still an innocence, a child-like view of what a relationship was, that she couldn't quite dissolve. Not yet. She wanted it to feel like the right time and whether that came before or after a marriage, she didn't really care. Ivan wasn't going anywhere and neither was she. And if she had a child, so be it. They would make good parents, she thought confidently. The only downside would be that she couldn't continue to ride throughout the pregnancy. For the first few months maybe, but after that she would have to be careful. And if that was her only concern, she had very little to worry about.

Of course, it wasn't her only concern. She had finished her morning jobs and was about to head to Ellendale when the trilling bell of the phone sounded across the yard.

"Can you come and get your brother, Stella?" Nelly Sweeney sounded harassed on the other end of the telephone. "Folk coming into the shop are ... *asking questions*."

She hung up and rang Leclercs' yard.

"I've got to sort some things with my brother," she told Danny Fearon.

He answered with a gruff, "Right."

"Can you let Ivan know I'll be late?"

She set off on her bike, peddling furiously. She *was* furious. Bloody Graeme! He couldn't even sort himself out by morning. Why didn't he have the capacity to find his own way home? Surely that shouldn't be beyond the capabilities of a man of thirty? He was *embarrassing* her *and* making her late for work. And why couldn't Nelly just kick him out herself?

She had worked up a good head of steam by the time she arrived. She burst through the door with such force the little bell above it flew across the shop and landed with a mewling tinkle on the floor a good ten feet away.

"Where is he?" she asked without preamble.

Standing behind the counter, Nelly jerked her head in the direction of the snug and turned her attention back to her customer with hunched shoulders.

Just then, a warbling voice issued from the room in question.

"*'Twas early one morning I walked 'long the strand ...*"

He was *singing*?

"*I happened to meet a young lady so grand ...*"

She glanced through the doorway and came back to Nelly immediately. "You gave him *drink*?"

Nelly rounded on her, standing to her considerable height, eyes blazing. "I did not! He took it. He paid, in fairness to him," she conceded, "but he was having that bottle and there was no way I was stopping him."

"*Me and my young wan of nineteen years old!*" Graeme voice rose then broke into a peal of hysterical giggling.

Estella closed her eyes in irritation. Or perhaps she was praying for divine calm. How would she manage him? One thing was certain: she wasn't leaving him here to make a show of himself and the Frayne surname. She knew the song and didn't really want him to get to the part about the 'young wan' unscrewing her wooden leg. Or the bit about her false teeth. And the glass eye rolling across the floor. Not in front the delicate souls who fetched their groceries at ten in the morning. There was already one woman queueing who looked deeply disconcerted by the voice emanating from the depths of the building.

Ignoring both curious and disapproving glances, Estella marched into the snug with her nose in the air. She was fed up using the gently-gently approach. Sometimes, an animal just needed to be shown who was in charge – it was the only way some would learn to respect you. There was no need for violence, just a firm hand. You respected them until they didn't show you the same courtesy. Graeme had barely acknowledged her existence, never mind anything more. It was time for a firm hand.

"*Graeme!*" Her sharp voice sliced through air thick with the lingering smell of smoke, men and alcohol.

Her brother started, smacking his knee on the underside of the table he was huddled at which, in turn, upended an empty glass and made the half-drunk bottle of whiskey rock precariously until he managed to swipe it off the table and cuddle it to his chest. It took a moment for his eyes to find her. His stare was contemptuous.

"*Whadidyedo tha' fur?*" he shouted.

"*Out. Now.*"

His gaze hardened instantly. "*No.*"

The use of reason didn't even cross her mind. He was beyond that. Instead, she strode across to him and kicked his stool, glad of the hard sole on her riding boot. The result was better than she could have imagined. The stool pinged out from underneath him and skittered away. A flailing Graeme landed hard on his backside, making the wooden floor shake. Even after he landed, his arms continued to wave, allowing Estella to swipe the bottle from his grasp with ease. She corked it and, ignoring Graeme's protestations as he continued to scrabble about, she walked out to Nelly, wordlessly handed her the bottle and went back to her brother. There was a sheen of sweat on his brow and he was breathing heavily but at least he had stopped flinging his limbs everywhere.

"Ye'd no right t' take that. 'S bought 'n' paid for."

"And I'm sure you'll have no problems drinking the rest of it tonight."

"No right …"

"*Get up!*" she said sharply. "And stop making a show of yourself."

"No one here." He flung an arm, gesturing to the sea of table and stool legs.

"I'm here. And I'm not no one. And neither are you. Have some self-respect."

He thought about that. "Can't get up."

She took three long strides, grabbed his arm in both hands and wrenched him to his feet with one clean jerk. Graeme staggered a little – both from shock and inebriation. Estella was strong for her size but didn't often show it. However, she was somewhat shocked herself by how easy it had been to lift her brother's almost dead-weight. He weighed much less than she expected. And his arm beneath her hands felt narrow under the thick weave of his jacket. Had he always been that thin? She couldn't think of the last time she had touched him so it was hard to know.

"Let's go."

After Graeme managed to find his car keys, she drove them home. The sour reek of stale sweat and fermenting alcohol permeated the vehicle, forcing Estella to open her window. Graeme huddled in the passenger seat, hands clamped tightly over his stomach.

"You eaten?"

"Don't want anything."

She stopped herself from replying. It wasn't worth the childish back and forth that would ensue. Instead, once they arrived home and she had removed her bike from the car, she followed him into the kitchen to make some food. He was already sitting at the table, a bottle in one hand and his mug in the other, glass and ceramic singing as his shaking hand knocked them together.

"Goodness' *sake*!" she spat, storming across the room to the Aga. "If you're going to keep drinking, you have to eat *something*."

"No, I don't."

To prove his point, he downed the mugful in one gulp, sneering at her over the rim. However, no sooner had the alcohol hit his stomach than his face changed. He shuddered, gasped. Lurching forward, he put his hands to his stomach, his mouth and eyes pinched in agony. And then he began to vomit.

Foul-smelling liquid spewed across the table, on the floor, down his front, as he heaved and retched, bringing up dark bile and froth. It ran down his chin, gushed from his nose and in between he sobbed and screeched like a child unable to fathom the sudden betrayal of his own body.

Estella stood paralysed. The waves continued to wash over her brother until he was on the floor – gagging, crying. But this wasn't what impelled her to move. What brought her back was the sight of the cat streaking out of the kitchen away from the horror. It surprised her. On multiple occasions, her father had performed surgeries out in the yard or on the kitchen floor with Sophie sitting on high watching every move he made. 'Like she's studying and I'm her teacher,' Reg used to say. Sitting perfectly upright with her front feet slightly turned out, Sophie had observed castrations, caesareans and the removal of intestinal blockages. Never had any sight or smell resulted in her high-tailing it out of the room. Yet in the face of Graeme's sudden expulsion of his abdominal contents (because this wasn't just from his stomach), Sophie's resilience had finally deserted her. Estella didn't have that luxury.

"Oh Jesus! Oh God!" Her words hurried the cat on her way. *"Graeme? Oh Christ!"*

She started forward and then stuttered, unwilling to step into the puddle around his knees. She saw the dark stain of it seeping into the fabric of his trousers and creeping up his knees. She felt the juices of her own stomach begin to rise but swallowed hard, breathing through her mouth. It helped but she still recoiled from the acid tang on her tongue. Doing the first thing that seemed sensible, she grabbed the back of Graeme's jacket and hauled him out of the pool since he looked like he was about to keel over in it. For the second time that morning, she landed him on his backside and he screeched, clutching at his stomach again. She didn't care. She was furious. White hot anger burned through her veins.

She had tried kindness and sympathy. It hadn't worked. Firmly suppressing the urge to empty her stomach, she took hold of his shoulders and removed his jacket with three swift tugs, careful not to touch the soiled front or cuffs. He tried to fight her off but she was stronger and much more coordinated. She burst the top few buttons on his shirt then ripped it off over his head as he sobbed, sagging like a ragdoll against her knees as she stood over him. Next, she grabbed him by the wrist and oxter then, with an almighty jerk, heaved him upright so that he was resting on her shoulders. He screamed and retched but brought little more up.

"*Undo your trousers,*" she ordered. He whimpered, shaking his head. "*Do it now or I will.*"

With a trembling hand, he managed to fumble with the belt and buttons. It was pitiful to watch his slow progress, but she didn't have enough hands to help even if she wanted to (which she didn't). Eventually he managed to drop them, almost overbalancing himself and Estella as he stepped out of them.

"*Upstairs. Now.*"

She half dragged him up to the bathroom. They were both panting by the time she deposited him on the toilet in his underpants, socks and vest. He was shivering violently. The pipes gurgled as she turned on the bath then fetched an enamel basin from the spare room and plunked it down on the floor beside the head of the bath.

"If you're going to throw up again, do it in this, not on the floor."

He looked uncomfortable at the thought.

"Do you need help into the bath or will you manage

yourself?" For a moment, she was reminded of all the times she had to help her father wash. But she cringed away from the thought.

"Manage," Graeme grunted, teeth chattering.

"I'll get you clean clothes."

That done, she trudged back down, only then realising she had worn her boots upstairs. At least the surfaces were all wood or linoleum and easy to clean. It was hardly a buoying thought as she returned to the sour alcoholic stench of the kitchen. But there was no point delaying the inevitable so, while keeping an ear out for her brother's movements above, she set about clearing up just as she had many times before.

The clothing was immediately dumped outside the back door. She then set about cleaning the table, chair and floor with what little hot water Graeme had left. Leaving the kettle boil in order to scald the wooden table, she used some cold water and Parozone to kill germs and the smell. The chlorine stung her nostrils but it was better than vomit any day. Anything was better than that, including the contents of an animal's bowels, she thought.

Kitchen now humming with the stench of bleach, she traipsed upstairs to check on Graeme. He was sitting in his bed, flannel pyjamas on, skin a pasty yellow. He was still shaking.

"Eat?" she asked. He shook his head and she saw dark spots appear on the covers as fine droplets of water fell from the ends of his wet hair. "You should dry that."

Turning about, she got a towel from the bathroom and came back to him with it just in time to see him hurriedly stuff a bottle behind his pillow. He knew she'd seen it. The look he gave her was a mixture of shame and defiance.

"If I take that one away, do you have another?"

"Yes," he answered.

"Are you going to tell me where it's hidden?"

"No."

She couldn't even bring herself to respond. Instead, she slammed his bedroom door shut as she left. He wailed in response. Probably because the noise upset his delicate constitution, she thought. She tore down the stairs, catching herself on the wall at the bottom. What was it about her family? Her mother, father, Graeme. And Joy. Poor, clueless Joy – nothing would ever make her better. One by one, her family were taken from her. She wanted to scream in frustration. She couldn't go through this again. She couldn't fight to save another family member who didn't want to be saved. Repeat the experience of caring for Reg with Graeme. But then could she stand by and do nothing?

The simple and definitive answer was no.

With heavy feet, she walked over to the telephone table and sat down. She dialled the number.

"Can you put me through to Doctor Adkins, please?"

She waited.

The doctor was in.

"Hello, Doctor Adkins, It's Estella Frayne – I'm good, thank you. How are you? – Yes, it's about my brother. Graeme." She glanced at the foot of the stairs and lowered her voice needlessly. "He's, well, he's an ... an alcoholic. I think. He's very poorly, sir. And," she felt her throat tighten, "and I really just don't know what to do."

Not only was Adkins a good doctor, he was a good

person too. "Well, Miss Frayne, I've got a few patients to see early in the afternoon but perhaps I can call out this evening. Have a – ah – *chat*. And maybe a look at our patient. Yes?"

After that, she rang Ellendale. This time, she got Ivan.

"You all right?" he asked immediately.

"I'm fine. It's Graeme." She had been about to tell him she would see him tomorrow but changed her mind. What was she going to do at home? Sit and wait for a thud to emanate from Graeme's room? "I'll be over after dinner to ride. I'll talk to you then."

It was cold – heartless – to leave him. She sat by the telephone a little longer and wondered about calling Ivan again to tell him she was staying. But she didn't.

Instead, she went outside, picked up Graeme's soiled garments and proceeded to sluice them under the pump, washing until her hands were shining red and stinging from the exposure to freezing spring water.

Chapter 34

After dinner, she checked on Graeme again, making plenty of noise on the stairs so he had time to hide his whiskey. If he was still drinking it, she didn't want to know. But when she looked in, he was lying in a ball, facing away from her.

"I'm off. Do you want anything?"

There was a grunt but nothing more. She closed the door and left.

Ellendale was relatively quiet when she arrived. The morning jobs were over and the evening ones yet to commence so without meeting anyone, she fetched a saddle and bridle then headed off to tack up her first horse. She had only just brushed the dust off its coat when a shadow fell across the stable as Ivan came in.

"Well?" he asked, leaning up against the wall.

"Shouldn't you be off doing something useful?" she asked lightly.

"I am. I'm keeping an eye on the staff. Making sure they're doing a good job. You missed a bit." He pointed at the horse's knee where there was a patch of dried mud.

She threw him a dirty look. "Muddy knees never did

anyone any harm."

"Really? I'm shocked. Little Iris Kellett is willing to stoop as low as riding a horse with a mucky knee?" He tutted.

"Fine," she sighed, bent down and ran the brush over the offending knobbly knee. "Satisfied?"

"Succeeded in getting you to stick your backside in the air without you even realising? *Very* satisfied. *Oi!*" He managed to catch the brush she had thrown at him. "No, seriously – is everything all right? What happened this morning?"

"Graeme happened."

"Oh?"

"He's in a bad way. Drink."

"Oh. How bad?"

"He's stopped eating."

"Oh."

They were both people who had been raised to believe that three square meals a day were essential to good health.

"He just … drinks instead. I had to collect him from Nelly's. She rang me this morning. And when I brought him home it … all came back up." Ivan's nose wrinkled. "And then he just drank some more. The doctor's coming to see him later but I don't know if he can really do anything. I'm worried the drinking has gone too far. That he's incapable of stopping."

Ivan scuffed the straw beneath his feet. "It's hard when they go that far. Neighbour of ours tried to dry out. It was nearly worse than the drinking. Anyway, he was dry for a while and then went back on the sauce. Killed him in the end. Sclerosis of the liver. But he had thirty years on your brother."

"I don't know if that means he has more of a chance to

get back to good health or a longer time to kill himself." Her tone was weary – flippant – but the truth of her own words hit her like a gut punch. She leant against the horse's shoulder.

A moment later, Ivan was holding her.

"If you want to go home, go."

She shook her head against his chest. "And sit around worrying? No, I'd rather work."

"All right then. Let's go."

It wasn't until they were out on the horses trotting towards the woods that Estella thought to ask, "Was Rebecca all right after last night?"

Ivan sucked in a slow breath and gave her a serious look.

"Oh no!" Estella's face fell. "She's not –"

"She's fine." They trotted on a little further. "Anstruther asked her to marry him on the way home last night."

"*What*?" Estella shrieked, making both horses shoot forward. "Oh! Sorry, pet!" She gave her horse a pat. "*What*?" she asked more quietly.

"Yep."

"No!"

"Yes!"

"*No!* And what did she say?"

"Apparently that she would *think about it*."

"Oh. Right. Sensible."

"That makes one of them." Ivan snorted. "What was Anstruther thinking? No – that's not right – he wasn't *thinking*."

"Don't be cruel!" she admonished. "She's your sister. And she's lovely!"

373

"I know that! But we know that because *we* know *her*. Howard's known her – what? – three months?"

"Successful marriages have been had on lesser acquaintance."

"And unsuccessful on greater."

"Don't be so cynical!"

"I just don't want to see her hurt again."

Ah. Estella slowed her horse to a walk. "Howard's a good man, Ivan. And his family are lovely, decent, honest people. I've known his parents for as long as I can remember and never heard a bad word against them. Or him." There weren't many people she would be prepared to give such a ringing endorsement. In fact, she couldn't think of a single man other than Howard of whom she would so wholeheartedly approve.

Ivan hunched in the saddle, brooding. "He seems good enough," he conceded reluctantly. "But ..."

"But?"

"Well," he cast her a furtive glance, "puts me under pressure, doesn't it?"

"It does?" She had no idea what he was talking about.

"Means I'll have to propose to you now too, doesn't it?"

She gawped at him then burst out laughing. He as good as told her they were going to be husband and wife the night before. But they were in no rush. Now, however, he had competition. Who would be the first to get married? Whatever Ivan thought, Estella was quite happy to stand back and watch someone else walk down the aisle first. She was in no hurry. But that didn't mean she couldn't have a little fun.

"Yes, you'll have to propose to me now. *Right* now."

He gaped at her. "Wha?"

She sat tall in her saddle, brushing down her clothing with one hand and pulling her plait over her shoulder so that it looked pretty. "I'm ready. But –" she held up a warning finger "– it better be a good one. All the right words and sentiments in the right order, yes?"

Ivan looked even more gormless and panicky. "I – I don't –"

"*Buuut …*" she cut him off, then suddenly squeezed her horse's flanks and leant forward, giving the gelding his head. The horse took its cue and launched itself forward into canter. "*You'll have to catch me first!*" she shouted over her shoulder.

They rode three horses apiece that afternoon. Ivan didn't propose. He didn't need to. They knew they were promised to one another. They would sort it out eventually. But, for now, they had too much to do.

As she cycled home, Estella's limbs felt heavier with every pedal-stroke. She didn't want to go back. She didn't want to have to deal with whatever it was that awaited her. That wasn't how it was supposed to be. Home was supposed to be a safe, comforting place. You went there for refuge, tranquillity after the hurly-burly of the world. But really, home only occasionally meant that for Estella. Her sense of calm and utter contentment came from horses, from Ivan. So often she crossed the threshold of her house fearing what she would find within – arguments, upset, anger, illness. Perhaps this was the lot of everyone entering their own home. But she couldn't picture a future with Ivan where she was afraid to go home. All she could think was that it would be something to look forward to. Surely everyone expected their life would be like that?

She didn't go in when she got back. Instead, she went around the yard and fields checking animals, feeding animals and generally spending as much time as she could on each job. She was just sweeping out the parlour having milked the cows when she heard a car coming up the lane.

"You look busy, Miss Frayne," Dr Adkins greeted her. "How's the patient?"

She hesitated. "I don't know. I haven't checked on him in a while."

They went straight in, took off their footwear and headed upstairs, socks muffling their tread. To appear polite, Estella knocked on the door and preceded the doctor into the room.

Graeme was curled up, knees to his chest but his sleeping face was now facing the door. The skin was puffy and the grey-yellow of gone-off porridge. His left hand peeped out from under the covers, dangling over the edge of the bed and below it on the floor was an empty bottle. She couldn't have staged the scene better to prove the point that her brother had a serious problem. Yet embarrassment still urged her to pick up the bottle. But she stoically left it where it was.

"*Ah* ..." The doctor's lips compressed. "Where did he get that?"

"I don't know. This morning, I thought he only had a bottle in the kitchen but he must have them hidden everywhere."

"*Hmm*, yes, they do that. They can be very resourceful."

"They?"

"Alcoholics."

"Oh. So he's definitely ..."

"Well, if the bottle wasn't enough of a giveaway, the jaundiced skin is certainly a concern." He leaned over Graeme and studied him carefully. "I assume the whites of his eyes are the same."

"Yellow? Yes."

"Unless I'm mistaken, I think your brother is suffering from alcoholic hepatitis. I've seen it quite often, I'm afraid. It means his liver is packing in. The liver filters toxins from the body," he explained.

"I know. It's the same in animals."

"Of course. Your father was a vet. I assume he's not eating either?"

"Not that I've seen."

They both stood and watched Graeme for a while.

"Should we wake him?" she asked.

"I think not. For now. He wouldn't thank us. And, well, if he's asleep then he's not drinking and it's imperative he doesn't do that."

Dr Adkins walked out, holding the door for her.

Back in the kitchen, Estella made tea. Once she was seated at the table, Sophie appeared and hopped onto her knee. The doctor's eyes rested on the cat.

"How long has Graeme been drinking?" He continued to focus on Sophie.

Estella thought. "I don't remember a time when he didn't. Except when he was very young. He and Daddy used to have awful arguments over it. But that just made him worse."

377

"Often does. What casual observers don't often realise is that once someone starts drinking heavily, it's desperately difficult to get them to stop. No matter how much chastising or cajoling you do. Alcoholics can be very difficult to save if they don't want to be. Even if they *do* want your help, the urge to drink can sometimes be too powerful."

"So, what's to be done?"

"Prevent his alcohol consumption. Immediately. If he continues to abuse his body in this way, he might not see the summer, never mind the end of the year."

She blenched at that. Her brother could be dead in a few months. She would be the last Frayne left in the house. Alone. "How do I stop him?" she asked hopelessly.

"We have to convince him. I take it you're close?" he added.

"No, not at all," she replied.

The doctor raised his eyebrows.

But it was the truth. Graeme may have been part of the fabric of her home but he was almost an inanimate feature – less sentient than some of the animals. She had a closer relationship with Sophie, with Beryl the donkey than her own brother, she thought guiltily.

"Ah. I thought you might be able to help me to persuade him. Lend the weight of your opinion …"

She gave a hollow laugh. "I think I'm more likely to drive him to it. He'd drink just to spite me."

Adkins sat back, tapping his lip. "Then perhaps myself and Mr Frayne should conduct this conversation alone. I'm wondering if we could persuade him into a bed in the hospital. It would be much more conducive to his recovery to be in a different, more public environment. And it would remove him from his secreted deposits of alcohol, no doubt scattered around the house."

"Yes," was all she could think to say in response.

They sat quietly until they heard a coughing fit overhead followed by groaning and what sounded like sobbing.

"That won't have done the pain in his stomach any good." The doctor got heavily to his feet. "Wish me luck," he said, heading for the stairs.

"Good luck," she mumbled, but he'd already disappeared.

Adkins was gone for nearly half an hour. "Your brother won't go to hospital," he said wearily on return. "Despite my telling him he mightn't last the year. I think, for now, you're going to have to manage him yourself. I'm sorry. I tried. But he's stubborn."

"Yes, he is."

"Try and get him to eat something first of all. He couldn't tell me the last time he ate which is worrying. He'll need good food to repair all the damage he's done. But it's going to be hard to get it into him. Especially when his stomach's so tender. Maybe try him with some bread and milk. Or milk and cereal. Or a lightly boiled egg."

"I'll see what I can do."

"But if he gets any worse, you'll have to get him into hospital one way or another."

"Knock him out with one of his empty bottles?" she asked sardonically.

The doctor chuckled. "I wouldn't rule it out just yet." He put a fatherly hand on her shoulder. "I know you're a good girl, Stella. You did a wonderful job with your father. I'm

379

afraid this might be something similar. Don't be afraid to ask for help, yes?"

"Yes. Thank you."

"I'm just at the other end of the telephone if you need me." His smile was solemn but encouraging. "You'll do fine."

With that, he left.

Estella continued to stand in the middle of the kitchen unsure what her next move should be. Sophie came over and weaved around her legs. She picked the cat up. "What do you think, Soph? Shall we do him an egg?" She kissed the soft fur between her ears. "Yes, I think we will."

Chapter 35

They didn't 'do fine' at all. Graeme was furious with her for calling the doctor.

"You had no business doing that!" he croaked, his usual volume quelled by weakness and an enflamed gullet. He pitched forward, grabbing at his stomach as he did so. "And I don't want your bloody food!"

She stood before him with a tray which she wordlessly placed on the foot of his bed.

She wanted to search his room for whatever cache of spare drink he had but as her eyes roved the room, he said, "Don't even think about it."

"You did hear it when the doctor said you won't see the end of the year if you keep going?"

His face was mutinous but he didn't reply.

"What about all your plans? Improvements, the animals? Don't you care about them anymore?"

"As if that's ever going to happen now." His voice was full of scorn. "I've got nothing to do improvements with. Less than nothing since Daddy left everything worth anything to *Golden Boy*."

"Did you manage to sort out that business with the woods?"

He didn't answer.

"Graeme?"

He still didn't answer.

"Did you tell Austin?"

"No."

"Graeme, you have to tell –"

"*Leave me alone!*" He threw himself back on the pillow and turned away.

"Oh for goodness' sake! Act your age! Take some responsibility for yourself, for the decisions you make. You're not a boy anymore. And Daddy's not here anymore to either fix or ruin anything. That's up to you now. But for now, will you just bloody eat something? Please!"

She didn't wait for a response. There was no point.

Once she was downstairs, she fixed herself supper and ate in silence. It wasn't until then that she realised how bone-achingly tired she was. With only a few hours' sleep and all the jobs to do around the yard as well as Ellendale, it seemed the day had gone on forever. She had been so happy this morning watching Ivan slip from her room, still feeling the heat of his presence beside her. Then in the space of a few short hours, the bubble burst and she was brought back to reality. She heard a thump on the floor upstairs and then the noise of heaving. She closed her eyes hoping, praying for guidance.

"*Stella!*"

Her eyes snapped open. She was on her feet, across the hall, taking the stairs two at a time. It was the tone of voice. The child-like panic, the unquestionable fear. He was still heaving and crying when she hit the landing. She charged

382

through the door and almost collided with her brother crouched on the floor, hugging the basin she had given him earlier in the day. However, it wasn't the figure on the floor that sent her reeling backwards. It was the eye-watering stench of strong alcohol seeping from an overturned bottle onto the bedclothes, the mattress and the floor. The food tray was also in disarray with crumbs and small amounts of egg adhering themselves to the bedding. He had obviously tried to eat but rather than relying on tea to wash down his supper, had decided whiskey was the only thing that would ease its passage to his stomach. After all, it had been easing the pain, dulling it, removing feeling altogether for years. Graeme knew this. And the doctor who told him otherwise was clearly talking out of his hat.

Leaning down to him, she wasn't sure whether to touch him. He seemed so racked by the pain in his body, she was afraid he might scream if she put a hand to him. Or, maybe, like with a distressed horse, her firm, reassuring contact would calm him.

"Graeme?" Her voice was deep, quiet, soothing – just like when she was dealing with an animal.

His sobs eased and slowly he sat up, arms cradling his stomach as if he was holding his torso together. "There's – there's b-blood in it …"

She had deliberately avoided looking in the basin but now she did. Sure enough, red ribbons shone livid against the white enamel. Graeme wailed again as she turned back to him. For someone who had grown up around animals and had two vets in the family, he was laughably squeamish. But Estella wasn't laughing now.

"I think you might have burst blood vessels. From all the retching."

"Does that mean I'm – I'm bleeding *inside*?"

"Yes."

If he was an unhealthy colour before, he turned an even worse one. His mouth opened and his top lip drew down, highlighting the smear of snot beneath his nose. "What if I bleed to death inside and don't even know it?"

"You've got about ten pints in you so I don't think you're gone quite that far yet. Although," she added, catching a flittering thought as it rushed past, "it'd probably be better to get it checked. To be sure. Peace of mind, you know?"

"Can you call the doctor back?"

"No, I think you'll have to go to hospital, Graeme." She extracted a hanky from her pocked and daubed his nose.

He allowed her ministrations for a moment, then snatched it from her with an impatient, shaking hand.

"I don't *want* to go to hospital."

She observed him for a moment, watching his eyes flicker from the empty bottle to the spilt bottle to the bottom of his wardrobe. *Ah.* "You just don't want to be somewhere where you can't get drink. When's the last day you actually remember *not* drinking?"

"I don't," he answered. "I … I can't remember lots of things. It's – I – what …"

Without warning, he burst into tears, clutching his belly. His face contorted and before Estella could put a comforting hand on his shoulder, he was lurching for the basin, throwing up again. This time, the redness predominated. He brought little up but what he did made him keen harder. She could see he was going to pieces before her. The more he moaned, the more erratic his breathing became, the more he retched. She was worried he would either choke or keel over and, trying to remain calm herself, she started to run her hand up and down his spine.

"*Shh*, it's all right, you're okay, calm down, good boy."

Good boy? He wasn't a bloody horse! But they were all phrases that worked with animals. And what mattered was her tone of voice, not the words she said. At this moment, she doubted Graeme was any more aware of what was being said than one of the frightened yearlings over at Ellendale.

Slowly, Graeme began to subside but his whole body was shaking. He could barely support his own weight on his trembling arms. Estella pulled him back to lean against the side of the bed.

"I'm taking you to hospital. Graeme. You can argue all you want but if I have to push you down the stairs to get you there, I will."

"I don't – I don't think I can stop," he whimpered. "I can't not ..." Slowly a juddering hand raised an imaginary glass to his lips. The eyes that stared at her – tears leaking from the lower lids – were haunted.

"We'll see what we can do," she said firmly. "We're not giving up on you yet."

The doctor sounded quite cheerful on the telephone when she rang to arrange Graeme's admission to the hospital in town. He even said, "Good, good!" when he heard about the latest turn. "We're heading in the right direction, at least. Getting him away from the source of the problem."

The patient in question had been left in the bathroom to clean himself up. She also thought this was a safer place than his room since it was unlikely there were concealed bottles in the pokey bathroom. Although, she hadn't checked the toilet cistern …

She packed some clothes and toiletries in a case for him, unsure how long he would be staying. But she reasoned that she could take him more when he needed them. If they could keep him in, that was.

The closer they got to departure, the more he dawdled. "Maybe I don't need to go," he said as he shakily rolled socks on to his long, bony feet. "'M feeling a bit better."

"You're going," she answered shortly, closing the case with a snap. "Come on. *Up!*"

He grumbled something that sounded very like the name of a farmyard animal but descended the stairs without the helpful push Estella offered.

Graeme sat in the car and said very little – most of that pertaining to his not needing to go to hospital at all. However, the power of his assertion was diluted somewhat when, halfway there, he threw up in the enamel basin hugged to his chest. He didn't say anything after that.

Much to Estella's surprise, the doctor was waiting for them when they arrived.

"Just to be sure he doesn't make a bolt for freedom," he said quietly to Estella as Graeme shuffled towards the austere concrete building.

In fact, the doctor was there to help sign him in – something Estella was glad to see Graeme did without complaint. He looked so pitiful, hunched in the glaring light above the admissions desk, cuddling the basin. The shadows under his eyes and stubble on his chin made what little of his face that wasn't yellow look grey. Standing back, she could see him sway slightly, not because of inebriation but because of fatigue. She was surprised he was managing to stay upright at all. He must have been so weak. But there was that stubbornness. There was no way he was going to walk into hospital and *look* like he needed to. He still had pride. She just prayed someone he knew didn't walk in. Because if that happened, he'd definitely take to his heels.

Bed allocated, Estella was glad to see a porter scoop her brother into a wheelchair. It did jar slightly seeing Graeme reduced to the same conveyance that had borne her father. The same thought seemed to pass through his mind too as he looked down at the metal and leather, cautiously rubbing his hand over the armrest. He turned dull eyes on her and held her gaze as the porter wheeled him away.

"Should I follow?" she asked Dr Adkins.

"No. I think it best to leave him to the nurses for the night. They'll get some fluids into him and then ... well, if we can keep him in here, they'll get him through the next forty-eight hours. It won't be pretty."

"What do you mean?"

"Well, I'd surmise that he's currently in the early stages of withdrawal since he hasn't been keeping anything down. And it has to get worse before it gets better."

"Worse. How worse?"

"More vomiting, headache, diarrhoea. He'll likely get very aggressive, possibly hallucinate."

"Oh."

"Quite. But I'm afraid it has to be done. For his own good. And the nurses will take good care of him, don't you worry. They'll get all the right things into him and give him the best possible chance to start over again."

Estella nodded. Yes, she was worried for her brother and what he was about to go through. But she was also worried for the nurses. She knew what Graeme could be like – how he could fly into a rage on the slightest provocation – and was afraid that he might injure one of the hospital staff either intentionally or inadvertently. If that happened, would they send him home and leave her to deal with him?

They said their goodbyes and headed to their respective vehicles. Sitting into the silent interior, Estella tried to think back to when she last drove a car on her own. She barely drove at all since most of her journeys were an easy bike-ride away. It was completely dark as she followed the narrow streets out of the town, past the turn for Claybourne's where Joy was safely tucked up for the night. It was strange to think that, tonight, two of her siblings were ensconced in hospitals – one allowing her sister to live in comfortable oblivion, the other trying to *save* her brother from oblivion. And she, for the first time in her life was knowingly returning to an empty house. Was this to be her future? If Graeme didn't get better, would she be alone in that big family home full of ghosts? She shuddered. You'd better sort yourself out, Graeme, she thought.

Chapter 36

When Estella got home, Ivan's car was in the yard. As soon as she saw him, the leaden feeling in her chest lifted with such rapidity it left her giddy. He had been lying back in his seat, probably resting. After all, he'd had even less sleep than she had. Indeed, the journey home had been such a struggle, she'd opened the window in the hope that the cold air would keep her awake. A kind of liquid contentment seemed to slide through her veins as she watched Ivan unfold himself from the car. She walked silently into his waiting arms and allowed his warmth, his smell to envelop her. His strong arms cocooned her and she smiled, sighing happily. It didn't matter that the house was empty – she was already home.

"Graeme?"

"I brought him to hospital. He hasn't been able to keep anything down so he needed fluids and, well, they're going to try and keep him in. Dry him out, you know?"

Ivan nodded, tucked her under his arm and led her to the door. "I came thinking you might need company if he was … being difficult."

"Were you waiting long?" She now noticed there was a slight chill to his clothes.

"Doesn't matter. Saves me having to listen to Mammy and Rebecca drafting a letter to some cousin of Anstruther's who's a solicitor. Trying to figure out if she's still married to that –" He hissed through his teeth. "Anyway, I'd prefer to come and help you deal with your alcoholic brother than be involved in that."

She knew Graeme was an alcoholic but hearing someone else say it still hurt, even if it was Ivan. She also felt a little swoop of guilt for not at least ringing Rebecca to check on her herself after the incident with Paul Craven. Tomorrow, she told herself, she would make sure to ring or call over.

In the kitchen, she disentangled herself from Ivan and put the kettle on to boil. "She's marrying Howard, then?"

"Seems to be. Decision was made by the time I got home."

"And you're not happy about it?"

"It's not that. I like Howard. I just … don't know what to think." He threw himself down in the armchair, making it creak.

"Do you know," she said thoughtfully as Ivan snaked an impossibly long arm around her waist and dragged her into his lap, "I remember when Dolly's older brother said he was getting married, the whole family was sort of … upset. Like they were grieving. And I think when things change, you can sometimes go into a kind of mourning. Because – like when someone dies – the household changes. The routines, the relationships all change." She wrapped her arms around his neck. "Maybe you're anticipating the change – the separation from Rebecca, from Harry."

He didn't reply but began gently stroking her back and her bare forearm. When the kettle started to sing, he reluctantly let her go.

"Do you want anything to eat?" The question reminded her that Graeme's supper was still scattered across the bedcovers and floor of his room. "Damn," she said softly.

"What?"

"I forgot I still have to clean up the mess in Graeme's room."

"Leave it."

"No."

He rolled his eyes. "All right. But sit down and have your tea while it's hot. And then we can both do it."

She sat on his knee again – at his insistence – and they drank their tea in silence while Sophie glowered from the other armchair. Estella felt she could close her eyes and sleep against Ivan's chest but she didn't want to cut off the blood flow to his legs. Wearily, she got to her feet and dragged him with her. He had offered to help, after all.

When he got up to the room, however, he looked as if he was seriously rethinking that offer. The lingering sourness of sweat and vomit still permeated the room along with the heady sharpness of alcohol, forcing them to breathe through their mouths.

With a muttered, "*Oh bloody hell,*" he crossed the floor and threw open a window. The curtains billowed and whipped into the space as if attempting to waft the stench of sickness away from their offended noses while they stripped the bed.

"I'll wash everything tomorrow. Watch! Don't stand in the egg!"

"*Eugh!*" he exclaimed as he hopped out of the way, trying to find a safe patch of floor for his socks.

"Sure this is better than listening to folk discussing a letter?"

"Of course," he grinned. "Because I'm getting to clean up with *you*."

She laughed. "Good answer!"

"I know. Proud of myself for coming up with that."

She sent him off to get some water to wash the floor while she took the bedding downstairs. How was it that he made even the terrible jobs seem easy? How was it that he had this gift to make life better and he was choosing to spend this gift on her? But then she thought, why question it? Just accept it. There was no point trying to rationalise love. It just … *was*.

"*Hurry up, will you!*" he called, hearing her tread on the stairs. "*The water's going cold. And I'm going to keel over and need to be dragged out by my foot if I have to breathe in these fumes for much longer.*"

"You're an awful lightweight if some fumes are enough to incapacitate you."

"It's more that they're whiskey fumes. I can't abide whiskey since the first and only time I drank it I sicked it back up my nose."

She snorted – despite how disgusting it was, despite what she had seen with her brother this morning. She took heart when she heard him mutter that he would never drink the God-awful stuff as long as he lived. At least, she thought, he would never have the problems Graeme had.

When she went to shut the window, he said, "Leave it open, give it a good airing."

She hesitated. "But what if someone tries to get in?"

"I'm here," he shrugged, then pulled her in for a cuddle. "I'll protect you."

"You're staying?"

"Yes. Unless you don't want me to …" He suddenly looked unsure.

"It's not that. What will your mother say when you don't come home?"

He grinned sheepishly. "I told her I might have to stay over and help with your brother."

"*Oh.*"

"Honestly, I don't think she believed me."

"No?"

"No. She said, *'Don't you go doing anything stupid now!'*" His voice was a shrill, unconvincing imitation of his mother. "*'Stella's a good girl and I don't want the pair of you messed up in any bad business.'*"

"What sort of 'bad business?"

"Suppose she doesn't want me to get you pregnant before we're wed."

Estella's stomach dropped. When she thought about it herself, it didn't seem to matter. When she imagined it in Edna Aylward's voice, it worried her. "And what did you say to her?"

"I said I was a very good boy who never got in trouble," he answered primly. "And I told her I thought it very cruel of her to describe children as 'bad business'. I mean, fine if you want to describe Rebecca in that way – she was always an awful little child. But me? I was angelic."

"And what did she say to that?"

"That I wasn't too old for her to wash my mouth out with soap. I told her she'd never reach. So she said she'd do it when I was asleep. And that decided me on staying here tonight. I wouldn't put it past her," he added, looking deadly serious. "I even brought a toothbrush and clean underwear."

Estella surveyed him for a moment. He was doing an excellent job of looking the innocent martyr. But she knew the playful, cheeky nature that was hidden underneath. And she loved it. "You'd better go and get them then," she said evenly though her heart fluttered.

He clattered down the stairs to his car but was back in no time with a small holdall, proudly brandishing his toothbrush.

"What about your underpants?"

He looked scandalised. "I'm not showing you my underwear!" His voice was high-pitched and he placed a protective hand over his chest.

She tittered and headed for her room. "Well, if you won't show me yours, I'm definitely not showing you mine." She expected a smart reply but he simply threw himself on her bed, smiling benignly.

However, he quickly began to squirm and poke at the covers beneath him. "This isn't a particularly comfortable bed, you know. Is there a bigger one here? I'm not sure I could manage another night crushed between you and the wall. I might not be able to get up in the morning."

"And we couldn't have *that*. There's a spare room that you're welcome to."

His hand swept across the blanket in a pensive fashion. "Do you know, I'm not sure *you* should be sleeping in this bed either," he said casually.

"Oh?"

"Could do untold damage to your back. I don't think you should spend another night in it."

"Really?" She tried very hard to keep the smile out of her voice. "I always thought it was the most comfortable bed in the house."

That seemed to stump him for a moment. But he recovered with, "And have you ever tried the bed in the spare room?"

"No," she admitted.

"Don't you think you should?"

"I wouldn't be a very good hostess if I expected the guests to share a bed with me, would I?"

"I wouldn't mind," he said too quickly.

"And anyway, there wouldn't be room in it for two people what with you being so big and needing so much room."

"I'm sure we'd manage."

The earnestness in his voice finally broke through her serious veneer. A low, naughty gurgling giggle swelled in her chest, rising, overflowing. Ivan's eyebrows shot up in surprise making her cover her mouth like a child who had accidentally revealed a secret. Yet her laughter continued until Ivan joined in and they collapsed into one another. It felt good to laugh after the day she'd had. Only a day! It felt like weeks had elapsed since she had danced in a pretty frock at the Hunt Ball. She had danced with Dolly more than with Ivan but it was his arms around her – the arms that held her now – that she remembered. Suddenly, she realised that she hadn't checked on Dolly. She never even thought to ring and make sure she got home safe. And why hadn't Dolly rung her either? But then maybe she had been out when she did. After all, the whole incident with Graeme had overtaken the rest of her thoughts.

"What?" Ivan was staring down at her.

"Nothing. Just thinking I should have checked on Dolly."

He snorted. "She's fine. By the sounds of things, she spent most of the day on the phone to my sister. I thought she *worked* at the telephone exchange, not sat there making her own phone calls all day."

"Have you never noticed women can do several things at once?"

"Depends on the woman."

"Depends on the man too," she countered.

He paused. "True. Now, do we think we could do one task and … get ready for bed?"

She thought she saw a little flush begin to creep up his neck and fought the urge to tease him. However, she could also feel the heat of her own skin and surmised that any jokes at his expense would amount to the pot calling the kettle black – or perhaps pink.

She sent Ivan off to the other room while she got ready for bed, dawdling as she listened to all his unfamiliar movements reverberate down the corridor. Tonight would be different. Tonight, she decided, she was going to share a proper bed with him. Tonight, there wouldn't be a blanket between them. Or maybe there would be? Did she really feel comfortable with the idea of sharing a bed with him? No. But did she *want* to go to bed with him? Absolutely. The thought of being so close to him, with nothing in between terrified and thrilled her in equal measure. She wanted to lie beside him, wanted to fall asleep with all of his body touching hers. She wanted a tangible human connection. Yet she didn't want it to descend into love-making. She wasn't brave enough to go that far.

When she eventually pushed open the door of the guest room, Ivan was lying in bed (she already knew this having heard the cessation of his footsteps) looking at her. She stood in the doorway, staring back. The bedside lamp cast an inviting glow across the room, highlighting the handsome lines of Ivan's face beautifully. The cover was pulled up to just below his bare chest exposing white skin and a smattering of dark hair. His pale shoulders were rounded by knotted muscles, stretched tight over his bones.

As he lay casually with a hand under his head, Estella felt the absurd urge to rush up to him and tickle his exposed armpit.

"If you keep staring at me, I'm going to think there's something wrong with me."

She looking away. "*Um*, you *are* wearing something on the bottom … half?" she asked, panicking slightly.

He grinned and casually threw back the cover, revealing striped pyjama bottoms similar to her own. The gesture was almost an invitation, beckoning her to the empty expanse of mattress beside him. She obliged by launching herself across the room and onto the bed, snatching the blankets from his hand and cocooning herself against the chill of the unused room. Yet the bedding too felt cool and damp. She was almost immediately drawn to the body radiating warmth beside her. Ivan casually arranged the covers around both of them and, when he had finished simply left his arm exactly where it was, draped heavily over her.

"Very smoothly done," she told him, interlocking her fingers with his and pulling herself closer.

"Yes, I thought so. God, you're cold!"

He cuddled her close and started chafing her body with his large hands. Slowly, however, the movements of his hands became less rhythmical. They ceased to follow the same plains and began to gently explore the contours of her body. At first, Estella stayed rigidly still, barely daring to breathe while his hands flowed over her. But then she began to brush her own fingertips across his exposed flesh, feeling the burning warmth that seemed to hit her in waves. Without even realising, she found her own breathing now matched his, calmed as she was by his solid reassuring touch. Her eyes met his – heavy, dark, languorous – and his hand slid under her pyjama top. Her breath caught and she cringed away but it was more a reaction to such an unfamiliar feeling than a rejection of his contact with her tender skin.

"We won't do anything," he promised, "but there might be some ... involuntary movement on my part."

She didn't know what to say to that so she simply nodded. Inch by inch, they wordlessly felt their way around each other's bodies, counting as fingers bumped over ribs, checking that each was comfortable with the exploration of this part or that with looks and nods of acquiescence. After a while, they both lay naked under the covers having pushed their night clothes out of the way. Limbs intertwined, chests and bellies pressed flat against one another, it would have been so easy for them to give in to their desire for one another. Yet neither of them tried to break past that one remaining barrier. Neither of them dared to move in case the moment – which stretched on and on – was broken. Finally, Ivan shifted a little – just enough for his lips to meet hers. Estella reached for him eagerly, her lips parting, kiss deepening until their tongues met. She did not think it was possible to be any more aroused by the situation, but the strange sensation of his tongue stroking hers stoked the fire already burning inside her. It was almost too much. She began to feel lightheaded, useless, lost in a gloriously, golden-hued sensory overload. His body seemed to be everywhere. She wasn't even sure her own limbs belonged to her anymore.

Eventually, Ivan pulled away, raggedly dragging air into his lungs. "*Ah!* No, I … I'm going to have to –' He tried to pull away but Estella held him fast. "Stella, I can't! I'm going to … to … to burst!"

She understood. Yet still she clung on. "No! Don't leave!"

"I'm not! I just … need to go to the bathroom."

"No." She whispered the word in his ear, nipping the soft flesh of his earlobe. He yelped. "Stay. We can … we can do this."

His hand shot to her cheek, held her face inches from his, his eyes darting back and forth as he read her expression. "Are you sure?"

"I'm sure about you, Ivan."

He kissed her again. She kissed back. Anticipation fizzed and bubbled through her veins. His hand was no longer on her face. He trailed it up her spine to her shoulder, his other arm wrapping around her lower back, pulling her flush against him. He broke away again, resting his damp forehead on hers.

"Really? You really want to…"

"*Yes.*"

And they did.

Chapter 37

The first thing Estella felt when she woke was heat. She was so hot, draped in Ivan, that it was almost unbearable. But then when she tried to pull away, it seemed their flesh was adhered together as if she had been subsumed into his body and they had become one and the same person. Next, she felt a withering, burning shame that was nothing to do with the warmth Ivan generated and everything to do with what had occurred the night before. How could she? When her brother lay in hospital – possibly dying. She should have at least prayed for his wellbeing instead of being consumed by the flesh. How could she have committed such a sinful act?

But it didn't feel sinful. The indolent yet insistent voice in her mind overtook her heavily burdened guilt. The glow of happiness swept joyfully around her head, through her limbs. It lay siege to another wave of shame, danced with her reawakening desire, overcame her worries with its buoyancy and made her realise that, if she could have the night over again, she wouldn't change a single bit of it.

Yes, she was a little sore but she knew that was to be expected. Really, the pain was worth the pleasure of such intimacy with the man she loved – adored. She turned in his heavy arms and drank in the newfound pleasure of his sleeping face. He looked younger with his hair tousled – a wave falling across his forehead. Tentatively, she reached up and brushed it back. But as soon as she let it go, it flopped back down again. She stifled a laugh then gently blew on the rogue strands. He frowned and twitched. She bit her lip to stop a giggle escaping, unsure whether she wanted him to wake or stay asleep so she could observe him. However, as she watched, his face continued to move as he slowly came to.

"Hello," he murmured hoarsely, a smile playing about his lips. Then his eyes lost focus and he grimaced. "*Ow!*"

"What?"

"Can't feel my arm," he moaned, heaving it uselessly from beneath her.

Estella lifted herself out of the way as he dragged his arm under his body and dropped it over the side of the bed. "*Ahhhh!*" He winced as the blood pooled at his fingertips.

"Sorry!"

"'S all right. Not your fault. Worth it." He grinned up at her and she lowered herself down beside him so they both lay on their fronts. He reached across and caressed her back, finally resting his hand on her buttocks. "Hello, you." He flexed his fingers. "You feeling all right?"

"Yes. You?"

His teeth flashed. "Never better. *Never.*" However, his smile faded. "Although we really shouldn't have done that."

"But I'm glad we did," Estella answered firmly.

"So am I."

Distantly, she heard the insistent trilling of the alarm

clock in her room and buried her head in the pillow with a dry sob of dismay. Ivan's hand glided up her back, brushed her hair out of the way and she felt him leave a trail of soft kisses over her shoulder and up her neck. "Up you get," he whispered when he got to her ear. Then, suddenly, he was gone. And the bedcovers went with him.

She yelped and drew her knees up, wrapping her arms across her chest. "*Ivan!*" She tried to look angry with him but was distracted by *his* nakedness.

He knelt back on the bed and leaned over her. "Now *there's* a sight to behold of a dull morning."

"I agree," she laughed.

He kissed her cheek. "*Up! C'mon!*"

"*No! No!*"

But he grabbed hold of her arm and easily dragged her to the edge of the mattress where she scrabbled to find her feet rather than falling face first onto the floor. There ensued much touching and tickling, kisses, the odd bite and a fair amount of clothes snatched away from their owners to be held out of reach (Ivan was particularly good at this). Eventually, however, both were somewhat respectably washed and dressed ready for a day's work. And, despite Ivan's protests that he would drop dead from starvation, the first thing they did was feed the animals.

It was strange how easily they slipped back into such mundanities after their intimacy the night before. Ivan asked for instructions and she gave them as they checked sheep, fed chickens and cows, then milked. By the time they were cleaning out the cow shed, even Estella was struggling with hunger pangs.

"Told you we should have eaten," Ivan teased.

The morning's cache of eggs was put to good use with both of them eating large helpings of scrambled eggs and toast.

Once the last of the scalding tea had been swallowed, Ivan stood, kissed her tenderly and bid her a reluctant farewell. "You'll be over later in the morning to ride though, won't you?" he asked, dawdling on the threshold.

"It'll depend on what the hospital says about Graeme. I'll ring them and see now. See you later."

The telephone call to the hospital was brief. Yes, Graeme was still on the ward. No, he was not particularly well but that was to be expected. Yes, they would let her know if anything changed. No, it would be best she didn't visit today since her brother was, "in a bad way".

She had barely put down the receiver when there was a great clatter at the back door.

"You weren't away long," she called ahead cheerfully but stopped dead as she entered the kitchen.

"Who'd you think I was?" asked Dolly, standing red-faced with her hands on her hips. She was breathing heavily, clearly having put some effort into cycling up to Robin Hill.

Estella's words immediately left her. Flashes of the previous night obscured her vision and for a moment all she could see was the person she assumed had come back. But then Dolly's curious face re-emerged and the sensual fog in her brain cleared.

"I thought you were Ivan."

"Very early for *Ivan* to be calling. Even earlier for him to be coming *back*." Dolly's eyebrow quirked. A challenge, a tease.

404

"He came to check everything was all right." She left out the fact that he had come the day *before* rather than this morning. "Graeme's gone into hospital."

Dolly gasped. "With what?"

"Drink."

"Bad?"

"Fairly."

"Oh."

"Tea?"

"Yeah."

While boiling the kettle, Estella gave her friend the sanitised version of Graeme's implosion the previous day but Dolly still winced and shivered in disgust.

"I knew something was up. Lucy Keane's back working the switchboards and she told me there'd been several calls to the doctor from Robin Hill when I came on shift last night. I tried ringing but ..."

Estella knew enough not to admonish her friend and colleague for nosing into other people's private business. Everyone accepted that the traffic at the local switchboard was virtually public property. "I was probably at the hospital by then."

Dolly sipped her tea. "It's been a long time coming."

"Suppose."

"How'd Ivan know before me?"

"I told him yesterday at Ellendale. He came to see if he could help."

"Have you seen Rebecca?"

"No, I was going to but Ivan said she was fine –"

"I did. Howard asked her to marry him!" Her face shone,

anticipating Estella's shocked reaction at such a revelation, but then it fell. "Oh. You already knew."

"Ivan told me. I *was* going to see her last night but then everything with Graeme ..." She frowned. "Probably shouldn't have even gone to Ellendale."

Dolly dismissed her guilt with a swat of her hand. "What were you going to do – sit on him? With Graeme it wasn't a case of 'if' but 'when'. You have to get on with things. It's up to Graeme to sort out his own problems. And that's if he *wants* to sort them out. Do you think he does?"

"I suppose," Estella sighed heavily. "Whether he has the determination to commit to what he needs to do is another matter. Well, he *is* determined. But I don't know will he use it for getting better ..."

"Or carrying on the same way like the stubborn old donkey he is."

"Now, now, don't insult my Beryl."

"True. Apologies to Beryl if those great donkey ears picked up something offensive."

They laughed and chatted about various things from then on, focusing on what had happened at the ball once Estella and Ivan left. There had been much talk of the incident involving Rebecca, with especial attention paid to the usually-quiet Howard Anstruther's role in proceedings. After his banishment, Paul Craven had eventually slunk back to the bar to join the group in the corner too drunk to care who was in their midst. A perfectly sober Jacqueline Hawes had fallen over someone else's feet and had hurt her hip and Dolly had discovered that Roy was a voluble if tuneless singer when he was well-oiled.

"Overall, I'd say it was an excellent outing!" Dolly concluded brightly.

Once their tea was finished, they stood, ready to get on with the rest of the day. Dolly reached over and wrapped her arms around her friend. Somewhat surprised, Estella stood rigid but soon relaxed into the embrace and hugged back.

"I really shouldn't have to say this but you know I'm always here for you, even if I do disappear a bit with Roy? Give me a shout anytime and I'll come running."

"I know. Although you'd never run up that hill. You're hard pressed to cycle it."

Dolly slapped her on the back. "Though I suppose you'd prefer it was Ivan who came running nowadays and not little old Dolly. Not that I blame you. I wouldn't mind being caught up in those big strong arms!" She gave Estella an extra-hard squeeze.

"*Ow!* You'll snap me clean in two!"

"Not a bit of it!" she scoffed. "But seriously," she continued. "You and Ivan, yes?"

"I think so. Yes."

Dolly squealed. "I *told* Roy. I said you were the prettiest couple there. And that you're perfect for one another. You're meant to be, Stella. I know it."

Estella felt her cheeks flame – this time, with pure girlish, passionate happiness. She gave her best friend an impetuous, joyous kiss on the cheek and a final bone-crushing cuddle. "You know what, Doll? I know it too."

Chapter 38

Two weeks of daily telephone calls to the hospital were Estella's only means of discovering how her brother progressed. During the first week, she always asked whether she could visit him, hoping that her presence might encourage or offer him some light relief. She thought he might want to know that everything on the farm was continuing as usual – that she had moved the new lambs and ewes to fresh pasture, for instance. But Graeme rejected all visitors.

In truth, Estella was glad her brother didn't want to see her. She rarely finished in the evening before dark and, if she did visit, couldn't imagine what she might say to him. It was enough to know that he was being cared for by people much better equipped to deal with his issues than she was. It was something of a relief to have a holiday from worrying about his health and whereabouts. Never in all the time she had lived in the family home had she only herself to care for. Yet again, she was struck by the notion that she was the last of the Fraynes left at Robin Hill. Even if the arrangement was only temporary, she found it both sad and quite enjoyable. With no fear of her brother coming back soon, Ivan was free to come and go as he pleased, making sure she didn't get too lonely up on the hill.

Indeed, it seemed she and Ivan couldn't be separated. There was an intensity, a seriousness to their commitment to one another that shielded them even from the teasing that so commonly came from the others at Ellendale. In fact, on one occasion, Ivan had simply grabbed hold of Estella in the middle of the yard and kissed her wetly in front of everyone.

"I remember a time when Barbara and I were like you two," Mr Leclerc told them, wiping the tears of laughter from his eyes as the whoops and cackles of the other lads dissipated against the walls of the courtyard. "Going to be a race up the aisle between you and your sister, eh?" he chortled.

"I can't believe they're telling everyone already," Ivan said as they drove into town the next day. It was a familiar refrain by now. But Estella had become increasingly quiet with each passing mile and he wanted to prompt a response.

"Why wouldn't they if they're in love?" she replied, already exasperated. She felt tetchy and couldn't sit still. They were going to Claybourne's to visit Joy first and then heading across town to see Graeme who was finally willing to admit well-wishers.

"But what if they fall out?" Ivan continued doggedly, trying to hide his smile. He enjoyed bickering with her even if it was a foregone conclusion that she would win.

"If we fell out, would you sod off and leave me at the altar?"

"No. I'd call ahead to make sure you only got as far as the church door. Save you some embarrassment, you know?"

She slapped his arm playfully. "Anyway, if there's anyone going to be left at the altar, it's you."

"*Me*?"

"Well, isn't it the men who wait at the top of the church for the women?"

"Yes, but why'd you say *me*? You could have said me and Anstruther. Or just him."

"Have you not seen Howard Anstruther?" she said seriously. "No one's leaving *him* at the altar."

"Are you suggesting he's more handsome than I am?"

"Of course! Haven't you noticed? He's got such lovely brown hair, such a kind face and he's so tall –"

"He's a bean pole," Ivan snorted.

"Now, now! Don't be cruel! You're just jealous."

"If you're so in love with yon reedy fella, why don't you off and marry him?"

"I can't. Your sister's marrying him."

"Yes, she is!"

"*Aha!* Caught you!"

"*Bugger*," Ivan muttered, though Estella couldn't help noticing he was trying very hard to hide a smile.

When they approached the gates to Claybourne's, Estella fell silent again.

"Are you sure you're happy for me to meet Joy? I don't have to if you don't want me to."

Each time Estella had visited Joy since Christmas, Ivan had dropped her off then gone into town. But following the last visit, he had asked if he could meet the final sibling since Estella now spoke about her more freely.

"I just feel I should, you know. Gain her approval or something," he had said in the car on the way home.

"But she probably won't even notice you're there,"

410

Estella reasoned. "Or worse, she might take against you on sight and that would just be upsetting for everyone."

Ivan didn't push it. However, the more she thought about it, the more she wanted Ivan to see Joy. Estella didn't want to have any secrets. And she now knew Ivan well enough to be sure he wouldn't turn against her on account of her sister as some men might. Yet Ivan was still a big, intimidating man. While she trusted him, there was no saying how Joy might react.

"No, you can come in if you want to. But just hang back for a minute until I see what sort of humour she's in."

Joy, of course, remained gloriously oblivious to the welfare of her older brother. Had circumstances been normal, it would have been Joy whom Estella discussed Graeme's illness with first, not Ivan or Dolly. The two sisters would have shared the burden of worry. She would have called with updates and Joy would have telephoned her in return. But there were no calls. Instead, Joy knelt in the gardens at Claybourne's working industriously on the flowerbeds, breaking off now and again to watch the birds hopping about her and murmur a contented "Chook-chook, *chook*!" It seemed her concerns were nothing more than the expanse of ground that filled her immediate vision – the life of flora and fauna rather than siblings.

"Your part of the garden looks lovely, doesn't it?" Estella said admiringly, sitting beside her sister on a hessian sack as she surveyed the late-spring flowers. "Daffodils are lovely, aren't they? So bright and cheerful. Mammy always loved them, didn't she?" She reached out and gently pinched the bright yellow petals.

411

Joy immediately froze. Her eyes darted to her sister's hand. She was suddenly hyper-alert, ready to react. Estella let go. She knew if she had pulled the petal, picked the flower, that Joy would begin to squeal and flail her arms – as if the snapping of the stem caused her physical pain.

Estella shifted back on her sack and neatly clasped her hands in her lap. Joy's eyes followed the movement peripherally, then, as if nothing had happened, continued to tend the soil. Estella sat and watched her elder sister's simple movements, silent observation allowing her mind to wander, to wonder. Perhaps the care her sister took with other living things – birds, plants – told of a more profound connection with them than with her own species. Who was Estella to say that her sister *didn't* know the pain a flower endured when it was ripped from the soil by greedy hands? Perhaps Joy did feel something. Maybe she heard it. There was no way Estella could ever know. But what she did know was that her sister would never have experienced the calm gentle stimulation of Claybourne's at home. Never could her father, brothers or (though she hated to admit it) she herself have accepted Joy's eccentricities – her alternative viewpoint on the world at large. They would – quite literally – have driven her mad.

As the thought crossed her mind, she spotted Ivan's imposing figure sauntering towards them, hands in his pockets. Forgetting her sister, Estella watched him walk along the flowerbeds, bending to admire the blooms. Her heart skittered as she saw his hand cup a flowerhead and she fought the urge to call out and warn him against plucking it. If he approached with a decapitated flower in his grasp, she was sure Joy would go wild. But, glancing up, he

412

withdrew his fingers then waved before clasping his hands in front of him, mirroring her own pose. Clearly, he had been studying proceedings carefully. Slowly, as he came nearer, he seemed to enfold his bulk into himself. He dropped his gaze and rounded his shoulders, just as she had seen him do with skittish horses at Ellendale. And while some people might have thought his gesture discourteous, Estella saw it for what it was. It was a recognition that Joy – like the animals he loved so dearly – was not always familiar with what was considered normal human signalling. Being open and friendly with Joy was never going to prompt a normal response. So trying an unorthodox approach, one that Ivan was at least familiar with, was perhaps quite appropriate.

Eventually he was crouching beside Estella who was now totally focused on Joy, alert to any signs of distress. But she continued to ignore them until Ivan absentmindedly put his arm around Estella's waist. Joy was suddenly looking directly at him. Ivan calmly gazed back, blinking benignly.

And that was it. Joy turned back to her work and carried on, quietly murmuring, "Chook-chook, *chook*," to a sparrow that hopped back and forth close to her hands.

Estella wondered if it was the same one she had seen her feeding all those months ago in the window seat with Susan. Estella's head jerked up. "Where's Susan?"

"Susan?" Ivan asked.

"Joy's friend."

As if called to them, Estella suddenly spotted her coming towards them carrying a shallow basket filled with plants. Susan's head bobbed and she smiled shyly as she arrived. She took in the group on the grass then, as if it had been her

413

plan all along, handed Ivan and Estella two primrose plants apiece before placing the rest beside Joy. Job done, she sat a little distance away to stare avidly at Joy who began boring holes in the cleared earth with a small trowel. Into these, she decanted the primroses from the basket. There was a silent precision, a rhythm to her movements. Not even when she reached for the plants proffered by Estella then Ivan did it change. Two taps on the base of the pot to loosen the contents, three wiggles of the stem to remove it, three gentle teases of the fingers to unknot the roots, into the hole and five handfuls of soil around it and three pats on the earth once it was snugly tucked away.

"Well! Didn't you do a grand job of that?" Estella remarked as Joy sat back to survey her work.

"Even I couldn't have done it better," Ivan agreed. "The whole garden's lovely. A credit to everyone."

"Joy likes the outdoors, don't you, Joy?"

Susan covered her giggling mouth with a slightly earthy fist as Joy brushed the soil from the basket into the flowerbed, filled it with her tools, then stood. The others followed suit and she wordlessly picked up the hessian sacks, folding them neatly. As Joy walked towards the potting shed, basket over her arm, Estella was struck by how much her sister resembled their mother. Trailing behind her, Estella felt like she was five again – following Prudie about the yard as she worked. The only thing that was missing from the image was the small squealing child who was forever clinging to her mother's hand, sleeve, skirt or leg. It suddenly struck Estella that she didn't know if Joy had been beside their mother when she died crossing the yard all

414

those years ago. If she wasn't then where had Joy been that morning? And if she was, what must that have done to her? Was it Prudie's death that finally closed Joy off to all other people in the world? If their mother had been there to guide her, to guard her, might she have improved? Led a better, happier life? Had even a few more words to articulate herself? At what point did she understand that their mother would not be coming back? Or had she ever understood?

Estella gasped and shuddered to a halt. Tears pricked her eyes and she clamped a hand over her mouth to stifle a sob. She didn't want to upset Joy.

"What? *What is it*?" Ivan was standing in front of her, gaze filled with concern.

"She was there," Estella choked out a whisper, watching Joy disappear behind Ivan's shoulder. "Joy was there when my mother – our mother – died. The 'chook-chook, *chook*!' It's what Mammy used to say when she was feeding the chickens. And she died feeding the chickens. Joy knows."

Ivan straightened a little and turned to look at the retreating figure. "Maybe. But you can't ever be sure."

But Estella was sure. "What if it's still upsetting her all this time later?"

"Well," Ivan began, choosing his words, "even if Joy *was* there, there's no knowing for certain how or if it affects her still. And there's probably very little you could do even if you did know. You know her better than I do, but she really does seem … contented here."

Joy re-emerged from the potting shed empty-handed, Susan hot on her heels.

Estella quickly swiped at the tears on her cheeks but the

gesture caught Joy's attention. She marched over, eyeing Ivan warily, contemptuously, and stood before them.

Estella laughed wetly as her sister gave her a questioning look. "It's all right, Joy, it's not his fault. He's nice, don't worry." She reached her hand out to Ivan and he took it.

"I'll look after your little sister, don't you worry, Joy. I'll make her a good husband."

Estella's mouth fell open. She stared at his bright, smiling face and felt his great paw squeeze her hand. "See? You don't need to worry your pretty head over me, Joy," she said. On impulse, she reached out and tucked a loose strand of short, chewed hair behind Joy's ear, trailing her fingers down her sibling's cheek. She couldn't think of the last time she had touched her sister's face. But it felt so natural, so loving, so maternal.

Joy looked slightly perturbed. Or was she embarrassed? Or pleased? Estella couldn't tell. However, a moment later, she knew.

Tentatively, Joy reached out, arms bent at the elbows, and hugged her little sister around the waist. Estella hardly dared to breathe, afraid to do something wrong, to ruin the moment. Slowly, she brought her own arms up and lightly cuddled her sibling. Joy's arms tightened and Estella let out a sigh, inhaling the smell of fresh soil, greenery and soap that clung to her sister's clothes.

"Chook-chook, *chook*!" Joy whispered in her ear.

"Yes, sweetheart," Estella murmured. "Chook-chook, *chook*!"

Chapter 39

It took Estella a little time to recover after their visit to Joy. Ivan watched her carefully over lunch as she oscillated between smiles, hysterical giggles and watering eyes (she insisted she wasn't crying).

"Are you sure you're up to visiting Graeme?" he asked as they emerged into the afternoon sunshine.

She nodded. "I told him I'd come. And I'm fine. I'm happy." She threaded her fingers through his and swung their hands. "I'm getting *married*!" she thrilled.

Ivan scanned the vicinity. "To who? Where is he? Let me at him!"

He dropped her at the hospital gates since he was meeting a lorry in Mountlennon's marketplace to unload and sell his pigs from the orchard. Wishing him luck, she began her ascent up the short tree-lined avenue leading to the front steps of the building, loitering to observe the crags of the bark and the soft new shoots just beginning to form. Life marched on, she thought. Trees grew, some were cut down in their prime, others succumbed to disease, were ravaged by time or simply died of old age. Their limbs stretched hopefully skywards and each year produced small changes, mostly noticeable to those who knew them best. Just like people.

As she walked, Estella gave a name to each one. Joy was first – foremost in her mind after her visit – a slightly chaotic-looking ash. Then there was Prudie, inseparable from the eldest daughter she hovered over. Beside her mother was a particularly craggy one she christened Reg. It suited his character. And there she was, smaller than the rest, right beside her father – a copper beech with smooth bark and upright trunk. There was a gap next where another tree had been cut down and beside it a diseased-looking ash cowered beneath the towering height of a final horse chestnut. These two were Graeme and Austin – one always overshadowing the other.

She found the real Graeme sitting by the large windows of the hospital's day room, a blanket over his knee despite the fact that the spring sun was heating the space quite nicely.

"Can't keep warm," he muttered. He had a fork in one hand and a plate of food beside him cut into childish fragments. "Can't eat that well yet either. Have to take it slow, otherwise it all comes back up."

"But isn't it cold by now?" Estella asked, viewing the congealed gravy and limp veg with distaste.

He shrugged. "Doesn't matter. Still edible. Can't really taste it."

"How are you feeling anyway?" She had barely recognised him when the nurse had shown her in. He had aged two decades in as many weeks, his complexion still greyish-yellow. Even his hands – hard farmer's hands – looked frail.

"I've felt worse." His mouth twisted ruefully. "Probably looked it too."

"*Wellll …*"

"Oh, *thanks*. And here I was thinking I was improving things."

"You are! You are. But it'll take time to get back to normal – to get better."

"I know. I'm getting better, I *feel* better. But I'd want to. The last two weeks have been –" His face darkened. "I didn't know if I could manage it at all. But the nurses … they've been very good. Even when I was … a bit nasty. But you'd know all about that too." His head dropped and the slightest tinge coloured his cheeks. "I've spent the last three days apologising to them. And I should apologise to you too."

"The farm's all good, in case you've been wondering." Estella spoke a little more loudly than she intended. Her brother's admission made her uncomfortable. She wasn't sure why. Perhaps because this version of Graeme was unfamiliar to her. The gruff, irascible man seemed … broken. It was terrifying to think how vulnerable that made him – that he would have to build himself back up again. Yes, he was drink-free now, but would he stay that way?

"I knew things at home would be fine with you in charge. You've always had a way with animals – you and Austin. I've never had that."

She scoffed. "Don't talk rubbish! You've been a grand farmer all these years."

He was already shaking his head. "But I haven't. No," he

said, stopping her from interrupting. "Since I was a boy, I've struggled with it. It's never felt natural to me. Not the way you are with, say, the horses. And … and I'm not sure I want keep on struggling with it."

Estella mouthed silently. "What … what does that mean?"

"I think … I think I don't want to farm anymore."

What? "But farming is what you've always wanted. Since you were, what, fourteen?"

"Is it? Daddy needed one of us to take over the farm and the other to take over the practice. He knew himself that one man couldn't manage both. But he still wanted it to stay in the family. What better way than making sure one of your sons farms it? And that was always going to be me. I never had Austin's brains. But I think, in a way, Daddy knew I didn't want it. And I think that's part of the reason he divided the place between the two of us. He was afraid I'd walk away from the whole thing and Robin Hill wouldn't be in the family anymore."

"But what about the woods? I thought you were selling them to buy Austin out. To get more land. To expand. To have it all."

"It was more a case of one of the lads asked me to sell it to him and I thought, 'Why not?' And … and I don't think you realise how much I was spending on drink. On silly card games too. I was an easy target for the card men." He paused. "There aren't many farms that could support that amount of spending for no return. And I was too addled to realise that when you're in a hole, you shouldn't keep digging. You should climb out. Right now, I think I can just about do that. I need to get out, Stella. Because if I stay, I'll be digging my own grave."

The starkness of the statement sent a chill down her spine. "But … but if you're not a farmer what are you going to do?"

He hesitated. "I've been thinking about that. Marion Ward has a brother who's a foreman over in Liverpool. I was thinking I might go over and see about doing some building work. Maybe she'd put in a good word for me."

"You do know she and Austin are an item, don't you?"

Had Graeme been standing, Estella reckoned he would have keeled over backwards. His face was such a picture, she couldn't help but burst into giggles.

"No! *Really? No!* Austin and – *no!*" He covered his mouth, stifling his laughter. But then he looked at his sister – her shining eyes, her conspiratorial smile – and suddenly they were siblings sharing a joke, tattling on their brother. He threw back his head and laughed. "Oh *Jesus!*" he eventually wheezed, wiping away the moisture on his cheeks, continuing to chuckle.

"I know."

They continued to shake their heads and giggle until Graeme eventually – after a sudden coughing fit – subsided into a pensive silence. They sat like this for a time, Estella studying the faults in her brother's face, trying to pick out the improvements. If he was physically weak, what was to say he wasn't quite in his right mind either. But he shook his head when she tentatively suggested it.

"I can see why you'd think that but I'm serious, Stella. I'll only end up in the same state again if I stay here. I'm not *happy*. And all the lads I call friends are just there to see what they can get out of me – whether that's a drink or a bit of land. I need distance. And, yes, I know I *might* fall in with a bad crowd wherever I go next, but I prefer the odds of 'might' somewhere else to 'definitely' here. This place isn't good for me. I have to leave."

A lump began to rise in Estella's throat. He meant it. He really did. Her brother was leaving Robin Hill. He was leaving her alone in that house, on that farm, because it was killing him. Maybe it was slowly doing the same to all of them and behind her mother and father, Graeme was next on the list. And if that was the case then she had to let him go. She swallowed her tears.

"What do you need me to do for you, Graeme?"

Chapter 40

It was late April before Graeme was home and able to begin planning his exit from Robin Hill. His appetite had improved but he still ate slowly and preferred the plainest of flavours in his dishes. Estella had been given a list of things to cook for him and stuck to it rigidly, determined to do all she could to aid his recovery. This did, however, mean she was run off her feet looking after him, his sheep and the cows at home. And she was also very much in demand at Ellendale since gymkhana season had started and they were exercising a string of horses every day and competing in showing and show jumping every weekend. Mr Leclerc had, of course, offered to give her the time off to manage things at home but she had immediately panicked and shouted him down. Working with the horses meant she had time to do something for herself each day (even though the animals belonged to someone else) and it was also where she now saw the most of Ivan. Their intimacy had been greatly curtailed by the return of Graeme so that now all they could steal were quick kisses and touches in the woods or around the yard.

"Although we'd better not do *that* again," Ivan told her, cheeks reddening one evening on the way home from table tennis as he gently broke off their kiss.

"Do *what* again?" she asked, poking him in the stomach just a little too low to be entirely playful.

"You know… *That*. That night. It was – well, you know it was –"

"Quite good?"

He tittered. "That's a bit of an understatement. But we shouldn't have done it. We'll have to make it official before we do it again."

Estella didn't disagree. She didn't regret the act itself but she certainly didn't want to go through the several weeks of worry before she was sure she wasn't going to have Ivan's baby. There was time for that yet. For now, she had enough to do riding Ellendale's horses and preparing everything for her brother's departure.

Though Graeme had argued his own capability at handling arrangements, Estella had persuaded him to allow her to talk to Marion Ward about a job with her brother.

In his often-drunk-or-hungover state, he was prone to rudeness and sometimes downright cruelty. People shrunk away from him or immediately went on the offensive which meant normal conversation was somewhat of a struggle. Graeme was aware of the change in himself and Estella could see it too. But that did not mean everyone else knew and would treat him accordingly. She felt the need to go everywhere ahead of him, warning them to treat her brother with kindness since he was making such a Trojan effort at self-improvement. But she couldn't. She had to let him deal with most of these encounters alone and allow him to brood on their uncomfortableness once he got home. However, the importance of Marion in the whole scheme meant she needed to be handled especially carefully.

Under the guise of collecting a drench for the sheep from the vets, Estella made her move on Marion. The conversation started routinely enough.

"Was your friend all right after that episode at the Hunt Ball with Paul Craven?"

"Rebecca? Oh, yes, she's fine. She's getting married! In a few months apparently."

"To Howard Anstruther?"

Estella could almost see her filing the information away in a little box in her head ready to be opened when there was a bit of gossip needed. "That's it."

"Lucky her," Marion said glumly, her face darkening. "There were plenty there that night who weren't so lucky, eh? Men!" she tutted. "They want you to put out but they don't want to give you anything in return."

That stumped Estella. Did she mean … "Oh?"

Marion ignored her. "You and your fella seemed wrapped fairly tight though. Coming along nicely, is it?"

"Ivan and I are getting on fine." She spoke carefully, aware of the edge in Marion's voice. "We're both working at Leclercs' so we have to!"

"Back at the horses then?" Just as suddenly as the darkness arrived, it left and was replaced with the bright-eyed Marion of old. "Your daddy would be delighted. He was always so proud of you with the horses."

Estella expected the statement to hurt, but all it did was

fill her with warmth. "I don't know how I filled my time without it. I'm constantly looking after something – horses, sheep, cows, Graeme."

"Graeme?"

Estella paused very deliberately. "He's been in hospital. The drinking finally caught up with him. He's been off it now for over a month."

"Oh? That's good. Again, your daddy would be delighted. He used to say that the drinking would be Graeme's end if he wasn't careful."

"He's making real progress. But ... but he doesn't think he wants to farm anymore."

Marion's perfectly drawn eyebrows shot up. "What d'you mean? What's he going to do instead?"

"Leave. He wants a fresh start away from the past, the bad influences."

"Where?"

Again, Estella hesitated. "Well, he was hoping to go to England. Maybe do something manual like building work."

Marion's eyes narrowed slightly. "What part of England?"

"He said you had a brother who was a foreman in Liverpool." There was no point pussyfooting around the obvious. Marion was far too clever for that.

"Ah. And dear old Graeme is hoping for a good reference from me, is he?"

"Tell your brother the truth," Estella said simply. "Graeme's a recovering alcoholic looking for a fresh start. He's used to the outdoors and is a good, strong, hard-working lad when he's sober. That is, if you're willing to say anything at all."

"I suppose we all deserve a second chance when we cock up, eh?" Marion tapped her pen against the vast account books on the counter in front of her. "I'll ring Adam tomorrow night and have a chat with him. No promises though."

"I know, I know. Thank you! But," she sobered suddenly, "do you think it'll annoy Austin if he hears you helped Graeme out?"

A flash seemed to light up Marion's eyes. "Stuff Austin!" she snapped. "He does what he likes so I can do whatever I like. Now," she said, getting laboriously to her feet, "I'll get you that sheep drench."

She left for the dispensary out the back. But not before Estella's eyes fell on the curves of Marion's elegant figure. However, there was an extra curve to her body that Estella hadn't anticipated. A swelling across her lower abdomen. Mind reeling, Estella cast back to the Hunt Ball, trying to recall what Marion wore. She seemed to remember something caught under the bust which gave no hint at any womanly shape from the waist down. Maybe, she thought, middle age was finally catching up on Marion and her swollen belly was simply the result of indulging in too many cakes. But Estella knew Marion. She would never let her figure slide. And then there was her uneasy movement and her 'Stuff Austin!' comment.

Marion, Estella surmised, was pregnant and Austin was the father.

Chapter 41

"Jesus, you think you know someone."

Graeme was sitting eating supper with Estella having spent most of the day pottering around the yard. He was getting stronger and she was glad to see he attacked his eggs and rashers with healthy, manly relish.

"What d'you mean? You don't *know* Austin. You've never got on."

He swallowed a mouthful of bread and sat back. "Just because we can't stand the sight of each other doesn't mean I don't notice things when I *do* see him. He was always a little perfectionist, by-the-book sort of lad. You'd think he'd be a good little boy and marry some pretty young one and settle down to have a perfect little family. Someone like your friend Rebecca. Not saying Marion isn't good-looking but she must nearly be old enough to be his mammy. And to get her … in the family way *before* marrying her. Well, pigs'll fly."

Estella snorted. Not so much at the content of his speech but the incredulous tone in which he delivered it. This verbosity was also new. Gruff Graeme was gone, replaced by this dry-humoured chattiness. In fact, he was like Austin when he was younger and their father before his accident. She actually enjoyed talking to him rather than dreading his company. It was sad to think he was leaving her now that they were finally on good terms. "Still, if Marion's got the hump with him, maybe she'll put in an extra good word for you just to irritate Austin."

As it turned out, they barely had to wait at all to witness Austin's ire. They were, again, sitting eating scones and jam after an evening's supper when they heard the familiar rumble of a car on the driveway. Graeme frowned at her but she shook her head, wondering if Ivan had decided to call before heading to Ellendale for a night of watching a mare on the brink of foaling. But she was soon dissuaded of the notion by a shout of, "*Austin! Austin, don't!*" From the yard.

A moment later, the man himself burst through the back door sending Sophie streaking out into the hall. He barely broke stride as he crossed the kitchen, blazing eyes boring into his brother.

Graeme had just enough time to push back his chair before Austin's hands closed around the lapels of his jacket, lifted him from his seat and slammed him into the wall behind. Estella gave a strangled shriek as Graeme's head thunked off the whitewash, his eyes wide with shock, mouth moving wordlessly.

"*Austin!*"

Estella jumped as Marion stormed by her and grabbed Austin's elbow. Her hair was coming out of its usual neat swirl at the base of her skull and her skin was flushed a

429

deep, angry red. She yanked at his arm but he didn't budge an inch.

"*Austin!* Don't be so *stupid!*"

He ignored her completely. "*What have you done?*" he snarled in his brother's face, shoving him further up the wall.

Graeme's toes scrabbled as the floor below him disappeared out of reach. "*What*? Whatisit I've done?" he choked out.

"*You know what you've done!*" he roared.

"For God's *sake!*" Marion let go of Austin and flapped her arms ineffectually, looking desperately to Estella for assistance.

Up to that point, Estella had remained rooted to the spot, at a loss. But suddenly a burning flash of rage ripped through her body, propelling her forward. She was angry. She was *livid*. And she was going to let Austin know it. Hurling herself at her brothers, she thrust her hand between them, caught Austin around the shoulder and dragged him backwards with all her might. Caught off balance, he stumbled backwards, dragging Graeme with him before letting go and crashing into a chair. He roared in frustration, in pain and clutched at his side where he had fallen against the chair back. Yet, undeterred, he gathered himself again and was about to launch another attack only to find his sister planted firmly between him and his quarry.

"Get out of the way, Stella!" he hissed. "This isn't your concern."

"This is *my* house," she snarled back. "And unless you get a grip of yourself right this minute, you're leaving and won't be coming back."

Austin simply sneered at her. "You love a lost cause, don't you, Stella?"

Her fist connected with his nose. She heard a kind of hollow 'pop' and his head snapped backwards. But not before she saw the look of complete shock in his eyes. There was pain there too – and not just the physical kind. She had hurt him deep within his heart's core. But he had done the same to her.

"*Ow!*" he whispered, cupping his hand over the centre of his face just in time to catch the blood. There wasn't much but it was still enough to turn his top lip and palm red. "You punched me."

"*Yes, she did. And if she hadn't, I would have.*"

Estella was surprised to hear those words in a woman's voice. She glanced to the side and saw Marion standing at her shoulder with her hands on her hips. She was grim-faced and tight-lipped. Austin, however, was getting a second wind. His discomfort was again turning to anger. Wiping his nose with his sleeve, he turned his attention on Graeme, still recovering his wheezing breath behind the others.

"Letting two women defend you, eh? You were always good at getting other people to do your dirty work."

He expected a reply from at least one of them. Yet no one spoke. The silence stretched on and on as each of them seemed to wordlessly agree not to dignify his vitriol with an answer. Even so, he stood like a prize-fighter poised to attack until eventually the tension ebbed and, with a final sneer, he turned away.

"Where's there a bloody towel?" he barked, dabbing at his nose.

"I'll get you a cloth." Estella spoke tonelessly as she

431

swept past him to fetch one from the cupboard before wetting it and handing it to him.

Sitting at the head of the table, he delicately ministered to his injury, wincing a little. "I think you've broken it."

"I doubt it," she replied off-hand as she stood over him, fearing he might launch another offensive on Graeme who now sat gingerly at the opposite end of the table. "I didn't hit you hard enough to do that."

"You hit fairly hard all the same."

"What is it that I've done, Austin?" Graeme's voice was quiet but clear. "Because I honestly don't know. But if you tell me, I'll do my best to fix it."

"*Fix* it? Bit late for that now."

"It's the woods," Marion answered, taking her position opposite Estella, leaning on the back of a chair. Austin threw her a dirty look but she didn't see it. She was observing his brother.

"I told a potential buyer I'd show him the land and the woods this evening because I'm looking to buy out Tommy Shannon's half of the practice. And when we drive down the lane there's not a tree in sight. The whole place gutted" – Austin slammed his fist on the table – "and a bloody great stack of logs up one side. And your man looking at me like I'm thick and me standing there like a total, utter gobshite without a clue as to what was going on!"

"*Ah*," Graeme nodded, "I was hoping I'd get to talk to you before you saw it."

"Talk? *Talk*? Shouldn't you have done that *before* you destroyed the entire bloody thing? I don't know, maybe asked my permission?"

432

"I know. It was all a terrible mistake. I wasn't in my right mind."

"Are you ever?"

Graeme locked his gaze with his brother's. "Yes," he replied crisply. "I am."

Austin snorted, winced. Estella felt her hand tingle with the urge to hit him again for his juvenility. "Graeme's been sober for more than a month now. Which you would know if you ever bothered to check in on us."

"Oh, I heard. Marion told me. She also told me you were looking for a reference with her brother in England. What was the plan – sell the woods and live it up across the water until the money ran out and you came crawling back?"

"Are you stupid or what?" Marion countered. "What would be the point in looking for a job with my Adam if he was going to be living off the money he already has?"

Austin's cocksure smirk withered slightly. "Well, I don't know, do I?" he blustered.

"Clearly."

Graeme's sure voice cut off Austin's retort. "I was not in my right mind when I sold the wood. I was drunk, as I often was this last while. And I really did think Daddy had left that part of the farm to me. So I thought I was selling something I owned. I know that's no excuse, but it's the truth. I wouldn't have known only Stella showed me Daddy's will."

Austin rounded on his sister. "You *knew*? And you didn't tell me?"

"Why would I when I knew this is how you'd react? Graeme said he'd fix it and that's what he's going to do."

433

"Oh yeah? And how are you going to *fix* it, Graeme?" Austin spat.

"Whatever is in my bank account right now, aside from what I need to go to England, is yours," Graeme answered calmly. "Anything I still owe, I'll pay you back with interest from what I earn over there. And whatever part of my land Stella doesn't want, you can rent out and keep what you get for it."

Estella knew this plan already. She had even helped him make it. But hearing her brother lay it out so calmly, so starkly, made her stomach drop with abject grief. It was just another strike in the dismantling of the life she had grown up with – another change to cope with, to grow through.

Another loaded silence met Graeme's words. The brothers gazed at one another across the expanse of the table strewn with the remains of supper – one calm, the other mutinous.

The women looked from one to the other until finally Marion said, "Well, you can't ask for fairer than that."

"Can't I?" Austin bit out.

"No. You can't," she answered coldly. "You'll get your money and that's all you wanted. Leave it."

"I could sue."

"If you do that, so help me, I'll take the boat to England with Graeme and you'll never see me or your child again."

That caught Austin's attention. He gaped stupidly at her, swallowed several times, then said hoarsely, "You can't do that."

"I can do whatever I damn-well please," she countered. "Stop being a boy, Austin. Stop your petty little rivalries with

434

your brother and sister and be a man. Be a *gentleman*."

Estella watched her brother shrink in on himself as Marion continued, lowering her tone.

"Where's the kindness, the sense of humour, the *good* man I fell in love with? Where did he go? And where did all this bitterness and aggression come from? Because it's impossible to deal with." She paused then haltingly asked, "Was it me? Did *I* do something wrong?"

"No!" he choked out as the tears began to well in his eyes. "No, it was me. All me. I just …" Austin looked to his siblings. "I can't cope anymore. I've just … I've been working so hard all this time. Working towards owning the practice when I've barely been a vet three years. Working on the plan Daddy set out before he died – even though I don't feel ready to do it all on my own. I always thought I'd have Daddy there to help me. And then, when he died …" Here he had to stop to daub at the stream of slightly bloody snot and tears running down his face. "When he died, I was so hell-bent on keeping going that I never really stopped to … to …"

"Grieve," Graeme finished quietly.

Slowly, the siblings all looked at one another and saw their own expressions mirrored on each other's faces. And in that moment, they all shared the same sadness. Estella felt the lump rise in her throat and swallowed hard. She didn't want to draw attention to herself by crying in front of everyone.

Then Graeme spoke.

"We three have all suffered the same losses but we've all experienced them in different ways. Yet rather than that bringing us together, we've turned on each other. And I'm

435

more guilty of it than either of you. I've pushed away help and not offered it to those who need it most." Here, he looked at Estella. "I was the most awful, horrible, cold bastard to our father. I was glad when he died. And I feel so guilty about that now. That for the last few years of our father's life, I hated him."

Austin clenched his fists, white knuckles protruding.

"That's time, that's hatred I can never take back," Graeme went on. "And I don't want to – I can't – do the same with the two of you. I want to have a little sister *and* a little brother. I want to deserve you. If you'll let me."

There was a long pause. Graeme wasn't daring to look up, instead inspecting the cleanliness of his fingernails with affected calm. No doubt he could feel Austin's blazing eyes boring into the crown of his skull.

Estella allowed her gaze to roam across the expanse of table between them. She was trying to calculate how great a distance it was and whether Austin could launch himself across it when Marion spoke.

"Well, that's a good place to start, Graeme." She glared pointedly at Austin. "And, sure, if you turn into an eejit again, you'll be all the way over in Blighty so it won't matter too much."

A beat followed before they all began to snigger. It was just the kind of levity they needed. Estella stepped over and squeezed Graeme's shoulder just as Sophie peeped her nose back into the kitchen sensing – as animals so often do – that the conflict was over and it was safe to look for a knee to curl up on.

"Tea?" Estella asked the room at large.

Conversation was easier after that – although there was still an undercurrent of tension which radiated from Austin towards the other three. Some of his comments were, at first, a little close to the bone – especially about Graeme's alcohol dependency – but the less they rose to his taunts, the more polite his exchanges became. And Marion was, of course, a godsend with her sense of humour and the distinct advantage of not having the Frayne surname. She simply had less history in the room and was, therefore, much better equipped to lighten the mood.

However, Estella surmised that it wouldn't be long before she *did* share their surname. As the evening progressed and they drank their second pot of tea, she noticed how Austin's gaze was so often drawn to Marion's still-youthful face. How small, tender smiles passed between them once her brother's temper cooled. Clearly the relationship between the siblings wasn't the only one repairing. Whatever impediment existed between Marion and Austin quietly slipped away with each sip of tea. Although Estella did wonder why they had arrived together if things really were as bad as she guessed from their conversation at the practice. Perhaps it was just a case of Marion and Austin both being quick-tempered individuals. She had seen it with Dolly too. Whenever any of her previous menfolk annoyed her, she still never passed up an opportunity to go somewhere with them if there was an outing or a free lift on offer. One day, she would hate a man and the next she would be planning their wedding.

The unfamiliar hum of conversation allowed Estella's mind to drift as she thought about all the couples she knew

– married and unmarried. The ones that loved each other deeply. The ones that couldn't stand the sight of each other. The ones that blew hot and cold, full of passion then corrupted by hatred. Dolly and Roy had a relationship seemingly built on teasing and mutual irritation. Yet there were no two who more publicly displayed their affection. Henry and Barbara Leclerc had completely intertwined interests and each a clear fondness for the other. Howard Anstruther seemed totally besotted with Rebecca who, in turn, appeared a little stunned having acquired such love. Looking at the couple in front of her, Estella hadn't the first clue what Marion and Austin's relationship was built on. And then there was herself and Ivan. What was their relationship built on?

'Horses' was the first word her brain offered up making her titter to herself. If that was all, why wasn't she in love with Mr Leclerc or old Danny Fearon or even Paul Craven?

Because they weren't Ivan.

It wasn't the best of explanations but it was the truth. Ivan was young, playful, kind, handsome, strong and made her feel more alive than she had in years. He helped her to be the best version of herself. They could be serious together, they could laugh until they cried. Every time she saw him, she longed to feel his arms wrap around her. She loved the way he looked at her, the way he smelled, the pattern of veins in the back of his hand. And she loved the way he laughed at her, with her. The way his smile grew and his eyes danced when he saw her coming his way. She had never felt anything like it, never seen that sort of synergy – partnership – between two people. It just so happened that the first man she had fallen in love with was the man she was *meant* to be with. Perhaps there was someone looking down on her, guiding her, bringing Ivan to her and she to him. She glanced at the kitchen ceiling and offered her silent gratitude just in case there was some celestial intervention that had laid their path to one another. Or maybe it was just good luck. After everything that had happened in her twenty-five years of life, surely it was about time it changed for the better.

"Hellooo! Wakey, wakey, Stella!"

She blinked. Austin's iodine-stained hand was waving lazily in front of her. They were all staring at her, including Sophie who gazed across the table from Marion's knee. If the cat accepted her, Estella thought, there mustn't be much wrong with her. Marion was going to be her sister! *Another* sister, she corrected herself. Throughout all the discussion, Joy had never once been mentioned – the forgotten part of the family. She wondered if her brothers even remembered there was a fourth Frayne sibling. They never spoke her name. They never even enquired about her wellbeing. She suddenly felt very angry with Austin and Graeme. For all their talk about becoming a family once again, they were forgetting a quarter piece of it. But then maybe Joy was the lucky one. Family feuds never touched her. She lived in a state that was separate from squabbling siblings. Alcohol dependency, monetary worries and social anxiety would never sink their claws into her back. Perhaps she was better off removed from such concerns. Perhaps it was better she existed on a different plane.

"Stella!"

They were all still looking at her – apart from Sophie who

had her leg cocked in the air to groom herself. Estella wanted to reproach her brothers for their lack of interest in Joy. She wanted to make them feel guilty, to make them care. But then would that do Joy any good? In this instance, forced regard was hardly better than none at all. And this evening had been about finally laying the past to rest – getting beyond their differences and moving forward. Estella swallowed her anger, drew thoughts of her sister back into her chest and closed the door, keeping her safe. She would remain the sole gatekeeper to Joy's delicate heart.

"Just thinking to myself," she murmured. "Don't mind me."

"Right. Well, I think we're going to head home," Austin said, frowning slightly. However, the frown cleared when Marion sidled up beside him and slipped her arm through his. No matter how much Estella liked Marion, seeing her like that with Austin was still going to take some getting used to.

Estella glanced at the clock and was surprised to see it was coming up to ten o'clock. "Yes, you'd better get going. I'd say you've an early start."

Austin rolled his eyes and grinned. "Always."

Sophie wound herself around everyone's ankles as they shuffled as one to the door with promises of calling again, handshakes and kisses (from Marion). Graeme and Estella stood in the doorway to wave them off just as another set of headlights lit up the driveway and the familiar rattle of Ivan's old car reverberated off the walls of the yard. He shouted pleasantries to Austin and Marion over the din of the engines but didn't stop to chat.

Graeme headed back inside once he had watched their taillights disappear. For some reason, Estella thought he seemed a little nervous or perhaps intimidated by Ivan's presence. Ivan, on the other hand, didn't notice Graeme's discomfort at all. He had eyes only for her. Bounding across the yard like an excited puppy first thing in the morning rather than a grown man well into the evening, he swept Estella off her feet in a bear hug.

"Did I miss a party? Or a brawl?"

"Which would you have preferred?"

"Either," he said promptly, following her into the kitchen. "Both can be quite entertaining."

She chuckled. "What are you doing here at this hour? I thought you were on foaling duty tonight."

"I was, but Danny arrived and said he'd take over. His wife's sister and her husband are staying and he said he couldn't stick another minute in the house with them. I didn't even know he was married. Did you?"

"I *think* I knew. I've never really thought about it."

"Oh, well at least I'm not the only one. I just assumed he lived alone since he's never talked about anyone at home."

"Danny doesn't talk, full stop."

"True. Although he said 'hello' to you two days ago."

"It was more of a 'lo' than a full 'hello'. But, yes, even I was surprised by that."

"Then you imagine how surprised I was when he spoke enough words to tell me he had a wife and a sister-in-law. I nearly keeled over."

"Did you need to dunk you head in the water trough to revive yourself?"

"Nope."

He bent to show her his dry hair and, without thinking, she ran her hand through it. He caught her arm and kissed the inside of her wrist. She smiled and brushed his hair away from his forehead all the better to see his face. "Not that I'm not happy to see you, but why are you here anyway?"

"I came to bring you back your coat," he told her. Straightening up, he looked around him. "Damn, I left it in the car."

"I could have just collected it tomorrow."

"But then you wouldn't have had the pleasure of seeing me just before going to bed." He grinned cheekily, eyebrows wiggling.

"Don't be naughty," she admonished, turning away, but his arms were around her in an instant, pulling her flush against him.

"I'm not *naughty*. Your head went there."

"Only because yours is there already."

There was a thump and shuffle from upstairs. Ivan looked up then, with a sad sigh, let her go. "Oh, to be alone with you in this house again."

"All you have to do is ask the right question. Tea?"

"Please," he said, sitting. "Can I stay tonight?"

"That's not the right question. I'm not having tea. I've already drunk a gallon of it with Austin and Marion."

"That's all right. As long as you don't mind me having a cup." He paused. "You mean *that* question, don't you?"

"But you should only ask it if you want to."

"You know I want to. And you'd definitely say yes? Because I wouldn't be able to stand it if you broke my poor little heart."

"Your heart's safe with me," she laughed.

"Good," he said, taking her hand as she walked past him. "I'll ask then. But I just have to find the right moment."

Epilogue

Estella was sitting on the end of Dolly Greer's bed, watching her best friend in the mirror as she pulled out a selection of perfectly placed hairpins and reinserted them in the exact same places.

"It's just not *right*," Dolly hissed in frustration, slamming the handful of little pearl-encrusted pins onto her dressing table.

It must be bad, thought Estella. since Dolly usually treated these pins – a twenty-first birthday present from an aunt – with a kind of beatific reverence. She worshiped at the altar of pretty things and relished the opportunity to show them off. But not today. All through the girls' preparations, Dolly had whinged and grumbled that her face looked haggard (it didn't), that her dress was unflattering (it wasn't) and that no matter what she did her hair just … wasn't … *right*. It also hadn't helped that Estella had turned up over an hour late for her allotted preparation time.

"And what can I do with you in only an hour?" Dolly had snapped as Estella arrived up the stairs panting with the effort of cycling over at speed in the humidity of late-summer.

Estella had to bite back her laughter as she took in the sight of Dolly with hands on hips and hair full of oversized curlers. She managed to turn it into a placating smile. "It won't take an hour for me to get ready. All I need is a quick *Dolly*-up and I'll be fine. No one will be looking at me anyway. But first I need a quick wash. I'm all sweaty."

She didn't try to make out the invectives that followed her downstairs to the kitchen for some hot water.

"Any improvement?" Dolly's mother asked anxiously when Estella appeared. "It's been like living with a half-tamed cat for days now. One minute she wants to curl up in your lap, the next she's tearing at you with her claws."

"She'll get over it," Estella assured Mrs Greer as she hurriedly filled a basin to take back up to have a quick sponge down before putting on her posh frock.

Dolly, meanwhile, stood tutting and tapping her foot, waiting for the right moment to attack Estella's head with a hairbrush. "What am I supposed to do with this?" she asked as she violently ripped the brush through the long strands.

Estella bore the punishment without complaint. "Whatever's handy for you. I don't mind."

Of course *Dolly* minded. Once her initial assault was over, she delicately arranged Estella's hair in an elegant up-do much like the one she had done for the Hunt Ball. The occupation seemed to give her a modicum of contentment and, for a while, she was much like the old Dolly as she faffed and fussed over Estella's appearance and tried to convince her to wear much more rouge than was necessary. All of this took barely more than half an hour by the end of which the Estella on the end of the bed was a much more presentable version of the one that had entered the room not so long ago. However, when it came to readying herself up, Dolly's mood slipped again.

"I don't know why I'm bothering," she huffed, having fixed whatever was wrong with her hair and moved on to reapplying her make-up.

Estella looked at her watch for the umpteenth time as she counted down the minutes she would have to spend alone with this testier version of Dolly. "Because the day will feel better if you feel good about yourself."

"Nobody wants me there," she snapped, dabbing a rosy pink colour onto her lips with her pinkie finger.

"Now you're just being silly," Estella retorted, losing patience. "It wasn't Rebecca's decision to make Howard's sisters the bridesmaids. It was his mother's. And *you* were the one who told Rebecca to agree to it so as to get off on the right foot with the rest of his family."

"But I didn't *mean* it!" she wailed, burying her face in her hands. "I was *so* looking forward to being a bridesmaid."

"Oh would you ever give over! Stop making a show of yourself, Dolly! What would Roy say if he saw you moping like this?"

It was the wrong thing to say. Dolly's eyes met hers in the mirror and welled with tears. "But ... but he's not ... not here!"

Estella was on her feet and had wrapped her arms around her friend in an instant.

"Mind my hair!" Dolly squawked as Estella leant over her to give a better hug.

"*You. Look. Perfect, Dolly Greer,*" she said firmly.

447

"We both do," Dolly sighed, rearranging her face into a smile. "You and I scrub up pretty well, eh?" She crossed her hands and held on to Estella's arms, resting her head against her friend's chest.

Estella studied their reflections. Despite her efforts, Dolly still looked sad. It was her eyes, Estella thought. There was no brightness to them, no matter how beautiful the rest of her looked. The brightest spark came from the small diamond that still felt heavy on the ring finger of Estella's left hand. Though she tried to focus on Dolly, her eyes were constantly drawn to it – shocked by it, admiring it.

Ivan hadn't got down on one knee. If he had, he might have been run over by a horse.

He had done it at a horse show one Saturday in June. To anyone else, it was an unremarkable day but to them it had been an unprecedented success. Of the eight Ellendale horses that had competed that day, all of them had won prizes. Several had gained qualifying places to compete later that summer in the prestigious Royal Dublin Society Horse Show and to cap it off, Estella and her own horse, Hedy, had won their class having returned to competitive show jumping only four weeks previously.

"*Little Iris Kellett strikes again!*" Henry Leclerc shouted at her as she collected her red rosette, cup and prize money. Ivan stood beside him clapping and had simply winked.

Having ridden her lap of honour she left the arena and allowed the horse to saunter back to the Leclercs' horse lorry on a loose rein. As she rode, long rosette tail ribbons fluttering from the pocket of her jacket, old friends looked up to congratulate her, tell her how glad they were to see her back where she belonged – on a horse.

By the time she got back to the lorry, Ivan was leaning against the side, hands in the pockets of his tweed show jacket, shiny black boots crossed at the ankles. He had, however, loosened his tie and removed his bowler hat though the shape of it still pasted his hair to the top of his head.

"Your hair looks ridiculous!" she laughed, stopping in front of him.

He pushed off the lorry and presented his head to her as he sometimes did now. He knew she loved his hair. "Fix it for me then." Reaching over, she ran her fingers over the crown of his skull and gently tugged the strands so that they stood on end before lovingly smoothing them back into position. "Thank you." He smiled up at her, squinting in the sunlight. It really was a beautiful day. He patted the horse then placed a hand on Estella's thigh. "Quite the day."

"I know! What a way to finish off!"

"It's not over yet, though."

"No? I don't think it can get much better!"

His hand was still on her thigh, keeping her in the saddle and she placed her own over it as he absentmindedly stroked the back of his fingers down the mare's shoulder. He stopped and put his hand in his pocket again. "I was hoping I could make it a *little* bit better."

He pulled his free hand from his pocket and brought it up to rest on the horse's mane. In it was a small black box. She gasped, fingers contracting over the hand on her thigh. Letting go of her reins entirely, she reached for the box and prised open the lid. The ring inside shone bright in its deep red surroundings and even brighter against Hedy's grey mane. Estella glanced down at Ivan to find he looked quite serious, almost nervous. She threw her head back and laughed then leant down and kissed him wetly on the mouth. His eyes sprang wide and his face cleared, splitting into a joyous grin.

"*Yes!*"

"Yes?"

"Yes!"

Catching her reins again, she slid off the horse straight into his arms. As they kissed again, a roar went up behind her, making Hedy dance sideways. "*Woah!*" She and Ivan spoke together and both reached over to pacify the horse. She turned and was met by a sea of smiling faces and Barbara Leclerc snapping a picture with her camera. Henry Leclerc, Rebecca, Howard and Jacqueline Hawes engulfed them as Danny Fearon wordlessly took the horse, grinning toothlessly.

"Let's see the ring then!" Jacqueline ordered.

"She hasn't even got it on yet!" Rebecca laughed.

"Wait, *wait!* It's not official till it's in position. She might do a bunk yet!" Mr Leclerc chortled.

Ivan turned to her, prying the ring from its bed. She offered her hand and, taking it firmly, he slipped the ring on her finger. Another whoop went up and the horses in the lorry stamped and clattered, clearly put out.

"Careful!" Ivan admonished. "You don't want any of them injured before they get to compete in Dublin."

Staring in the mirror, the whole scene played out in Estella's mind's eye. Really, Ivan couldn't have picked a better moment to propose to her. Now, every day when she rode Hedy she would look down at the horse's grey mane and remember the little black box perched on the coarse hair. It never failed to make her smile.

"Why don't you wear it all the time?" Dolly asked, picking up her hand to inspect the ring.

"I'm afraid I'll lose it or get it dirty or catch it in something."

"Doesn't Ivan mind?"

"No. I even asked him. Jewellery has no place in the yard. But on days out, like this one, of course I'll wear it."

"It's so pretty," she said wistfully. "Don't suppose I'll ever wear one now."

"How many times do I have to say it, Roy was *delayed*. He didn't realise how long it would take to settle all the affairs after his father died. I know what that's like. I had to do the same with Daddy. It takes time. And he promised he'd be back as soon as he could."

"He also promised he'd be back for the wedding," she said wetly.

There was a rumble of an engine in the distance and Estella almost cried out in relief. "Here's Ivan!" she shouted. "Are you ready to go?" She placed her hands on her friend's shoulders. "You look beautiful, Dolly."

Ivan looked distinctly harried as they sat into his car ready to be waved off by Mrs Greer. "Your hair's still wet," Estella commented, reaching over.

"Most of me's still wet. I got Danny to hose me down before I got changed. I think he enjoyed it a little bit too much."

451

"You did not!"

"No. I hosed myself down actually. Now I know why the horses aren't keen on it – my *God* is it cold! You both look lovely, by the way," he added, smiling at Dolly in the rear-view as he tooted the horn and drove out the gate, after leaving a cloud of dust in their wake.

"Thank you. You mean you brought your suit to Ellendale?"

"Had it in the car. I knew I wouldn't get home. There was too much to do. I mean, who holds a wedding on a bank holiday Monday? And two days before Dublin Horse Show!" He shook his head. It had been his refrain ever since he got the invite.

"Just be glad they aren't having it later on in the week," Dolly answered.

"I wouldn't have bloody gone if that was the case. I've already seen her married once. I don't suppose the second time round is much different."

They all looked at one another then tittered nervously. They had all thought about the fact that this was Rebecca's second marriage but no one had mentioned it up until now.

"Let's just hope this one's more successful than the last," Estella muttered.

"It better be. Because I like it here and it'd be terrible if I had to leave for murdering one of the local landed gentry …"

Harry Bruce's face was a picture as he preceded his mother up the aisle. Rebecca looked radiant as Ivan walked with her, putting on an excellent show of this being the exact place he wanted to be.

"True what they say then about it making you glow, eh?" Dolly whispered in Estella's ear.

Estella swiped at her. "*Shh!* You don't want anyone to hear," she hissed.

Dolly rolled her eyes. "They'll know soon enough when a full-sized baby arrives four or five months after the wedding. Most of them aren't complete idiots."

"I never should've told you."

Ivan had told her six weeks ago. "You'd never think Anstruther had it in him, would you?" he said half angry, half amused.

"I wouldn't have thought Rebecca did either. Even though she's got Harry. I would've thought she's the sort to do things in the proper order."

"I would've thought the same about you," Ivan teased. "But when the moment takes you ..."

"But that was only because it was you. Any woman would be hard pressed not to lose the run of themselves with you in their bed. But Howard –"

"Gangly bean pole –"

"Doesn't exactly inspire ideas of mad passion. Not with me anyway."

"I should count myself lucky then."

"I've eyes only for you," she assured him.

"And every single animal within a mile radius ..."

"Not fair ... only a half mile ..."

When the meal was over, a slow version of musical chairs ensued as guests began swapping tables to sit beside people they knew or move away from people they didn't.

"My *goodness*, does Jacqueline Hawes talk about anything other than dogs and horses?" Dolly huffed as she plumped down beside Estella. Ivan had just vacated his seat under the pretence of going to the bathroom but they both knew he was off to talk horses with one of the other guests. Estella, who had begun rolling bits of ribbon from the favours to bring to Joy and Susan on her next visit, was glad of the company since Ivan would doubtless be gone a while.

"They *are* her life so – Oh! Hello, Jacqueline!"

Dolly cringed as the lady in question sat down beside her.

"Well, Stella, all set for a triumphant return to Dublin? You've some top horses there. Should be in the line-up with a few at least."

Dolly mimed falling asleep as Estella talked across her. "Hopefully! What about you? You've two going, don't you?"

Jacqueline tutted as Dolly shot Estella a warning look. "Not sure, not sure. The three-year-old was a bit lame on the back foot there on Friday so I'm hoping he'll be all right by tomorrow. Your brother reckons he will be at least. Seen much of Austin lately?"

"No, I haven't." She had seen him briefly when he'd come to treat horses at Ellendale but hadn't really talked to him since the night Graeme had attempted to make amends. He hadn't even come to see Graeme off when he sailed for England.

"Or his secretary for that matter," Jacqueline continued. "Do you know she's in foal? Only a few weeks left I'd say. But I'm no expert. And no man. And she's not young either."

"Yes, I heard that," Estella answered vaguely, looking around, wishing someone would come and save her. "How's your dog, by the way? You said he had a dickie tummy the last time I saw you."

"Oh yes, vomiting everywhere! But now …"

Estella wasn't really listening. She was thinking about Marion still working in the practice though she was merely days away from her due date – still working with Austin. And he was no closer to marrying her either. He "didn't have time". And for some reason Marion wasn't pushing him.

"He says he's not annoyed at me helping Graeme but I know it irritated him," she said. "So I did it anyway. And Graeme deserves help. He's trying. Besides, we're living together so we're as good as married. But don't tell that to anyone because I'd never be allowed into someone's shop or home again."

"Jacqueline, darling! *Cooey!*" Mrs Anstruther was waving at her from across the room.

"Oh! Talk later, girls!" Jacqueline smiled and departed.

"Thank *goodness* for that!" Dolly slid down in her chair in mock exhaustion. "I was ready to *scream* if she gave another detailed description of her mutt's bowel movements. How often can one dog defecate?"

Estella was still laughing when Ivan returned, parking himself firmly in his seat. He looked distinctly browbeaten.

"What happened to you?"

He winced. "Mammy wanted me to do the first dance with Rebecca. You know, instead of the father of the bride. But I'd already told Anstruther I wasn't doing it. She's not best pleased with me."

"When are you going to start calling him 'Howard'?" Dolly asked. "He *is* your brother now."

"Don't know. I just like the way 'Anstruther' sounds when I say it. *Anstruther*," he demonstrated richly as the band struck up at the end of the room and the new Mr and Mrs Anstruther took to the floor. Ivan winced, eyes on the musicians. "Thank Christ I didn't have to pay for all this," he muttered. "You'd be marrying a pauper if I had."

"I'm not marrying you for your money," Estella said, kissing his cheek. She liked it when he spoke of their getting married.

"Or my dance moves."

"Definitely not!" Estella glanced at Dolly to share the joke but she was too busy watching the happy couple, a glum look on her face. "Poor Dolly …" she murmured quietly.

Once the first dance was over, more pairings flooded the floor and Dolly's face fell further.

"Do you mind if I …" Ivan whispered, gesturing to Dolly. Estella grinned up at him and nodded enthusiastically. Ivan kissed her then pounced on Dolly. "Come on, you! *Up-we-get!*" he cried in a sing-song voice, dragging her onto the floor where he whirled her around in a kind of loose-limbed mad gallop that drew the eyes and smiles of nearly everyone except Edna Aylward who looked furious until Mr Leclerc led *her* onto the floor where she blushed like a schoolgirl.

By nine o'clock, Ivan, Estella and Dolly were all lounging about in their chairs, fanning themselves from the exertions on the dancefloor. "These shoes aren't designed for walking in, never mind *dancing*," Dolly told them as she removed them and massaged her feet.

Ivan grunted in reply but Estella said nothing. She was suddenly very alert but all her attention was directed towards the door. "Dolly ..." she said cautiously.

"*Mmm?*"

"You should put your shoes back on."

"What? Why? There's no way I'm dancing anymore with your great galumphing elephant. You can keep him. No offence, Ivan."

"Some taken," he said mildly.

"No, you're not dancing with Ivan anymore. He's mine."

"Bit late to be getting possessive, isn't it? You've been sharing him all night."

"I am sitting right here, you know." Ivan sat up to make his point.

"Yes, you are," Estella said, her eyes dancing, her smile wide. "But she doesn't need you anymore because her man is standing over there." She pointed.

All of a sudden, Dolly's chair was empty as she bolted stocking-footed across the room into the waiting arms of Roy Oaks who stood in the doorway. Her screech of happiness and their ensuing passionate kiss made everyone stare. Estella was almost embarrassed watching them.

"How come I don't get a welcome like that every time I walk in?" Ivan asked quietly from behind her, his lips close to her ear.

"Because you and I have never been separated for two whole months. And if I said hello to you like that every time we met, I think your back would have given out by now."

"Oh, I'm not sure about that." Slowly, he crept his fingers around her waist, wrapping her in his arms. "I reckon I'd manage. There's not much to you," he added, giving her a squeeze and kissing her neck.

"There's enough in the right places," she answered as his hands stealthily crept over her body while everyone was looking in the other direction. "But there's not much to you either." She stood, bringing him with her and leant back into his chest, feeling the familiar shape of his body pressed close to hers.

"There's enough. In the right places." He pulled her even closer.

"Oh … I know that," she replied. Then, swiftly checking around them, she turned to face him and wrapped her arms around his neck. He bent his knees and easily lifted her off her feet. She giggled like a little girl. "Outside?"

Out on the patio, the air was cool but still retained the scent of greenery and honeysuckle. Ivan wordlessly removed his jacket and draped it over her shoulders as they came to sit on a white wrought-iron bench. She cuddled into his warmth, feeling his chest vibrate as he said, "Us next, eh?"

"*Mmm!*" she agreed, hugging him tight.

"Ours'll be a bit different though, eh? Smaller."

"More intimate. I'm thinking about asking Mr Leclerc to give me away."

She saw Ivan's white teeth grin at her in the dusk. "You'll make his year."

"It's already been made with so many of his horses going to Dublin."

Ivan groaned. "To think we've got to get up early tomorrow and head off up there with eight horses. No one's going to be able to stand, never mind help."

"I will be. And so will you. Because the horses come first."

458

"Always."

"I've had another idea for the wedding too ..."

"Oh?"

She sat up and held his hands, vibrating with excitement. "You know the way Howard organised the horse-drawn carriage?"

Ivan snorted. "I hope you're not wanting one of them too."

"*No!* I thought we could ride away from the church."

"Ride off into the sunset." He grinned. "I like the sound of that. I could ride Bella since, in a way, it was her taking off on Christmas Day that started this whole thing."

"Sounds like a plan. And I can ride Hedy, since you gave her back to me." She snuggled into his warmth again and he kissed her hair. They sat in silence, enjoying the feeling of being alone with one another. Then another thought struck her. "Really, if you think about it, it's just common sense to ride a grey horse when you're wearing a white dress."

"I agree," he nodded.

"We always do. Almost ..."

"*Almost*," Ivan agreed, grinning.

Estella smiled in return. Then, reaching up, she brushed the hair from his face and kissed him.

THE END

www.ingramcontent.com/pod-product-compliance
Lightning Source LLC
Chambersburg PA
CBHW021119260626
47169CB00005B/1351